spaniels,
She loves Jane Ausand has a passion for

🐦 @georgiawrites
📘 www.facebook.com/georgiahillauthor
www.georgiahill.co.uk

The Little Book Café

Georgia Hill writes rom-coms and historical fiction and is published by HarperImpulse.

She divides her time between the beautiful counties of Herefordshire and Devon and lives with her two beloved spaniels, a husband (also beloved) and a ghost called Zoë. She loves Jane Austen, eats far too much Belgian chocolate and has a passion for Strictly Come Dancing.

@georgiawrites
www.facebook.com/georgiahillauthor
www.georgiahill.co.uk

The Little Book Café

Georgia Hill

A division of HarperCollins*Publishers*
www.harpercollins.co.uk

Harper*Impulse* an imprint of
HarperCollins*Publishers*
The News Building
1 London Bridge Street
London SE1 9GF

www.harpercollins.co.uk

This paperback edition 2018

First published in Great Britain in ebook format by
HarperCollins*Publishers* 2018

A catalogue record for this book
is available from the British Library

ISBN: 978-0-00-828130-4

This novel is entirely a work of fiction.
The names, characters and incidents portrayed in it are
the work of the author's imagination. Any resemblance to
actual persons, living or dead, events or localities is
entirely coincidental.

Typeset in Birka by Palimpsest Book Production Ltd,
Falkirk, Stirlingshire

Printed and bound by CPI Group (UK) Ltd, Croydon, CR0 4YY

MIX
Paper from
responsible sources
FSC
www.fsc.org   FSC® C007454

To Bertie, with love and cuddles.

To Bernie, with love and cuddles

PART ONE

Tash's Story

Chapter 1

'Is that really what you're wearing to this book club thing?' Adrian frowned at Tash's reflection in the mirrored door of the wardrobe in their fitted bedroom.

'Yes, what's wrong with it?' Tash looked down at her mini-skirt and wedge sandals.

'Oh, I don't know. You wear skirts all the time for work. Why not try those palazzo pants I bought for you last week? And that black sweater?'

'Ade. It's August.'

'Aren't you meeting up in that chapel Millie's converted? Those sorts of places are always freezing.' He smiled and, lifting her hair out of the way, bit her ear. 'Or you could always stay home with me.' He reached around her waist and covered a breast with each hand, finding the nipples and pinching hard. 'I might have plans for you. Plans that would keep you very warm.' He nuzzled his mouth into her neck and nipped.

Tash took his hands off her and stepped away. 'You know I promised Emma I'd go with her for the first time. It's only this once, Adrian.'

He flung himself onto the bed and pouted. 'Well, if you prefer the company of a load of boring old women instead

3

of a night of hot passion with me...' He spread his legs and rubbed his crotch, grinning.

Tash looked away, revolted. Adrian's sexual appetite was getting wearisome. 'I'll change into those trousers and then I'd better get going. I'm late already.'

'You sure you don't want me to give you a lift?'

Tash hurried into the next bedroom, the one she used as a dressing room. 'No, it's fine. I need the fresh air and exercise.' She yanked her skirt off and pulled the trousers on. She needed to get out. Fast.

'Plenty of opportunity for exercise here,' Adrian called from the bed. 'I'll get you hot and sweaty.'

Tash grabbed her bag and ran down the stairs. 'Won't be late. Don't wait up!' Please don't wait up, she added silently. The thought of his body grinding over hers yet again was nauseating. How had it come to this? She slammed the door decisively on her way out.

'You okay, Tash?' Emma asked as they walked along Berecombe's seaside promenade.

'Yes, I'm fine!' Tash replied curtly.

'No need to snap my head off.'

'Sorry, Em. Lot on my mind.'

'Yeah, work was manic today. That's three take-ons this week and it's only Wednesday. Good, innit?'

'Excellent.' Tash shoved her bag onto her shoulder as a group of men ambled past.

'Evening girls,' one cackled. Another wolf-whistled.

She put an arm through Emma's and hurried her on. 'Honestly, why men feel they can just, just—'

'Just what?'

'Oh, I don't know.'

'Lighten up, Tash. They were only being friendly. If I didn't know you better, I'd say you were the one who was nervous about this book club, not me.'

'Well, that's just rubbish, isn't it? I'm never nervous about anything.' Tash slowed down as they approached Millie Vanilla's Cafe. It was brightly lit and still had a few customers sitting outside, enjoying a pot of tea in the golden evening sunshine.

Emma pointedly took Tash's arm from out of hers. 'You never used to be. You used to be fun, Natasha. Until you moved in with Adrian Williams.'

Tash's eyes glittered. 'You've gone too far, Emma. Remember I'm your boss.'

'Not at this precise second, you're not.' Emma reached out and took hold of her friend's hand. 'I'm worried about you, Tash. You seem tense all the time, jumpy.'

'I'm just tired, that's all. As you pointed out, it's been a hell of a week. And now, to top it all, instead of drinking a good white, curled up on the sofa in front of the telly, you've got me coming along to this.'

'It'll be fun, you'll see.' Emma tugged on Tash's hand gently. 'Come on, we hardly ever go out on girly nights any more. And, besides, aren't you dying to find out what Millie has done with the old chapel?'

'Yeah. Suppose.' Tash had gone to school with Millie. Although not close friends, they often bumped into each other at events to promote businesses in Berecombe. Tash admired Millie's work ethic and was a regular at her café. Scuffing her foot on the sandy prom, she noted that the hem of her trousers was already getting frayed. She should have worn her heels but Adrian didn't like her in them. She was already a good four inches taller than him in bare feet. Something he hated. 'Lead me on then, girlfriend.' She shook her finger at Emma. 'But I warn you, if it's boring or the wine is undrinkable, I'm out of there.'

Chapter 2

The book group was being held in the new extension to Millie Vanilla's Café. When Millie had bought up the old seaman's chapel next to the café, the town had been agog to see what she had planned for it. There were some who voiced disappointment when it had been announced it was going to be an extension to the café and a bookshop. They'd hoped for a Rick-Stein-style fish restaurant. After all, it hadn't done Padstow's tourist industry any harm, had it? The builders working on the continuing refurbishment of the newly launched Henville Manor Hotel had moonlighted and, after a few short months, the refit was complete.

Even the most ardent Rick fan had been won over. A wide glass walkway had been built to connect the original café building to the chapel's side door. The whole of the west side of the building had been removed and replaced with two-storey-high windows which looked over the harbour and the sunsets. Even the terrace had been extended right around both buildings to create a huge open space. In the pinkening light of the sunset, with the bunting fluttering and people milling about in front, it looked wonderful.

Despite her preoccupation with Adrian, Tash gasped as she

walked in. She'd only ever walked past the building before and had ignored it in its boarded-up state. When she'd heard it was on the market her interest as an estate agent had been pricked, but as soon as it had gone up for sale it had been snapped up. Not long after she'd heard Millie and Jed had bought it and she'd joined in with the rest of Berecombe in wondering just what they had planned. They'd done an amazing job in a very short space of time, she thought, as she looked around in awe. Running around the inside, giving access to the upper floor, was a wide walkway, wider where it butted up against the double-height window. There, low leather chairs and sofas had been arranged to make a cosy reading space – that's if you could tear your gaze away from the stunning sunset. There were bookshelves everywhere, with old-fashioned sliding ladders dotted about. The part nearest the glass corridor was set up as an extension to the café, with scrubbed pine tables and benches. A few people had gathered there, clutching wine glasses and chatting.

Amy Chilcombe, the bookshop's manager, greeted them. 'Natasha, Emma, how great to see you. Come on over and grab some wine. I'll introduce everyone once we're all sitting down in the reading area.' She caught Tash's glance and her huge blue eyes blinked nervously. 'Not all the stocks of books have arrived yet. The grand opening isn't for a while.' She nodded to the far end of the building, where some makeshift screens had been put up. 'And the children's area is still under construction too.'

'Just as well you're not open yet then, isn't it?' Tash said and received a sharp elbow from Emma.

'Be nice,' her friend hissed.

Tash apologised. 'Sorry Amy. Came out sharper than intended. I'm in a foul mood.' Things between them could be awkward and she never really understood why Amy was so nervous around her. True, Tash's first boyfriend had dumped her to go out with Amy but that hadn't ended well either. If anything, she and Amy should have bonded in female solidarity against unreliable men but it had never happened. She attempted a friendly smile. 'We'll get a glass and then where do we go?'

Amy blushed and cast a worried look at Tash. 'The reading area is up there, on the mezzanine level.' She pointed to the comfortable-looking area that Tash had spotted earlier. 'I hope we've got room for everyone. More have turned up than I anticipated.'

'Probably just want to have a nosey around,' Tash said, without thinking. 'You know what people are like in Berecombe when there's something new.'

'But they might stay on for the book group,' Emma added, more helpfully. As Amy went to greet two men who had just walked in, she rounded on Tash. 'What has got into you tonight? Would it hurt to even try to be nice? You know how shy and unconfident Amy can be.'

'I thought I was being nice? I can't help it if Amy jumps like a cat whenever I'm around,' Tash retorted, immediately regretting it when she saw the hurt look on Emma's face. She should have stayed at home. She couldn't seem to snap out of her mood.

'Sometimes I feel I just don't know you any more, Tash.' Emma paused, on the verge of saying something else, before she decided not to. 'I'll get us some wine, you go on up. I'm not sure you're fit company for anyone tonight. I don't know why you bothered to come.'

She turned away before Tash could apologise. Tash stared after her friend for a second and then made her way to the spiral staircase before she could change her mind and go home. The image of Adrian lying on their bed grinning had her running up the stairs and tripping on her long trousers.

'Careful.'

Tash would have fallen had the owner of the voice not grabbed her arm. A man was coming up the stairs behind her.

'They shouldn't put such dangerous stairs in a place like this,' Tash said. 'I could sue.'

The man smiled. 'More haste, less speed.' He pointed to the hem of her trousers. 'And I think any case for damages might have failed on the grounds of personal negligence,' he added, mildly.

She followed his look and saw the hem of one leg of her palazzo pants had completely unravelled. 'Well, this evening started off badly and is just getting worse.' Turning away, she took the rest of the stairs more carefully. She flopped onto the nearest chair, annoyed to see him take the one next to it. Just what she needed. Another arrogant man, telling her what to do. She had it at work, she suffered it at home and now had to endure it in her free time too.

'Why, because of a hem coming down?'

She ignored the remark.

He held out a hand. 'Kit Oakley.'

Tash gritted her teeth and then remembered Emma's comment about not being fit company. 'Natasha Taylor,' she offered, grudgingly.

'Oh,' he said, raising his eyebrows. 'The estate agent.'

'Yes. And before you say anything, some of us are quite human.'

'I believe *some* of you are.'

Tash resisted the barb. She was tired of the jokes, the criticism her profession received. If only people realised how hard they all worked. Then a thought stopped her. 'Hang on, Oakley? I sold a bungalow belonging to a Mrs Oakley last month. Over Southleigh way.'

Kit grinned. 'My mother. She said you worked tirelessly.'

'Yes, it all got a bit tricky just before exchange. Problems over a questionable access, I remember.' Tash relaxed a little. She loved talking about work. 'Glad it went through though. She's lovely.'

'I'll tell her. She'll be delighted.'

'Where's she gone to?' Tash was curious. Mrs Oakley had always been welcoming and they'd shared a pot of tea once, but she'd not mentioned where she was moving to. 'All I knew was that it was a no chain sale.'

'Moved in with me, for my sins.' He raised his eyebrows again. 'I've bought up a ramshackle of a place with land. It's on the outskirts of Colyton. Mum's got the lodge.'

'Oh, the old Fairbairn farm?'

'You know it?'

'Only farm big enough around here to have a lodge house.'

'You're good!'

'It's my job.'

They smiled at one another warily, stowing their weapons and sensing a truce.

Emma arrived, carrying two glasses of wine. She handed

one to Tash without a word and then settled in the chair next to Kit and began chatting to him.

So much for Emma being nervous, Tash thought as she grinned. She sipped her wine which, to her relief, was delicious and found herself studying the man next to her. She couldn't say he was good-looking, not in any conventional sense. Actually, not in any sense. He was very tall and she could see he had a well-muscled build even though it was disguised under a pair of baggy jeans and a grey hoodie. A powerful nose separated deep set eyes and he had a scrubby beard, a slightly darker brown than his hair. Clearly he felt he could dress up, Tash thought to herself sarcastically. He and Emma suddenly looked at her and, for one second, she was worried she may have said it out loud. An unaccustomed blush stole over her cheeks and she finished her wine in one gulp. She really was in no fit state to be out.

Chapter 3

The chairs and sofa in the reading area gradually filled up. Millie welcomed everyone, said they were all invited to the grand opening in a few weeks' time and then explained she was handing over to Amy who was going to run the group.

'Thank you, Millie. And thank you for providing the wine and the sandwiches and coffee for later.' Amy's hands fluttered. 'Perhaps we could go round the group and tell each other who we are and a little bit about what we do, what we like to read? I know most of us know one another but it might help those of us who don't. Know one another, I mean.'

Emma rescued her. 'Great idea, Amy. Shall I go first?' She beamed at the group. 'I'm Emma Tizzard and you all probably know, I work with Natasha at Hughes and Widrow, the estate agent's up in town. I absolutely love to read and I'll read anything. I'm working my way through the *Poldark* series at the moment. The main problem is time.' She looked around. 'It's probably something we all battle with. Finding the time to read.' A few nodded. 'Well, that's me...' She tailed off and looked to Kit.

'I'm Kit Oakley,' he said after clearing his throat. 'Just moved into the area. I'm in the middle of setting up the farm I've just bought. Like Emma, I love to read and will read anything too, although I don't sleep much so finding the time is maybe easier. Reading at night means I get through an awful lot of reading material.'

There were one or two murmurs of sympathy and then Tash realised it was her turn. 'I'm Natasha, although most people call me Tash. As Emma said, we work together at the estate agents. I'm the manager. I live up on the new estate on the edge of town and I don't have much time to read at all but when I do I like something escapist, a good beach read.' There was no reaction to this at all. Sod them. Tash stopped talking and turned to the woman next to her.

'Well, you all know me,' she began, stoutly. 'I'm Biddy Roulestone, used to be Treeby, as I've not long married.' One or two giggled. Biddy glared and they shut up. 'I like a good biography or a bit of Dickens and I'm partial to erotica, as long as it's well written, that is.'

Tash smothered a laugh. She knew Biddy by reputation. Pete, her manager before his promotion, had dealt with Biddy when she'd bought the huge house on the hill. She'd been a cash buyer. He claimed he'd never recovered from the experience.

One by one, they all introduced themselves. The only other man present caused a slight stir when he said he was Patrick Carroll and a writer. Tash saw the blush creep over Amy's face and didn't blame her. The man, with his black hair and vivid blue eyes, was gorgeous.

A woman in an arty linen smock and large earrings introduced herself last. 'I'm Marti Cavendish and I live on the new development too.' She smirked at the group as if they should all be impressed by the fact.

Tash had noticed her when she'd come in. She thought she looked familiar and now recognised her from the six-bedroom detached at the end of the cul-de-sac. It was the biggest, most expensive house on the estate. She often flashed past Tash's house in her Audi convertible.

'You probably know me as I volunteer in the charity shop,' Marti preened. 'I love to read too and I read most things but not those big books with the gold lettering.' She gave a delicate shudder. 'I don't read trash.' She gave Tash a quick look as if in challenge.

Tash was about to retaliate and then remembered, as an estate agent in a small town, it wasn't politic to annoy anyone. You never knew whose house you were going to sell next.

Amy beamed. 'Millie, do you want to add anything?'

Millie smiled. 'Just that you all know me, Millie Fudge, or rather Millie Henville now. I was ecstatic to buy this old place and rescue it. Owning a bookshop is a real bucket list tick for me, because I've always loved to read and belonged to the library's book club for years, when it was running. Or tried to. Work kept getting in the way.' She shrugged, her brown hair falling over her face. 'I just love reading, talking about books. Any kind of books. I never had the chance to go to university, so I've been trying to make up for it ever since, I suppose. To get people together and discussing what they've read is a dream and I'm determined, now I've got a full-time manager in the café, to be fully committed to a book group this time.' She turned to Tash before she continued. 'And I love escapist beach reads too. Oh, and I also promise to provide good food and wine!' Everyone laughed. They knew Millie's reputation for great catering.

'Thanks Millie,' Amy said. She looked around and blushed again. 'Well, that's everyone. Thank you for coming. Our next task is to decide which book we want to read for this month.'

'I'll go and get some more wine, shall I?' Millie offered. 'This could take some time.'

It did.

No one could agree. Emma suggested one of the *Poldark* books, Patrick offered a travelogue about walking in the Hindu Kush and Biddy wanted *A Tale of Two Cities*. Tash kept out of it. After all, she'd only agreed to come with Em for this first meeting, she had no intention of coming again and certainly wouldn't bother reading any of the books. The arguments even continued throughout Millie's excellent sandwiches and coffee. They re-grouped back in the reading area, with topped up wine glasses.

'What about *Wuthering Heights*?' Kit put in. Everyone stopped bickering and looked at him. He had a way of commanding attention. Perhaps it was the deep, authoritative voice. The sun had lowered almost into the sea and, as it shone through the huge windows, imbued the reading area with a warm orange glow. It deepened his suntan and picked out the red highlights in his hair.

'Oh, I loved that when we had to read it at school,' Tash said, impulsively.

'I so adore the classics,' Marti gushed. 'Oh, Charlotte Brontë. The Mahler of the literary world, as I always like to think of her.'

The women who had come with her looked on admiringly and nodded.

'It's Emily Brontë, actually,' Tash said.

Marti blinked. 'Did I say Charlotte? I meant Emily, of course.' She flushed unbecomingly.

'It's easy to mix them up,' Emma said, ever the diplomat. 'I never have a clue who wrote what.'

'Haven't read any Brontë for years,' Biddy said. 'And I was born in that part of the world. Be good to reread it. Cruel book though,' she added and shuddered.

Amy looked from one face to the other. '*Wuthering Heights*, then? I mean, we could discuss a few more?'

'I think most of us are in agreement, Amy,' Kit said, looking around. The others gave a collective sigh, obviously relieved something had been decided. He looked at his watch. 'And it's getting quite late. I have to get back to put the chickens away.'

That was the cue for people to begin gathering their coats and bags.

'Millie,' Biddy roared, getting up and going over to her. 'Got a new recipe for chocolate brownies. Think they might go down a storm in the caff.'

'Same time in three weeks,' Amy spluttered, aware she was losing control of the group and trying to regain it desperately. 'I've got all your email addresses so I'll be in touch. Thank you all for coming,' she called, as they tripped down the spiral staircase and drifted out into the night. 'And don't forget the bookshop's grand opening in a couple of weeks!'

Taking pity on her and seeing Millie had been ambushed by Biddy, Tash volunteered Emma and herself to help tidy up. They pushed the chairs back into position to the soundtrack of Amy's effusive thanks. Kit glanced at Marti, as she ushered her coterie out. She was talking loudly about the importance of Emmaline Brontë's poetry. He blew out a frustrated breath and began to collect glasses.

'Put them in the kitchen in the café please, Kit,' Millie said, having escaped Biddy's clutches. Kit nodded and hefted a tray downstairs. 'Nice man,' she said, as the women watched him disappear.

'Strangely attractive too, in a weird way,' Emma added. 'Scything muscles to die for.'

Tash looked at them in disdain. 'Close your mouth Em, you're salivating. And get a grip, you've got Ollie. I can't see the attraction, personally. Big nose. Felt a bit sorry for you, Amy. He practically took over.'

'I didn't mind, actually.' Amy blushed. 'It was getting a bit out of hand, wasn't it? I never thought we'd agree on a book. I was so relieved when he suggested *Wuthering Heights*. Thanks again for helping to clear up,' she added and looked around, checking one last time. 'See you next time.'

Tash followed Emma downstairs, careful to hold up the legs of her trousers. As they got outside she stopped for a minute and lifted her head to the night. 'It's so clear tonight. Look at the stars.' She took a deep, cleansing breath and realised she felt much better, far more relaxed. Perhaps coming out had helped after all?

A tall, bulky figure strode out of the newly-installed bi-fold doors at the front of Millie Vanilla's. Kit. He put up a hand in farewell and disappeared onto the promenade. With his long, loping strides, he'd reached halfway in seconds.

Emma followed Tash's gaze as she watched his progress. 'You going to come back for the next meeting, then?'

'Maybe. Maybe I just will.'

They began the walk home, following in Kit's footsteps along the prom.

A familiar deep-throated growl of an engine sounded. It was Adrian in his Porsche, coming towards them. He drove along the road bordering the promenade, slowed when he passed Kit and then accelerated again, before skidding to a halt in front of Emma and Tash.

The window buzzed down. 'Thought I'd save you the walk up the hill,' he called out cheerfully. 'Hop in. You too, Emma, room for a little one in the back.'

'Thanks Adrian,' Emma said, as she clambered onto the miniscule back seat. 'Great timing.'

Tash got into the passenger seat and clipped on her seatbelt. She could feel him staring at her.

'That's what I thought,' he said and gunned the engine down the side street to home.

Chapter 4

The next evening, as Tash parked her car on the drive after a long day at work, she felt her shoulders drop. She'd been on the phone for most of the day trying to persuade some clients not to pull out at the last moment. There was nothing the matter with the property they were buying, they were just nervous first-time buyers. The problem being the buying chain depended on them and would collapse if they changed their mind. Having flitted between them and their solicitor and the vendor of the house they were buying, she'd eventually coaxed them into agreeing to exchange the next week. A disaster had been narrowly averted and she'd driven home feeling satisfied. The challenges of her job were the things she loved most. Especially if theend result was a happy one.

As she slid her key in the lock and opened the front door, the aroma of chicken casserole, rich with herbs and wine, hit her. Glancing into the dining room, she saw the table was set with lit candles and their best Jasper Conran. A bottle of prosecco sat in the cooler. The exhilaration of a difficult day doing what she loved best and doing it well, fled. The seduction scene unnerved her. It was only too familiar. Adrian wanted something and she wondered what.

From the sounds upstairs, he was in the shower. Half of her wanted to sneak back outside and grab a pizza and beer with Emma. But if she came in late and smelling of alcohol, it would only make matters worse.

Biting her lip, she hung up her suit jacket and slipped off her heels. She padded into the dining room and poured herself a glass of prosecco. How had it come to this? She was skulking around in her own home, trying to second-guess just what might provoke Adrian into a mood.

It had all been so different this time two years ago. She'd met Adrian at a summer charity ball. She'd gone along with Pete Hingham, to represent Hughes and Widrow. Pete had recently been promoted to area manager, leaving the way clear for her to step up into the role of manager of the busy Berecombe office. Both she and Pete were in high spirits, looking forward to some good food and copious amounts of champagne. The evening had been warm and sultry and the doors to the terrace had been flung open to a starry midsummer night. Maybe she'd had too much fizz, or maybe she'd just been carried away by the romance of the night but she'd tripped onto the terrace, longing for some cooler air after dancing for hours.

Adrian had been leaning against the low stone balustrade, sipping from his champagne flute and staring into the darkened garden. As he heard her, he turned and smiled.

'Of all the terraces in all the world, you had to walk onto this one.' He held out a second glass and she took it.

It was a complete romantic cliché. She'd not even wondered why he had two glasses when he was alone, but had fallen for it. She had perched on the stone wall and chatted. He was very handsome and, even in a room full of sharply tuxedoed men, he stood out. Glossy dark hair, piercing blue eyes and the whitest, most perfect teeth she'd ever seen. It was only when he took her back into the ballroom for a slow dance that she realised he was shorter than her by several inches. Usually, things like that mattered to her a lot; she put a premium on how things looked. Being with a short man, especially as she was addicted to perilously high heels, just didn't look right.

Adrian Williams was older than her, an established property developer, obviously monied and the most sophisticated man who had ever taken an interest. At first, she had been fiercely attracted. After that initial evening, he took her out on a series of imaginative dates. They enjoyed a helicopter ride along the coast and attended a Mozart concerto followed by the most sumptuous Thai meal Tash had ever eaten. After Adrian had discovered Tash's love of penguins, he'd even arranged a picnic next to the penguin pool at Bristol Zoo. And he'd not laid a finger on her. It had made her even more desperate for him. They'd finally consummated the relationship while on a long weekend in Paris. The fact that he'd booked separate rooms decided it for her. The sex had been mind-blowing. It hadn't been much of a leap when he'd asked her to move in with him in the executive detached he'd just bought on the outskirts of Berecombe.

When she'd queried why he'd bought it, he'd laughed and said he spent his working life on building sites and wanted something easy to come home to. Then he'd grabbed her by the waist and kissed her until her lips were numb.

Emma warned her she was rushing into something, but her

mother seemed delighted she was happy, and Pete was ecstatic as she was on fire at work and exceeded all her monthly targets. Tash ignored them all and found, to her surprise, that she enjoyed coming home to the same man every night. The sex continued to be amazing even if, occasionally, Adrian coaxed her into doing it when she really didn't feel like it.

And then, when the honeymoon glow had faded, another side of the genial, indulgent Adrian emerged. Earlier in the summer he began buying clothes that he wanted her to wear. Tash didn't mind so much the racy underwear and peephole bras; she found them hugely funny. She was less of a fan of the wide-legged trousers he insisted on, the expensive but figure-concealing cashmere sweaters. He pouted and sulked when she tugged on the slim skirts and jackets she preferred for work. 'Wouldn't you rather be warm and comfortable?' he wheedled, as he held out the tunic he'd just brought home.

Tash surveyed the navy blue top with dismay, looking at its high V-neck and discreet pattern. Her lip curled. 'It's lovely, Ade,' she said without thinking. 'But it's something my mother would wear. Thank you but it's just not my thing.' She'd registered his suddenly shuttered look and wondered what she'd said. That night, after he cajoled her into a marathon bout of sex, they had their first row. She'd hurt his feelings, Adrian said. Rejected his generosity. Tash felt guilty. The top was obviously expensive. She agreed to wear it at the weekend.

He developed other weird habits too. Flying into a jealous rage if she talked about Pete too much, picking her up after a night out with her girlfriends saying it was so she could have a drink but always too early, when the evening had only just got going.

Tash had toyed with the idea of leaving but something always tugged her back to her original feelings for him. After a tantrum, Adrian lavished attention on her. He talked about taking a long holiday in south Africa, of buying an apartment in Paris. The house was convenient for work and she liked the kudos of his money. She put his moods down to work stress; when things were tough, he suffered stomach problems. Besides, how would it look if the relationship folded? Everyone told her she had the perfect life. How could she admit it was anything but? So, she shrugged his contrariness off. She knew loads of friends who had problems in their relationships. She was a strong, confident woman. She could handle a man like Adrian.

Chapter 5

He came up behind her as she sipped her wine. Reaching up, he kissed her neck and exclaimed, 'Good, you're back! Just in time.' He smelled of shower gel.

Tash felt a rush of affection for him and was relieved. Maybe things weren't so bad, after all? She turned and smiled. 'You've gone to so much trouble.'

'I know you love my casserole. Creamy mash to go with it, loads of butter. You sit down and I'll serve. Pour me some fizz, will you? I held off until you were back.'

'I'll get fat,' Tash complained, filling his glass and topping up her own.

'Nonsense,' he called through from the kitchen. He reappeared, wearing his butcher's striped apron and carrying a casserole pot. 'Besides—' he winked '—I like some meat on my women.' He placed the dish on the trivet and disappeared to get the potatoes.

Once they'd eaten, Tash sat back replete. 'That was one of your best, Ade. Delicious. I'm going to have to unbutton my skirt though. I've eaten far too much.' She reached around to the back of her work skirt and sighed as the waistband eased.

Adrian gave her an odd look. He stared at her stomach

intently and then took a breath. 'You're not ... you don't think we're pregnant?' He paused, and stared owlishly at her.

'God, no. At least I bloody well hope not.' Tash shuddered.

'Don't swear Natasha, you know I don't like it.' He picked up his flute of prosecco and sipped thoughtfully. 'I wouldn't mind, actually. Having a baby, I mean.'

'Well, I would,' Tash answered, robustly. 'It's not the right time for me. I want to make area manager before I'm thirty and try to set up on my own eventually. A baby wouldn't fit into that.'

'You could always give up work.' Adrian clocked her horrified expression and back-tracked. 'Or go part-time?'

'No,' she said firmly. 'No babies. Not now.' Not ever, she added silently. *And not with you*, came the echo.

'Well, that told me,' Adrian said but cheerfully enough. 'A discussion for another time. Shall we take the coffee into the sitting room? I'll clear up later, there isn't much to do.'

Ensconced on the sofa leaning against Adrian, with some Puccini on in the background, Tash felt more mellow. She looked around at the cream and white décor and couldn't help feeling slightly smug. She'd had a great day at work, a man who had cooked her a superb meal and this wonderfully luxurious house to come back to. At this very moment, her life seemed as perfect as the image she tried so hard to put out to the world. To those who had bullied her at school and made her feel as if her life would never amount to much.

'Perhaps we should do Glyndebourne next year?' Adrian said.

Tash shifted against him. 'That's come out of the blue.'

'Not really. I used to go every year before I met you.'

'It's funny. You've never really talked about then. Before me, I mean. Have you had many girlfriends?' She twisted her head round to look up at him and caught his quizzical smile.

'Never a very ladylike thing to ask, Natasha.' He laughed softly. 'I had my fair share, I suppose. What about you?'

'Not the most gentlemanly thing to ask,' she countered. 'I was always too busy concentrating on work. Only had one boyfriend before you.'

'Really?' Adrian sounded pleased.

'And at school I was always the fat one with glasses. Had my eyes lasered as soon as I could. None of the boys wanted to know until I was twenty-four and I'd lost three stone and the bottom of bottle specs.' Tash giggled but there was an underlying note of hurt. 'Then I had the satisfaction of telling them where to go.'

'I bet you did. I really can't imagine you fat.' He pinched her thigh quite hard. 'Who was this one boyfriend, then?'

'Lee Styles. He got engaged to Amy Chilcombe last year but dumped her at the altar.'

'How awful,' Adrian murmured. 'Who's Amy Chilcombe?'

'She's running Millie's new bookshop. The one where the book club was held last night.' Tash could have sawed out her tongue with a blunt knife. The book club was a touchy subject. The Puccini ended and the room fell ominously silent. She tensed for Adrian's inevitable quicksilver change of mood.

'You still haven't told me who was there.' Adrian still sounded relaxed but Tash detected an edge to his voice.

'Oh, you know, the usual.' She felt the muscles in his arm stiffen.

'I don't know, actually. Tell me.'

'Millie, Amy, Emma of course. Oh, and Biddy, and some snob called Marti and a few of her acolytes. She lives on the estate.'

'Natasha please. Executive housing development. It's hardly an estate.' Adrian chuckled and then his mood changed. 'Any men?' This time there was definite steel in his voice.

'Erm, a couple. A writer called Patrick Carroll or something and some bloke called Kit, I think.' Tash said, deliberately vague.

'Ah. And was that one of them walking back along the promenade when I picked you up?'

'Dunno. Might have been.' Tash hated how defensive Adrian made her feel.

'Tall chap. Scruffy. Wearing a disreputable beanie.'

'Sounds like the Kit bloke,' Tash admitted. She'd have to tell him the truth; he had a way of finding out when she lied. 'He helped Millie clear up.' She waited for Adrian's reaction, without daring to breathe.

'Ah.'

Tash forced herself to relax. He'd taken it quite well.

Adrian kissed the top of her head. 'And now, my darling, I think it's time for bed.'

He made her dress up in the PVC nurse's outfit. When she complained, he pouted and said that after all the trouble he'd gone to with dinner, it was the least she could do. But, apart from that, the sex was fairly normal. For once.

Chapter 6

On her day off Tash decided to go for a walk. She hardly ever went for walks. It wasn't something she and Adrian did. Meals in expensive restaurants or drinks parties with his business contacts were more their style. Or rather Adrian's style. She missed the simpler pleasures she'd enjoyed before him. It was funny how life with Adrian had consumed her. She used to love walking her parents' dog. She hadn't seen them for ages, or Benji, their over-indulged Westie. So she decided – once Adrian had left for work, she'd go and have a coffee with her mother and borrow the dog for a few hours.

She waved Adrian off at dawn on a peerlessly beautiful August day. The house martins chattered above them as she saw him into his car. He was going on one of his regular trips to Manchester to reccie possible development projects and was grumpy. He hated going away.

Looking up at the birds, he grumbled, 'We'll have to clear the guttering before they nest next year. They've made a right mess. Put netting up. Bloody things.'

Tash smiled tightly. She handed him his briefcase as he squeezed into the Porsche. She wasn't the only one putting on weight. 'Drive safely.'

'Will do, don't want to risk any more points on the licence. Cops spot this car and think it's fair game. I'll give you a ring tonight.' He slammed the car door hard, revved the engine and gave a loud toot as he went.

Tash winced as she saw curtains twitch in the house opposite. It was very early. She wished Adrian would be a little more considerate sometimes. Giving a conciliatory wave to her neighbour who had opened her bedroom window and glared, she fled inside. She tried to ignore the flush of freedom that a few days without Adrian always produced.

'This is more like it,' Tash chatted to Benji as he scampered up the hill. She'd driven to a local spot popular with dog walkers on the outskirts of Berecombe. Once an old hill fort, it had spectacular views over Chesil Beach and towards Portland. As it was still early, there were few others about and a cool breeze softened the hot day which promised.

It had been a good summer. The town was full to bursting with tourists and the place was revving up for Lifeboat Month. Some complained the grockles got in the way, that you couldn't walk along the pavements and there was never anywhere to park but Tash loved the buzz. As she'd driven through town yesterday, on the way to the office, the bunting was being strung up across the main street; she adored its frivolity.

She wandered to the eastern side of the hill and perched on one of the benches, enjoying the sight of the sea, a smudge of silvered pink in the early morning haze. Benji nosed contentedly around at her feet. Tash closed her eyes. She felt very peaceful and curiously free. She had two whole days to herself. Adrian wasn't back until Thursday. She concentrated on the sound of a bird, a skylark maybe, high above her and the snuffle of Benji's nose as he discovered fascinating new smells. His sudden bark had her eyes open in a flash.

'Hello there.'

A man was standing a little way away from her. He had his hand on the collar of the most enormous dog Tash had ever seen. It was grey and rangy with a noble head. Not unlike its owner. 'Kit. Hello.'

'I'm sorry. Did I disturb you?'

The Westie had his hackles up and had begun to growl. 'Benji, stop that,' Tash scolded and clipped the terrier back on the lead. 'Sorry, he can be a bit of a grump with other dogs sometimes.'

'Not a problem. Merlin can look upon dogs smaller than him as prey but he's very laidback most of the time. May I join you, or would you rather have the place to yourself?'

It seemed churlish not to share the bench so Tash shuffled up. Besides, she was curious about Merlin. 'What breed is he?' she asked, after he and Benji had sniffed each other thoroughly, decided there was no threat on either side and then gone on to ignore each other.

'Irish wolfhound.'

'Does he come across many dogs bigger than him?'

'Sorry?'

'You said Merlin treats dogs smaller than him as prey. I'm surprised he meets any bigger.' She reached over and rubbed the dog's head.

Kit laughed. 'He's a gentle giant but, when people meet him for the first time, he can come across as a tad alarming. I tend to be on the defensive.'

Merlin whickered in agreement.

'He has the most intelligent eyes,' Tash said. She pulled on the dog's ears gently.

'A wise old man's soul in a dog's body, this one.' Kit ruffled Merlin's head and his and Tash's hands met.

Tash snatched hers away. Their eyes met and she felt herself blushing. Desperate to fill the charged silence, she blurted out the obvious. 'Beautiful day.'

'It is. Can't argue with you on that. Hadn't pegged you as a dog person.' Kit nodded to Benji who had stretched out next to her feet.

'Oh, Benji's not mine. He belongs to my parents. Spoiled rotten too. I haven't got a dog, Adrian doesn't like the mess they make so I borrow Benji every now and again.'

'Adrian?'

'My boyfriend.' Tash felt her face grow hot again. Why should she be embarrassed about admitting to Adrian?

'Oh.' Tash could see Kit processing the information. 'Well,' he conceded, 'they can make an awful lot of mess. Lot of work too.'

'Yes, doubt if I could cope, what with working full-time.' Tash tried to keep the longing out of her voice. She'd happily put up with a bit of disruption if it meant she could have a dog. It was Adrian who had flatly refused to have any kind of pet. He'd even put his foot down about the idea of a hamster. 'They smell,' he'd moaned.

'Probably best to borrow one once in a while then. Dogs like someone around and it's tricky if you work.'

'Do you? Work, I mean?' It wasn't just Merlin Tash was curious about.

Kit chuckled. 'I have a dog, two cats, a brood of

argumentative chickens, one or two goats and three donkeys. Plus an orchard I can't decide what to do with on top of an awful lot of land. I count that as work.'

'But you haven't always had the farm, have you? What did you do before?'

She felt Kit's gaze, hot on her face. He leaned nearer. He smelled of old-fashioned coal tar soap, with an earthy undertone. It wasn't unpleasant and a world away from Adrian's sluiced-on Paco Rabanne.

'Can you keep a secret?'

'Oh yes,' Tash smiled. 'I'm good at keeping secrets.'

'Part of your job, I suppose?'

'Well, client confidentiality is important.' It wasn't what she had meant but she let it go. 'What's this secret then?' This was fun, she realised. It was almost like flirting.

'I had a lottery win.'

'No! Really?' Tash was delighted, it seemed so incongruous. 'Why keep it secret though?'

Kit shrugged. 'I'm a private kind of a person. Mum is too. I bought the winning ticket but gave it to her for a birthday present. She persuaded me to buy the farm with the half she gave me. It was great at first. Then we got the piles of begging letters. Some were obviously fake but most were genuine. Mum decided to donate what she could but couldn't cope. So we shut the doors and decided not to tell anyone.' Kit picked a grass seed out of Merlin's coat, frowning. 'Money changes how people react to you. Not always for the better. Not that I'm complaining though. Mum's got a nice home, I get to do what I've always wanted to. Have a bit of land, a few animals. Thinking about what to do next.'

'What were you before you won?' Tash was agog. She'd never met a big-time lottery winner before. She wondered how much money was involved but it seemed rude to ask.

'That's the other secret.' Kit gave an impish grin. 'I was a dentist.' He shrugged. 'Not sure which is the more unpopular. Estate agent. Dentist. The two most loathed professions.'

Tash roared. She hadn't laughed so much in ages. When she'd calmed down, she said, 'Dentists, estate agents, we get some real stick, don't we?' She looked at him properly, for the first time. Still no better looking, she decided, but she couldn't deny he was sexy. With his shabby beanie hat and scrubby stubble she couldn't imagine a less likely dentist, though. She said as much.

'Oh, I agree,' he said, affably. 'I enjoyed it while I did it but the hours were epic and I was stuck in a surgery all day looking down people's throats.' He grinned. 'I was glad to get out of it. Much prefer the fresh air and freedom.'

'So now you spend your day with animals instead. At least you'll know what to do if one of the donkeys has toothache.'

'Ha ha. As far as I know, animal dentistry is a whole other ball game. And if anyone had walked in to my surgery with teeth like a donkey, I think I would have run. Speaking of which—' he glanced at his watch '—that's what I have to do now. It's getting too hot for Merlin and I've got the donkeys to muck out.'

'Now that is hard work,' Tash agreed. 'I used to help out at a stable when I was a horse-mad teenager. Aren't they out to pasture at this time of the year though?' They stood up and began to walk back to the car park.

'Rescues,' Kit said, as a way of explanation. 'Someone

attacked them one night and they still get spooked being out in the paddock when it's dark. Owner couldn't cope so I re-homed them.' He sighed. 'Have to stable them at the moment.'

'That's awful!' Tash stopped dead and looked up at him, her mouth open in disgust. She hated any cruelty to animals.

Kit shrugged. 'I'm trying to find ways of gradually getting them used to being outside but nothing's working at the moment.'

'Maybe get in touch with the donkey sanctuary over at Sidmouth?'

'I'll have to do that.'

As they reached what Tash assumed was his car, a dusty Freelander, she smiled at him. 'It's been great bumping into you.' Giving Merlin a stroke, she added, 'And you too, Merlin.'

'Come over and see the farm one day.' Kit opened the Freelander's tailgate and the dog leaped up gracefully. 'I'm hoping to acquire some ducks soon.'

'How could I resist?'

'How, indeed?' He came to her and looked down. 'And it's been lovely bumping into you too, Natasha Taylor the estate agent. Come for a coffee. Mum would love to see you again.'

'I will.' By the time she'd persuaded a reluctant Benji to get into her car, Kit had driven off. 'What a great start to my day off,' she said to a completely uninterested terrier. The sun had risen in the sky and the heat in the car had built up to a suffocating level. She buzzed all the windows down. Once she'd dropped Benji off, the garden and a book beckoned. She was ready to top off her tan with Heathcliff for company. 'A perfect day,' she added. In her pocket her phone came to life as it got a signal. On it were fifteen texts from Adrian asking where she was and why she wasn't answering her mobile.

Chapter 7

'But I want to do it. I like raising money for the RNLI. I happen to think it's important.' Tash tried to keep the petulance out of her voice. She really couldn't see why Adrian was so dead set against a fun run. 'It's for Lifeboat Month.' She opened the kitchen door and went into the hall.

'I know exactly what it's for, Natasha,' Adrian said, following her so closely she could feel his breath hot on her neck. 'I just don't see why you need to go out three times a week dressed like that.'

'If I'm going to take part, I want to train for it. I don't intend on coming in last. And, for goodness sake Adrian, what the hell do you expect me to wear to go running? A winceyette dressing gown? Of course I'll wear my shorts. Stop being so ridiculous.' It was the second time they'd argued about it. The last time Adrian had got round her and taken her to bed so she'd missed the training run with Emma. She needed to train; there was no way she was going to be beaten by a girl who thought a crisp sandwich was health food. Tash thought she'd gone too far with the last comment but Adrian just made what she privately termed his cat's arse face.

'I was going to make my special cottage pie. With cheesy potatoes.'

His voice had a whining quality that had Tash taking several deep breaths before she trusted herself to answer. 'That would have been lovely Ade, but I need to cut my carbs if I'm going to be serious about this.' She went into the hall and sat on the vintage pew that they'd sourced from a very expensive antiques centre in Exeter. She slipped her feet into her running shoes and began tying the laces.

His mood changed, as unpredictable as ever. 'Serious? It's a fun run for charity, Natasha, not the London bloody Marathon.'

Tash tried to disarm him. 'Don't swear Adrian. I don't like it.' Getting up, she faced him. The attempt at humour hadn't worked. Out of the corner of her eye she could see her car keys hanging on the hooks by the front door. If necessary, she was sure she could grab them and be out of the door before he – she bit off the thought. What did she think he was going to do? Hit her? No. He'd never do that. He loved her.

He took a step towards her. His eyes bulged a little and he'd broken out into a clammy sweat.

Tash sucked in a sharp breath as his hand fisted to white knuckles. Her fingers inched towards her keys. Then she saw his shoulders relax and the tension splintered.

'I just don't understand why you don't want to spend any time with me nowadays.' His voice had gone back to wheedling. 'You're either at work late, off at this book club or out running.' He reached out a hand and stroked her bare arm. Tash willed herself not to flinch. 'Why not spend the evening with me. Nice bottle of white in the garden. We

40

could go through those conservatory catalogues. You've always wanted a conservatory. Natasha, it's too hot to go running.'

'But I want to. It's important to me. For lots of reasons, Adrian. Not just the fun run but to get fitter too. I had to use an elastic band to fasten my work skirt this morning. I need to lose a few pounds.' She warmed to her theme as he seemed to be taking it calmly. 'And I enjoy my job, I want to do well. Like yours, it's not nine to five and that's one reason I love it. For the variety.' She put her head on one side, her pulse calming as he'd shown no reaction. 'And, the book club? Really? I've been once so far. We both work hard. We both play hard. I seem to remember that was what you liked about me when we met. Both ambitious, you said.'

'We are.' He took her hand. 'And yes, I did love that about you. Still do, Natasha. I can't help it,' he sighed. 'You're just so gorgeous, you make me want to spend all my time with you. I love you so very much.' His hand sneaked around her waist and he pulled her to him. He kissed her, backing her into the mirror on the wall. Tash's head banged against it. She used to find his roughness sexy. Took it as a sign of his passion. He trailed a kiss across to her collarbone and fisted a hand into her hair, holding her prisoner. 'We could have a baby, Natasha,' he murmured throatily. 'We could make a baby tonight. If you had a baby to look after, you wouldn't have time for running.'

Finding all the strength she had, she pushed him off. 'Not that again, Ade.' She looked into his lust-blurred eyes. 'It's not the right time for me. Not now.' She saw a tightening of his jaw. He was angry again. 'Look, I'll just go for a short run tonight. I'll be back by ten. We can still have that drink in the garden.' She'd lifted her keys and had escaped before she could gauge his reaction. Something told her she'd pay, in some way, on her return.

Chapter 8

'What *are* you wearing?' Tash looked up from the office's main computer. 'Morning to you too, Emma. You're late, by the way.'

'Soz. Couldn't shift Stevie out of the bathroom. Little bro has turned thirteen and discovered girls. And the shower. Used up all my shampoo.'

'You need to find a place to yourself.' Tash slumped back onto her desk chair and fanned herself. It was the beginning of another hot day and tourists were already thronging Berecombe's main street. On her way from the car park, Tash had ducked around several suntan-anointed families heading to the beach. Pausing before unlocking the agency's front door, she'd gazed after them wistfully, wishing her life was so carefree.

'No argument from me there. Can I have a pay rise then?' When Tash didn't rise to the bait, Emma said, 'So what are you wearing? Baggy's never been your thing. And how long is that skirt?' Emma twisted and peered down at Tash's feet. 'And flats?' Her eyes widened. 'The heel of your foot is never in contact with the ground!'

'Well, it is today. Haven't you got to put the coffee on?'

Emma flicked on her computer and got up. She went into the little kitchen and called through, as she boiled the kettle and rummaged for biscuits. 'Not up to high heels this morning? Bit stiff after the run last night?'

'You could say that.' Tash was sore but not for the reasons Emma was hinting at. She'd been right, she'd had to pay for defying Adrian. And what he'd done to her in bed had made her feel demeaned. It hadn't been even close to the erotic experience he'd promised her. But after a bottle of wine each, he'd persuaded her to let him do it. The final humiliation had been waking up to find he'd gone in early to work, leaving some clothes for her laid out in the dressing room. She'd hunted for her usual skirt suits and stilettos but they'd disappeared. In their place was the midi skirt, loose blouse and expensive-looking leather pumps that she was currently wearing. They were marginally smarter than the only other clothes left in the wardrobe.

Emma reappeared carrying two mugs of coffee. 'Great crowd last night. Brilliant that Millie and Jed turned up although I think Amy's going to struggle.'

Tash took her mug. 'Well, she's a bit of a lardy-arse.'

'That's so unkind, Tash! I seem to remember you weren't all that svelte not that long ago.'

'Yeah. And I did something about it.'

'Well, maybe Amy is trying to as well. It's not always easy.'

Tash bit her lip. Why was she such a cow sometimes? *Because you're unhappy*, said the voice in her head. She sipped her coffee. 'Sorry, I know it isn't. Sorry Em,' she repeated. 'I'm in a foul mood this morning.'

Emma raised an eloquent eyebrow. 'Just this morning?'

'Point taken.' Tash sat up straighter and took in a great gulp of breath. It was a gorgeous summer day, she lived and worked in a beautiful seaside town. She loved her job. Life was good, wasn't it? Glancing across at Emma she wondered if she'd understand? Emma was younger by a few years and happy in what seemed a loving and uncomplicated relationship with Ollie. Did he play mind games the way Adrian did? She was about to ask when Biddy Roulestone flung herself through the door, a hot-looking poodle trailing behind her.

'Need a house,' she boomed unceremoniously. 'For Arthur and me. Thinking ahead, you see.' She tapped the side of her nose. 'Neither of us getting any younger. Bungalow would be good. Want to release a bit of equity too. Got my sights on a silver swingers' holiday in Lanzarote, amongst other things.' She hmphed. 'Can't persuade Arthur though. Might have to leave him here with Elvis.' The poodle, recognising his name, looked up and wagged his tail. 'Oh,' Biddy added. 'Having a go at baking. Got a bit addicted to *Bake Off* and thought it couldn't be that difficult. Thought I'd have a bash.' She slung a Tupperware box onto Emma's desk. 'See how you get on with my special brownies. Stick me on your property hotlist, won't you?' She waved as she began to leave. 'Come on Elvis,' she muttered to a reluctant-looking dog. 'And, if you can find me the right house, you might have mine and Arthur's to sell and all.' She cackled. 'That'll up your commission!'

Once she'd gone, leaving dust motes swirling in the morning sunshine, Tash looked at Emma and said, 'Arthur Roulestone must be a saint.' They burst out laughing and it broke the tense mood.

Emma opened the box and sniffed the brownies cautiously.

'Well, they smell good.' She picked one up and bit into it. 'Taste good as well. It was great that Kit came running too,' she said through a full mouth, returning to the subject. 'We had such a great time in the Old Harbour afterwards. Shame you had to get off home. God, he looked good in those sweats. Never seen a man with such long legs.'

Tash's bad mood threatened to return. She'd not mentioned Kit's presence to Adrian when he asked who had gone running. It had seemed easier. She thought back to how Kit had loped along, his long legs making light work of the two-kilometre run. He'd been a good running companion. Not talked too much, had gone through the stretches with her. Easy company. The run hadn't taxed her all that much either but the group had decided, to be fair to the beginners, to start with a short distance and build up. The fun run itself was only five kilometres but they had less than a month to train up. 'Waste of training, if you go and get hammered in the pub afterwards,' she snapped, conveniently forgetting the bottle of white she'd drunk. 'And now, when you've finished with gossiping perhaps we can sort out the day diary? I'd like you to value the Morrisons' bungalow today. And this time Emma, try and get them to sign us up.'

Emma looked mutinous for a second. The Morrisons had Hughes and Widrow over at least twice a year to value their crumbling 1930s bungalow, with absolutely no intention of putting it on the market. But she knew better than to argue with Tash in her present mood. 'Yes boss,' she sighed and hid her resentment in her coffee mug.

Chapter 9

'Salad tonight?' Tash called from the kitchen, as she heard Adrian open the front door. 'Too hot to eat anything else. Feta and some nice juicy beef tomatoes.'

'Do we have to? What happened to those steaks I bought?'

'Thought we'd have them on Friday. Celebrate the fact it's the weekend.' Tash kept her tone light. 'I'll get a bottle of your favourite Rioja to go with them.'

'Oh, okay.' Adrian brightened for a moment. 'I'll go and get changed. Won't be a sec.'

They ate in the garden. A light mist was coming in with the tide, cooling the end of another hot day. Sometimes Tash thought it would be fun to live nearer the sea, like Millie did, but in August it was good to leave the hustle and bustle of the seafront behind. She waited until Adrian was halfway down his second Bud before she began.

'I couldn't find my work clothes this morning.' Adrian remained silent so she continued. 'I had to wear that long skirt you bought me in the spring. Couldn't really go to the office in these.' She gestured to her cut offs. 'Do you happen to know what happened to my suits? I can't find them anywhere.'

Adrian put his beer bottle down. 'Sorry darling? Miles away. Lovely salad, by the way. You were right about the tomatoes.'

'I said, do you know where my works suits are?' Adrian was stalling. She could see him thinking up answers.

'Oh! Your work suits? Yes. I took them into the dry cleaner's on the way to the site in Taunton.'

'You took my clothes to a dry cleaner's? On a Monday morning when you knew I'd need something for work?'

Adrian stared at her innocently. He wrinkled his nose. 'I thought it a bit odd when you asked me to. Wondered what you'd wear.' He drained his beer.

'I didn't ask you to do anything with my suits.'

Adrian got up and strolled through the French doors into the kitchen. 'Of course you did, darling.'

Tash heard the fridge door open and close and the hiss of air as he opened another beer.

'Remember, you said with all this hot weather they needed a clean.'

'When?' She twisted her neck around to glare at him as he sauntered back into the garden. 'When did we have this conversation?'

'The other night.' He waggled his beer bottle. 'Mind you, you'd had the best part of a bottle of red so perhaps that's why you don't remember. I distinctly recall you saying that if I was going over Taunton direction to drop them off.'

Tash was certain she'd said no such thing. 'And did you take my shoes to the dry cleaner's too?'

Adrian chuckled. 'Why would I take your work shoes to the dry cleaner's?'

'I couldn't find them either this morning.'

A blackbird flew low across the garden, calling its warning as it went.

Adrian watched as the bird flew up into a tree and disappeared. 'Oh, I had a quick tidy up while you were still in the land of nod. I put them in the cupboard in the spare room. You were sleeping so beautifully I didn't want to wake you up to tell you.' He pointed the beer bottle at her. 'You know, you're working too hard. Maybe you should go part-time? If you can't remember these things maybe you're too stressed at work.'

Tash ignored the last comment. She stared at Adrian. His behaviour was getting increasingly irrational. 'I looked all over the house for my shoes this morning. I looked in that cupboard. They weren't there.'

'Oh darling, are you sure?' He put his head on one side in a bid to appear sympathetic. 'That's where I put them. Perhaps you need to pop into the optician's. Have your eyes checked.'

'There's nothing wrong with my eyesight,' Tash said through gritted teeth.

'You mentioned having them lasered. Maybe it's wearing off? No harm done to have an eye test.'

Tash lapsed into silence. She watched the dusk lengthen the shadows created by the six-foot-high fence Adrian had insisted on having. They'd begun to plan the garden but hadn't got very far. She shivered. Putting in plants which would bloom next summer hinted at a permanence she was no longer sure she wanted. She glanced across. At least not with Adrian.

'You cold, darling? Shall we go in?' He grinned, wolfishly. 'Shall I warm you up?'

'I'm fine,' she snapped, then had a rethink. 'Actually, I'm not,' she added in a more conciliatory tone. 'I'll go and get my sweatshirt. You stay here. It's too nice an evening to go in yet. And it's the end of the summer. We don't know how much more of this lovely weather we'll get.'

Padding up the thickly carpeted stairs, she looked around. She loved this house. Its luxury. The status it gave her. The way eyes widened appreciatively when she explained where she lived. She was seen as the local girl made good. All those nay-sayers who'd bullied her and told her she was a nobody had been proved wrong. *She'd* proved them wrong. The house was a symbol of her success and the success to come. As her hand rested on the door handle of the spare bedroom, she paused. But were people really so bothered about something so avidly materialistic? The book group members had been indifferent when Marti Cavendish had tried to impress them in the same way. Would it be such a big wrench to leave? Was it stupid to hang on to a lifestyle that no longer gave her any joy? Her stomach turned at the thought. Would Adrian even let her leave? Pushing the bedroom door open she cast a fearful look behind her, took a deep breath and went in.

She opened the cupboard door with a hand that trembled. She'd looked in there that morning. It had been empty. She recoiled violently. It wasn't anymore. Stacked neatly in pairs, on the shoe racks she'd bought especially, were her stilettos. The ones she wore with her smart little suits for work. She blinked, then blinked again hard. They were still there. She shook her head and thought back. She was certain the cupboard had been completely empty that morning. Or was she? She'd been tired, in a rush, maybe she'd not looked properly. Maybe Adrian was right and she did need her eyesight testing? After all, what purpose would he have for doing something so petty as to hide her shoes? She heard him call from the garden and eased the cupboard door shut. Nipping into her dressing room, she had the sense to pick up a sweatshirt on her way back to him. A headache threatened. None of this made any sense.

Chapter 10

'Find it?' Adrian asked casually.

'What?'

'Darling, you jumped a foot. I asked if you'd found your sweatshirt. Ah yes, I see you have. And you were quite right as always. It's too nice to go in just yet. Autumn will be upon us before we know it.' He patted the space beside him. 'Come and cuddle up on the bench. Drink?' When she shook her head he asked, 'Is everything alright, Natasha? You look awfully pale.'

'Headache,' she mumbled as she slid in next to him.

'Oh my darling, why didn't you say? Shoulder massage?' Without waiting for an answer, he got up and began kneading her muscles. 'My, there's a lot of tension here. No wonder you've got a bad head. You really do work too hard, Natasha.'

She let her head loll back. Adrian was good at rubbing away her headaches.

'Perhaps we should look into booking a break? Somewhere hot where we can do nothing but lie in the sun. Or a city break? I know you've always wanted to go to Italy. Florence maybe?'

'I'm not sure I can take the time off.'

'Well, not immediately but maybe November or December.' He stopped massaging for a moment. 'Oh Natasha! What about a Christmas holiday? Iceland or somewhere really wintry? Just think, sleigh rides, ice hotels, vodka shots.'

'It sounds wonderful.' It did but Tash had never been away from her parents at Christmas and she was their only child. Would it seem like a proper Christmas for them if she didn't see them for lunch? And December was a long way away. Over four months. If she committed to going to Iceland, it would be even harder to break away. Did she really want to leave? She opened her eyes wide. Was she serious about leaving Adrian? She watched as he wandered into the kitchen murmuring something about finding aspirin. He could be very kind. He looked after her, treated her like a porcelain doll. She must have made a mistake about the shoes. There were too many bedrooms and too many cupboards in the house. It would be an easy mistake to make.

Adrian returned with a packet of tablets and a tall glass. 'Elderflower cordial,' he said. 'Lots of ice.' He smiled benevolently as she took the pills and drank.

'Delicious. Maybe that's what I needed. Dehydrated, probably.'

'Easily done in this hot weather. Maybe we should talk more about snow and ice hotels to cool us down?'

Tash laughed.

'That's better.' Adrian looked at her thoughtfully. 'You know, I haven't heard you laugh for quite a while. I've missed it.' He sat next to her and took her hand. 'I'm worried about you, darling. You seem so busy all the time.' He gestured to the garden. 'If you didn't work you could be here more. Look after the garden, the house.' He squeezed her hand reassuringly. 'You don't have to, you know. We could afford for you to stop work quite easily. If the Manchester job comes off, I'm targeting half a mill profit.'

Tash eased her hand away. Adrian had never before suggested she give up work. He'd nagged at her for working too hard, wanted her to cut her hours but this was new. She put the glass down carefully. 'I love my job, Adrian.'

'I know you do, my sweet. But you don't see what it's doing to you. Always running late, never having enough time to do the things you enjoy.' He paused. 'Getting forgetful,' he added, meaningfully.

'Am I?' Tash frowned. She didn't recognise the picture he was painting. She'd always been efficient, organised, focused.

Adrian smiled. 'Why don't you have an early night? I'll bring you up a cup of tea. *Pretty Woman* is on later, we could watch it in bed?'

It seemed easier, the less exhausting thing, to agree.

Chapter 11

The grand opening of Millie's Little Bookshop Café was in full throttle by the time Tash and Adrian got there. Despite knowing Tash wanted to go, Adrian had got home long after he'd promised and then had insisted they ate before leaving. As a result, they were late.

Light spilled from the enormous windows overlooking the harbour and as it was another sultry evening, the double doors were flung open onto the paved space beyond. Fairy lights bedecked the outside of the building and the night air hummed with the scent of potted scarlet nicotania, purple petunias and the saline from the black sea crashing onto the beach beyond.

'Millie always knew how to hold a party,' Tash said, as she and Adrian fought through the crowd. 'Is that a seafood bar over there? And a cocktail bar as well. Wow!'

'Folks will always turn up if there's free booze on offer,' Adrian grumbled. 'Doesn't make it the most sophisticated of events.'

'Oh, stop moaning and let's have a drink.' When he was about to start whining again, she added, 'Look isn't that Barry from the planning committee? Might have some work to put your way.' She watched as Adrian darted off in Barry's direction. He never missed an opportunity to network.

Collecting a mojito, she spotted Millie. 'It all looks amazing,' Tash kissed her on the cheek. 'Congratulations. You must be a miracle worker to get all this done in the time.'

'Thanks Tash. I'm not sure how we got it finished to be honest. And between you and me, there's still a lot more to do.' She winked. 'I bribed the builders working on the hotel Jed's brother owns to moonlight. My lemon drizzle will do it every time.'

Tash laughed and raised her glass. 'It will. I know, I've tasted it and it's my favourite.' She groaned. 'Not allowed it at the moment. On a diet.'

'You? On a diet?' Millie was incredulous. 'There's nothing of you at the moment. Won't the training for the fun run help?'

Tash glanced over to where Adrian was talking to Barry. Patrick Carroll had joined them and looked bored. 'It would if I didn't keep missing sessions.' She rolled her eyes. 'You know what it's like. Work.'

'I do but I've learned the hard way to step back every now and again.' Millie raised her eyebrows. 'And with the wedding planning business, the café and now this place, I have to delegate. Still love it all though.'

Tash looked around at the shelves groaning with books. 'Do you think you'll turn over a profit with this place?' She'd just ordered thirty pounds worth of paperbacks from Amazon and felt guilty. It was all too quick and convenient to buy books online. She wondered if Millie was doing the right thing.

'Yes. Yes, I do.' Millie sounded determined. 'I still think there's a place in the world for a well-stocked, old-fashioned bookshop and Amy is working so hard. As well as the book group, we're going to run children's events, readathons, puppet shows, that sort of thing. The organisers of the literary festival want to use us as a base too. And it's great to have more covers for the café. We're so busy and popular these days we've had to turn custom away.' Millie looked so horrified Tash laughed again. 'Books and cake,' Millie went on. 'Two of my very favourite things.'

'And at least books don't have calories,' Tash observed.

'That's true. How are you getting on with *Wuthering Heights*?'

Tash pulled a face. 'Not very well. Only got as far as Lockwood seeing the ghost.' Tash shivered. 'I'd forgotten how bleak that book is. I started reading it while sitting in the garden on my day off and it still puts the wind up me.'

'Talking *Wuthering Heights*?' A booming voice sounded as Biddy joined them, Elvis, her deaf assistance poodle, loyally trotting behind. 'Could never abide Heathcliff the first time I read it and I haven't changed my mind. Cruel man.'

'I remember completely falling for him when I read the book at school,' Tash put in. 'I loved his wildness. His passion. The way he dominated the book.'

'Well, reckon when you're seventeen that's what takes your fancy.' Biddy slugged down her drink. 'Too controlling by half, in my opinion. I'll just go and get another cosmopolitan. Excellent cocktails, Millie. Excellent.' She strode off.

'She might have a point,' Millie said. 'About Heathcliff I mean. I'd never thought of him that way.' She wrinkled her nose. 'Have to confess I haven't even started the book yet. The spirit is willing but the work schedule isn't. I may have to cheat and do the SparkNotes.' Someone called to her and she excused herself, squeezing through the crowds.

Chapter 12

Tash picked up another cocktail and wandered outside. She left the crowds behind and went to sit on the café's terrace. Millie had been clever. She'd made the most of the café's best asset by joining it up with the open space outside the bookshop. Now there was one large terrace lit by pretty fairy lights and fragranced by bedding plants. It would be the perfect spot to idle away a few hours with a good book and a pot of Millie's famously excellent coffee. Maybe she was right about the bookshop being a success. It had all the right ingredients.

It was a balmy evening – one of those rare English summer nights when it was comfortably warm enough to linger outside. The murmuring sea shifted gently under a fingernail moon and one or two people had drifted onto the beach. Tash could hear shushed giggles and the occasional chink of glasses. She perched on the low wall which separated the terrace from the beach and breathed in the sweet-scented heliotropes. Millie loved her potted plants. She and her husband Jed radiated happiness. Tash had seen him earlier whispering jokes into Millie's ear when she'd looked a little flustered at the volume of people who had turned up. He was supportive. Her rock.

It was lovely seeing Millie blossom in the way she had since marrying Jed. Tash knew she hadn't had an easy time of it after her parents died. She'd never complained, had made the best with what she had, drove a rusty old car and lived in the flat above the café. She and Jed still lived there. No five-bedroom detached on an executive housing development and a top of the range Porsche for them. They seemed happy without the trappings of the life that she and Adrian had so carefully carved out for themselves. Tash sipped her cocktail. Did it make her happy? She'd thought at one point a big house and a flash car would be all that it took. But she wasn't so sure lately. The more she grasped at material things the more happiness sidled out of reach.

Tash sighed. Maybe she should leave Adrian. Start over again. But the voice of the chubby, bespectacled teenager, the girl who all the boys overlooked, wheedled in her subconscious. *You'll be on your own again. Adrian is the only man who has ever really loved you. Look how kind and generous he is.*

'That's a heartfelt sigh.' It was Kit. 'I seem to make a habit of coming across you in moments of introspection. I called your name but you were miles away.'

Tash forced a smile. 'Hi.'

'May I join you? If you'd like to be on your own I understand.'

She gestured to the space on the wall beside her. 'Do you know, I'd really like some company. I was in danger of getting maudlin and it's too beautiful a night for that.'

'It is.' Kit straddled the wall and put his beer down in the space in between them. He stared into the night and at the distant lights of West Bay.

Tash took the opportunity to study him in the dim light given off by the fairy lights. Tonight he had forsaken the beanie hat. His hair had been shaved into a buzzcut and, with his collarless shirt straining over hulking shoulders, he looked the sort of man she'd cross the road at night to avoid. But Tash had seen how tenderly he'd treated Merlin, had witnessed his self-deprecating humour. She was beginning to appreciate that, under the muscles, lurked a gentle, caring man. And a very sexy one. A year ago she wouldn't have looked at him twice. Too scruffy. Too many He-Man muscles. Not slick enough. But now? Now she could sense her skin prickling in his presence, feel the beat of her heart skipping out a little dance. She sighed again. The last complication she needed at the moment was to fall for a man like Kit.

'Lot of sighing going on,' he said mildly.

'Just mulling over a few things.' She expected him to ask what those things were, but he just lifted a leg onto the wall and rested his arm on his knee. No questions. No interrogation as Adrian would have done. No fussing over her. He simply let her be, in her own space. It was curiously soothing.

They sat in silence for a while enjoying the night and the sounds of the party in the background.

Kit picked up his glass and drained it. It broke the mood.

'Not tempted by one of Millie's cocktails?' she asked. 'My mojito is good.'

'Not really a cocktail sort of a bloke. More of a real ale guy.'

'Figures,' Tash said and saw one brow rise.

'And you,' he pointed with his empty glass. 'Are very much a mojito sort of a girl.'

'Guilty as charged, m'Lud. I can't help it.'

'Goes with the outfit.'

Tash looked down at her silk jumpsuit. She'd thrown it on at the last minute. It was vividly patterned in oranges and pinks and showed off her black hair and summer tan. Adrian hated it which was probably why she'd worn it. 'One of my favourites.' She held up a foot to display the hot pink stilettos. 'Goes with my fave shoes.'

Kit grinned. 'So I see. You look very beautiful tonight, Tash.'

If she leaned forward, she could kiss him. Her eyes dropped to his lips. Kit had a generous bottom lip and a moody upper one. How could she have not seen what Emma and the others saw? He was drop dead gorgeous. She found herself inching closer, wondering if his stubble would scratch when their lips locked.

'Can never fathom how women walk in heels like that.'

The comment threw cold water over her lustful thoughts. Just as well. She was getting a bit carried away there. 'Practice,' she said, airily. 'Lots of practice.' Tash was vaguely aware of the alcohol seeping into her bloodstream. The evening was getting fuzzy around the edges. Although Adrian had heated up a frozen pizza before they'd left, she'd only had a slice. Too churned up to eat. 'And they add inches.' She jumped off the wall and demonstrated with only a very slight wobble. 'See. Bet I'm nearly as tall as you.'

'Doubt it.'

'Stand up then and we'll see.' Tash could never resist a challenge.

'Tash, I'm six foot three.'

'And these are five-inch heels. Come on, real ale man, show

me your credentials.' She giggled. She hadn't had this much fun in ages.

Reluctantly, Kit stood up. Placing his beer glass on the wall next to Tash's cocktail glass, he stood next to her. 'See? Much taller.'

'No,' she complained. 'We've got to do it properly. Stand back to back like you used to do at school.' She tripped to stand behind him and stood on tiptoe. The movement pressed her back against his and the heat from his hard muscles radiated through her silk jumpsuit. She wiggled a little, enjoying the seductive slip of the thin material against her over-heated body.

'How do I know you're not going to cheat?' Kit laughed, a delightful low rumble beginning from somewhere deep inside. Tash felt the laugh vibrate through him and then through her. It was all becoming incredibly erotic.

She giggled and wheeled round to face him. As she stumbled he caught her by the waist, pulling her against him. She felt his belt buckle push into the soft flesh of her stomach, felt his erection nudge her. The night fell away. All she could feel was Kit's powerful arms around her waist, all she could see was him.

Again, she realised that if she reached up, she could kiss him. 'Me cheat?' she breathed as she gazed up at him. 'What sort of girl do you think I am?'

'I don't know, Natasha. What sort of girl *are* you?'

It was Adrian.

Chapter 13

'I'm not sure I know you anymore.' Adrian shoved the Porsche into third and accelerated loudly up the hill out of town.

'Oh Ade, it was only a bit of fun.'

After he'd sneaked up on them, Adrian had coldly introduced himself to Kit and had then grabbed Tash by the arm so tightly she knew she'd have bruises later. He'd marched her through the street to where he'd parked the car and ordered her to get in.

'You're drunk!'

'I was at a party. I was having a good time. Or I was until you did your gorilla act.' She rubbed her arm. 'You hurt me, Adrian.'

'That got through. I'm sorry.' He turned into the entrance to the estate. 'I am sorry, Natasha. You make me get jealous. You don't laugh like that with me.'

'Maybe it's because you're always banging on about babies and me giving up work,' Tash grumbled.

Adrian pulled onto the drive of their house and killed the engine. He eased round to face her, which was difficult in the confined space of the sports car. 'I love you Natasha. I love you very much. Perhaps too much.' He put a finger and thumb to the bridge of his nose and frowned. 'When I saw you flirting with that hulk, the red mist descended. I'm sorry if you think I was heavy-handed but there were people at the party who are influential in this town. Dennis Hall and Arthur Roulestone to name but two. I couldn't have you making a fool of yourself.'

'Why? Because you'd lose a building contract? Come off it, Adrian.'

'Because *you* have standing in this town, Natasha. I thought you said your career was everything to you? That you wanted your own agency? Do you think people are going to take you seriously as a businesswoman if they see you falling over drunk?' He got out and slammed the car door.

Tash stumbled after him. Had she really been that drunk? She hadn't thought so. Just mildly tipsy, like most of the other guests. And did it even matter all that much? She followed Adrian into the hall. The bright light bouncing off the white walls and huge silver-framed mirror blinded her for a second and she staggered.

'Some coffee, I think,' Adrian said coldly.

Tash went into the kitchen and perched on a bar stool. 'You've been drunk lots of times at works dos. Who gives a shit?'

'Language, Natasha,' Adrian said automatically. 'Who indeed? Probably the Morrisons who were staring at you with outright disapproval.'

Tash hooted. 'The Morrisons? Oh, come on Ade, they're not serious about moving. They ask us in to value their grotty old bungalow out of habit.'

Adrian paused in the act of filling the kettle. He turned to her. 'Really? You hadn't heard then, that their daughter is ill and they need to move to be nearer her?'

Tash stared at him. She hadn't heard that. As its only resident estate agent, she needed to be on top of Berecombe's news and gossip and it wasn't usually difficult. The town was a small place. Gossip quite often led to business and business meant commission. She usually knew who was getting married, who was getting divorced,, who had died, got a new job, was expecting another child. All triggers to putting a house on the market. Her mouth fell open. Had she slipped up? She'd sent Emma in to value the Morrisons' home but she hadn't checked to see if Em had bothered to follow up. And, as the manager, it was her responsibility.

Adrian clicked on the kettle. 'I doubt very much if they'll bother to give Hughes and Widrow their business having seen the exhibition you made of yourself tonight.'

Tash screwed up her face with the effort of remembering what awful things she'd done. Had a giggle with Millie, drunk a few cocktails. Had a laugh with Kit. There was nothing else, was there?

'You're obviously having trouble remembering spilling your drink all over Marti Cavendish, knocking over a tray of glasses and reading aloud passages from the more erotic section of the bookshelves.'

'I didn't do any of that.'

'I think you'll find you did, Natasha.'

She felt suddenly very sick. The cocktails had been strong and she'd drunk on a practically empty stomach but she was certain she hadn't done any of those things. 'Why are you making things up about me?'

'I'm not, Natasha. And if you really can't remember the evening you must be more inebriated than I thought. Perhaps you should go to bed. I'll bring you up your coffee and some water.' He turned his back to her and Tash could see rigid disapproval in every muscle. 'I'll sleep in the spare room tonight.'

Tash fled. She staggered upstairs wondering what was going on in her head. Had she thrown her drink over Marti? The woman had bumped into her in the crush, that much was true. And a tray of glasses had been knocked over, that was why Millie had been called away but Tash had been nowhere near it. Or she didn't think she had. Her memories of the night had been eclipsed by the joy she'd felt when flirting with Kit – and made fuzzy by the cocktails. She flopped down onto the bed. And she didn't think she'd read any erotica out loud although, out of everything Adrian had mentioned, it was the one thing she would be most likely to do. She shook her head to clear it. Had she really behaved like that? She was pretty sure she hadn't. But if she hadn't, why would Adrian make it all up? Why would he want to lie?

Chapter 14

Tash woke up the following morning with a sore head and a gritty mouth. She couldn't believe how hungover she felt after only a few cocktails. Staggering into the shower, she blasted herself with water as cold as she could stand. She regarded her reflection in the bathroom mirror. Even through the condensation she could see shadows under her eyes and a face that was too thin. Gripping the basin, she vomited suddenly and copiously. 'Never again,' she croaked. 'I'm going teetotal.' Leaning forward she wiped the mirror but she didn't look much better. Her reflection was still misty and hazy round the edges. It was a bit like her sense of herself; she felt the true Natasha Taylor was slipping away.

'You look awful!' was Emma's greeting as Tash walked into the office.

'Thanks, Em.' Tash sank onto her chair.

'Too many of Millie's cocktails last night?'

'I don't think so. I didn't drink that much.'

'Might be the bug that's doing the rounds. Stevie says half his friends have gone down with it.'

Of course, that was why she was feeling so ill. Tash leaned back in relief. It explained why she felt so out of it. Maybe even explained why she had such a hazy memory of the party.

'You enjoyed yourself last night then? Saw you talking to Kit. Really nice man.'

'Yes, he is.' Tash sat up slowly. 'Em, was I out of order?'

'What do you mean?'

'Did I seem too drunk?'

Emma shook her head. 'Nah, don't think so. You seemed normal drunk. Bit tipsy. Having a good time.'

Tash took a deep breath. This was mortifying. 'I didn't do anything too outrageous then?'

'Not that I saw.' Emma shrugged. 'But I went to sit on the beach for a bit. I got hot – if you know what I mean.' She winked. 'Me and Ol have to make the most of any opportunity we can.'

'I didn't ... I didn't do anything like read the naughty bits out of books?'

Emma hooted. 'Wouldn't put it past you but, like I said, I was otherwise occupied with erotic thoughts of my own. You just looked like you were having a good time, Tash. Why all the questions?'

Tash didn't reply. She was too embarrassed to press Emma on the matter. A wave of nausea overwhelmed her and she shot off to the bathroom.

When she returned Emma insisted she go home, assuring her she would cope with any appointments booked and would cancel those she couldn't cover. Steering Tash towards the door, she said, 'And if management don't like that, they can sodding well put in another person. We've been saying for months we can't cope with just the two of us now Pete has been promoted. You alright to drive home? If not, I can drop you off on the way to the Smiths' place.'

Tash nodded and staggered up the hill to where she'd parked her car half an hour earlier. She was never ill. She fumed to herself, – she couldn't afford to take time off.

The estate was deserted when she drove onto the drive. The house seemed hushed and slightly disapproving as she padded upstairs, took off her work clothes and sank into bed.

She came to a few hours later feeling much better and, to her surprise, hungry. Taking some dry toast and a glass of water into the garden, she sat in the shade. It was hot and the cloudless blue sky hurt her eyes. Going back in to find her sunglasses, she was distracted by the plop of a letter onto the doormat. The post. She was rarely at home when it arrived. Adrian was more often back from work before her and he put her post on the kitchen island. Not that she got all that much. Picking up the letter she frowned. It was to a Mrs Anna Williams. Right address, though. She flipped it over but there was no clue where it had come from. Probably a rookie postie seeing the surname and assuming it was for them. Williams was a common enough surname. Putting it on the kitchen table she found her sunglasses and went back to the garden. She'd investigate later and return it to the sender.

Adrian got back from work early. When she told him, she thought she had a stomach bug his attitude changed. He fussed over her, insisted she return to bed and said he'd go to his meeting on his own. Tash gave in to him with relief; the dinners with his business contacts were excruciatingly boring. She went back to bed, slept for another two hours and woke up feeling her old self. Coming downstairs in her dressing gown to watch some mindless television, she noted without interest that the misdirected letter had disappeared. Adrian must have dealt with it.

Chapter 15

'We missed you on Saturday night.'

Tash tore her eyes away from the computer screen where she was updating the agency's website and glanced up at Emma in surprise. It was Monday morning and, after a quiet weekend at home insisted upon by Adrian, she was fully recovered. 'What do you mean?'

'Well, I assume you were still too poorly to come but thought you might have rung me back. We'd arranged to go out to Laughsinnit, remember?' Laughsinnit was the new open mic comedy slot at the Regent, Berecombe's little theatre.

Tash pushed her chair away from her computer and looked blank. Her heart began to pound. Was this something else she had forgotten? She put a thumb to her temple and massaged. Was she going mad? Having a breakdown? She had been working too hard for months now, probably because, as Emma had said, Pete's promotion had left them short-handed. 'I don't remember.'

'I rang you on Saturday morning,' Emma explained impatiently. 'I mean, fair enough, it was all a bit last minute, but I thought it was just your sort of thing. Millie mentioned it at training, which you also missed. Honestly Tash we hardly see you these days. Amy came along, Millie and Jed were there and Kit tagged along too. He said he'd hoped to see you,' she added meaningfully. 'It was brilliant fun. Why didn't you want to come?'

'I didn't know about it! Did you ring the mobile or the landline?'

'Your mobile was dead, so I left a message on the landline. Didn't you get it?'

'No.' Tash thought quickly. She'd slept in on Saturday morning and Adrian had gone to get the papers but they had an answerphone. 'Maybe the phone's not working properly. It goes through phases like that. I've missed one or two messages from Mum as well. I'll get Ade to have a look at it. He normally fixes it.'

Emma gave her an odd look. 'Well, shame you missed out, it was a good night. They're doing them monthly though so maybe you can come for September's?'

'I'd like that.' Tash smiled. She felt her well-ordered, efficient life was being eaten away at the edges. She hated this sense of losing control.

'Training tonight. You going to come? Feeling up to it?'

Tash nodded and then picked up the ringing phone. 'Good morning, Hughes and Widrow Estate Agents. Tash speaking, how may I help you?' She took a deep breath. 'Ah, hello Mrs Morrison.'

Chapter 16

Tash jogged to the end of the beach and stopped, putting her hands on her knees. She was out of puff and they'd only been running for ten minutes. The rest of them were way ahead of her so she straightened and concentrated on getting her breathing controlled. Maybe she wasn't over the stomach bug quite yet.

She'd checked the answerphone when she'd got home. It was blank. All old messages deleted, it stated. Adrian had arrived home as she was reading the user manual. Assuring her he would sort it, he'd suggested she went for her run. For once, he seemed desperate for her to go out. She'd shrugged and had run upstairs to get changed. She really couldn't keep up with his moods these days. Maybe Emma had rung the wrong number? Maybe the phone was faulty? The things were so complicated.

Putting it to the back of her mind, she concentrated on the view instead. The light was just going, leaving a rippled orange streak above the dark sea. It was very calm this evening, with barely a suggestion of a wave at the shoreline. The pubs and restaurants in town were packed and there was a steady stream of people wandering along the promenade. They stopped every now and again to admire the scenery or enjoy the planted flowerbeds. Berecombe was dressed in its summer party outfit, with red and orange begonias bursting out. It was still warm and Tash felt sweat cooling on her neck. Tying her hair up in a ponytail and repeating her thigh stretches, she hoped it was still the after-effects of her illness. Otherwise, it meant she had let herself become very unfit.

Emma jogged back to her. 'What did Mrs Morrison want?' She stretched her arms over her head. 'Was it a complaint about me?'

Tash straightened. 'No, actually. She wants one of us to go over and discuss the house going on the market.' She grinned. 'Mrs Morrison especially asked for the enthusiastic young lady who was so positive about her conservatory and was a big *Poldark* fan.'

Emma giggled. 'That would be me.' She pulled a face. 'And *conservatory?* It's a mildewed lean-to. It'll take some selling, that place.'

'It'll sell as long as it's on at the right price. The market down here is hot at the moment.'

'All the more reason to have another agent working with us.' They began jogging along the beach to catch up with the others.

'I agree, Em. I'll mention it to Pete at the next meeting. Again. Oh, and here's a thought. Maybe Biddy and Arthur might like a look at the Morrisons' place?'

'Worth a try.' Emma hiked up the strap of her running vest. 'We deffo need another member of staff, though. I mean, look at you, Tash,' she continued. 'You're never ill and you've been really poorly lately. We're both doing too much and we can't keep up. When was the last time you had any time off? And being off sick doesn't count.'

As they joined the group, Kit looked over at Emma's indignant voice.

Tash shot Emma a warning look. 'Hi everyone,' she said. 'Didn't mean to hold anyone up.'

'You didn't,' Kit answered. 'We're just taking a breather before tackling the hill.' He came closer. 'Are you alright? You disappeared very quickly the other night.'

Tash looked up at him. She couldn't help but take in the way his jogging bottoms clung to his muscles, how strong his arms looked and, more importantly, the warm concern in his eyes. She wished she could tell him what was happening. But she wasn't even sure herself. Was she losing her mind? Was she run down or was she simply overworked as Emma had pointed out? 'I'm fine. Thanks. Just laid low with some bug or other.' She smiled at him and felt something fluttering inside. It was happiness. He made her happy and she hadn't felt that for so long. She liked him. Would like to get to know him more. She gave herself a little shake. She'd told Emma off when she'd lusted after him and here she was, doing the same. Except it wasn't just physical. She sensed a gentleness in Kit. A deep-rooted gentleness borne from his innate confidence. He was content being who he was. Adrian was always twitchily looking to see what other people had got, what they drove, how much they earned. Where he sat in the order. How he could get one in front of them. Kit was simply Kit. Happy to be who he was. And she didn't think winning money had anything to do with it. She thought it had everything to do with the man himself.

'Are you okay Tash?'

His hand, firm and warm on her bare arm, brought her back. 'Yes,' she managed. 'Just getting my breath back.'

'Ready to carry on?'

'Ready.'

As one, the group turned and began running back along the promenade. As they jogged past the bookshop, Amy peeled off apologetically. They dodged through the crowds that were gathering on Millie's terrace to enjoy the sunset and Emma, Millie, Jed and some of the others soon gained speed and surged ahead. Tash, still feeling under the weather, maintained a steadier pace and was pleased when Kit slowed to run alongside her. They didn't speak but she was comforted by his presence. They skirted around the tourists until making their way to the narrow lane which ran steeply parallel to the main street. It was a quieter route out of town, away from the throngs of people and the fumes of the traffic.

Tash had to pull up halfway. Leaning against an oak tree, she pressed a hand to her side and gasped in pain at the stitch which had developed. Kit took her by the shoulders and led her to a gap in the hedge. Next to the kissing gate leading onto the coastal path was a bench. Guiding her to it, he sat her down and let her breathe through it.

Eventually she was well enough to sit up. Taking the water bottle he offered, she murmured, 'Thanks.' They sat in silence. Screened from the streetlights, it was dark, with only the occasional car headlights flaring briefly. The air smelled damp and bosky, of deep greenness and secrecy. An owl hooted somewhere. It made Tash jump and she laughed.

'Noisy at this time of the year. Out hunting I expect,' Kit

said and they lapsed into silence again.

Tash concentrated on the moment and felt her shoulders relax. Her whole body relaxed. It was very peaceful sitting here. She'd forgotten the bench had such a fantastic view over Berecombe. She used to walk Benji along the coastal path but hadn't done it for months. They often used to sit on this bench before the rest of the walk. Benji was lazy and demanded frequent rests. A laugh rippled through her as she remembered how he'd squat on his fat little bottom, refusing to move.

'Wonderful view,' Kit said quietly, echoing her thoughts.

It was. Tash's eyes followed the trickle of white houses descending the river valley. The white lights strung along the prom like a diamond necklace leading to the harbour and its still, black water. 'I love it here,' she whispered, not knowing if she meant Berecombe or the intimate peace of the bench shaded in its arbour of trees. She turned to Kit. He seemed very close. She could hear his breathing. It was uneven and ragged. Was it possible he felt what she did? He inched nearer. She sensed rather than saw his lips move towards hers.

'Tash?'

'Oh, Kit.'

A flare of headlights blinded her and she jolted back. What was she thinking? She was in a relationship. 'I have to go,' she panicked. 'I have to get back to Adrian.'

'Of course,' Kit muttered.

Was that regret in his voice, or was it her fevered imagination?

Chapter 17

Adrian bounced into the sitting room brandishing an enormous bouquet. 'Roses for my rose. Lilies for my lily,' he exclaimed.

Tash was touched. He used to buy her flowers every week when they first got together. She took them and inhaled. 'Oh, they're gorgeous Ade. And the creams and whites even match the colours in the room. I'll go and find a vase. They'll look perfect on the sideboard. Thank you.'

Adrian looked abashed. He pursed his lips. 'Thought they might make up for my behaviour lately. I know I've been a grump. Work's a bit—' he paused '—tense at the moment.'

Tash stood up. 'Oh Ade, why didn't you say?' She gave him a hug. 'You know you can talk to me about stuff. It's not good to bottle it all up.'

'Yes well, I don't like to bring it home.' He huffed. 'Nothing more tedious than a work bore. Your training going well?'

Tash, disconcerted by the change of subject, disentangled herself. She went into the utility and hunted for the Waterford crystal vase she'd stashed in the cupboard. A pang of guilt shot through her as she remembered the bliss of sitting on the bench next to Kit. Of so nearly kissing him. 'Yes, fine. Didn't I say?'

Adrian followed her. He lifted her hair off her neck and kissed it, sucking hard. It would leave a bruise later. 'You just headed for the shower last night without a word.' He gave a short laugh.

Tash frowned as she cut off the cellophane. She was sure they'd had a brief conversation about how far she'd run. She dismissed the thought and concentrated on arranging the flowers. Adrian was so thoughtful sometimes. He really liked to spoil her. 'You still up for the meal at my parents on Friday? I'd like to spend some time with them before they go on holiday.'

Adrian pouted and then rearranged his face as he caught her look at him. 'Nice to be able to jet off to the Algarve for six weeks.'

Tash didn't rise to the bait. 'Well, Dad worked hard. He retired early so he could do things like that and he loves his golf.' She pressed her nose into the bouquet. Disappointingly, they had no scent. She wasn't sure why Adrian was so jealous of her father. Tweaking the flowers, she said, 'These are really lovely Ade. You'll enjoy the meal when you get there. They always make such a fuss over you.'

As it turned out, Tash and Adrian didn't make the meal with her parents. Just as they were about to leave, Adrian rushed to the bathroom and Tash heard him being violently sick. Coming out, he clutched his stomach saying he must have caught the bug she'd had.

Tash got him to bed. Putting a glass of water by his bedside, she was about to leave when he caught her hand.

'Don't go, Natasha,' he pleaded. 'You know how awful I am at being ill.'

She sat on the edge of the bed. 'Oh Ade, it's the last time I'll see Mum and Dad before they go on holiday.'

He pouted. 'They're only going to Portugal. They'll be back before you know it.' When she didn't say anything, he continued. 'I don't see my parents from one year to the next.'

This was true. Adrian was detached from his family; he rarely saw them. Tash had never met them. 'That's not fair Adrian, they all live in Cumbria. It's not easy for you to get to see yours. And you know how close I am to mine.'

'I wouldn't be ill if it wasn't for you.' He sighed mutinously. 'This must be the bug you had.'

'That's not fair either. I recovered days ago. It might just be something you ate.' The words came out more sharply than she intended and made her feel guilty.

'Oh Tash, stay,' he pleaded as he grabbed her hand. 'Keep me company. Let's watch some television and be all cosy.' He jack-knifed in the bed and groaned. 'I feel awful.'

Tash looked at him in concern. Adrian was prone to stress-related stomach upsets and was a dreadful patient, but this looked much worse. He was clammy with sweat and had gone a peculiar puce. Perhaps she shouldn't leave him. It was doubtful it was the same bug she'd had after the party; she'd been fine after sleeping it off. 'Should I call a doctor?'

'No, no,' he answered weakly. 'They always take ages to come out after hours.' He turned and opened his eyes, a brilliant blue in his flushed face. 'I'll be okay as long as you stay with me, darling.'

Tash gave in. 'I'll just go and ring them and apologise.'

'Good girl.' He pulled the duvet up around his shoulders and relaxed. 'And put the heating on, will you? I'm freezing.'

Tash's parents were understanding. 'I haven't seen you for weeks, though, Tash,' her father said on the phone. 'I missed you when you collected Benji the other day. And didn't you get the message your mother left on Thursday?'

'That must be the answerphone having a fit,' she explained. 'It's been a bit erratic lately. Look, I'll try and pop over in the morning before you go. Have a quick coffee.' After chatting a little more, she hung up and went back upstairs.

Two hours later, after a couple of episodes of *The Crown*, Adrian declared himself suddenly better. 'And you know what?' He said with a grin. 'I'm ravenous!'

Chapter 18

The following morning, Tash arrived at her parents' house to find them in a state of panic.

'Tash darling,' Keith Taylor kissed his daughter. 'Thank goodness you're here. The kennels have just rung to say there's been a mix up with the booking and they can't take Benji. Your mother's on the phone to them now.'

The Westie cowered in the corner of the hall, looking deeply unhappy.

Tash picked him up and soothed him. She kissed the top of his white head. 'Poor Benji.' His trembling lessened slightly. 'He hates the sight of suitcases.'

They went into the kitchen where Nadia, Tash's mother, was having a terse conversation on the phone. Tash could tell from her clipped speech that her mother was furious. She sat down with Benji on her lap and fed the dog a sneaky fragment of biscuit. Keith gestured to the coffee pot and she nodded.

Nadia put the receiver down very, very carefully. 'Well, that's that. I'm never, *ever* using them again.' She registered Tash's arrival, gave her a swift kiss and stroked the dog's ears. 'Poor boy. Homeless.' She sighed, melodramatically and sank onto a kitchen chair.

'Have you tried anywhere else?' Tash pushed a mug of coffee towards her.

'Of course I have! And once they realised their appalling mistake, the kennels rang around everyone they knew.' Nadia spread her hands wide. 'It's August. Everyone's on holiday. Everywhere they tried was fully booked.'

'It's outrageous,' Keith began.

'Darling,' Nadia warned. 'Think of your blood pressure.'

'But we've got to go in an hour. You know what security's like nowadays, it takes forever to get through it.'

'They've not been the same since the new owners took over. Basil and Jenny were so good.' Nadia drank her coffee and then pulled a face. 'Ugh. No sugar. I must have yours, Tash.'

They swapped mugs. 'I'll have to have him,' Tash offered.

Nadia stared at her daughter. 'But you can't.'

'Why not?' She gave the dog a hug. 'We'll get on just fine. Don't you trust me?'

'Of course I trust you,' her mother snapped. 'But you work twenty-four hours a day.'

'Mum, calm down. Think of *your* blood pressure. I'll find a way to work round it. He can have a basket in the back of the office and stay in the car when I'm on a viewing.'

'In this heat? He'll suffocate! You'll have to have all the windows open. And make sure he wears his doggie seatbelt.'

'I can probably take him in with me to the clients I know well. But if I have to leave him in the car, I'll make sure I park it in the shade and with the windows open, I promise. And put his seatbelt on.'

'And what about Adrian?' He father put in, meaningfully.

There was a tense pause. Adrian's antipathy to Benji was legendary – but Tash had already decided. It was give and take in a relationship. She'd given in enough times over the last few weeks, Adrian would have to compromise on this. 'Adrian will understand,' she said. 'And, after all, it's only six weeks.'

'Well, I suppose you could try a few kennels later in the month,' Nadia conceded. 'Things go quieter after the bank holiday. But make sure you ring me so I can approve. I'm not having my baby go anywhere I don't know.'

'I promise.' Tash grinned. 'Hadn't you better think about getting organised? You don't want to leave too late, you know what the traffic's like at this time of year. Don't worry, I'll wash the mugs and lock up. And yes,' she added, as her mother began to fuss. 'I'll pop in every couple of days to get the post and water the garden.'

Chapter 19

Adrian's reaction to her arrival home with a dog and all the bits and pieces her mother had insisted Benji needed was predictable.

'If you think I'm having that thing mess up my house,' he blustered, 'you've got another thing coming.' He blocked her in the hall.

Tash knelt and put a protective hand on Benji's back. 'He's perfectly house-trained, has just been clipped so he won't shed that much, and I always thought it was our house, Adrian?'

'The mortgage is in my name.'

'Well, if that's how you feel about it, I'll just go and live at Mum and Dad's for six weeks.'

'No. No, don't do that.' Adrian subsided. 'But honestly Natasha, what were you thinking? How can you look after a dog?'

'I'll just have to work around him.' Tash looked down at Benji who was looking confused and scared at the loud voices. 'It'll be fine,' she said confidently, trying to convince herself. 'And look, Ade, if it's really impossible, I'll investigate kennels and dog-sitters.'

Adrian backed away and looked down at the little dog in

disgust. 'I suggest you do that. God, I hate dogs. Dirty, smelly, flea-ridden things.'

'Don't listen to a word, Benji. We both know if you had even one flea my mother would hang her head in shame. Come on, let's put your basket in the utility, shall we?'

'In the house?' Adrian roared. 'Hasn't it got an outside kennel or something?'

'If you force my mother's dog to sleep outside you'll have her to answer to,' Tash answered serenely and sensed him shudder. He was always very careful around her mother. 'I'll take him out of your way later this afternoon, don't worry.' She put the basket in the corner by the radiator and tidied away Benji's many toys and brushes in a cupboard. To do so she had to put all the washing powder boxes and conditioners on the counter top. 'Well Adrian will have to live with the place looking untidy for a few weeks,' she whispered to the dog. 'Won't he?'

Benji sniffed his basket suspiciously then waddled into it, turned around three times and settled down with a sigh of recognition. Tash's heart melted. He'd looked so lost all morning. He was spoiled, stubborn and lazy but it wasn't his fault he'd been made temporarily homeless. 'We'll go and see the Red Arrows later, shall we? That'll be fun.'

Chapter 20

Adrian sulked all afternoon so Tash clipped on Benji's lead, called out a cursory, 'Off to walk the dog. See you later,' and left without waiting for an answer.

She made her way down the steep lane to Berecombe seafront and followed the crowds to the beach. Benji trotted along happily as if glad to be doing something. As she neared Millie's café, she heard her name being called.

'Tash, we're over here. We've got a good spot.' It was Emma.

Tash eased her way along the congested promenade, to where Emma, along with her boyfriend Ollie, was sitting at a bench on the extended terrace in front of Millie's bookshop. 'Wow, the town's rammed isn't it?' Tash squeezed herself onto the bench next to Emma. 'Hi both.'

'Hi Tash,' Ollie replied, pushing his dark fringe off his eyes. 'Red Arrows always bring in the crowds. Car parks full by eleven this morning, apparently.'

Emma rolled her eyes. 'He likes to know boring things like that.'

Tash smiled and picked up Benji to put on her lap. Emma wasn't always very nice to her boyfriend. Ollie was a saint to put up with it.

'Won't be boring when you're complaining about having to walk back up the hill. You'll be glad of a lift,' he answered placidly.

'Got you there, Em.'

'Nah. I'm at my physical peak. Fun runners be afraid. Be very afraid. I'm going to win.'

'Aren't you supposed to be raising money for the RNLI?' Ollie asked. 'Thought that was the point.'

'And I can aim for first place while I'm at it.' Emma poked him in the ribs with an elbow and gave Benji some fuss.

Tash looked at her suspiciously. The girl was flushed and her eyes were over-bright. Maybe it was just relief at finishing work for the weekend. She and Emma took turns at manning the office on Saturday mornings. 'Why can't I sit on the bench on the other side of the table?' she asked. 'It's a bit squashed with you two and the dog.'

'Kit and Amy have gone to get drinks and some food, I hope. I'm starving. Busy morning in the office. I didn't have time to eat. Phone never stopped and the grockles were in trying to buy their dream home by the sea.'

'Oh.' Tash felt herself blush. She wasn't sure how to react to seeing Kit again. 'Good that it was busy.'

'Yeah, it was manic. To top it all, that Biddy came in. I gave her the draft details of the Morrisons' bungalow. She seemed interested. Gave me some more of her brownies. It's the only thing I've managed to eat all day.' Emma craned her neck. 'Oh good, here they are. Hope they've got some of Millie's sausage baguettes. They're delish.'

Ollie waggled his eyebrows at Tash. 'In the peak of physical health and eating sausage baguettes.'

Kit stepped over the bench and straddled it. 'Great buzz in town and I love that café. I've got the coffees and Millie's special cherry and almond cake and Amy's got the sandwiches.' He put the pink tin tray with the flowery mugs down on the table. 'Will that do you, Emma?' He clocked Tash. 'Oh, didn't see you there. Hi Tash.' He began to stand up. 'I'll go back and get you something, shall I? What do you fancy?'

Tash looked up at him mutely. 'You,' she wanted to say. Instead she smiled. 'I'm sure there'll be more than enough.'

Amy perched next to him. 'Think there's enough to feed half of Berecombe here. Millie's portions are huge.' She began to dole out sandwiches. 'Only one sausage baguette left so that's yours Emma. I've got tuna mayo. Hand-carved ham and mustard, Ollie and Kit? You can share my tuna if you like, Tash. I won't eat all of it.'

Amy would be able to eat the entire picnic, Tash was sure. But like a lot of chubby women, she was too self-conscious to eat too much in public. Tash knew the signs. She'd been like it once. 'That's really kind, Amy, thank you. It's great this, isn't it? I love the Red Arrows.'

Emma looked at her through narrowed eyes. 'You're in an unusually good mood. And why have you got Benji?'

Tash tightened her hold on the dog as he got a sniff of ham and sausage and wriggled. 'Parents flew out to Portugal this morning and the kennels cocked up. He's staying with me for the duration.'

'And how does Adrian feel about that?' Emma's eyes went huge. 'He hates dogs. Won't it mess up his perfect shag-pile?'

'Adrian's fine with it all,' Tash lied. 'And we don't have shag-pile, as well you know,' she said stiffly. She felt Kit's eyes on her and her face heated. 'Let's dig in, shall we? I'm hungry too.' She accepted the half a sandwich Amy offered. 'Bookshop not open today?'

'Millie's given me a couple of hours off.' Amy blushed. 'Patrick's covering. He'll do a lot better than me. Knows much more about books.'

'I'm sure that's not true.'

'I'll go back in once it's over. The Red Arrows bring a lot of people into town and I've done a display of books about them and stuff,' Amy added eagerly.

Tash warmed to her. She'd thought the girl was a bit of a milksop when she first met her but she came alive at the mention of books. 'I'm sure that will go down well.'

The cheers from the crowds on the beach told them something was beginning to happen and a roar of planes swooping in low over the cliffs behind them, followed by trails of coloured smoke, told them the Red Arrows had arrived.

Chapter 21

Kit accompanied Tash and Benji back along the prom. The crowds were gradually dispersing but there was still a buzz about the place. Cars inched along the road, heading out of town, windows down, music blaring.

'I love it when it's like this,' Tash said. 'All happy faces and suntan lotion, buckets and spades and sandy feet on the prom.'

Kit scuffed his feet through a puddle of sand on the hot concrete. 'Certainly half the beach along here. Have you always lived in Berecombe?'

'Yes. Berecombe born and bred. I couldn't ever imagine living away from the sea.'

He followed her gaze to the sea, a vividly deep blue, glistening in the hot sunshine. 'I take your point.'

'What about you?' Tash steered Benji past a yappy dachshund. He was getting tired after his long walk, and grumpy.

'Oh, lived all over the place. Grew up in Bristol, trained in London, ended up here.'

Tash looked up at him. He wasn't giving much away. 'And no girlfriends or wives lurking in any of those places?' She bit her lip, horrified that the question had slipped out.

'I was married once. Briefly. A long time ago.' He flashed a grin at Tash. 'All ended amicably I'm happy to say and she's now living in the States with her new husband.' He laughed. 'And much happier.'

'What happened?' Benji dragged her to a bin where he sniffed with interest. Tash leaned against the railings separating the prom from the beach below, letting the dog explore. She lifted her face to the sun, drinking it in. It really had been the most glorious summer. Then she realised what she'd asked. 'I'm so sorry. That was nosy.'

Kit joined her, his shoulder resting companionably against hers. 'It's not rude at all. Just curious. We met when we were dental students. Rushed into something too young too soon. I think Melanie was fully-formed at twenty-two but I most certainly wasn't. She's still a friend and having a lovely life with another dentist. Howard is a great bloke.'

'You're very calm about life, aren't you?' Tash wasn't sure how she felt about Kit having an ex-wife somewhere. She knew she had no right to be jealous but she was. Great swooping waves of jealousy filled her. She stamped down on them. 'You're very—' she searched for the right word '—*zen*, aren't you?'

Kit laughed. 'Am I? I suppose I am. Takes a lot to get me riled.'

Tash turned and leaned her elbows on the railings behind her. She held her hair out of her eyes and looked at him. 'Tell me then, Kit Oakley, what gets you riled?'

He scuffed his feet again, maybe embarrassed. 'Oh, I don't know. Injustice, cruelty, unfairness. That sort of thing.' He looked up and locked gaze. 'I hate to see animals mistreated.

And I hate to see people unhappy.' Reaching out a hand, he put it on her arm. 'I hate to see you unhappy, Tash.'

'What makes you think I'm unhappy?' It came out as a strangled whisper. His touch was hot on her bare skin. She longed to tell him everything. Ached for the comfort of his strong hold. For the feel of his body on hers. He was very close. She was mesmerised by his mouth and the urgent need to kiss it. The crowds melted away. There was only her and Kit and the hot sun drilling down. The moment crystallised. She reached forward and gave in to impulse. His lips were firm and warm and welcoming and she wanted to drink him in.

She leaped back, appalled at what she'd allowed herself to do.

Scrubbing a hand across her mouth, she shook her head in a desperate attempt to clear it. 'I've got nothing to be unhappy about,' she said through clenched teeth. 'I've got everything I've always wanted. A gorgeous house, a good job, a great boyfriend.'

Kit stared at her intently. 'Who are you trying to convince, Tash?' he said. 'Me or yourself?' He took his hand away and Tash shivered, despite the hot sun. 'You put on a front. All brittleness and confidence,' he went on in a hoarse voice. 'You keep telling us how great your life is but you're far too thin and you've got shadows under your eyes. You look haunted, Tash. You look like you're being eaten alive.' He ignored her gasp of horror. 'You know, you can always come to me if you need to.'

'How dare you!' Tash spluttered. 'What right have you to say that?' She pulled herself up. 'You hardly know me.' She turned to go but Kit put out a hand to stop her.

'You're right, I hardly know you but I see what I see. You look like you could do with a friend, Natasha Taylor the estate agent. And when you do, I'll be there.'

Tash wrenched her arm away. How could she have kissed him? And now he felt he had the right to say these horrible things to her. She'd let him get too close. He'd seen too much and she hated it. 'I've got friends,' she spat. 'Plenty of them. I've got a boyfriend waiting for me. I don't need you. I'll never need you because, Kit, unlike you with your donkeys for company, I've got the perfect life.' A shudder rippled through her. 'And now, if you'd let me, I'd quite like to get back to it.' She stomped off, bumping into a family with a Labrador on the way. The dogs' leads got entangled for a moment, thoroughly spoiling her attempt at a dramatic exit. When she'd freed Benji she looked back to where Kit stood. He'd gone.

Chapter 22

'Where have you been?' An ashen-faced Adrian met her at the door. He ran a hand through his hair, leaving it sticking up on end. 'I've been worried sick.'

'I took Benji out for a walk. Didn't you hear me? I shouted where I was going.'

'I didn't hear anything, Natasha. I had my music on. You've been gone for hours, darling.' He followed her as she took an exhausted Benji through to the utility room and gave him some water. 'I tried your mobile but you had it switched off. Natasha, I insist you stop fussing over that dog and talk to me!'

'I told you where I was going, Ade. I didn't hear any music playing when I left.' Tash blew her fringe off her hot face. She was in no mood to deal with Adrian.

'Well, of course not.' Adrian huffed irritably. 'I had headphones on.'

'Not much I could have done to make you hear, then.'

'You could have come into the study. I was really worried, Natasha.'

Tash felt the burn of Kit's kiss on her lips. 'Yes, I could have done. Sorry.' She was exhausted. Still smarting from Kit's words, she didn't want an argument with another man and hadn't the energy for a mental dance around Adrian's moods. A pang of guilt shot through her. 'Look on the bright side, I've walked Benji further than he's been in years so he'll sleep like a baby tonight.' She took his arm and led him through to the kitchen. 'How about we make do with a pizza tonight? I'll make a nice salad and we can open a bottle of Rioja. Have a lazy night in front of the TV.'

Adrian smiled, mollified. 'That sounds good.' He took her by the arms. 'I'm sorry I get so het up. It's just that I love you so much. I worry about you.' He wrapped her in his arms. 'I want to know where you are every minute of the day. Every second. Every millisecond.'

'I don't know what you think might happen to me in Berecombe, Ade.' She tensed for his reaction then, to her relief, felt a ripple of a laugh go through him.

'I know. I'm a silly old man.' He kissed her. 'Did you see the Red Arrows go over? Did they frighten the dog?'

Tash disentangled herself. She hunted in the dresser for a couple of glasses, hiding her burning face behind the cupboard door. Guilt gnawed at her insides. Why couldn't she just tell him the truth? That she'd bumped into friends and watched the display with them. And then had launched herself at one of them and kissed him. She screwed up her eyes. 'Yes, I had a good view of the planes. They were fantastic as usual. Be an angel and fetch a bottle of wine from the garage, will you? I forgot to get a new one out.'

Adrian came to her again. He kissed her cheek. 'Honestly, what would you do if you didn't have me to look after you? You can be so disorganised sometimes.' He went out humming, happy to be useful.

Tash went to the window and looked out at the garden. She clung onto the icy sides of the Belfast sink, willing the cold porcelain to shock her senses. She and Adrian had spent weeks finding just the right one and even longer hunting down the taps to go with it. This kitchen was her pride and joy. She took immense pleasure in the black granite work surfaces, in the state of the art NEFF oven, in the gadgets that she and Adrian had collected but rarely had time to use. He loved her. He really loved her. Look at what they'd created together. Then why was it now flawed? If she was able to kiss another man, to contemplate going much further, then what was the future for her and Adrian? Thoughts of Kit filled her. Consumed her. The very core of her being ached for him. She hardly knew Kit and yet he'd managed to sum her up after a few weeks' acquaintance. She concentrated on her breathing then splashed cold water over her face. This was her life. Her perfect life. This house and Adrian was all she'd ever wanted. And it was no longer enough. Adrian was no longer enough.

When he returned she greeted him with a smile.

The evening passed companionably. Adrian had drawn the line at the dog coming into the sitting room. When Benji woke them in the middle of the night howling, Adrian was too stupefied by wine, an Americano and a bout of vigorous sex to complain too much.

After seeing to the dog, Tash lay wide awake, staring at the ceiling. She didn't know herself any more.

Chapter 23

'Oh, hello Benji,' Emma crooned. She got up to help Tash with the dog bed. 'We'll put you just here, shall we?' She took the bed off Tash and put it in the back corner of the office. Bending down she stroked his ears. 'You won't be any trouble at all, will you?'

'Do you think this will be alright?' Tash flung her briefcase onto her desk and went through to the kitchen to stow Benji's supplies. 'It doesn't look very professional. Having a dog in the workplace, I mean,' she shouted through. 'Adrian said it might lose us clients.'

'I think it makes us look friendlier,' Emma replied, stoutly. 'Besides, Berecombe's known to be dog-friendly and all the tourists come in with theirs. If anyone is really bothered we can always put him in the kitchen.'

'Poor Benji. He's being pushed from pillar to post. He had us up both nights at the weekend. He's just not used to sleeping on his own. Mum lets him sleep on her bed.'

'And I expect Adrian won't tolerate that.'

'No need to be snippy.' Tash returned and collapsed onto her chair. 'You're right though. Ade won't hear of Benji being anywhere in the house apart from the garden and the utility.

He must be so lonely. Mum dotes on him, spoils him rotten.' The little dog trotted up to her and rested his nose on her knee. 'I'd live at Mum and Dad's while they're away but Adrian won't hear of it.'

'I bet he won't.'

'What's that supposed to mean?'

'He does like to keep tabs on you, doesn't he?'

Tash thought about defending him and decided she didn't have the energy. 'You're right. He does. But it's only because he cares so much.'

'Hmph.' Emma went into the kitchen and clicked on the kettle. 'You've got to have space though, Tash.'

'Like you and Ollie, you mean?'

Emma poked her head around the door. 'Oi. Nothing wrong with *my* relationship, thank you.'

Tash hadn't had enough sleep for an argument. 'Nothing that Aidan Turner wouldn't solve.'

Emma grinned. 'Think that man would solve anything.' She disappeared. 'But only dressed as Ross Poldark.' She returned with a packet of crisps. 'Breakfast?' She offered Tash one.

Tash shuddered. 'How can you eat cheese and onion at this hour?' As the phone began to ring, she added, 'And don't give any to Benji!' She picked up the receiver. 'Oh, hello Ade. Yes, of course I got to work alright. Why?'

Emma rolled her eyes and crunched her way through the crisps while waiting for Tash to finish on the phone. Making faces at Benji, she slipped him the tiniest morsel. When Tash put the receiver down, she exclaimed, 'I can't believe he rang you. You've only just left the house!'

'Accident on the A35. He wanted to check I was okay.'

'You don't even come that way.'

'Oh. Yes. Hadn't thought about that.'

'Tash, are you alright? Have you got over that bug? You just don't seem yourself. Haven't for ages.'

'I'm perfectly fine,' Tash said repressively. 'It's just lack of sleep.'

'Okay,' Emma said, not sounding convinced. 'Well,' she went on more cheerfully. 'This should buck you up. The Morrisons called and, guess what, we've got their business. They definitely want us to market their bungalow.'

'Oh Em, that's fantastic news. Well done.'

'I'll ring Biddy to say it's definitely on the market, if she's interested, and I'll chase up the brochure and make sure the pic gets pole position in the window. I'm going over this afternoon. I promised to give them some staging advice.'

Tash thought of the cluttered bungalow with its floral wallpaper and mis-matched carpets and, despite her tiredness, giggled. 'Good luck with that then.'

Emma laughed too. 'Yeah. Not sure how I'm going to get them to de-clutter that collection of Beswick figurines but I'll give it my best shot. You going to the book club next week?'

'Is it next week? That's come round quickly. I haven't even read the book yet.'

'I wouldn't worry about that. I bumped into Millie on Friday and she said the same. Said I'd email her the SparkNotes. You want them too?'

Tash nodded gratefully. 'Brill. Yes please.' Then a thought struck. She'd have to face Kit. And she wasn't sure how she felt about that.

Chapter 24

Despite Tash's worries about leaving Benji on his own for the evening, Adrian insisted he take her out.

'Look, the house is detached,' he grumbled. 'He won't disturb the neighbours.'

'I'm not worried about him barking, I'm more worried about him being on his own. Mum doesn't leave him. And what if he trashes the utility room?'

Adrian's eyes narrowed. Tash could tell he was on the edge of losing his temper. 'Natasha,' he began. 'Is it too much to ask to have an evening with you without that fleabag hanging around?'

Tash thought it through. If she made a fuss over this, he might be difficult about her going to the book group next week. Despite everything she was desperate to go. Benji couldn't do all that much damage to a room full of white goods, could he? And she'd make sure he had all his favourite toys with him and leave the radio on. 'Oh, alright then.'

'You could sound a little more enthusiastic. I have a very special night planned.'

'I'm sorry, Adrian.' Tash forced a smile. 'I'm tired. Busy day at the office.'

'And yet, you still insist on working.' Adrian compressed his lips. It made him look slightly sinister.

'Let's not go over that again, Ade.' Everything was a battle between them at the moment. Her heart sank at the thought of one of Ade's 'Very Special Nights.' It usually involved something extra-energetic after dinner. She was finding she shared Adrian's sexual tastes less and less these days. Giving herself a shake, she scolded herself silently. For goodness' sake, the man was offering to take her out, spoil her and she was being a real misery. 'I'll go and get ready then, shall I?'

Adrian's eyes gleamed. 'Put something sexy on, darling.'

'Will do.' Tash ran upstairs wondering what her problem was. A few months ago she would have jumped at the chance to be taken somewhere nice by Adrian. Now she longed for a night on the sofa in front of some brainless telly, cuddling the dog. 'Must be getting old,' she muttered to herself as she opened the wardrobe door. 'Little black dress and heels it is then.' It was the option that involved the least thought.

Adrian took her to Samphyre in Exeter. He loved seafood but, despite being brought up by the sea, Tash could take it or leave it. As they got out of the Porsche, she rebelled and wondered why he hadn't bothered to ask her where she would have liked to go – she was dying to try the new Italian that had just opened – but she damped down on the thought as unworthy. Adrian tried so hard to please her sometimes. She smiled at him as he opened the restaurant door for her. 'Lovely,' she said brightly.

As they were led to their table she thought Adrian seemed nervous. There was a tic going in his cheek and he made a huge fuss about insisting they had the best table available.

Everyone stared at them during his loud conversation with the maitre d' and Tash got embarrassed. 'Let's just sit down, shall we, Ade?' she hissed. Eventually they were settled, with snowy white napkins spread on their laps. A bottle of champagne in an ice bucket arrived. Adrian did his usual performance of tasting the wine and, after two glasses were poured, it was placed on an elaborate stand next to the table. Tash was beginning to sense this was something more than just a nice meal out and became uneasy.

'Champagne midweek is a bit extravagant, isn't it?' she asked.

'Not for tonight,' he beamed. 'I want to make it as special as possible.'

The evening continued uneventfully. The food was exquisite, the wine flowed and Tash found herself relaxing. Life with Adrian *was* good, she decided. She stopped glancing at her watch and worrying about Benji.

After their mains had been served, Adrian had had a furtive conversation with the waiter. Tash hadn't given it much thought at the time but now, as she saw a huge ice-cream sundae coming her way, with a sparkler fizzing on top, she knew. 'Oh Adrian,' she whispered. 'Please say you're not about to—'

The sundae was placed in front of her. The waiter melted away tactfully and Adrian said, 'Look at the sparkler darling. It's a very special one. In fact, it hides another sparkler but of a different kind.'

Tash looked. Hanging off the sparkler, which had now fizzled out, was a diamond solitaire. The biggest diamond solitaire she'd ever seen.

'Natasha Taylor,' Adrian said and then slid off his chair

and went down on one knee. Tash was aware of every other diner watching them avidly. 'Will you do me the very great honour of becoming my wife?'

A ripple of a sigh went through the restaurant and someone began to clap. Someone else joined in and soon the whole room was filled with cheers and applause.

Tash looked about her, stricken. The delicious food she'd just eaten threatened to return. 'I—' she began.

'That's a yes folks,' Adrian yelled. He jumped up, took the ring off the sparkler and slid it on Tash's finger. He kissed her hard on the lips, his fingers biting into her shoulders as he clutched them. More cheers and applause resounded and a fresh bottle of champagne arrived.

Tash was dazed. How could she tell him in front of everyone? How could she say every nerve in her being rebelled against the idea of being married to him? He'd gone to so much trouble but hadn't even waited for an answer. Just steamrolled her into submission. As usual. A wave of hot anger flooded her. How dare he put her in this impossible position? She picked up her champagne flute and drained it in one.

'Happy darling?' Adrian reached over and caressed her hand. 'I am. You've made me the happiest man in the world.' When she didn't answer, he added, 'Don't want your pudding? What a shame. Toffee ice-cream sundae is your favourite. Too emotional to eat, hey?' He chuckled and pulled the dish over. 'Waste not, want not then. This evening has cost me a pretty packet. Not to mention the bling. Do you like it? Three carats,' he boasted. 'Only the best for my fiancée.'

For the remainder of the evening Tash let Adrian chatter on. He seemed oblivious to her silence and talked endlessly about getting a newer, bigger house, perhaps out in the country, another car, maybe a Range Rover, about how happy he was, that they should throw a party to celebrate. As they left he yelled at the maitre d' that they'd be back to toast the first of the babies.

Benji was exhausted and whimpering when they returned, Tash assumed from barking. He'd also left a puddle by the back door. Numbly, she went to get the mop.

'Don't be long, darling,' Adrian called from upstairs, with a snigger. 'I've got a long night ahead planned for you.'

The light caught on the enormous diamond on her finger as she mopped up dog wee. Tash had never felt more trapped or more unhappy. And she had no idea how she was going to let Adrian down.

Chapter 25

Tash, only too aware that Benji's presence was causing Adrian stress and wanting to keep him sweet so she could get to the book group, kept her feelings on the engagement quiet. She hated herself for being so cowardly but couldn't face another argument. She was also frightened about how physically dominant he was getting. Part of Tash was shocked to the core that she could consider the possibility that Adrian might be violent towards her. The other part of her couldn't deny he had been getting increasingly rough. In the way he touched her, in the way he made love. In the way he had begun to force her to do things she wasn't happy about. So, for a few days, she let Adrian chatter on about plans for their future. The more she let him talk, the more she realised, just like the proposal itself, all the plans were about him and what he wanted. He never discussed them with her beforehand, just assumed she would go along with whatever he suggested. How had she morphed into this compliant creature lacking in self-confidence? She thought back over the last year. Adrian had gradually taken over her life. Sorted all the house admin, planned what they were going to eat, even insisting he did things like put new tyres on her car. He booked the holidays and presented them as a fait accompli. It was all done with love, he said. She was far too busy at work to be bothered over such things and, besides, he was better at stuff like that. At first Tash had been grateful to have time freed up so she could concentrate on her job. Now, looking back, Tash could see how controlling he had become and how it had sapped her confidence. Reflecting on Emma's words that she'd been much more fun before Adrian, she felt her stomach drop. It was true. She'd lost herself.

She needed to leave but knew she had to think through what to do and what to say. Adrian would argue, try to persuade her to stay. He'd be shocked and hurt. He loved her in his way but she knew he'd manipulate the situation to get what he wanted. With a sinking heart she realised that was the problem: Adrian was a manipulative man. And she couldn't stay with someone like that. It was time to consider what she wanted. To put herself first.

She avoided the next few group training sessions and went running on her own. It gave her some space from Adrian and meant she avoided having to see Kit. He had been right but she couldn't face having to apologise to him and admit her perfect life was shattered into a million pieces. She took Benji along on her runs and the little dog was looking much more fit and trimmer. It also meant she didn't have to leave him with Adrian.

Chapter 26

'Still think it's a cruel book,' Biddy launched in.

The book group had convened again, and up for discussion was *Wuthering Heights*.

Amy bit her lip, looking put out. 'I'd hoped I could introduce the book and perhaps put it into context?' She glanced around, appealing for help.

'Great idea Amy,' Kit said, giving her a supportive smile.

'Perhaps we could take a few minutes to decide how we're going to run the discussions?' offered Millie. 'Before we start on the actual book.'

There was a general murmuring of agreement, with the exception of Biddy who muttered something about there being too much messing about going on.

Tash had been half-dreading, half-counting down the minutes until the book group. She'd been frantic that Adrian would pull a stunt and force her to stay at home. She'd been stupidly gullible to fall for his lie when he'd insisted he was too ill to go to her parents' dinner. A lot of things were falling into place. The way he steamrolled over every decision of their lives, the weird business over her work clothes, his attempts to cut her off from her friends and family – she'd double-checked the answerphone and it was working. She assumed Adrian had erased the messages from her mother and from Emma, for whatever reason. In a spare moment at work she'd googled manipulative behaviour and what he was doing was a classic example. She'd looked up gas-lighting and, with a dawning sense of horror, realised that was what Adrian had been doing too.

'What do you think Tash?' Amy asked.

She came back to the book group with a bump. 'Sorry, miles away. You sure you don't mind me bringing Benji? I didn't want to leave him on his own. He gets distressed.'

'It's no problem, Tash.' Amy smiled kindly. 'I've heard he's become quite a celeb in town these past few days. And he seems to get on with Elvis.' She nodded to where the two dogs had cuddled up together in the middle of the reading area, in a sort of black and white curled up comma.

Biddy grunted. 'Wonders will never cease.' She huffed. 'Still, as a hearing assistance dog, Elvis is entitled to be here.'

'And we'd never dream of saying otherwise,' Millie put in. 'So how are we going to do these meetings then?'

There followed some discussion on how it would all work. Tash remained silent, acutely aware of Kit's presence in the chair next to her. As people were wont to do, everyone had sat in exactly the same spot as they had during the very first meeting. All had been taken by the time Tash had arrived. She'd been trying to get a non-compliant Benji to have a wee on the beach beforehand and had come in last. She felt Kit's nearness acutely. Could hear the rustle of his shirt sleeve as he reached for his glass of wine, could hear him crunch into the upmarket crisps Millie had provided. It was as if every sense had been super-powered. She hadn't been able to meet his eyes, or even mutter a greeting. Kit, on the other hand, had treated her as he always had.

'So,' Amy began, blushing a little. 'If I could begin.' She went on to put the book into context, explaining it fell into the gothic genre and that she felt its themes were destructive love and the hope that a new generation could bring. As she continued to talk, her blushes and halting speech evaporated and a new confidence shone out. 'Perhaps we could now go round the group sharing our thoughts. Biddy, would you like to start? What do you think of Heathcliff?'

Biddy grunted and swallowed her glass of wine in one. 'Manipulative, that's what he is,' she boomed. 'Pulling strings. Making Linton woo Catherine, abusing Hindley and Isabella.'

Tash hid a grin as she saw Marti flip feverishly through her copy. It was pristine with the spine unbroken.

'A lot of people see him as a romantic hero,' Emma argued. 'There's no doubting his love for Cathy. He loves her so much.'

'Piffle. Real love isn't about possession.'

'I happen to think you're right Biddy,' Kit said. 'I think real love is stepping back and letting the person you love make mistakes, even if it's painful to watch. Giving them the freedom to discover themselves and what they can be.' He paused. 'Even if it means, in the end, they might go away from you.'

Tash shifted uncomfortably. All this was too close to her realisations about Adrian and she didn't like it. Heathcliff, the romantic hero she'd loved so passionately when she'd read the book at school, was being revealed as a controlling bully. At seventeen she'd longed for a strong, dominant man to love her possessively as Heathcliff had loved Cathy. The reality of being loved like that was terrifying.

'Oh, but Heathcliff has been betrayed by Cathy. That's what has made him act so vindictively,' said Emma, ever ready to see the good in people.

'Doesn't excuse the things he did,' Biddy declared. 'Terrorising Nelly, that poor puppy.' She shuddered, and Elvis whined in his sleep as if he sympathised.

'Shall we move on?' Amy suggested. 'The role of the unreliable narrator plays a huge part in this novel. Marti, what do you think?'

Marti started. Tash watched with interest. She'd bet a month's commission the woman hadn't even opened the book.

'Oh yes,' Marti blustered. 'I just love great literature, don't you?' She nodded enthusiastically, her long earrings jangling violently. 'I think the unreliable narrator plays a very vital role.'

Biddy hmphed in disgust. 'Speak up woman. Some of us don't hear so well.'

Tash bit her lip to stop a giggle escape. Marti had spoken perfectly audibly. Biddy was having fun at the woman's expense.

'Come on,' Biddy continued. 'We're all waiting on your pearls of wisdom. Make your views known. How specifically does the unreliable narrator affect how we read the book?'

Marti went scarlet and hid her face in her immaculate copy of *Wuthering Heights*. She stuttered something anodyne until Amy rescued her.

Chapter 27

When everyone moved downstairs to eat Millie's sandwiches, Tash stayed put. She picked up the wine bottle and re-filled her glass thoughtfully. It had been a fascinating evening but some of the discussion had been painfully close to home. Adrian might not have been physically violent yet but he was certainly as manipulative as Heathcliff, and did it all in the name of love. Heathcliff and Cathy had long been her model for a perfect passionate and romantic love. Now Tash knew she needed to break the chains of the warped love Adrian had bound her with.

Weirdly, the deciding moment that told her it had ended had been over something trivial. It had happened a few days ago. The thing that made her determined to get away from Adrian had been, of all things, a lipstick. Emma had passed the iconic Dior cylinder onto her explaining she'd won it in a competition but the vibrant red wouldn't suit her. With Tash's jet-black hair and tanned colouring, it would look fabulous. It did. Tash had been admiring its effect in the bathroom mirror one morning after applying.

'What on earth have you got on?' Adrian asked, after barging in without knocking. 'You've been in here for ages.

Aren't you going to be late for work?' He peered closer. 'Your lips aren't that shape, Natasha.'

Tash looked at him, puzzled. 'What do you mean?'

'You don't have lips that shape. Why have you put lipstick on in a way to make them look like that? And why on earth would you want to wear lipstick that bright anyway? It makes you look cheap, Natasha. Oh, and here's your engagement ring. You left it on the bedside table. Anyone would think you didn't like it. Up to Manchester again today and might have to stay over. I'll miss my darling fiancée.' He kissed her on the cheek, groped her bottom and left.

Tash stared at her reflection, absorbing the relief flooding through her. A whole day, maybe two, without Adrian. And he hadn't mentioned the book group. She was free to go. In fact, if he stayed in Manchester overnight, he wouldn't even know. She stared at her lips. The matte red made them appear fuller, more sensual, but they were still the same shape they'd always been. She leaned closer and pouted. A glimmer of the old Tash reflected back. The confident, fun person who had been eroded by months of Adrian's controlling behaviour. 'Where did she go to?' Tash whispered. Before she'd gone out with him, bright red lipstick had been a favourite. Adrian had bought her a nude shade as one of her presents for their first Christmas together. 'Christian Louboutin,' he'd said proudly, when she opened it. She'd looked it up a few days later and had been amazed to see it sold for seventy pounds. At the time things like that had mattered. Now she'd settle for a Boots own brand as long as it was given without the expectation that she change to suit someone else's agenda.

Defiantly, she patted the Dior red down with a tissue and

applied another coat. Leaving the engagement ring on the bathroom sink, she had gone down to collect Benji to go into work.

'Penny for them?'

Tash jumped. Biddy had climbed back upstairs to check on a sleepy Elvis, who was still snoring alongside Benji. 'Brought you some food. Looks like you could do with some, in my opinion.'

'Thank you.' Tash took the plate loaded with coronation chicken sandwiches. She wasn't sure she could eat any of it.

'Try a morsel, child,' Biddy said, stoutly. 'Lemon drizzle to follow. Brought some of my special brownies as well.'

Tash nibbled on the corner of a sandwich and, to her surprise, found herself ravenous.

'That's more like it. You got troubles?'

Tash looked at Biddy. She hardly knew the woman, except by reputation. She wasn't exactly the person she wanted to confide in but, somehow, she did. And once she'd begun, the relief was so acute, she couldn't stop. She told Biddy everything.

When she'd finished Biddy simply nodded, then said, 'You have to make a plan. Rehearse what you're going to say because the bastard will screw you round otherwise. And have things ready for when you go. It's the most dangerous time. Many a woman has got hit the moment she told her bloke it was all over. It's the time you're most vulnerable in an abusive relationship.'

Tash swallowed down the last tiny crumb of cake. It stuck in her throat. 'Do you think that's what it is? Abusive? Adrian's never actually hurt me.' She winced as she thought back to that one night. 'Well, not deliberately.'

123

'From my experience that'll be next,' Biddy said. 'Get out while you can, girl. You got somewhere to go?'

Tash nodded. 'I can go to my parents' house.'

'Good.' Biddy got up, easing her back as she did. 'Oof. Too much time sitting down tonight. You want any help, just ask, you hear?' Then she winked. 'We got the measure of that snob Marti, didn't we?' She shook her head and cackled. 'Bet my bottom dollar she's not got past the first page. Had to chuckle when she asked who Nelly was! Can't abide a book snob.' She whistled to Elvis, waved a hand and made her way carefully down the spiral staircase. 'Hello there, young Kit,' Tash heard her say. 'Yes, go on up, she's still there.'

Chapter 28

'I've come to say sorry,' he began. 'For making all those assumptions the other day. I had no right.'

Tash waved his apology away. 'Oh Kit, it should be me saying that to you. I'm so sorry. You were only trying to help.' She bit her lip, keeping the sudden tears at bay. She never let herself cry and certainly wouldn't break down in front of Kit.

He resumed his seat beside her. 'Life can be shitty sometimes.'

Tash looked away. That he didn't ask questions, didn't insist on an explanation for her awful behaviour, made tears threaten again. She took several deep, gulping breaths and concentrated hard on reading the poster advertising the Fun Dog Show. 'Entry five pounds,' it proclaimed. 'All proceeds to the RNLI.' When she'd recovered, she turned back to him. 'Was your divorce really awful?'

Kit didn't seem fazed by the abrupt question. Pursing his lips, he gave a little nod and blew out a breath. 'It was. At the time. Took a while for the legal stuff to be sorted and Mel and I didn't talk for a few years.' He leaned forward. 'But the one thing we had was a deep friendship, as well as a married life together. In the end that resurfaced.' He shrugged. 'When we'd got to a point where we were both happy in our lives, we became those good friends again. I'm genuinely happy she's happy with her American dentist. And Mel would be the same if it ever happened for me again.'

Tash stared into his deep set eyes. They were green, she noticed. A deep, forest green. How could she ever have thought him unattractive? 'And has it?' she breathed. 'Happened for you again?'

Kit looked down. He picked a dog hair off his jeans. 'Possibly. Too early to tell. There are complications. Wish it would get sorted soon though. One legacy of divorce is that it's left me unable to sleep without someone else in the bed.' He scrubbed a hand over his face. 'Permanently tired.'

'Oh.' Tash ached to know who the woman was. 'She must be someone very special.'

'She is.' Kit grinned. 'Come on,' he said, standing up. 'I'm sure Amy is desperate to lock up. She was saying earlier that the meeting had overrun and she needed to get home.'

Tash became very busy. Clicking her tongue at Benji, she gathered up his water bowl and chew and stuffed them into her backpack. Maybe it was Amy who had captured this man's heart? He was always so kind to her. She slung the backpack on, thrusting her arms through its loops. She hoped they'd be very happy. Amy, with her shy, gentle ways was a good match for him. But, despite her preoccupation with Adrian, she felt her heart break a little further.

'Don't forget your book.' Kit picked it up and passed it to her. 'Hang on, I'll put it in your rucksack for you. Save you taking it off again.'

His fingers brushed hers as he took back the book. He

went to stand behind her and the heat from his body radiated out. His breathing tickled her ear, making her long to turn and capture his mouth with hers. Hearing him unzip the bag and feeling it sag made Tash's breath hitch. It was a curiously intimate act, as if he was unzipping her clothes. Screwing her eyes tightly shut, she forced back the tears which, once again, threatened. The zip closing had a note of finality.

'All done.' Kit patted her on the shoulder. 'Come on, time to go. Try not to fall on the stairs this time.'

'I'll try my best.' Tash forced a cheery note into her voice.

They called goodnight to Amy who, as Kit had predicted, was waiting to lock up, and went out into the night.

It was very still and clear. A late seagull cried mournfully as it glided overhead, its underbelly lit bright white by the lights on the prom. Tash could hear the sea shift in the distance and smell the pungent seaweed. She loved her home town, had never felt the need to move away. She had everything here that she needed or wanted. A fresh wave of misery washed over her as she contemplated having to face those who would crow and gossip over the ruins of her once perfect life. And, for the first time, she questioned how easy it would be living in a small town with an ex in the background. An ex like Adrian.

'I hope I don't have to move away,' she blurted out.

Kit came very near. He traced a finger down her cheek. 'Why would you need to do that?' His curiosity was intense.

'I don't know,' she floundered. 'I just might have to.'

'I've said it before and I'll say it again. If you need any help, you know where I am. Come to me.' He smiled slightly. 'Benji too. Plenty of room.'

She longed to kiss him, craved the solidity of his touch.

She wanted him to make her feel safe. That was what had been missing from her life with Adrian, she realised, especially in the last few months. She'd been spoiled, indulged, but caged like a bird with clipped wings. And never made to feel safe.

She made a move towards him then stopped. She ought to go. With Adrian in Manchester, it would be the ideal opportunity to pack up some things. She'd stow them in her car boot. He'd never notice if she was careful with what she packed. The temptation to linger with Kit was strong, though. She wished they'd met at a simpler time. She wished there was no woman in his life who 'might become special.' She wished he'd kiss her until she had no breath left. Then she froze. She heard the roar of a car coming along the prom towards them. She knew that sound. It was unique. No other car in Berceombe sounded like that. It was Adrian's Porsche.

'I've got to go,' she whispered and ran away from him. As she reached the start of the promenade behind Millie's café, the Porsche had parked up. It sat, a malevolent red creature, the engine still running with Adrian tapping his fingers on the steering wheel.

'Sorted Manchester sooner than I expected. Thought I'd come and collect you from book group,' he called out cheerfully. 'Aren't I clever to remember you were going?'

'I'd rather walk home, Adrian. I've got the dog.'

'Of course you've got the dog. You've always got that bloody dog. Oh get in, Natasha. I'll put up with the animal just this once.'

Tash clambered in, clutching Benji close to her on her lap. She had no idea how much Adrian knew but, from the underlying violence in his tone, it was enough.

Chapter 29

'Natasha, will you get home and stop this dog from yapping?'

Pulling the car over, Tash took the message on her mobile. It had been one of those mornings. She'd left Emma in the office manning the phones chasing up fifty or so queries and had been out taking on three new clients. They'd all taken longer than expected. Adding to her stress was that Benji had thrown up in the early hours. She'd left him at home, thinking it unfair for him to be in a warm car while she worked. It meant leaving him with Adrian who was working at home.

The journey home from the book group had been under-taken in a tense silence. Surprisingly, Adrian had accepted Tash's plea of exhaustion and the need for a shower and an early night. Tash hadn't slept but had lain rigidly on her back, as far away from Adrian as possible. It had almost been a relief to get up and see to Benji. After cleaning up, she'd slept on the sofa to be nearer to the dog. Or that was the excuse she gave herself.

She and Adrian had tiptoed politely around one another that morning but he'd agreed to keep an eye on Benji when she explained she had to leave the dog behind. 'He'll be no trouble,' had been her parting words as she rushed out.

Pressing a thumb to her temple, she tried to return Adrian's message but his phone went to voicemail. She let her head loll back on the headrest for a second. She was exhausted. Not just from lack of sleep but from the situation and from her lack of action. It was unlike her. She was the sort of person who, when faced with a problem, decided what possible solutions there were and tried them out. Or she used to be that person. Switching the engine back on, she did a swift U-turn and headed for home. The very fact that Adrian was being so unusually accommodating worried her. Remembering Biddy's words, she knew she had to handle it all calmly and have a plan.

The house was silent when she unlocked the front door. Going through the kitchen into an empty utility room she breathed a sigh of relief when she saw Adrian out in the garden with Benji. The dog was running around. He must be feeling better. She left her bag on the work surface and went outside. She was about to call out when she saw, to her horror, that Adrian was chasing the dog. And it was no game. Benji had slid behind the rose arbour and lay, cowed and panting, his eyes wide with fright.

'You little fucker!' Adrian yelled, puce in the face and aimed a kick. Benji screamed in pain.

'Adrian,' Tash roared. 'What the hell is going on?' She ran to the arbour, putting herself between dog and man, spreading her arms wide as a barricade. As she did so Adrian kicked again, missing the dog but grazing Tash's ankle painfully.

'Adrian, stop it. You've hurt me!'

For a second everything froze. Tash waited, watching rage and guilt chase across Adrian's face. Watching a shade of ashen white replace the red flush of fury. She held her breath, listening to Benji whine. He'd hurt the dog. Was she going to be next?

The moment held and then broke.

Adrian staggered back. He collapsed onto the bench, breathing heavily.

In a lightning response, Tash turned to the dog and took him by the collar. Benji refused to come out, so she dragged him from his hiding place and picked him up. Holding him close, she tried to soothe him with a shaking hand. She levelled a stare at Adrian. 'What did you think you were doing?'

Adrian went on the attack. 'Oh, so now you come back. After the little shit has puked all over the garden.' He thrust a hand towards the path where Tash could see a puddle of vomit. 'About fucking time.' He reared up.

Tash felt Benji begin a growl and clutched him harder. That he was willing to protect her, even having been attacked, brought tears to her eyes. She willed them away, sensing that if she showed the slightest sign of weakness, Adrian would go for her next.

Adrian lurched close. He put his face into hers. Tash forced herself to stare back, refusing to back down. She could smell his sour breath, feel the fury dagger off him.

'You—' Adrian snarled. His finger stabbed at her chest. 'You can fucking clean up after this little shit.' For a horrible, wrenching second, Tash felt his wavering need, his desperation to hurt her some more. Then he barged past her, knocking her shoulder roughly.

Tash heard the front door slam and the roar of the Porsche's engine as it skidded off the drive. She held the terrified dog closer to her; he was whimpering. 'Oh Benji, I'm so sorry,' she sobbed. 'I should never have left you with him. Has he hurt you?' Standing Benji on the garden table, tears pouring down her face, she felt over the dog's flanks and then ran a hand down each leg. He didn't react except to wince and then tremble some more. Tash's legs wouldn't hold her. She sank onto the bench, cuddling Benji on her lap. Sinking her face into the dog's silky fur, she screwed her eyes shut and willed herself to think.

She made her decision. 'Come on little man, we need to pack up and go.' She lifted him carefully down and ran into the utility. He followed her like a shadow.

Heart pounding, Tash shoved Benji's stuff into a bag. Putting him on the lead, she whispered, 'You've got to be very brave and stay in the car for a minute while I go and pack. Do you think you can do that?' Then Tash froze for a second. Fear paralysed her. Should she put Benji and his things in the car first, or stack it up by the front door? What if Adrian came back before she'd gone? If he could mistreat a defenceless dog like that, what might he do to her? She'd tasted enough flashes of Adrian's temper to know he ran on a knife-edge and had been doing so for some time. She didn't care if it was work stress that was causing it, she didn't want to hang around any longer to be his next victim. What if he was watching the house? Ready to stop her as she made her escape?

Thoughts were wheeling hysterically. She took some deep breaths. Leaving a whimpering Benji in the utility, she went into the garage from the access door in the garden. She opened one of the garage doors an inch and peered out. The estate was perfectly quiet. Next door's cat shimmied past but otherwise no one was about. A blanket of heat lay over the place. Everything was normal, the house windows blankly ignoring the personal drama taking place. Tash ran out, opened the garage doors fully and backed her car in. Unlocking the tailgate, she left all doors open for a quick escape if needed.

She ferried all of Benji's things to the car and then told the still shivering dog that she had to go upstairs. Keeping one eye out through the windows at the front of the house, she shoved underwear, jeans, some toiletries into an overnight bag and ran back down, nearly tripping in her haste. She felt sick. It had all taken far too long. It was nearly half an hour since Adrian had roared off. Long enough for him to have driven around and let go of most of his temper and plenty of time for him to think up excuses for what she'd witnessed.

Benji nearly scuppered the whole escape. With the car stuffed with a random collection of belongings, he sat on his bottom and refused to get in the passenger side. Tash bit down on her impatience and then when he showed no enthusiasm for getting into the vehicle but just sat and shook, she picked him up and bundled him in. Running around to the driver's side, she froze in horror, her hand on the door handle. She heard the distinct note of Adrian's Porsche. Throwing herself in, she rammed the car into gear, shot down the drive and turned right.

It was, of all people, Marti Cavendish who bought her time. At the entrance to the estate, she had pulled in front of Adrian's car, blocking him in and at an angle which suggested he had committed some kind of road rage. Marti stood at his open driver window yelling at him.

Tash caught a fleeting glimpse of Adrian's furiously red face as she sped past.

Where could she go? At the junction Tash grasped the steering wheel in a white-knuckled grip. It made sense to turn right and go to her parents' but Adrian would guess and follow. The house was empty and Tash had no desire to be alone with Adrian ever again. Kit! Kit had said she would be welcome any time. That if she needed a friend, he'd be there. Glancing down at Benji, who had two paws over his nose as if trying to block out the memory of the morning, Tash wondered what else Adrian had done to him. She couldn't risk Adrian finding the dog. She turned left and headed out of town.

Chapter 30

Once clear of Berecombe, Tash pulled into a lay-by and backed up tight in front of a juggernaut. It was pink and called Priscilla-Louise. Weird the things you noticed in times of stress. Priscilla-Louise was enormous and might hide her if Adrian had followed. She called the office and begged Emma to hold the fort for the afternoon. Explaining briefly what had happened and warning that Adrian might go into the office to look for her, she was heartened by the amount of sympathetic swearing on the other end of the line. Emma promised to get Pete in as back-up. She had to cut her off as Benji was beginning to retch. Reaching over him, she opened the passenger door and pointed the dog's nose onto the grass verge just as he threw up. When he'd finished, Tash lay back on the driver's seat and wondered how much more she could take. She stroked Benji's trembling body, soothing him. When she was sure there was nothing more to come up, she got out of the car and ran around to close the passenger door. As she did so, a flash of red roared past.

Adrian.

Ducking down, she hoped and prayed Priscilla-Louise had done her job. Getting back in the car, she exited a swift U-turn and sped off in the opposite direction.

As she'd detoured an extra twenty miles, it took her an hour to get to Kit's. She stayed on the main roads, not wanting to be stuck down a single-track and risk being boxed in by Adrian. As she drove, she couldn't believe she was thinking this way about him. Although, if she'd been honest with herself, she realised, all the signs had been there for months.

'I've just been deluding myself and putting up with it for the sake of a nice lifestyle,' she said bitterly to Benji who, having dislodged whatever was making him ill, was looking brighter. 'Well, more fool me. What have I got to show for it now? Out on the streets with a carful of belongings.' Slowing the car, she turned off onto the lane that she knew would bring her to Kit's farm. She turned in past the lodge and bumped up a pot-holed drive, barely registering her surroundings. Scattering some indignant chickens, she let the car come to a rest in front of the house. The adrenaline drained. Covering her face with her hands, she sat unable to move. The engine ticked and, in the distance a dog barked. Benji whined in response. A roaring exploded in her head and all sounds faded. The car filled with her ragged breathing.

'Tash?' Kit opened the car door and was looking in. 'Whatever's happened?'

'Hello, Kit,' she managed. 'Do you think you could get Benji some water? He's not very well.'

The next few minutes were a blur. Tash was vaguely aware of a woman helping her out of the car and taking her somewhere cool and dark. She had a cold glass of water pressed into her hand and hoped Benji was getting the same. A violent shaking overtook her and the water was taken away. The sofa sank next to her and the woman held her hand until the panic attack passed. Merlin's woolly head rested on her knee and two wise canine eyes looked up at her in concern. Tash burst into tears.

'Feeling better?'

The storm had passed and Tash felt a lot better. She blew her nose on the handkerchief which had been offered. It was a large white cotton one. A proper man's handkerchief, not the scraps of tissue she usually used. 'Yes,' she said and then realised nothing had sounded. 'Yes, thank you.' She looked at the woman who had looked after her and saw it was Kit's mother.

'Excellent. Kit's making us all a cup of tea. And then perhaps you can tell us what's been going on and why the crisply efficient Natasha Taylor has arrived at my house looking, quite frankly my dear, as if she's been to the ends of hell and back.'

Tash nodded and managed a tight smile. Kit chose that moment to come in bearing a tray of tea things. He dwarfed the room and looked so incongruous among the faded décor that Tash wanted to laugh. She wondered if she was a little hysterical. Benji trotted at his heels, gazing up adoringly.

'You look a lot better,' Kit said and put the tea tray on a table. He came to sit on an armchair opposite. 'You had us a bit worried for a while. We couldn't get any sense out of you.'

Tash fondled Merlin's soft ears. The dog was still pressed to her knees. 'I'm so sorry to barge in on you. I didn't feel—' To her shame, her voice began to crack again. Biting down on more tears, she continued. 'I didn't have anywhere else to go.'

Mrs Oakley patted her arm and then rose. 'Seeing as I am, shall I be mother? Lots of sugar I think.'

'Thank you, Mrs Oakley.'

'It's Marianne and I hardly think pouring you a cup of tea warrants such an outburst of gratitude. Garibaldi?'

Tash stifled a watery grin and shook her head. She'd forgotten how eccentric Kit's mother could be. She took the tea gratefully, trying not to let the cup rattle in its saucer.

As if sensing she needed a little more time to recover herself, Marianne Oakley began a conversation with her son. It was something about the price of a sack of carrots for the donkeys.

Tash let the details wash over her. She lay back on the sofa and sipped her tea. As its heat coursed through her, she felt revived and took in her surroundings. High-ceilinged, the room had white-panelled walls and an air of decaying grandeur. A faded rug covered the floorboards and two chintzy armchairs and the sofa she sat on were grouped around an enormous stone fireplace. All looked well-worn and much loved. It was a million miles away from the executive housing estate and the clinically cream-and-white house she had shared with Adrian. Tash let her thoughts drift. How had she been so blind? So stupid? Why had she let herself disappear into Adrian's life?

The sofa sank again, signalling Marianne's return. 'More tea, dear?' When Tash nodded, she added, 'Fill her up Kit. Ready to tell your tale of woe?'

Tash nodded again and began to speak.

Chapter 31

'Oh my giddy goodness!' Marianne exclaimed. 'No wonder you wanted to get away. Poor you and poor little Benji.' She scooped up the dog and cooed over him. 'You did absolutely the right thing in coming here. Didn't she, Kit?'

Kit hadn't said a word during her long and rambling explanation. He blew out a long-held breath. 'I knew things weren't good for you Tash, but I didn't know it had got quite that bad. How could he kick a defenceless dog? Bastard.'

'Language, Timothy,' Marianne reproved, to the bafflement of Tash. 'There will always be men who lash out at animals, as well you know. I think Natasha here has had a lucky escape. It would have been her next. That's usually the way.' She patted Tash's hand. 'But perhaps we'd do better to consider practicalities? I have just the one bedroom, alas, so you will have to stay here. I'm sure you left in rather a hurry so if you need anything, nighties and such, I will provide.' She got up, dislodging a reluctant Benji. 'Kit will show you to the spare room. It's in the older part of the house, the only bit of Devon longhouse that the Georgians left. I think we're aiming for shabby chic in terms of décor, so you'll have to bear with us. I'll dig out some bedding. Is there anything else we can do for you, dear girl?'

'No, you've both been very kind. Too kind. Actually, there is one more thing,' Tash added, eyeing Benji's gait as he shuffled across to her. 'I'd like to get Benji to a vet. He's been ill and I'd like to have him checked over for any injuries too.'

'Why don't I do that?' Kit offered. 'Having so many animals, we're regulars at Holmefields, and they're very good. Mum, if you can get Tash sorted, I'll go and ring them now.'

Tash stood, alarmed at how wobbly she still felt. 'You know there's no need for you to put me up, I can easily go to my parents' house. They're in Portugal but they wouldn't mind me camping out in my old room. I'm more worried about Benji and Adrian getting hold of him. If he could stay here then I could—'

'No.' Kit said it with finality. 'You're staying here. At least for a day or two. It'll give you time to think through what you ought to do, take legal advice if needed. We don't mind a bit.'

'That's settled then,' Marianne added cheerfully. She wagged a finger. 'We'll be delighted to have you. With all the animals around here, another human balances things up rather.' She shooed Kit away. 'Off you go, phone the vet.' Turning back to Tash, she added, 'Shall we take your things up to your room?'

Three hours later, Tash had stowed her meagre belongings in the farmhouse's spare room, had phoned Pete to ask for leave and had rung Emma again. She'd been relieved to hear that the office had been quiet and, more importantly, that Adrian hadn't been in. She and Emma had often discussed security but, in a quiet, friendly town like Berecombe, they'd never felt particularly uneasy. That time might have come. Pete had accepted her sudden request for leave without quibble and had promised to take on her workload. Tash found this strange. She liked Pete and he was an okay boss, but he wasn't usually so understanding. In the shower she shrugged off worries over work with some foamy gel donated by Marianne. It smelled expensively of orange and bergamot and was soothing. Tash sighed as she towelled herself dry. She just didn't want to face any more responsibilities today.

Her exhaustion morphed into a not unpleasant floating sensation. Dressed in jeans and a soft sweatshirt, she made her way along the track to the lodge house. Marianne had insisted she cook for them all. Merlin loped along with her, stopping every now and again to sniff something interesting. He hadn't left her side once since she'd arrived, parking himself on the landing outside her bedroom. As she walked, Tash's stomach growled; she hadn't eaten since breakfast. She couldn't believe that was only eleven hours ago. She felt as if she'd lived most of her life in one short day.

Stopping halfway, she leaned on the fence to enjoy the tranquillity. A couple of donkeys grazed in the field next to the track and Tash could hear geese and chickens scatting about in the farmyard behind her. The sun was melting into a pink cloud and a premature fingernail moon winked down at her. It was all very green and end-of-summer lush. She looked back at the farmhouse. At some point, its Georgian owner had come into money and had attempted to obliterate the old longhouse original. The front had been remodelled into symmetrical lines but, as she'd seen, the back had been left. Maybe the owners had fallen on hard times before the upgrade had been finished? The bedroom she'd been put in was older and the roof above it, thatched. It was a world away from the red brick and sterile hard lines of the housing estate.

Tash took in a deep, cleansing breath. She felt very tired but calm. She had made the right decision. Merlin put a soft mouth into her hand and she walked on.

The door to the lodge opened at her first knock and an ecstatic Benji leaped up at her.

Kit followed. 'Vet says he's absolutely fine. Had eaten something he shouldn't and that's what caused the sickness but nothing serious.' He caught her look. 'And some nasty bruising. But, on the whole, he's been lucky.'

Tash picked up a wriggling dog and hugged him. 'Thank God.'

'Indeed. Ah, hello Merlin,' Kit added. 'Been looking after our guest?'

'He's been a wonderful companion.'

'Well, not that much of a guard dog but big and ugly enough to be a good deterrent.'

Tash gazed at Kit. 'I hadn't thought of him like that. That was thoughtful.'

Kit smiled down at her. 'Not really. His bark can draw thunder.' He raised his eyebrows. 'And then he'll lick you to death.'

They stood, smiling idiotically at one another, framed by the fragrant honeysuckle which grew around the door. Kit brushed a drowsy bee away and opened his mouth to speak.

'Are you going to let the girl come in?' called Marianne from the depths of the house. 'I'm dying for a glass of something chilled.'

'You'd better come in,' Kit said. He smiled ruefully and stood aside and let her go first.

Tash smelled the heat from his body as she went past.

Chapter 32

Tash rolled over in bed and came up against Benji, who, taking advantage of the situation, was cuddling up against her. Sun streamed through the thin curtains and the room was filled with early morning sunshine and birdsong.

The bedroom mirrored the shabby sitting room downstairs. Faded cabbage roses danced around the walls and the iron bedstead looked nearly as old as the house. Easing herself up, she drank some water and lay against the bed head enjoying the tranquillity. Benji snored beside her and then had a yapping dream, kicking out his stubby legs.

Tash slipped from the bed, not wanting to wake him. She went to the windows and drew the curtains back. The walls were a good two feet thick and the window was set high, nearly into the thatched roof above. She could hear furious tweeting going on from the sparrows burying into the straw.

Last night had been filled with restoring food and good wine, to the background of Marianne's odd snatches of conversation and Kit's quiet presence. She'd gradually relaxed and then Kit had walked her back along the track, with the dogs snuffling along, excited at the night smells. Then she'd slept.

Now, she had to face up to her future. Find somewhere to

live, collect the rest of her things, get back to work. And, worse, she had to ring her mother and explain what had happened to her beloved Westie.

She put it off by going downstairs to make a coffee. She let Benji and Merlin out and sipped while they did what they had to. Returning upstairs, she decided to have a shower before facing her mother's wrath. Yawning, she pushed open the bathroom door to be faced with Kit, a skimpy towel clinging around his narrow hips. He stood at the basin, a shaver held mid-air.

'Oh,' she gasped. 'Sorry.' She tried to look away and failed. He was simply glorious. Broad shoulders, bulging pecs and biceps she wanted to curl up and die on. He'd obviously just jumped out of the shower because water beaded on his tanned body. It was all unbelievably erotic. Her face heated furiously and she glimpsed his grin before she turned and ran out.

As she reached her room, she heard him call out, 'If we're going to share a bathroom, remind me to put a lock on the door!'

'Oh Benji,' she gathered the dog up and cuddled him. 'That'll teach me for putting off phoning Mum.' She clicked on her mobile and rang Portugal, her mind still full of the sight of Kit in his half-naked glory.

Her mother began by insisting they cut their holiday short and fly home, to demanding a full vet report, to finally calming down and actually listening to what Tash had to say. Tash ended the call, having reassured Nadia that both her and Benji were absolutely fine and wouldn't be going anywhere near Adrian again. She hadn't had time to draw breath before her phone rang. It was Pete Hingham.

'Oh Pete, I'm so sorry about all this. I'll get in as soon as I can,' Tash began.

'No worries. I can cover until things get hectic in September. You take all the time you need.' He hesitated and cleared his throat before continuing. 'Actually, Tash, I'm feeling a bit guilty about this whole thing. Some information came to light a while back about Adrian and I should have passed it on. But, you know, you seemed happy together and I wasn't sure if it was just gossip. It came from Rob Eaton over at Iver Construction. You know they're building that big development over Wellington way?'

Tash swallowed. All the carefully built up calm and security from last night swirled around the sunny bedroom and disappeared. 'Just tell me, Pete.'

'Okay.' He coughed again. 'Thing is, Rob seems to think Adrian is married and has got a wife in the north somewhere.'

Tash's world shrank to the bedroom and its dancing cabbage roses. A butterfly flickered in and landed on the curtain, its wings stilled to drink in the sun. A wife? In some part of her brain it made perfect sense. She thought of his trips away and his refusal to discuss what he'd done, saying it had just been 'boring business.' Then she remembered his over-the-top proposal and felt sick. 'What else do you know, Pete?'

'You sure you want to know? Again, it's hearsay. I don't know how much truth there is in it.'

'Tell me. I need to know everything.'

'Well,' Pete sounded unsure. 'Rob used to work with Adrian when he lived up north. The bloke had a reputation. With women, I mean. Used to swank all over the place, trying to impress them with his cash and when they were slow to give him what he wanted, he used to spike their drinks. Or that's what Rob heard. And all the time, he had a wife at home. This is a while ago, of course, well before he moved to Berecombe.'

Tash's insides went to liquid. Her head pounded. She thought it might explode. Everything was falling into place. Her constant dragging tiredness, her foggy brain – had Adrian been putting something in her food? And what about the letter to an Anna Williams that had mysteriously disappeared? Was that his wife? Her eye was caught by Benji vigorously scratching himself. Had Adrian drugged him too? Was that why he'd been sick? She gathered the dog to her. 'Oh God.'

'I know, it's a shocker. He's always come across as a decent bloke too. And, as I said, it's gossip Tash. He seemed on the level whenever I met him. And all this stuff that Rob said happened a long time ago. Adrian might even be divorced by now.'

'Yes. He might be,' Tash said, hollowly, somehow knowing it wasn't true.

'So, you take all the time you need, okay? Emma and I can manage things. I'm on the lookout for another staff member too. You've done a great job but you need an extra pair of hands in there. Take it easy.'

'Will do.' She gulped and clicked off the call. Hugging a now protesting Benji to her, the tears began to roll down her cheeks. She sobbed quietly for a while, her heart breaking. Then she reached for a tissue, scrubbed her face and pulled herself together. Her world, the world that she had so carefully created with Adrian had been a false one. It had shattered into a million fragments and was stained by his sordid betrayal. For a second, Tash felt so desolate, her pride so battered, that she didn't know how she was going to face the world again. Then, thankfully, a surge of pure white-hot anger powered through her. 'The bastard,' she seethed, to a startled Benji. 'The absolute bastard!'

Chapter 33

Tash went downstairs and out into the farmyard to find Kit feeding the chickens, talking quietly to them as he did. She watched him unobserved for a few minutes. She liked how such an enormous man could be so gentle to the birds at his feet. The image of his impressive muscles flashed back into her vision. He must be strong but he rarely chose to demonstrate it. Adrian would be bragging about how many hours he spent in the gym, if he had even half the muscle tone. They were very different men.

She took in a huge, healing breath and nearly choked as the ripe stench of goat wafted over from the field.

Kit glanced up as he heard her cough. 'Countryside smells can take a bit of getting used to.' He laughed then registered her tear-stained face. 'News?'

She nodded.

'Into the kitchen then. Tea, toast and you can tell me all about it.'

Once they were settled at the life-marked pine table in the kitchen and had drunk their first pot of tea, she began, haltingly, to tell Kit what she'd just found out.

Kit's reaction was gratifyingly dramatic. 'I'll kill him,' he roared as he jumped up, sending his chair screeching across the quarry tiles. Merlin growled and Benji went to hide behind Tash's knees.

'Kit, you can't kill him. I'd quite like you around for a bit and not in prison. Sit down, you're frightening the dogs.'

'The fucker.' He subsided and, collecting the chair, sat back down again. 'How can you be so calm?'

'I've had a whole twenty minutes longer to get used to it. I can assure you I wasn't remotely calm when I found out.'

Kit poured more tea. He shook his head. 'How can he do these things? How can he sleep at night? I can't sleep and the only thing on my conscience is a parking ticket.'

Tash rubbed a hand over her face. She felt suddenly very tired. 'I don't know.' She shrugged. 'I thought I knew him but it's all been a web of lies.' Her bottom lip trembled. 'He wanted to marry me, wanted me to have his babies and it looks like he was already married. And the way he messed with my head. Making up stuff and letting me believe I was going crazy.' She looked out at the sunny August morning, staring hard until the tears were under control again.

'What are you going to do?'

'I don't know.' She looked Kit in the eyes. 'If he was drugging me and poor Benji, I haven't got any proof. Whatever it was will have long disappeared from my system by now. And, although he proposed—' at this Tash shuddered '—he didn't actually get as far as committing bigamy.' She swallowed. 'So, I suppose there's little more I can do except go back to work, find somewhere to live and pick up the pieces of my life.'

'Jeez.' Kit was silently thoughtful for a moment. 'You can stay here as long as you like. Until your parents get back or until you find a place.' His lips twisted with sudden humour. 'There's plenty of room, only one working bathroom being the exception. And besides, I seem to make a habit of taking in waifs and strays. I've got a batch of ex-battery chickens coming over later.'

'Perhaps that's what you should do,' Tash said, glad of the change of subject though not happy with the idea of being thought of as either a waif or a stray. 'Turn this into an animal sanctuary, I mean.'

'It's a thought.' Kit gave Merlin and Benji a crust of toast each. 'Not sure how I'd make it pay though.'

'Sponsorship? Paying visitors?' Tash shrugged. 'I don't know. How do other places do it?'

'I've absolutely no idea. I'd have to look into it. But, more importantly, what are you going to do next? Take some kind of revenge?'

She shook her head.

'Why not?'

'Because I know Adrian and that's exactly what he wants. I'm not going to give him the satisfaction of knowing I care.' She lifted her chin. 'The only thing I want Adrian Williams to know is that he's out of my life. Forever.'

Chapter 34

Tash, despite Pete advising her otherwise, returned to work immediately. She left Benji with Marianne who was delighted to have him and said he'd be company as she gardened. Adrian hadn't tried to contact her but he loomed, threateningly, in the background. Once, Tash woke in a panic, convinced she'd heard the Porsche's engine gunning along the lane to the farmhouse. She'd lain awake, heart racing, listening to the owls hoot and the rustle of something nocturnal outside but nothing had come of it. She'd clasped a snoring Benji to her and had eventually slept.

Emma was hugely relieved to have her back and they treated themselves to a girly lunch to catch up. She was as confused as Kit had been to hear Tash was going to ignore Adrian.

'But don't you want to go and cut up his suits, or key his car or something? I know I would. I know,' Emma squealed, jumping up and down in her chair in the beer garden of the Old Harbour. 'Sew pilchards into his curtains. They go off when the heating gets put on and he won't be able to find out where the smell is coming from!'

Tash laughed. She'd been right to get back to normal as

soon as possible. This was doing her good. She picked up a chip and dipped it into ketchup. 'Nope. I'm doing nothing.'

Emma blinked. 'I don't understand. Why not?'

'Because realising I don't care enough to do anything spiteful to get back at him is going to annoy the hell out of him.'

'Has a certain logic to it, I suppose.' Emma frowned. 'You'll want to get your stuff back though, won't you?'

Tash sighed. It had been preying on her mind. She needed to go to the house to pack the rest of her belongings. 'Yes, I'll need to do that. I suppose I could just rock up.' She bit her lip and shivered, despite the hot sunshine. 'I can't face going back to that house though.'

'I'll come with you, if you like.'

Tash smiled at her friend. Emma loved a bit of drama.

'Thank God the mortgage is in his name.' Emma picked up her lemonade. They had to go back to the office that afternoon and Tash had insisted on soft drinks. 'You can have a clean break. Just walk away.'

'And that is precisely what I intend to do. Now, tell me what's been happening at work. Any viewings on the Morrisons' bungalow?'

'Sod the Morrisons.' Emma leaned forward. 'I want to hear all about the divine Mr Oakley and whether you've done the dirty with him yet?'

Tash grinned and then blushed.

'I knew it. I knew it!' Emma said in triumph. 'All that rubbish about how you couldn't see why we thought he was sexy.' She made a face. 'And all the time you had the lusty thoughts for him.'

'It's not that simple though, is it?'

'Isn't it?'

'No. I'm living under his roof. I can't just jump his bones.'

'Why not?'

Tash put down her chip. She'd lost her appetite. 'It's all too soon. I need some time on my own first. I don't want to go straight into anything new. Besides, I'm not even sure he's interested.'

'Oh come on, Tash.' Emma was scathing. 'Anyone with half a brain can see he's drooling after you.'

Tash picked at a splinter in the rough wood of the Old Harbour's picnic table. 'Not sure about that. He's just being very, very kind.'

'You always have the men falling at your feet. Think even Pete's got a bit of a thing for you.' Emma picked up her glass, drained it and pointed it at Tash. 'It's cos you're so beautiful.'

'Am I?' Tash was genuinely surprised. 'I can't see it.'

Emma shook her head. 'Arsehole Adrian's got a lot to answer for. He's nearly destroyed you. You're clever, funny and top dollar gorgeous, Tash, and you'd better believe it. And he's had you thinking the opposite. I could see how he affected you. I've seen it for ages.'

'Why didn't you say something?'

'Oh, come on. Would you have listened?'

'Probably not.' Tash grinned and straightened her shoulders. 'I'm just glad I'm out of it.' She tensed. 'Did you hear a car?'

Emma looked around. 'No. Only cars allowed this far along the harbour are the fishermens' trucks. And I can't see one of them. Old Davey's makes a hell of a racket.'

Tash took a gulping breath. She needed to stop jumping at shadows. It was over with Adrian. All over.

When they got back to the office, Emma frowned down at the bouquet resting against the locked door. 'What's this, flowers from a grateful client? We haven't completed on anything this week.' Picking up the lily and rose bouquet, she added, 'Oh, there's a note.' She passed it over to Tash, unlocked the door and disappeared into the office. 'They're gorgeous though, aren't they? I'll find a vase.'

Tash opened the tiny envelope. The note held only two words: 'I'm watching.'

Chapter 35

Tash's hand trembled as she slid the key into what used to be her front door. It slipped and her fingers became clumsy. 'Oh God Em, I think he's changed the locks.'

Emma glanced behind her anxiously. 'Try it again.'

'Maybe we should just go. I don't want to come face to face with him. I couldn't bear it.'

'Look, it's our only chance. Pete's friend Rob said Adrian was on the site in Wellington and was going to be there all day. And we've got Kit watching the road. We'll shove as much stuff into the bags as we can and scarper.'

'Scarper? Where did you get a word like that from?'

'I read a lot. Go on. Try the lock again.'

This time it gave. The women fell into the hall. Tash looked around. It looked exactly as it always had done. White, minimalist, sterile. Then she gasped. The mirror, the one Adrian preened in before he left the house, was shattered into three jagged pieces.

'Looks like our Adrian had a hissy fit,' Emma observed. 'Come on, let's get started. I'll do upstairs, it'll be easier for me to spot what's yours.' She took a bundle of the laundry bags off Tash and headed for the stairs. 'Get a move on, Tash,' she hissed. 'Don't just stand there!'

Tash staggered into the sitting room, her legs were refusing to work properly. There was hardly anything she wanted. Going to the mantelpiece over the fake white wood burner, she recovered the Wedgewood box her mother had given her. Then she added the photograph of her parents' wedding and one of her as a teenager. Getting into her stride she added the grey and cream union jack cushions. She'd bought them with her first commission when she'd begun at Hughes and Widrow. They were definitely hers. She'd brought them from her bedroom at her parents' house and Adrian had always moaned they didn't go. She went to the window and peered out at Kit standing guard at the end of the drive. The sight reassured her. Glancing at the row of expensively-framed photographs on the windowsill, of her and Adrian, she was surprised he hadn't done anything crass like cut her out. She didn't want any of them.

Heading into the kitchen, she shoved the omelette pan her mother had bought her into another bag, then added a few mugs she knew were hers. A collection of cooking knives went in next, along with a couple of saucepans and that was about it.

Suddenly, an urgent anger at the fact that she had to do this took hold. It gave her a furious energy. She ran into the utility and began to gather her coats which were hung on the back of the door. As she heaped them on the floor, one of Adrian's jackets fell off. It was his favourite leather one. Tash regarded it with distaste; he'd worn it on the night he'd proposed. Holding it between finger and thumb, she picked it up and hung it back on the hook. As she did so a plastic bottle bounced out and skittered across the tiles. Nudging it with her foot, she could see it contained small white pills. She gasped. Could this be the evidence that would prove Adrian had drugged her? Heart pounding, she took several photos on her phone. She went to pick up her bundle of coats and stopped. Fishing out a tissue, she picked the bottle up and put it back into the pocket it had fallen from. Then, making sure she didn't touch it, she took several more photos. She had no idea if they would even count as evidence but it was her only chance. Releasing a breath she hadn't realised she'd been holding, she grabbed her coats and ran into the hall. Putting the bags by the front door, she flung the coats on top.

On trembling legs, she went upstairs to give Emma a hand but was stopped on the landing.

'All done,' Emma proclaimed over-brightly. 'Let's get out. This place is giving me the wiggins. How could you live in a completely white house?' She shuddered and blocked Tash from going into the main bedroom. 'No need to go in there, I've got all your clothes here.' She gestured to the pile of bags on the landing.

'I just want to check you've got everything.'

'Yup. All of it. Even your stilettos.'

'Let me past, Em.'

Emma refused to move. 'You don't want to go in there, Tash. Trust me.' She stopped her by the arm.

'Emma, let me go.' Tash pushed past and went into the bedroom she'd shared with Adrian. And gasped in horror. The once pristine white bedding was covered in an ugly dark stain.

Lined up, against the headboard, were the beheaded remains of the cuddly penguins that Adrian had bought her. They too, were splattered with gore. She went nearer.

'Don't touch it, Tash. I don't know what it is.' Emma had come in silently behind her.

'Do you think, do you think it's—'

'Blood? God knows. It certainly dries like that. He's done a number in the ensuite too.'

Dazed, Tash went into the shower room. Obscenities screamed at her, written in lipstick, from the mirror. Her blood ran cold. Adrian had lined up the ruined lipsticks in rigid height order. They stood, like a line of defeated soldiers, awaiting execution.

'He's gone bloody loopy. Emma touched Tash's arm. 'Come on, let's get out of here.'

'Wait.' Tash took photos of the bathroom and of the bedding. Her hands shook so much she worried they would all be blurred beyond recognition.

Before they left, Tash bent to the ruined bedding. She lifted the duvet cover and sniffed cautiously.

'Tash, what are doing?' Emma recoiled.

'I think it's only ketchup or tomato soup.' Tash replied, relieved. She straightened. 'Not blood.'

'Still major weirdness though.' Emma took her arm. 'Come on, kiddo. Let's go.'

Kit, noting their ashen faces, said nothing as he helped them shove the bags into his Freelander. Emma filled him in on the drive back to the farm. Tash sat in silence, staring at the scenery flying past, trying not to look out for a red Porsche.

Chapter 36

It took several hours before Tash could stop shaking. Eventually, Kit ordered her to take a long hot bath. Afterwards she joined him in the garden of the farmhouse, where he sat, nursing a beer, the dogs lying at his feet.

She sat on the other side of the dilapidated table and poured herself a glass of wine, relieved to see her hands were almost steady. They sat in silence, letting the cool, evening air slide over them. House martins and swallows dived overhead and an early owl hooted softly from the trees. It made Tash remember the owl which had startled her when she'd had to pull up on the run. She and Kit had sat in silence then too. He was an easy man to be with. She glanced across and caught him watching her. She had so much to thank him for. Here was the only place she felt totally safe. She began to stutter out her thanks.

He cut her off. 'No need. What Emma said, was it all true?'

Tash nodded.

He blew out a breath. 'And there's me thinking she was exaggerating. You should take this to the police, Tash.'

Tash nodded. 'I didn't think I had any evidence but it's all adding up. And...' She paused. 'I didn't tell Emma this but I found some pills too. Adrian wasn't on any medication, to my knowledge. He hated taking tablets. Whatever those pills were, I don't think he was taking them for headaches.'

'It could be viewed as circumstantial.'

'Maybe,' Tash admitted. 'But I'll have to take that risk. I can't let him get away with this, Kit.' She laughed shortly. 'It's not the actions of a sane man and what he's done to me, he could go on to do to other women. Maybe already has.'

'There's his wife too. And all the other women who had the misfortune to encounter him.'

Tash's throat ached with unshed tears. 'I know. Perhaps it'll give her the courage to press charges as well.' She rubbed a weary hand over her eyes. 'Oh, I'm so tired from all this. I just want him to go away. I'm struggling to think about anyone else. I know it's selfish.'

'Not selfish. Trying to survive. And you know I'll back you all the way. You won't be alone in this, Tash.'

'I'd forgotten you were used to dealing with waifs and strays, Kit.'

He shrugged. 'Only they usually come with four legs.'

Tash managed a grin. 'What about the chickens?'

'Oh yes. The ex-batteries. Hardly any feathers. Poor things. I've been trying to teach them how to jump onto the roost at night. They'd only known a cage.'

'I know how that feels,' Tash said, with feeling. 'Do you think my feathers will ever grow back?'

'Of course,' Kit answered, equably. 'I think you're well on the way already. Today was just a setback, give it time.'

Tash sipped her wine. 'Don't think I'll ever be a one-egg-a-day layer.' To her surprise, she found herself giggling.

Kit pursed his lips. 'You'd better stick to selling houses then. And I repeat, you can stay here as long as you want to, you know. I quite like having you around, to be honest. Even if you are an estate agent.'

Tash watched as Benji snuggled closer to Merlin who blew out a dramatic breath in his sleep and put a long leg over him. It was comical how the wolfhound dwarfed the little Westie. 'They make an odd pair,' she said. 'But they seem to get on.'

Kit flicked her a glance. 'Bit like us then.'

Chapter 37

Tash sucked in a long shuddering breath, her hand hovering over the door to Berecombe's police station. Easing the kinks from her neck, she hardened her resolve and went in.

To her relief, it was Paul Cash behind the desk. He was older, fatherly. He might just understand.

'Hi Tash. What can I do for you?'

'Can I talk about...' Tash struggled to find the words. 'I need to report something. Domestic abuse. A possible drug spiking incident.' She floundered. 'I don't know how to explain.'

Paul's blue eyes widened. Then he assumed his professional veneer. 'Let's find a room, shall we? Somewhere quiet and you can tell me all about it.'

Chapter 38

The town was buzzing. The day of the fun run dawned, warm and sultry.

'Just as well they've got loads of vollies giving out bottles of water,' Emma said, as she hung onto Tash stretching out her quads. 'Going to be hot.' She nodded to a man behind them. 'Can't believe some are doing it in fancy dress!' They were standing outside the Old Harbour Inn, waiting for the off. The sun, already high in an azure sky, was beating down relentlessly. It might be the beginning of autumn but no one had told the weather.

Tash had thought she was looking forward to the run. Usually, she loved Berecombe when everyone came out for events like this. The family run had already started and she could see a long trail of children straggling along the promenade. Race marshals were handing out water and encouragement, their collecting buckets already groaning with donations. Everything was set for another brilliant Berecombe community event. She knew most of the people taking part, as well as those doing their bit by cheering the runners on. It should have been the highlight of the summer. But, standing with Emma and the other runners, Tash had never felt more alone or vulnerable.

She'd been trying hard to get her life back on track, refusing to let what had happened with Adrian impact any more than it already had. She was concentrating on work and, once the early autumn rush was over, she'd begin to look around for somewhere to live. Living with Kit was all too comfortable. He was laidback, not that she saw all that much of him; he was always out looking after his growing menagerie. They spent their evenings poring over documentation about setting up an animal sanctuary. Tash found Kit easy to get on with and undemanding. That was as long as she damped down the nagging desire she had for him. In the few short days since she'd left Adrian, life had got back to normal. Well, nearly normal. It was almost an anti-climax that Adrian hadn't followed up the threat implied by his message in the flowers and she couldn't help glance around, her heart jolting every time she spied a red car. Underneath the shimmering heat bouncing off the water in the harbour, lurked the still, cold fear that he might be here. Watching.

She focused back on the race. She refused to dwell on Adrian today. The route would take them from the harbour, along the prom and then up the killer hill on the way out of town. The main race's finishing line was at Berecombe's football club, on the only flat stretch of town at the top of the hill.

'Going to ace this,' Emma said, confidently. She looked at Tash in concern. 'Unless you want me to stick with you?'

'Who says I'm not going to leave you for dead, girlfriend?'

'Er, cos you hardly came to training?'

Tash hmphed. 'If you're going to split hairs.' She nudged Emma so that she staggered off balance on the uneven cobbles of the harbour.

'Foul play! Referee, this woman's trying to nobble me.'

'Wrong sport, Em.' Ollie jogged up behind them. 'And I'll run with Tash if you're insisting on going all Mo Farah.'

'Do you two mind?' Tash put her hands on her hips. 'I'm perfectly capable of looking after myself. It's been three days since I went back to the house and Adrian hasn't done a thing. I'm hoping he's gone back to Manchester for good.'

Emma pulled a face. 'We're all hoping that, if only so you can get together with Kit.' She looked around. 'Where is he anyway?'

'He had a crisis with one of the donkeys. Had to call the vet out. Said he'd try and get here in time for the start.' Tash glanced nervously as the runner in fancy dress took off his enormous rabbit head. She relaxed as she saw it was Percy from the butcher's. She pulled herself together. The idea of Adrian dressing up in fancy dress just to tail her in the race was farcical. Even so, she wished Kit was here.

'Kit had better hurry up,' Emma said. 'Arthur's about to start the race.'

'Nah,' Ollie said. 'He'll make a speech first. He always does. But, even if Kit's late starting, he'll catch up.'

'It's those long legs of his,' Emma sighed.

Tash grinned. She had to agree. Kit's legs were a wonder to behold but she wondered how Ollie felt when his girlfriend said things like that. She didn't have time to think any further as Arthur gave his speech and then fired the starting pistol. They were off!

Emma and Ollie sped off ahead. For a while, Millie and Jed kept pace with her along the terrace in front of the book-shop and onto the promenade but then Millie pulled up, bent double with stitch. She waved Jed on and retraced her steps to her café. At the bottom of the hill Jed went on ahead, his easy loping stride eating up the difficult incline.

Tash got to the oak tree where she'd had to stop during the training run, and had to stop again this time. Her lungs were bursting, and her thighs burned. She made her way through the kissing gate and collapsed onto the bench, sipping from her water bottle. It was too hot a day for a run like this. She wiped sweat off and sat back, concentrating on getting her breath back. Drifting up on a slight sea breeze, she could hear the cheers from the crowds on the front. The town really came together for things like this and she hoped the RNLI would make loads. She let her eyes close, enjoying the sun on her face, listening to the cheering and the odd gasp as a runner struggled up the lane behind her.

'Let yourself go, haven't you Natasha.'

Tash leapt up, heart pounding. Adrian leaned on the gate, a dangerous smirk on his face.

Chapter 39

'You know I always suspected those training sessions weren't what they seemed. I've been watching you. You've been really struggling to keep up, haven't you? I'm not sure you ever went to training. Too busy doing something, or should I say, *someone* else.'

'What do you want, Adrian?'

He stroked the gate with a forefinger, looking down. 'Do I have to want anything to talk to my fiancée?' He was icily calm.

'I'm not your fiancée anymore.'

'Would have been the polite thing to tell me that.'

'I would have thought my actions were clear.'

Adrian lifted himself away from the gate and took a step nearer. Tash tried not to flinch. She felt horribly vulnerable in her skimpy vest and running shorts.

'You came to my house.'

'I went to get my things. *My* things, Adrian. I didn't take anything that belonged to you or that we had bought together. I only took what was mine.'

He took another step, close enough that she could now feel his breath on her face. Running a finger down her cheek, he said, 'And I hear there's been someone taking what's mine. Running sessions, book club.' He spat. 'Oh, how could you be so transparent, Natasha? I expected, if you were going to cheat on me, that you would have a little more finesse.'

'*I* haven't done anything.' Tash made a concerted effort to straighten her shoulders and was gratified to see that, even in her running shoes, she was still taller than Adrian. 'And it wasn't me who kicked the dog.'

Adrian sneered. 'That sodding fleabag. You cared more about that little fucker than you did about me.'

'I did. I do.' Tash nodded, anger beginning to bite. 'At least Benji didn't try to control me.'

Adrian huffed out a breath. 'I gave you everything. You were just too selfish to appreciate it. You wanted to go and sell your stupid houses? I was the one who bought you the time to do it. Spoiled little daddy's girl. Think you're a big thing, don't you? In this scrappy sewer of a goldfish bowl.'

'You know what, Adrian,' Tash said, squaring up to him, too furious to care. She jabbed his chest. 'I am a big thing in this town. I do a good job and I can hold up my head with pride. What have you got? A boring house and a shiny Porsche on HP. Where are your friends, Adrian? Where's your family? Not much to show for someone your age.' She raised her eyebrows, enjoying the moment, despite everything. 'And now you can add a failed relationship.'

He moved so swiftly Tash had no time to react. He grabbed her wrist in a grip so tight it squeezed the blood from her hand. With his other hand, he pushed her backwards. Tash knew if she tripped, if she fell onto the ground, she'd be defenceless. Acting on instinct and with all the strength she could muster, she raised her knee and thrust it hard into his groin. When he fell off her, bent double in agony, she cast frantically about and found a stick. Holding it above his head, in both hands, she yelled, 'That's for all the women you've bullied, abused and made their lives a fucking misery. You're a sicko, Adrian Williams, and I never, ever want to set eyes on you again.'

He looked up at her, his face suffused with crimson, a vein standing on his forehead. 'I'll have you for assault,' he gasped. 'You crazy fucking woman.'

Tash laughed. 'Really? You're going to the police? Good! They'll be fascinated to hear all about your Rohypnol-fuelled exploits in the bars of Manchester. Oh, and how you planned to commit bigamy. As far as I know that's still a criminal offence in this country.'

Adrian blanched. The mention of Rohypnol had hit home. He straightened with difficulty, stumbling over a tree branch. 'You women are all the same.' He pointed a wavering finger. 'You want the cars, the clothes, the swanky meals in expensive restaurants. But you won't give a man a fuck in return.' He sneered. 'All the money I spent on you and you ended up being as frigid as the rest of them.' He swaggered a little, pushing out his chest. 'So what if I slip a little something into their drinks? Most of them are so drunk they don't notice. And drunk on the champagne I buy them! You're no different. You lapped up all the things I bought you. Even with all your airs and graces, you're just a whore like the rest of them. And I'll get you with the last breath I draw.'

Tash gasped. She stumbled back and came up against the bench for support. So it was true. Adrian had done all those awful things and had done the same to her. Her head throbbed but she knew she needed to keep in control or goodness only knew what he might do. 'You sad little man,' she began slowly. 'You're evil. Taking what you want and when you can't get it, forcing people to do it all the same.'

Adrian flinched and Tash sensed her advantage. 'You're a bully. Just like all those kids who bullied me at school because I was fat. Once someone stands up to them, they crumble away. I'm not scared of you,' she added, realising the truth with a glorious sense of freedom. 'I'm not afraid of you anymore.' She brandished the stick at him. 'And if you dare come near me, I'll go straight to the police for a restraining order.' She grinned. 'They're already looking into what I've reported. I'm sure they'll be extremely interested in this new information. This confession of yours.'

'You fucking bitch,' Adrian began. Then he laughed. 'You've got no evidence.'

'I'd ask you to not address my friend that way.'

Neither had seen Kit come through the gate. He was breathing heavily as if he'd run at pace up the hill.

'Oh, the knight in shining armour, come to the rescue. And all the time shagging my fiancée.' Adrian smirked but with wavering conviction.

'Actually, from what I can see, Tash is doing a pretty good job of rescuing herself,' Kit said casually. He leaned against the gate and folded his arms. 'I've just come to watch the show.'

For a second Tash wondered if Adrian was going to risk having a go at Kit. She saw his brain work as he weighed up the options, taking in Kit's height and muscles. She looked at

Kit. Apparently calm, but she knew him well enough by now to know anger simmered not far below the surface.

'You, you—' He pointed first at Tash and then at Kit. 'You deserve one another.'

Kit took one long stride and was towering over Adrian in a second. 'Then do us a favour and get out of our lives. And, as for evidence...' He waggled his mobile, previously concealed in his hand. 'Your interesting little exchange with Tash has all been recorded on here. You're going away, my friend. Locked up for a very long time.'

Adrian began to stutter something out, then thought better of it. Stumbling towards the gate, he disappeared.

Kit opened his arms and Tash ran into their comforting embrace.

Chapter 40

'He didn't!' Emma said, indignation evident in every pore. 'He did.' Kit grimaced and reached for his glass.

They had regrouped at Millie Vanilla's and were sitting on the terrace in front of the bookshop. Millie and Jed sat at one side of the table along with Ollie, and Emma perched on the edge of the bench opposite with Kit and Tash.

Tash had spent the last twenty minutes explaining what had happened with Adrian. After a scalding hot shower back at the farmhouse, a pot of tea and a chunk of Marianne's fruit cake, she was feeling a lot less shaky. 'And Paul Cash rang me. He's got a cousin in Salford CID. There are two women up there wanting to press charges against Adrian. With Kit's evidence on his phone and my photos, there should be enough of a case.' Tash blew out a breath. 'He said they were sending the boys round to his house to do a search tonight.'

'The complete nut-job!'

'Can't disagree with you there, Em,' Tash said.

'Will you have to go to court?'

'Maybe. I'm prepared to.' Tash felt her voice waver and was glad of Kit's solid, warm bulk next to her.' She shook her head. 'But I don't want to spend any more time talking about that waste of space. It's over.' She grinned determinately at Jed. 'Any more of that delicious champagne? What a brilliant idea to toast the race with it.'

'I thought, as it's the most glorious evening, it seemed the thing to do,' he replied, with a charming smile and topped up her glass with the last of the bottle.

'You not having any, Millie?' Tash asked, seeing their host's glass full of homemade lemonade. 'Going back to work afterwards?'

Millie blushed. 'I just fancied something long and cool as it's such a warm evening. And no, Petra is working out brilliantly as the new manager. She's amazingly efficient. I've given myself the night off. I never thought I'd like having someone else running Millie Vanilla's but it's actually great.' She laughed and gave Jed a sidelong glance. 'Maybe I'm getting lazy in my old age.'

Jed pulled his wife close and kissed her on the cheek. 'Jeez, Mil, you're the least lazy person I know. And now, with all you've got on, it's about time you delegated.'

'Amen to that,' Tash sipped her champagne. 'Listen up Millie. One thing I've learned over the last few weeks is to make time for the things and the people you *really* want.' The group lapsed into silence, too tired from the run in the heat to make much attempt at conversation.

The sun had long since dipped into the sea, the collection buckets had been gathered in and the crowds had returned to enjoy another balmy evening on Berecombe seafront. Families drifted across in front of them, scattering giggling children who skidded along on the sandy concrete.

Tash took in a deep breath as she watched them. 'It's been

quite a month.' Then she changed the subject and added, 'Does anyone know how much the fun run raised?'

'In the region of three thousand, I think. Good result,' Ollie supplied.

'Trust you to know that.' Emma grinned at him. 'But hey, forget about the run, Tash, did you really knee Arsehole Adrian?'

'Yup and I couldn't care less. It's finished. He's so out of my life as to be falling off the edge. And, if he dares to come anywhere near me, I'll just knee him again.'

'Trust me,' Kit put in. 'I've seen Tash in action.' He grinned. 'You don't want to get the wrong side of her.'

Emma pointed her champagne flute at him. 'You're telling me! Don't forget, I've worked with her for the last four years.' Realising her glass was empty she stared into it hopefully.

Jed took the hint. 'I'll go and get another one, shall I?'

'And I'll get that plate of canapés I made,' Millie added and stood up. 'Although I might spare you the brownies Biddy provided.'

The others looked at her questioningly.

'Haven't you heard? She'd only gone and put marijuana in them. Supposed to be good for arthritis, allegedly. Went down a storm at the WI until they realised. Arthur is furious with her.'

Emma roared. 'No wonder I was so giggly when I ate the ones she dropped off at the office!'

Millie shook her head. 'Nothing Biddy does surprises me. Says she got the weed from her younger sister. Apparently Angela is the black sheep of the family. I can't even *begin* to imagine what that means. Emma and Ollie, can you give me a hand bringing the food out?'

Emma looked up in surprise. 'Just how much food have you made, Millie?'

Ollie cleared his throat. 'I don't think that's what Millie meant.' He nodded meaningfully at Kit and Tash sitting close together.

'Oh. Ah. I get it.' Emma scrambled off the bench. 'Yes, some food would be good. I love those mini filled Yorkshire puddings you make.'

'Emma, I know it's the beginning of September but it still feels like summer,' Millie grinned. 'I've done salmon and watercress tartlets.'

Emma followed them as they walked to the café. 'Ace. Don't see the problem with Yorkies in the summer though.'

Kit looked at Tash and smiled gently. 'Hardly subtle.'

'Hardly.'

'You know what? I fancy a walk. Care to join me?' He stood and held out a hand.

'I'd love to,' Tash answered, taking it.

Chapter 41

They walked to the end of the harbour wall, where it curled back round on itself until it faced the town. Tash left her hand in Kit's, enjoying its warmth as it enclosed hers. She was so tired and dreamy from the champagne that she felt she was floating. Or maybe it was the beginnings of happiness? They found a dilapidated bench at the very far end of the harbour and sat down. As Kit leaned back, it creaked under his bulk.

In front of them, across the still dark sea, Berecombe's lights twinkled against the velvety night. The only sound was that of the waves washing softly against the harbour wall. Few ventured this far along the harbour at night and, apart from an optimistic gull strutting amongst the crab pots, they had it to themselves.

Tash found Kit's hand again and held it tightly. 'It's been quite a day.'

'It's been quite a month. And I still haven't finished *Wuthering Heights*.'

Tash managed a laugh. 'Neither have I. Poor Cathy and Heathcliff. Emily Brontë deserves to be read to the end.'

'Think I'll listen to the Kate Bush version. I've heard it summarises the salient points.'

'Amy will never forgive us, but I might too.' She blew out a breath. 'Think I've had enough of brooding anti-heroes and blasted heaths. Funnily enough, I've really gone off domineering men.'

'Hardly surprising.'

'Kit, I really appreciate all you've done for me. Letting me stay at the farm. Turning up this morning.'

'Haven't done anything really. You looked like you were handling that bastard by yourself.'

'But you were ready to leap in, weren't you?'

'Oh yes,' Kit said in a grim voice, with an edge of violence to it. 'I wanted to wring his scrawny, cowardly neck.'

Tash stared at his profile in the gloom. She could sense he was rigid with anger. 'So this is Kit Oakley all riled up?'

Kit laced his fingers between hers. 'Yup.'

'You don't say much, do you?'

'Nope.'

'Suits me.'

'Tash, about me and you. About us, I mean. I know it's way too soon but I just want you to know I care about you very much and, when the time is right for you, I'll be there. I can wait. I'm patient. Actually, I'm not feeling very patient about this at all but I will wait until you feel you're ready. I'm happy to go at your pace. That's if you want anything to do with men ever again.'

Tash smiled. 'So, I'm the woman with possibilities but complications?'

'Of course you were. Are,' he corrected himself. 'Always have been. But I know another relationship is probably the last thing on your mind at the moment.'

'I thought you didn't say much?'

He turned and rested one arm along the back of the bench. 'Always the exception that proves the rule.' He lifted her hand and kissed the back of it.

They sat for a while longer, enjoying the quiet. Enjoying being together.

'I seem to spend a lot of time sitting on benches with you,' Tash said. 'In the dark.' She heard the low rumble of his laughter.

'Is that a good thing?'

'I think so. I find you a very ... um ... calming presence.'

Kit laughed again. 'Now that's definitely *not* a good thing.'

Tash turned to him. 'Don't you want to be a calming influence on me?'

'Not really.' He put an arm along the back of her shoulders and pulled her close. 'It's not really what I want at this precise second.'

Tash inched nearer. 'Then what do you want?'

'This.' He kissed her. Slow, lingering and with so much underlying, humming passion, it left her aching for more.

'That was good,' Tash breathed.

'Not too calming?'

'Not calming at all. Just the opposite, I'd say.'

'Not too much too soon?'

'Possibly. But I'll risk it. In fact, I'd very much like you to do it again.'

So he did.

PART TWO

Emma's Story

Chapter 42

'Emma, what have you done now?' Linda Tizzard shrieked as she opened the bathroom door and stared at her daughter, open-mouthed.

Emma shot up guiltily. She mopped at a lock of her now bright tangerine hair with a stained towel. 'Thought I'd go auburn. For a change.'

Her mother thinned her lips in a way Emma remembered only too well from childhood misdeeds. She was in trouble. Big trouble.

'Auburn? You mean Tango orange, don't you? Get this bathroom cleaned up now. It's turned the bath orange. Why on earth didn't you come into the salon and have it done properly, child?' Linda grabbed a flannel and began scrubbing.

Emma pursed her lips. 'Maybe 'cos I can't afford Klassy Kutz prices?'

Linda paused in her cleaning and looked at her daughter in exasperation. 'You never stop to think, do you? Just like your father. You could have come in as a model or had one of the apprentice stylists. Suki wouldn't have minded.'

Emma chose not to answer. Suki owned the salon Linda worked in as a stylist. And she thought Suki would have minded very much. Although her mother adored the woman, Emma thought she was little more than a slave driver. She ran the shower hose attachment over the orange-splattered basin. 'I really don't know why you don't start up on your own, Mum, rather than renting a chair at Suki's.'

'You think we've got that sort of money?' Linda glared up at her daughter. 'You need to get your head out of those clouds.' She resumed scrubbing.

'You could always go mobile. There's always a need for mobile hairdressers and all the money would be yours then.' Emma sighed knowing it was no use. Her mother was permanently in a bad mood. Emma knew it was worry over money but it didn't make it any easier to live with. She knew Linda would never leave the salon. Her mother always chose the safe option. 'Owning businesses isn't for the likes of us,' she always said. 'Know your place and keep your head below the parapet,' was her mother's much-repeated motto.

'I've got a perfectly good job at the salon, thank you very much,' Linda said predictably. 'And we need the money coming in, what with your dad's job looking dicey. Seems there's no call for a traditional vacuum cleaner nowadays. Folk all want those fancy cordless ones.'

Emma lapsed into silence again. Her family seemed to lurch from one crisis to another. Last week it had been one of her mother's regulars moving away from Berecombe. As she'd been a twice a week set and blow-dry customer, it meant a loss of income. Lurking in the background was the constant threat to her father's job as office manager at a local manufacturer and this week Stevie, her thirteen-year-old brother, had got into trouble at school. She stared out of the bathroom window at the back garden. The small patch of lawn suffered from Stevie's keepy-uppy competitions and the flower beds, now it was early autumn, had lost their summer glory. Her father's beloved greenhouse was in one corner and the guinea-pig hutch was in another. It was just the sort of boring garden replicated in every Thirties semi on their street. She sighed again. Everything seemed so ordinary, so dull. Nothing happened to compare with anything in any of the books she read. It was one reason why she'd tried to spice things up. Dyeing her hair at least made a change. The other had been her longing to be more Demelza. 'Be More Demelza' was Emma's new mantra. Passionate, forthright, wild with an independence of spirit Emma admired. That and the fact she'd married one of literature's most gorgeous men, Ross Poldark.

'Be More Demelza!'

She hadn't realized she'd said it out loud until the arrival of Stevie, barging into the bathroom, brought her back to the muddled, overcrowded, monotonous life that was her existence.

'What the f—' he began and then remembered Linda banned any swearing in her hearing. 'What's been going on in here, then?' He caught a glimpse of Emma's hair. 'Oh boy! Look at you, you ginge.'

Linda reared up. 'That's enough. Now you're back from school, you can clean out those guinea pigs.' When he began to protest, she continued, 'Steven, you promised to do them at the weekend. They're in a right mess. *You* wanted them, so you look after them. Off you go and no Xbox until your homework's done.' Turning on Emma, she thrust the flannel into her hand. 'And you, madam, can finish cleaning up in here. I want it spotless before your father gets home.'

Linda pushed her son out and followed him downstairs. Emma could hear them bickering as they went. She scowled. There was always too much noise and too many arguments going on in this house. And, at the same time, nothing ever changed. Glancing out of the window and hearing the guinea pigs squeal a hunger protest, she promised herself she'd find somewhere of her own to live. And soon. It was either that or go mad.

Chapter 43

Emma pushed open the front door of Hughes and Widrow Estate Agents, catching sight of her hair in the shop window as she did. Self-consciously tweaking her fringe, she grimaced. She'd aimed for the subtle auburn with vivid lights promised on the box but she must have left it on too long. When she'd met up with boyfriend Ollie for a drink in the Old Harbour, he'd laughed at first and then asked when she was going to wash it out. If only she'd checked the small print. Instead of the wash-in wash-out she thought she'd bought, she'd picked up a box of permanent colour by mistake. Ollie hadn't been impressed when she explained. They'd had a row over it – one of many, recently. He was so serious these days. She'd told him to lighten up and had left him to his RNLI pals. She just hoped her boss, Tash, would see the funny side.

As her eyes adjusted from the bright sunlight outside, she could make out a willowy blonde standing by Tash's desk. She was talking earnestly to her manager and they didn't see her enter.

'Morning,' she said brightly and tried not to notice the shock on Tash's face and the superciliously raised eyebrows on the stranger's. Flinging her bag onto her desk, she switched on her computer and went into the little kitchen behind the office space to make coffee. 'I will never dye my hair again,' she vowed.

'I'm very glad to hear it.' Tash stood in the doorway, grinning. 'It's certainly a bold statement. Come and meet Leona, our new recruit.'

Emma groaned. She'd forgotten the new member of their team was due to start today. The blonde with the patrician features and superior air must be the new estate agent and not a client. 'Be right out, Tash. How does Leona like her coffee?'

Tash looked blank. 'Think she said she preferred mint tea. We'll have to get some in.' She ducked out and Emma could hear a muted conversation. Tash reappeared. 'Just some hot water.'

Emma muttered, 'Who, in their right mind, drinks plain hot water?' to herself while she waited for the kettle to boil. Finding the packet of chocolate digestives, she crammed one in her mouth and carried the tray of mugs through.

Tash had set three chairs around her desk and she and Leona were already sitting down and peering at the computer monitor. Emma could see the agent's website being displayed. She put the tray down and slid onto the third chair. It was slightly away from the others and made her feel excluded.

'Hi Leona,' she said, through a mouthful of digestive crumbs. 'Welcome to the team.' She wiped her chocolate-smudged hand on her trousers and held it out.

The woman eyed her coolly. 'So, you're Emma,' she drawled, in Sloaney-tones. She offered a fingertip handshake. 'I've heard so much about you from Tash. I would have said hello when you walked in but I took you to be a cl—'

'Who? The cleaner?' Emma grinned but the joke misfired. Leona stared back at her blankly. 'No, I meant I thought you might be a *client*.'

'No probs,' Emma went on genially. 'Most folk in Berecombe can't believe I'm an estate agent either.' No response. Not much of a sense of humour, then. Shame. She and Tash got through most days having a bit of banter or a laugh. It cut through the stress sometimes. Having someone so po-faced in the office would change things. Still, maybe Leona was just nervous. Understandable on her first day. She picked up another biscuit and crunched into it. 'In Berecombe you'll find everyone says good morning to everyone. In fact, sometimes it's hard to walk down the high street without someone striking up a conversation – whether you want it or not. We're friendly like that in this town.'

'I'm sure I have much to learn.' Leona smiled without it reaching her eyes. She half-turned so that Emma was given the cold shoulder. Literally.

Whoops. From the sour look on Leona's face, that hadn't gone down well. Emma didn't want to start out on the wrong foot. They'd be working in a small team and it helped to get on together but it seemed whatever she said to the woman got misconstrued. Without thinking, she launched into a jokey apology. 'Oops. Soz. Me and my big mouth. I didn't mean to imply you're unfriendly. It's just that a small town is different from a big city.' It couldn't have been a worse thing to say.

'In so many ways,' Leona replied, without turning.

Stop talking now, Emma said to herself. You're just digging that hole even deeper, girlfriend. She sucked her lips shut and made a mute appeal to Tash.

Tash glanced between the two. 'I'm sure there's no offence taken, Em.'

Leona shrugged her thin shoulders ever so slightly. 'Of course not.'

'You've been handpicked by our ex-manager Pete, haven't you?' Tash added, pointedly changing the subject. 'And you're on the fast-track programme? That's fantastic. And a degree as well?'

Leona preened. 'That's right, Tash. In Business Studies from Plymouth uni. A first, actually.' She gave Emma a look from under immaculate mink-shaded eyelashes. 'Can I ask your backgrounds?'

Tash explained she'd come straight into the job from A levels. 'It's the only thing I've ever wanted to do,' she added. 'And I really wanted to learn on the job. 'Made it to become the youngest branch manager in the company a year ago.'

'How marvellous,' Leona said. 'And what about you, Erin?'

Emma refused to rise to the bait. In truth, she didn't know how to. She got on with most people she met and was fairly easy-going. This immediate and undeserved antagonism was new to her. 'It's Emma,' she answered, equably. 'And I never really knew what I wanted to do.' She shrugged. 'Did a few dead-end jobs, pubs and waitressing mostly, and then joined here when I was twenty-two. Liked it, so I stayed.'

'Emma's skill is her ability to hone in on what people want,' Tash said, loyally. 'I've yet to meet anyone she couldn't charm. In this business it's people skills as well as qualifications that get the job done.' She smiled. 'That, and the ability to stay calm when all around you is chaos.'

'And that is my real talent,' Emma put in, laughing. 'If you live with a family like mine, it's a developed survival tactic.'

'Fascinating,' Leona said, making it clear it was anything but. 'So neither of you have any qualifications beyond school?'

Tash and Emma's eyes met. 'Nope,' they said in unison.

'Oh.'

The phone rang, piercing the frozen silence and making them jump. Emma rose to answer it. 'I don't know if I'll be able to manage this,' she muttered. 'What with only my GCSEs and all.'

Tash shot her a look. 'Let's go into the back office, shall we, Leona? I can fill you in a bit more and we can agree on your workload for this week.' They got up and disappeared through the kitchen.

Emma watched them. She and Tash got on well and had done so ever since they'd begun working together. Despite Tash being her boss, they were more like friends. She hoped the arrival of Leona, who had the makings of being a prize A bitch, wouldn't change that. Fervently praying that it was just first day nerves that had made the woman so unlikeable, she picked up the phone. She put on her best estate agent's voice and answered it.

Chapter 44

The creamy evening September sunshine, shining through the vast, double-height windows of the reading area in Millie's bookshop, turned everyone a mellow autumnal shade. Since its launch, the previous month, the bookshop had turned into a roaring success. Much to the relief of owners, married couple Millie and Jed, and manager Amy. Even at this late hour there were people downstairs in the main shop, browsing the bookshelves and enjoying its unique, chilled atmosphere.

Emma looked around at the mezzanine reading area with admiration. 'Another book group.' She rubbed her hands together. 'I love it! Millie and Jed have made a real success of this place – and in such a short space of time too. It's a fabby extension to their café.'

'I know,' Tash answered. 'Doesn't seem five minutes since the launch party last month. I'm so pleased for her. I really admire her – so hardworking. She had a shitty time when her parents died. Had to give up going to university and everything. Instead of feeling sorry for herself, she took over the café and worked 24-7. And it's lovely to see her so happy with Jed too. She deserves all the happiness she can get.' She sipped her wine appreciatively. 'The catering is always great at book club too.'

Emma eyed her. 'You going soft in your old age? Not like you to be sentimental.'

'Nothing sentimental about it. Millie just gets on with things and I respect that. I've got to know her a bit better lately at the commerce meetings and she's always full of enthusiasm about everything she does. And she's got a lot on her plate too. The café, the wedding planning business, and now this place.'

'Just as well she's got Petra in to manage the café, then.' Emma winked salaciously. 'Mind you, I'd be pretty motivated to get into work too, if I worked alongside a husband who looked like Jed Henville. There's something about him that makes me very . . . enthusiastic.'

Tash laughed. 'Emma, it's about time you stopped lusting over other men, isn't it? What with you having the lovely Ollie in tow.'

'Ollie *is* lovely,' Emma said, robustly. 'But I've still got eyes, haven't I? And hormones. No harm in looking. Keeps the blood flowing, or so my Auntie Tess says.' She screwed up her face in a leer, a picture of Jed's blond hair, wicked brown eyes and long legs springing into her mind. 'And come on, Tash, have you *seen* the man?'

'He's very easy on the eye, I agree,' Tash agreed, serenely. 'And, more importantly, he is completely and utterly besotted with his wife, Millie,' she said, emphasizing the word "wife".

'As if I'd do anything to stop that! Even if I could. Great believer in the sanctity of marriage, me.'

'Are you?' Tash looked at her curiously. 'I never knew that.'

'Yup. You might think it's old-fashioned but I think marriage is the only way. Got some great examples in my family. Mum and Dad, Uncle Ken and Aunty Tess. They bicker like crazy but they love each other to bits, really. That's what I want. Eventually.' Emma stuck her nose into her glass and swallowed some wine, aware she might have revealed too much. She and Tash didn't often get this deep. She deflected the focus back onto Tash. 'And here's you, all loved up with a fit new man.' Emma made googly eyes. 'You're still at the stage when you don't notice anyone else, let alone a hottie. Maybe it'll be you asking Millie to plan a wedding next. How long's it been now?'

'Since I got together with Kit?'

'And said bye-bye to Arsehole Adrian.'

'Two weeks, one day and . . .' Tash glanced at her watch. 'Three hours.'

'Aw. So sweet. Still counting the hours,' Emma teased. 'Seriously, though, I can't tell you how happy I am for you, babe. You look as if you've won the Lottery.'

Tash burst out laughing and Emma wondered why. 'Something like that.' She smiled, radiating joy. 'I can't believe I've only known Kit for a month or so. It feels like a lifetime.'

'Hopefully in the right way.'

'Oh yes. In absolutely the right way.'

'Any news on the legal stuff?' Tash's ex-boyfriend had been accused of raping several women in Manchester and Emma knew the pending court case was hovering like a thundercloud over Tash's new life with Kit. Because Adrian had abused Tash too, she might be called to give evidence.

Tash shook her head. 'Early days yet.' She forced a bright smile. 'Let's not spoil a good evening at the book club with mention of any of that, shall we?'

Emma put a finger to her lips. 'Point taken, boss.' In an attempt to lighten the atmosphere, she added, 'At least my hair won't be quite as obvious this evening.' She giggled as they sat down and she glanced around. 'Everyone's gone orange in this light.'

Tash looked amused. 'Why on earth did you want to dye it, Em? Your natural light brown is lovely.'

'Mouse, you mean.' Emma took a mouthful of wine. 'Boring.' She shrugged. 'Just wanted a change. Be more Demelza.'

'Who?'

'Tash!' Emma said, aghast. '*Demelza*. You know. Married Ross Poldark. "Be More Demelza" is my new mantra for life.'

'Oh right. *Poldark*. Watched bits of the first series but never really got into it.'

Emma watched as Tash's eyes were drawn to where Kit was sitting talking to Biddy, another book group member.

'And I don't have time for TV now,' Tash said. 'We're expecting another donkey this weekend. Had to get another stable ready.'

'You and Kit really going ahead with this animal sanctuary idea, then?'

'Think so. It seems a good way to use the land he's bought and you wouldn't believe how many need a safe home, especially horses. Kit's so passionate about rescuing animals. He's had yet another batch of battery chickens this week. He's marvellous with them.' Kit sensed he was being discussed and looked over. Tash blushed.

Emma's lips curled in amusement. 'So loved-up,' she teased.

'You could say that.'

'And you're sure Arsehole Adrian hasn't made contact? No more creepy stalkery stuff?'

'Nope. Thank God.'

Emma reached for the wine bottle and refilled their glasses, then grabbed a handful of kettle chips. She was munching a mouthful when a woman joined them.

'Hello, Natasha – oh, and Emma too.' It was Marti Cavendish, another book group member and an ex-neighbour of Tash's. She slid herself down onto the sofa next to them and sipped her wine, one little finger cocked. 'I hadn't realized you were selling up?'

'What do you mean, Marti?'

Emma felt her friend go rigid and cursed Marti. Tash had had a rough time last month and, with the court case pending, she was finding it difficult to get closure over her life with Adrian. She didn't need any reminders about her abusive ex-boyfriend and his executive four bed on the new estate on the edge of town.

Marti made an innocent face. 'Oh dear. Have I made a teeny faux pas? There's a for sale sign outside where you lived with Adrian. Of course, I may have the wrong house but you are number forty-seven, aren't you?'

'Used to be. I moved out.'

'I had wondered.' Marti batted her eyelashes. 'I hadn't seen you or Adrian around recently. And there's no Porsche on the drive.'

'Well, thank you for letting me know. As the house was in Adrian's name, it's entirely up to him what he does with it,' Tash said, through gritted teeth. 'And, quite honestly, I couldn't care less. As long as he stays away from me, that's all I'm bothered about.'

Marti sucked in a sly breath. She couldn't resist digging

further. 'It's such a shame he didn't want to use Hughes and Widrow, though. Seeing as you work for them.'

Emma had had enough. She knew Tash hated talking about her and Adrian splitting up. Swallowing the last crisp, she leaned forward and said sharply, 'As he and Tash parted on less than friendly terms, it's no loss to Hughes and Widrow that he didn't want to sell with us. Besides, we've got more than enough work on at the moment. I doubt very much that we could have taken on another client.'

Marti subsided in shock. Emma was known as the peace-keeper. She hardly ever raised her voice. Luckily, any further conversation was drowned out by Amy bringing the book group meeting to order and asking for suggestions for September's choice.

Emma couldn't believe they agreed on *Demelza*, the second in Winston Graham's series of *Poldark* books. Writer Patrick always seemed to suggest some obscure travelogue, while Biddy hankered after the classics, and Amy was keen on the latest Booker prizewinner. Millie summed up everyone's enthusiasm when she said it would be great to read something more accessible than *Wuthering Heights*, the group's last choice. 'And it would be wonderful to read one of the books seeing as the new TV series is starting this month.'

Emma nodded vigorously. 'Of course, they're way ahead on the telly but it would be ace to go back to the books them-selves. And we all seem to have read the first book, so choosing the second is a no-brainer.'

'Fine writer, Winston Graham,' Biddy put in. Elvis, her deaf assistance poodle, snickered in agreement.

'And Ross Poldark is such a hero,' Emma replied.

'Not so sure about that, child,' Biddy barked. Pensioner Biddy was always forthcoming with her opinions. 'He's guilty of more than one sin. Reckon Demelza is the real hero of those books.'

Emma was about to launch into a spirited defence when Amy cut her short. 'Just as well we're reading her book then, isn't it? And a discussion about what makes a literary hero could be for the next meeting, I think.' She turned to Millie hopefully. 'Time for sandwiches and coffee?'

'Just before we break,' Patrick said. 'Could I tell you all about something that my friend Joel is doing?'

'Oh yes,' Millie exclaimed. 'I meant to mention that before we began the meeting. Brain like a sieve at the moment. Please,' she gestured to Patrick. 'Go ahead. You know all the details anyway.'

'Could we talk about it over food?' Emma groaned. 'I'm starving.'

Everyone laughed. Emma was well-known for her bottom-less stomach.

'Excellent idea,' Biddy boomed. 'Need to stretch the old pins.'

As everyone began to move downstairs, to the bookshop's café, Millie added on a laugh, 'Can't promise you crisp sand-wiches, Em, even though know they're your favourite.'

'Don't know what you're missing, Millie. Have you ever had ready-salted and tomato ketchup on a thickly buttered white slice?' She watched in alarm as Millie turned green.

'Excuse me for a moment,' she said. 'Amy, can you do the honours with the coffee and food? I'm really not feeling all that well.'

Chapter 45

Emma backed Patrick into a corner after he'd explained to the group what Joel had planned. 'So, a four-week beginner's literature course?' she demanded, her face aglow with enthusiasm.

'Are you interested then, Emma? Sure, I wouldn't have had you down as someone who was interested in evening classes, especially in literature.'

'Why not?' Emma bridled. Leona's smug university-educated face and her jibes over her lack of education swam into her vision. 'I love books and reading. Otherwise, why would I be here, at the book club?'

'But evening classes? Is that really for you? It'll be classic stuff, not Winston Graham.'

'Oi Patrick, who was the only book group member who actually finished *Wuthering Heights?*'

'Point taken.' His blue eyes twinkled. He saluted her with his wine glass. 'And didn't you not only finish the book but defend our Mr Heathcliff with an informed passion, I seem to recall. I really shouldn't be such a literary snob. It's a bad habit.'

'No, you shouldn't.' Emma grinned at him smugly, enjoying

how his Irish accent slipped out occasionally. 'Or I'll make you sit next to Marti Cavendish at the next meeting.'

Patrick laughed in horror. 'Don't you be doing that! But evening classes? Is that really your thing?'

Emma shrugged. 'Look,' she began, 'I love my job and I love living in Berecombe, but sometimes it gets a bit boring round here. Especially out of season. I just want the old grey cells rattled a bit.'

'I can appreciate that. It's just . . .' He paused. 'Aw, how can I say this without insulting you further? Joel is quite highbrow. I love the man dearly but, if I'm honest, he's the last person I would have expected to teach these outreach programmes. Don't get me wrong,' he added hastily, 'I think they're a great idea, so I do. Anything that gets people reading and appreciating literature has my vote. I'm just not sure he'll be able to make it accessible enough. I wouldn't want you to be put off your studies right at the beginning and I certainly wouldn't want you to waste your money.'

'I hadn't thought about the cost. Me and Ollie are trying to save for a place of our own, so money's a bit tight,' Emma said gloomily. 'And I suppose this Joel bloke will be used to brainy undergrads. I messed about so much at school that college was never on the cards for me. Maybe I'll give it a miss.' Her face fell.

Patrick looked at her intently. 'And now I'm sorry. Maybe I've put you off?' He chewed his lip, obviously thinking. 'You know, I think I've underestimated you, Emma. You're probably exactly the sort of person these courses are designed for.' He grinned. 'And, do you know, I'd quite like to see you take Joel on.'

Emma preened a little. 'Always up for a challenge, me.'

'Well, isn't that good. You know, Joel can get a bit esoteric sometimes. It would do him good to step out of his ivory tower for once. He tends to live in a pretty rarefied plane of existence most of the time.'

'Who are you calling rarefied?' A deep voice sounded behind them. Neither had seen the man come into the bookshop.

Patrick laughed. 'Speak of the devil and he shall appear.' He turned to Emma. 'This is the man himself, so it is. Emma Tizzard, may I introduce you to my old mucker, Joel Dillon.'

Emma blinked. The man in front of them was tall; as tall as Tash's new boyfriend Kit. But, in contrast to Kit, he was lean and elegant. Sun-streaked brown hair flopped overlong onto the collar of his linen jacket. He smiled and the edges of his eyes crinkled in a very sexy Hugh Grant sort of a way.

Clasping Emma's hand, Joel stared into her eyes. 'I can now quite see the appeal of your little book group, Patrick. Hello, Emma Tizzard. You appear to have stepped straight out from a Hardy novel. What wonderful hair. It's alight.' He dropped her hand and Emma felt as if the sun had suddenly gone in. 'I'm early for our meal,' he said to Patrick. 'So I thought I'd drop in and see where I'm to be teaching.'

'I'll get you a glass of wine,' Patrick said. 'And then we can get off to have something to eat. I'll leave you in the capable hands of Emma here. She's interested in doing your course but I'm not entirely sure you'll be man enough for her.' Patrick's eyes flashed with humour.

Joel turned his laser gaze back to her. 'Now there's a

challenge,' he said, softly. 'How could I resist? Tell me why you want to learn great things, Emma.'

Emma stared up at him, feeling hot. He was looking at her as if she was the most captivating thing he'd ever seen. No one, not even Ollie, had ever looked at her with such fascination. His interest was incredibly exciting. Maybe this was someone who could actually encourage her to use her brain? Aware that Joel was waiting for her answer, she tried to put into words what she wanted. And failed. 'I've looked at evening classes before but they're all in Exeter or Bridport,' she stuttered, aware she sounded trite. 'Too far away. To have them here in Berecombe would be majorly cool.' That wasn't the real reason and she could see Joel didn't believe it. She took a deep breath. 'Look, like a lot of kids, I cocked up at school. Didn't concentrate. Couldn't wait to leave. Never thought of A levels or anything. Wanted some cash in my pocket, I suppose.'

Joel edged nearer. 'And you spent too long daydreaming and staring out of the window, I'll wager. Too imaginative. Bored with some very boring teaching.'

Emma blushed. How did he know?

He smiled. 'It happens so often. Agile minds let down by an unimpressive education system which treats its gentle charges as nothing more than sausages in a machine.'

Emma wasn't entirely sure what he meant but nodded vigorously. She could listen to his voice forever. It was smooth and cultured, with a sophisticated drawl.

He waved a hand. 'Sausage in. Pricked. Baked. Tested. Tested some more. Sent out into the world unsatisfied and dulled by the tedium of it all.'

'I like sausages,' Emma breathed and, to her horror, realized she'd said it out loud.

Joel roared with laughter. 'Patrick is right. You are perfect for me. And you will be a challenge. One I need.'

'I need a challenge too. I want to find out if I'm up to it.'

'And you want to be excited, I can tell.' He put his head on one side. 'And great literature can do that.' He clapped his hands together in a way that should have been effeminate but just came across as enthusiastic. 'Oh, Emma Tizzard, I can show you so much. Teach you so much. There are so many riches I can lead you to discover.'

It was all getting a bit heady. 'So you'll teach the course here, in the bookshop?' she asked, in an attempt to bring the conversation down to a more normal level.

Joel spread his arms wide. 'Where better? I think the idea is to hold them where the optimum number can attend. As you say, not everyone is capable of getting to Exeter.' He paused and then went on importantly, 'Should you want to, attendance can count towards a foundation course and then a degree. But we can talk more about that. I can bring some information to the first class. Do you think you're up to it, Emma? And more saliently, do you think you're up to me?' He raised one eyebrow.

Emma felt her face begin to burn with possibilities. 'I don't have any A levels and I haven't really done anything like this before.'

'But you read?'

Emma nodded.

'And love books? The worlds they offer? The escape from the tedium of everyday life?

He understood. Somehow, he knew that was why she disappeared into reading. Books were a way out. A way of forgetting the dragging fear over her father's job. The way her mother was worrying herself thin. The dull suburban life they led. She gazed up at him, enraptured. She'd never met anyone quite like him before.

'I need you, Emma with the flaming hair. I need you on my course.' He took her hand and looked mournful. 'Say yes or I shall leave here a bitterly disappointed man.'

'Yes,' Emma said, her eyes shining. 'Yes!'

Joel nodded, satisfied. 'And now, will you excuse me? I must away to find Patrick.'

Emma watched him go. 'Wowzers,' she breathed. 'What a hero.' He was every teacher she'd ever dreamed of, rolled into one. It was a world away – and more – from her days at Berecombe Comp. Turning away and seeing the last rays of the sun dip into the sea, she murmured, 'I could do this. I could actually do this!'

Chapter 46

'So, how was she today?' Ollie drained his pint. He nodded to her empty glass. 'Another?'

They'd met, as usual, for a drink in the Old Harbour. As they were saving every penny they could, their social life had become fairly limited. Tonight they were sitting outside in the balmy September air. The sun had long since disappeared but there were still streaks of blue and gold in the sky and it was warm. The sea lapped against the shore and one or two walkers strolled along the beach, dogs gambolling between their legs. It was an idyllic scene but one Emma had grown up with and took for granted. The only thing she could see was Joel's finely drawn features and the passion for literature burning in his eyes.

'Em? You're miles away. I asked if you'd like another drink.'

She nodded briefly and watched as Ollie got up and went into the bar, greeting one or two fellow volunteers from the RNLI as he went.

On his return he put her half of cider and packet of crisps down on the rough wooden table. It occurred to her that he knew her so well he didn't have to ask what she wanted. They'd met at school and had been going out ever since. Oliver

Lacey had been part of her life for as long as she could remember. Every now and again they'd split up, see other people, but had always drifted back to each other. Her family adored him and Emma treated his mum as her own. Then, last year, after another break up, they'd got back together and things had got more serious; they'd decided to start saving hard to buy their own house. The only problem being, in Berecombe, housing stock was limited and expensive. Emma couldn't really see it ever happening. Renting would be nearly as expensive and in seasonal demand and she didn't want to have to move out every April to make way for the holiday lets; she wanted her own place. Somewhere permanent. Preferably without the anaglypta wallpaper and neat flower beds of her parents' house.

Dave Curzon, who ran the newsagents, and his girlfriend Lola stopped to chat. Mostly to Ollie. Everyone loved Ollie. She listened as the men moaned about Berecombe football club's terrible start to the season. Ollie needed a haircut, she thought. His unruly black hair was flopping over his eyes and he kept having to flip it back impatiently. She'd have to get her mum to do it. Since he'd been training with the RNLI crew, he'd put on muscle weight and had bulked up. His shoulders had broadened and he was almost stocky. Or maybe he was just transitioning from a lanky boy into a man? Emotion shifted inside her. She knew she didn't always treat him as well as he deserved but, deep down, she loved him.

Dave and Lola drifted off and Ollie took a swig of his shandy and grinned. 'So, come on, tell me what's Her Ladyship done now?'

It was their name for Leona. It had taken one day for Tash and Emma to get the measure of their new colleague.

Emma's lips twisted. 'Today's hissy fit was over me using her mug. Apparently, I don't wash up hygienically enough and she doesn't want my germs.' Emma's eyes were huge and indignant.

Ollie laughed. 'She might have a point there.'

'And she had a go at me for eating crisp sandwiches for breakfast.' Emma drew herself up. '"You are what you eat apparently."' She rolled her eyes. 'I think it's up to me what I eat. And *then* I caught her using wet wipes to wipe the phone receiver before she used it. By the time she'd answered it, they'd rung off!'

'It takes all sorts, I suppose,' Ollie said equably. 'Dawn in the office is like that but not quite as bad.' Ollie worked for the town council. He had a dull but reasonably paid job which was, most importantly, local enough for him to get to a RNLI shout when on call. 'Let's hope she gets fast-tracked and disappears up to head office.' He put his hand on Emma's. 'Chill, Em. It's not like you to get so worked up.'

Emma sipped her cider gloomily. She didn't really like it but it was the cheapest alcohol the Old Harbour did. 'No, it isn't.' It was true, she rarely worked up a sweat about anything. Lately though, she'd been feeling unsettled, irritated, bored. She shook off Ollie's hand restlessly. 'Trouble is, if she does, it'll be Tash's job she takes. And there's no way in hell I could work for a boss like Leona. Tash isn't happy about it at all. And Leona, bless her, doesn't miss an opportunity to remind us she's the one with the degree. It's doing my head in.'

'Don't think a degree is going to equip her to deal with

Biddy Treeby. Or should I say Roulestone, now? Keep forgetting she married poor old Arthur. Is she still interested in the Morrisons' bungalow?' He batted a moth away.

Emma managed a giggle. 'Early doors yet. If I didn't want the commission so badly, I'd hand over the Morrison-Roulestone sale to Lady Muck.' She opened her crisps. 'Would like to see Her Ladyship cope with that.' She crunched down hard on salt and vinegar. '*And*,' she added, offering the bag to Ollie, 'when Tash and I explained about the carnival float we do for Hughes and Widrow, she flatly refused to take part. Said there was no way she was going to dress up as a St Trinian's schoolgirl. Talk about a killjoy. The woman's not human. No sense of humour and closed up like a scallop.'

'Maybe she's just feeling her feet? You and Tash make a formidable team, you know. You're good friends too. Can't be easy slotting in.' He took a slug of his pint. 'Probably nerves. It's not easy starting somewhere new sometimes.'

'We try to help her fit in, Ollie, honestly we really do. But with some people there's no helping.'

Ollie pointed his glass at Emma. 'You just breeze into places, expecting everyone to love you instantly.' He smiled at her, fondly. 'And they do.' He took her hand and kissed it.

'That's because I'm so gorgeous.'

Ollie knew his cue. 'That's because you're so gorgeous. So, naughty schoolgirls, eh?' He visibly perked up. 'Is that your theme this time?'

'Thought that might get your attention. Yeah. Should be good fun. We're going to squirt water pistols and throw sweets to the kids. You collecting, again?'

'Suppose. Or doing the car park.'

Berecombe Carnival was held every two years and was one of the town's highlights. The season seemed to get longer every year. When the schools went back, the type of tourist changed. More couples, fewer families, older visitors. The carnival, though, was more a celebration for the locals rather than visitors. Along with the funfair which camped out on the square outside the theatre, it marked the end of the summer season.

'Would prefer bucket shaking to be honest,' Ollie said. 'Overseeing the parking can get boring. And it would give me a chance to make the most of you dressed up as a schoolgirl.'

Emma smiled at him wistfully. 'If we had our own place, I could do that for you every night.'

He reached for her hand again. 'It'll happen, Em. One day.'

'I like your optimism.'

He grinned and reached for his pint again. 'That's me, Mr Optimistic. Now tell me all about this evening class you want to do.'

Chapter 47

Emma couldn't contain herself. She got to Millie's bookshop far too early for the first class and the reading area was deserted. Amy greeted her at the door and said she'd be along later. She also said there would be a few familiar faces at the class so Emma assumed some of the other book club members were attending. She found a sofa facing the harbour view and tried to compose herself. She wrote the date and title in the notebook especially bought for the class and then closed it again and hugged it to her. Would she be able to do this? Screwing up her eyes at the memory of school, she clamped down on the fear of failure.

She had been a bundle of nerves and excitement all day. When she'd knocked a mug of coffee all over an incandescent Leona, Tash had ordered her out of the office. She'd made a courtesy call on the Morrisons and had then driven out into the countryside on the edge of town to a thatched cottage they'd just taken on. She spent a while taking the photographs for the sales brochure, enjoying the tranquillity of its setting and its sea views. The old couple selling insisted she join them for tea and cake in the garden. Emma sat with them in the afternoon sunshine while they reminisced about how happy they'd been there. She could see why. Down a track off a B-road, it sat in the vee of the valley overlooking the distant sea. She couldn't think of a more wonderful place to live.

'Oh, you're far too young to be burying yourself out here in the country,' Mrs Grey had laughed when she'd mentioned it. 'You young folk want the bright lights and nightlife of a city, don't you?'

It had made Emma think all the way back to the office. Part of her could see Ollie and her in a house like the Greys'. A spaniel running about, a few chickens, maybe a couple of children – her mother would ecstatic at the thought of grand-children. Ever since she and Ollie had got back together, the idea of marriage hung around them, unspoken but expected. As she'd said to Tash, she was a big marriage fan but part of her wondered if marrying Ollie would be all too easy – if they were slipping into something because there was no other option. She loved Ollie, she really did, but every time she tried to imagine Ollie in the garden, playing with the dog or holding a toddler, the only face which swam into her vision was that of Joel. He'd said she looked as if she'd stepped out from a Hardy novel and the cottage she'd just left couldn't be more Hardy-esque. When she tried to picture a man inside the house, it was Joel she saw sitting at the ancient desk in the corner; Joel who stood at the Aga stirring a pan of something delicious, a glass of wine in his hand.

'Emma Tizzard. My auburn-haired queen.'

Emma blinked and looked up. The man himself stood in front of her. For a moment she wondered if she was still in her fantasy because he held a glass of red in one long-fingered hand.

'I don't intend the classes to be formal,' he smiled down at her, waggling the glass. 'Millie has provided some rather wonderful wine and nibbles. She'll be attending too, along with Amy and someone called Biddy?' He raised his brows.

Emma's heart sank. Biddy had a tendency to dominate most situations. She couldn't even begin to imagine why she'd want to do the classes.

'I gather she has a rather colourful past.'

'You could say that. The rumour is she was a madame in London at one time. One of Berecombe's most characterful residents. Deffo one of its loudest. Married to a local councillor and the talk of the town.'

Joel's brows shot up. 'Really? How utterly fascinating.' He slid onto the sofa next to her. 'I love how small places like this embrace its eccentrics.'

Emma smiled wryly. 'With Biddy I don't think it has a choice.' She tried to ignore the way his presence made her throat constrict. She wondered where he lived. Exeter, she assumed.

'So, it will be a lively set of classes. How very splendid.' He leaned nearer. 'I have to confess to not being able to contain my excitement at the thought of seeing you again. I have a passion for opening up young minds, of introducing them to all there is to explore.' He locked gaze and Emma felt her breath hitch. 'There is so much we can do together, my wonderful Emma.'

She stared at him. Was he coming onto her? She wasn't sure how to feel about that. Was it allowed? Then she remembered she wasn't at school any more. He wasn't a school teacher but a university lecturer. They were both adults. She thought of Ollie and a pang of guilt shot through her. The moment fractured as Amy and Millie clattered into the space and she heard Biddy's strident tones as she struggled up the spiral staircase behind them.

Chapter 48

After the first hour, Emma came out into the cool, salt-laden air in a daze. It might have been an introductory class, but Joel had taken no prisoners. After a quick discussion about why literature was relevant, Joel had launched straight into a lecture on Chaucer and had given them *The Wife of Bath* to read for homework. She wondered just what she'd taken on.

Biddy followed her out and stood next to her, rubbing her hands in glee. 'Think I'm going to like this Wife person. Woman after my own heart. Got to use your natural gifts to get ahead, like she said.' When she didn't get an answer, she humphed and added, 'I'm going back in to grab a sandwich. Don't stay out here, young Emma my girl, or you'll miss out. Brains need feeding.'

Emma went to sit on the low wall which separated the seating area outside the book shop from the beach. Although it had been warm during the day, there was a distinct autumnal nip developing tonight. She shivered. Doubts assailed her. No one at home could understand why this was so important to her. When she'd mentioned it, her mother had thinned her lips and warned her about trying things 'not meant for the likes of us. Fine words don't bring the money in,' she'd added and had gone on to complain about the state Emma had left her bedroom in. Stevie had scoffed about her wanting to go back to school when he couldn't stand the place and her father had fallen asleep in front of Man U on the television. They didn't understand why she was doing this. And certainly weren't offering any support. She sighed. No wonder she'd dropped out of school as soon as possible. No one in her family valued anything to do with education. Her Uncle Ken was a painter and firmly anti-establishment. Auntie Tess was a baker and had given up hoping that any of her three boys would show signs of being academic. Even Ollie had blanched when she'd told him how much the classes cost. Why on earth was she putting herself through this?

'Having doubts, Emma?' Joel's melodious voice floated into the night and shifted with the sea. He sat on the wall beside her. 'You were very quiet back there.'

Emma stayed silent. She didn't want to admit most of what had been discussed had gone straight over her head.

'What was the last book you read, Emma?' Joel put his hand on hers.

'*Poldark*.' Emma answered without thinking. His touch had taken her by surprise. 'I've just started *Demelza* for the book club and before that I read *Wuthering Heights*. I'm a big *Poldark* fan,' she added, self-consciously.

'And what do you like about the *Poldark* books?'

'Well, I know they're not high literature—'

'Have to stop you there. Nothing wrong with Winston Graham. Fine writer. But it's true, we can't quite class them as high literature. Tell me, in your own words and without overthinking it, why you love reading them so much.'

Emma blinked out into the night. Behind them, she could hear Amy calling to Millie that they needed another pot of coffee. She felt suddenly tearful. How could she explain? 'I don't know what to say.' She concentrated very hard on the distant flashing of the Portland lighthouse.

'Take your time.' Joel's voice was very gentle. 'Just say it like it is.'

Emma blew out an enormous breath. 'Mum and Dad weren't bothered about school and they didn't mind me leaving as soon as I could. Mum would be happy if I got married, had a few kids. Ollie, my boyfriend, would like that too. Especially the kids part. Life's been a breeze, I suppose. I've drifted along, picking up jobs where I can. The estate agent's job has been the one I've stuck at the longest, although I'm still not sure if it's what I want to do forever.' She shifted on the cold stone, smiling as she thought of all the dead-end jobs she'd done, mostly seasonal, all low-paid. Now she'd begun talking, it all tumbled out. 'I always wondered if there was something else out there. The book group is a big thing for me. For the first time I had people to talk about books to. No one at home is interested and all Ollie bangs on about is his latest RNLI exercise.' She glanced at Joel. 'He's just started volunteering for them.'

Joel nodded but didn't speak. His attention was intense. No one had ever really listened to her like this. It was an intoxicating experience.

'I've got a nice life, don't get me wrong,' Emma went on. 'I live in a great town.' She gestured to the white lights along the prom, reflections bobbing prettily on a shifting black sea. 'Who wouldn't want to live here? I've got a pretty good job – for round here, that is – and a decent boyfriend. It's not that I'm desperate to live anywhere else.'

'But you sense there's more.'

'Yes! And books give that to me. I love reading about Cornwall. I love how Ross Poldark is such a complicated man. Not a hero all the time. He's got flaws. Big ones. Everything's bigger in books. More vivid. More . . .' she shrugged, 'Oh, I don't know, more *everything*.' She gave a gutsy sigh. 'I'm not making much sense.'

'Yes, you are. You're making perfect sense. And this is what you need to say in class.'

Emma frowned. 'What, about the town and Ollie and stuff?'

'Maybe nothing quite that personal.' Joel laughed. 'But you can say how the characters you read about make you feel. How you relate to them. What relevance the words have for you.' He squeezed her hand. 'Don't give up, Emma. Words entertain us, make us think about the world. They matter. They matter to you. Words shape your world, may even change your world. They are powerful things. And you're just at the beginning of your journey with them. Ease yourself in gradually. Learn how to express how they make you feel. Your opinion is as valid as anyone's in that room. It's just that the brain is a muscle. It needs exercising to get it to do what you want.'

'Thank you, Joel.' Emma let out a breath in relief. She had a suspicion no one else she knew would understand the way he had.

'It's my absolute pleasure. I think you've got real potential.

224

And I'd like, if I may, to help you unlock it.' He lifted her hand to his lips and brushed it softly with a kiss. 'I'd like to think we can unlock many things together. Exciting things. And now, if you'll excuse me, the aroma of Millie's coffee is proving too enticing.' He stood up. 'See you after the break. I refuse to accept you not coming back in, Emma Tizzard!'

Chapter 49

Emma jogged along the corridor of the Arts Workshop and burst into the main hall. She was late. Despite this, she took a moment to enjoy the view with familial pride. There was a satisfying bustle of activity focused around Hughes and Widrow's float entry into Berecombe carnival.

She watched as Uncle Ken stood back for a second to decide what to paint next. He shoved a paintbrush into the front pocket of his tattered dungarees, oblivious to the smear of grey it left. The Workshop was his pride and joy. His fourth baby after his sons. Some might argue it was his favourite creation. Set up a year ago, its aim was to develop arts and crafts in the town – and to give its young people something to do other than hang around in the shelters on the promenade. It was slowly establishing itself and Ken was overcoming his innate reluctance to deal with those in authority and had recently been working with Jed Henville on securing Arts Council funding. The ceramic and calligraphy courses had waiting lists. Even those youths who considered themselves too hardcore for anything arty were drawn to the graffiti workshops run by Ken. He had probably done over and above the things they imagined they had, Emma thought, with a smile.

Carnival was a big event in Berecombe, the culmination of the season before everyone slid, exhausted, into winter. Everyone looked forward to the carnival parade and the old-fashioned fair that set up in town. Entrants went to extraordinary lengths to create the perfect float and competition was fierce. The best ones even made it to parade in the ultimate street carnival at Bridgwater later in the year. Under the embellishments, all floats were fundamentally the same: a sort of giant open box made of chipboard, big enough to hold a group of people but light enough to be lifted and fixed onto a vehicle, usually some kind of flatbed truck.

Ken spotted his niece and went up to her. 'Not too bad a turn out, then.' He surveyed the room with satisfaction. 'Shame your dad's had to take the boys to footie practice.'

Emma greeted him with a fond kiss. 'Yep. And Mum's doing a late night at the salon but it's good that Tash, Biddy and George volunteered and Millie said she'd be along later with sarnies.'

'You can always rely on Millie for food. Think Hughes and Widrow will be dead chuffed with it.' He gave Emma an exasperated look. 'Shame they can't send no one from head office to help. Always left to us,' he grumbled.

Emma took his arm and hugged it. 'You know they never do and you love it like this,' she said, humouring him. 'You'd hate Pete Hingham turning up getting in the way and worrying he'd got paint all over his suit.'

'Suppose.'

'I see Auntie Tess has put herself in charge.' Emma looked over to where Tessa was showing Tash how to paint a straight line on the St Trinian's-themed float.

Ken's lips twisted in humour. 'You can always rely on my better half to do that.' He cackled. 'She thinks she's in charge but she ain't got a clue.' He slung an arm around his niece's shoulders. 'We'd better get stuck in then, hadn't we? Otherwise we'll get accused of slacking. What colour do you want the sides?'

Tess bustled over and overheard. 'Hi, Em love,' she called, in her strident Brummie tones. 'We're going for grey all over to make it look like the walls of the school. Then we'll paint in lines to make it look like stonework and trim it with navy and gold stripes for a bit of bling. It'll match the uniforms we can get hold of from Berecombe Comp.'

Emma shuddered. 'Never thought I'd be wearing that uniform again.'

'You didn't take to school, kiddo, did you?' Tess eyed her with humour. 'Me neither. Not done us any harm, has it? Mind you, the schools in my part of Brum were as rough as an old badger's backside. Couldn't wait to get out. And don't you worry, our kid. Once Biddy has got hold of your uniform you won't recognize it.' She grinned. 'We're going seriously sexy here.'

Biddy came to join them. 'Your Sean's done a good job on the frame,' she boomed.

'That's my boy,' Tess said with pride. 'They let him knock up most of it at work, over at the picture framers. Then he and George shipped the pieces in, flat-pack like, and put them together in here. They let him have some off cuts of wood and he's shaped the top to look like an old stone building. It'll be fab when we've finished painting it. '

'Looks marvellous already,' Biddy added, stoutly. 'Even got

the crenellated edges, if that's what you mean by it looking like an old stone building.'

'Suppose it looks a bit Hogwarts. It's certainly big enough.' Ken went to the far end and screwed up his face, speculatively. 'Just as well we've got double doors to get it back out again,' he said. 'What's it going on?'

Local farmer and ex-school friend George Small rose from a crouching position on the other side of the float. Despite it being big, his rugby muscled bulk dwarfed it. George Small was only small in name. 'It's going on my flat-loader,' he explained. He nodded to Emma. 'Evening, Emma, my lovely. Nice of you to turn up at last.'

'Cheeky sod. I had to have a long telephone call with your Auntie Cheryl before I could leave work, if you must know.'

Cheryl Morrison was George's great-aunt. He winced in sympathy. 'She does like a chat.'

'Well, putting your house on the market is stressful. All part of the job.'

'That's my girl,' came Tash's disembodied voice from somewhere behind the float.

Emma preened and then stopped short as a thought occurred. 'This thing's not going on the truck you take the pigs to the abattoir on?'

'It had better not be,' Tash yelled.

George laughed. 'If you knew anything about my farm, you'd know I've got a trailer for that.' He shook his head. 'Just as well you're an estate agent and not a farmer.'

'I completely agree.' Emma leaned in closer to him, took an exaggerated sniff and wrinkled her nose.

'Oi!' George went to flick his paintbrush at her but Ken intervened.

'Children, behave. Paint goes on the float and not on anything else,' he grinned.

'I love the carnivals down here,' Tessa said. 'It always brings folk together.' Everyone laughed. 'Seriously, though, kids, you lot in the south west do an ace job. We don't have anything like it in the midlands.'

'Think you're an honorary west country person now, Auntie Tess. You've been here long enough,' Emma said, giving her a peck on the cheek.

Tessa made kissy noises at her niece and then bent down and picked up Elvis. Cuddling him, she said, 'You reckon, bab? As soon as I opens my mouth folk know I ain't from round here.'

'Well, that goes for quite a few of us.' Biddy glared. 'Put my dog down, Tessa. He doesn't like to be fussed. And we'd better go and get on with these costumes, hadn't we? Otherwise the girls will be getting on that float with even less on.' She bore Tessa off, with Elvis scampering behind.

'Who did you say was in charge?' Ken asked and winked.

They went to the far side of the float and joined Tash who had resumed painting, the pink tip of her tongue sticking out in concentration. She glanced up briefly. 'No Ollie tonight?'

Emma picked up a paintbrush and dipped it into the grey paint. 'No, he's got his RNLI training again.' She let slip a sigh.

Ken watched as she applied some paint. 'You'd do better to sweep the brush side to side and don't load your brush too much for the first coat. Better to build up the colour gradually.' When she was doing it to his satisfaction, he gave his niece a penetrating look and asked, 'How often does he have to train then?'

'Twice a week at the moment.' Emma narrowed her eyes as she tried to paint as instructed. 'What with my evening classes and the book group and him being out on a Wednesday night and a Sunday afternoon, we hardly see one another. And when he's made it to crew and on call, it'll mean even more disruption,' she added, gloomily.

'Just as well he's got an understanding boss.' Ken said. 'The council don't mind him having to disappear at a moment's notice?'

'Nah. Gary, his manager, used to crew when he was younger. He's all for it.'

'So he should. They do an amazing job,' Tash put in. 'You should be very proud of Ollie. I think it's marvellous.'

'I'd think it more marvellous if it brought a few pennies in.'

'Wouldn't be the same if it was paid.' Ken shook his head vigorously. 'It's the real strength of the RNLI that it's independent. Can you imagine what would happen if this lot in the government got hold of it? It'd be management heavy and bogged down with targets. No. Paid for with voluntary contributions. Always has been and always should be.'

Tash eyed Ken. 'How did your first evening class go, Em?' she said in an attempt to change the subject. Once Ken got onto politics he didn't shut up.

Emma stood up and stretched. 'Now that *was* marvellous. First hour on Chaucer. Second on *Hamlet*.'

Tash pulled a face. 'Bit heavy, isn't it? For an outreach literature class.'

'I don't mind.' Emma shook her head. 'Joel makes it all fascinating. We're doing a whistle-stop tour of the highlights of the English literary world. Words are important. They can change you. They can change the world.' Her eyes shone. 'I could listen to Joel talk great literature all night.'

'I'm sure.' This time it was Tash who eyed her friend keenly. She'd never heard Emma talk like this. She was pretty sure she was quoting her tutor verbatim. 'So you're going to stick with it, then?'

''Course. It's only four weeks. Just hope I can find some peace and quiet at home to do the reading. You know what it's like.'

Ken joined them again. 'Madhouse, your place,' he agreed. He pointed at Emma's brush. 'And words may be important, my girl. But so is my floor. You're dripping paint all over it.'

Chapter 50

'Em, are you sure this is the right way?' Ollie peered through the windscreen at the narrow Cornish lane. 'Hate to think what will happen if we meet something coming the other way.'

'Then we'll find a passing place.'

'Haven't seen one for the past half a mile.' He changed down a gear as the road narrowed even more dramatically.

'Oh, cheer up, Ollie. It's our day off. The one day we've had together for ages. Let's make the most of it. And as long as we keep the sea to our left we can't go far wrong.'

He looked about him. 'Weird countryside. Not Devon, is it?'

'No that's 'cos it's Cornwall,' Emma said, trying to be patient. She'd thought this was a good idea. She'd suggested a day out on the one day off that she and Ollie could take together. She had researched a few places used as locations for the filming of *Poldark* and suggested they head for the far tip of the county. Millie, knowing how strapped for cash the couple were, had packed up one of her special picnic baskets, saying it was on the house. Emma had thought a picnic and a laze on a lonely beach was just the thing she and Ollie needed to connect again. They hardly saw one another and when they did meet for a quick drink, he was more interested in hanging out with his new RNLI pals. The talk was all about rescue methods of pulling bodies from the sea and first-aid techniques. While she admired what Ollie was doing and was secretly proud of him, the conversation bored her rigid. She'd sit there, sipping her cider slowly to make it last and dreaming into the sunset of Joel explaining the theme of 'seeming' in *Hamlet*.

Getting back to the driver next to her, she could feel Ollie rigid with frustration. He hated getting lost. 'Look, as long as we keep going downhill,' she pointed put logically, 'we'll find the sea eventually.'

Fate must have been listening. They rounded a blind bend, eased past a white cottage, and came to a building right next to a tiny cove.

'Car park sign that way,' Emma pointed.

Once they'd parked, there was the usual scramble for change for the meter. Ollie cheered up when the sun came out from behind a cloud and he spotted the café – the building they'd driven past to get to the car park. 'At least we can get a cuppa,' he said, as he lifted the wicker picnic basket from the boot of his Focus.

'What are you like? Fifty?' Emma teased. Now she was here, she couldn't contain her excitement. She couldn't wait to see the first film location. 'Come on, let's get down to the beach.'

They navigated the narrow opening to the cove and found somewhere to sit. There wasn't much choice because the beach was tiny. Ollie insisted on putting up the sun umbrella he'd borrowed from his mum. 'Can't have you burning, especially now you're a redhead,' he said, grinning and ruffling her still vibrant hair.

'Ha ha.'

He scanned the sky. 'And if it rains, it'll keep us dry.' Sitting down, he looked around as Emma delved into the basket. 'Is this it? Not much sand. More shingle and rock. It's not what I expected. Why were you so desperate to come here and not somewhere a bit bigger like Rock or Penzance?'

Emma blushed and busied herself getting the sandwiches out. 'Ooh. Smoked salmon and cream cheese,' she said and handed him one. 'Good old Millie.'

It didn't get past Ollie. The penny dropped. 'Oh, hang on. I get it. This is something to do with *Poldark*, isn't it?'

'Might be.'

'Oh, Emma!'

'Well, it's not a bad place to spend lunchtime is it?' She looked up at the steep cut in the cliffs next to them. 'Quiet, too. Away from the crowds. You know what Biddy always says, "September's the season of the newlyweds and the nearly deads."' She looked over her shoulder at an elderly couple sitting on the bench behind them.

Ollie laughed. 'And we're neither.'

Emma blushed again. Marriage had only vaguely been on the agenda. 'Is that a proposal, Oliver Lacey?'

'Do you want it to be, Emma Tizzard?'

His use of her full name had her thinking about Joel. Her brain muddled with a confusion of excitement and guilt. She couldn't look Ollie in the eye. And she couldn't speak.

He took it as a refusal. 'Yeah, well . . .' he said, staring out to sea, blinking hard. 'Weddings are expensive.' He bit into his sandwich, ending the scrap of conversation.

'I might have said yes had you asked me properly,' Emma

muttered into the picnic basket. 'And if you'd bothered to be a bit more romantic.' Taking a sandwich she stifled her frustration with food.

Millie had done them proud. As well as salmon sandwiches, she'd included a pavlova, complete with a tub of clotted cream and a flask of iced ginger-and-elderflower cordial. The delicious food was in direct contrast to the mood that had built up. They ate in an awkward silence and Emma wondered how it had got like this between them. They used to be able to talk about anything.

Lunch finished, they managed to find enough beach in between the rocks to lie down. In a gesture of reconciliation, Emma took Ollie's hand and snuggled into his side.

He sighed heavily. 'So, go on then, tell me what they filmed here,' he said in a sleepy voice.

Emma began to explain about the key smuggling scene but, within seconds of her talking, she could hear Ollie's gentle snores. He was fast asleep. Turning onto her side she watched how his straight hair had flopped back from his tanned face. He was lovely. He'd always been lovely. 'I love you, Ollie, I really do.' She bit her lip, inexplicably on the verge of tears. 'It's just sometimes you make it so hard.' Sitting up, she wiped her eyes and reached into her bag for her book. The day wasn't turning out quite as she hoped. 'You're not quite most people's idea of beach reading,' she told *The Wife of Bath*, 'but you'll have to do.' She opened the book and, as she read, all she could hear was Joel's smooth voice as he described the five times married pilgrim. 'Gat-toothed was she, experienced in the ways of men . . .'

Chapter 51

'Hi, Emma,' Tash greeted her, as she walked into the office on the following day. 'Have a good day off? Where did you go?'

Emma hung her bag on the back of her chair and flopped down. 'It was a disaster, Tash.' She thrust her hands into her orange hair. 'And I was looking forward to it so much.'

Tash looked at her in alarm. Emma, who although enjoyed other people's dramas, was usually placid and easy-going. 'I'll get the coffee and you can tell me all about it before Her Ladyship gets in. She's gone straight out on a viewing.'

Twenty minutes, two mugs of coffee and half a packet of digestives later, Emma had told Tash everything. She slumped back on her chair, staring gloomily into her Hughes and Widrow mug.

'So, you hadn't told Ollie the real reason why you wanted to go to Cornwall for the day? He was under the impression you wanted a romantic day out?'

Emma squirmed. 'And I did. As well. Oh, come on Tash, he should have guessed it was something *Poldark* related.' She pouted. 'He's so bloomin' obsessed with this RNLI stuff, he never takes any notice of me any more.'

'What happened after you went to this place, Porth – what?'

'Porthgwarra. It's where they filmed the smuggling scenes and the one where Ross swims watched by Demelza. Ollie got a bit arsey about me not telling him it was a *Poldark* reccie but then we compromised. He agreed to stop at Botallack – that's the Wheal Leisure Mine – as long as we went home via St Agnes. Then we got stuck in traffic which Ollie hates. He wanted to see the lifeboat.' Emma made a sarcastic face. 'It's a D-Class apparently. Completely different to the B-Class he crews on.'

'He's got it bad,' Tash said, laughing.

'Tell me about it. It's all he ever talks about. It's majorly boring.'

'Whereas you talking all things *Poldark* isn't to him?'

'Okay, okay,' Emma huffed. 'I just thought a day out in Cornwall would be romantic.'

'Except Ollie knows all you're doing is lusting after another man.'

Emma's head shot up. 'What do you mean?' she said sharply.

'Ross Poldark. Why, who did you think I meant?' Tash's voice was curious.

'Oh yes, him.'

'Isn't that why you went? To see where your breeches-wearing hero once stood? Bearing in mind he's completely fictitious, of course.'

'Don't get snarky, Tash. I'm at a crossroads in my life.'

Tash, by now thoroughly intrigued, perched on the edge of Emma's desk. 'Really? Why?'

'Well, the M-word reared its ugly head.'

'Oh Em, Ollie wants to marry you?'

'I don't know.' Emma fiddled with her mug and then put it onto the desk with a bang. 'And I don't know if I want to marry him.'

'Maybe you should try sitting down and talking about it?' Tash said gently.

'That's if we can ever be in the same room at the same time ever again. It's sod's law that his training and my evening class are on different nights. And, when I do see him, it's all he can do to keep his eyes open. He's knackered after all this training. Apparently, they were practising the man overboard drill on Sunday. He said it was exhausting.'

'Emma, it's a good thing he's doing. Heroic. Really heroic. Not like your blokes in books.'

'I know. I know that,' Emma said irritably. 'And his boss Gary did it and his uncle. They're all bloody saints.'

'He's a keeper and a good man.'

'I know that too. It's just we don't have anything in common any more.' She looked up at Tash, her hazel eyes enormous and troubled. 'And that's a biggie, isn't it? Especially if we're talking marriage.'

Tash shrugged. 'Kit and I don't have anything in common and it works for us.'

'Yeah, maybe.' Emma stared unseeing at the computer monitor. 'Maybe I just need to go somewhere else. World's a big place. Bigger than flamin' Berecombe.'

'Maybe you just need to find a place of your own. Still chaos at home?'

Emma picked up a paperclip and straightened it. 'Yup. Mum's working all hours for that cow Sukie. Dad's in a permanently bad mood and Stevie keeps forgetting to feed Todger and Snog. I've had to do it the last three times. Poor things.'

'Todger and Snog?' Tash pulled an incredulous face.

'The guinea pigs. It's what he calls them when Mum's not around. Real names are Tina and Sammy. They must have an identity crisis. Bit like me,' she added gloomily.

The conversation came to an abrupt halt as the door opened, letting in a blast of hot September sunshine. Leona sashayed in. 'You two look very cosy,' she drawled, looking down her nose at them.

Emma felt a pang of sympathy for Leona. It couldn't be easy trying to slide in between her and Tash. They were such a tight little team and good friends as well. She vowed to make more of an effort with her.

'Morning, Leona,' Tash said, sliding off the edge of Emma's desk. 'How did the viewing go?'

'Oh, it took an age. Time wasters, I think. Emma, are you heading into the kitchen? Be a sweetie and make me some mint tea, would you?' Leona sank into the chair Emma had just vacated. 'I see the hair hasn't faded. If anything it's brighter than ever. Probably the sun's bleaching it. What did you think you were doing?'

As Emma stomped moodily into the kitchen Tash mouthed the words, 'Talk to Ollie.' Emma nodded back, pulling an evil face at Leona as she went. Any promise to be friendlier to her fled.

Chapter 52

Later that afternoon Emma's ears pricked up when she heard Leona gush about the Morrisons' bungalow to the familiar-looking couple who had come in after lunch.

'Of course it needs quite a lot of work,' she was saying, 'but that's reflected in the price and the vendor is very motivated. I can arrange an accompanied viewing – would that suit?'

Emma knew better than to interrupt a sales conversation but, as soon as the couple left the office, she went over to Leona's desk and, putting her hands on her hips, glared down. 'The Morrisons' bungalow is sold.'

Leona looked up. 'Is it?' One perfectly groomed eyebrow rose.

'Yes, to Biddy and Arthur Roulestone.'

'I don't see a STC sticker on the details,' Leona smirked.

'Well, they haven't actually made an offer yet, but they're close. Biddy was getting a few quotes for the work needed on the conservatory.'

'And until they offer, it's still on the market,' Leona said with infuriating logic.

'Well, yes, I suppose, but it's not how we operate here. If we know someone is interested and is a solid buyer, we back off a bit. Let the sale have a chance to develop.'

'Really? What a remarkable business model. And how do you think the Morrisons feel about possible buyers being discouraged to view?'

'I think they'd rather have a quick sale, which Biddy is in a position to do, than have time wasters poke around who haven't the slightest interest in doing any work on a property and are just using it as an excuse to put in an insultingly low offer.' Emma was aware her voice had risen.

Leona thinned her lips. 'And what evidence have you for suspecting that of my clients?' Her voice was glacial.

'Instinct. Experience. I can spot their sort miles off.' Emma narrowed her eyes. 'In fact, I remember now. I *thought* they looked familiar. They came in this time last year and tried the same thing on a house near the seafront. The bloke runs a property development company. Buys up stuff at the lowest price he can, does it up and then sells it on at a profit. I advised Mrs Etham not to accept the offer.'

'You lost her a sale?' Two pink spots appeared in Leona's pale face.

'I lost her that one. I thought she could get more. I found her a buyer two months later who paid what I thought the house was worth.' Emma was getting angry. How could Leona not see the argument? 'Mrs Etham was elderly and she was on her own. I didn't like seeing her getting ripped off. She got near the asking price and that meant she could afford an apartment with a balcony and a view over the garden in the sheltered housing block she moved to.'

'How very socially minded of you.' Leona made it sound the worst of insults. 'Maybe, just maybe, we should be thinking of making our company money instead of cosseting geriatrics?

And, here's an idea. Perhaps it might be better to let the vendor make the decisions?' Leona stood up and matched Emma's fury.

'I did. I advised her what to do. Gave her all the info, gave her the options.'

'And then dictated to her what she should do.'

'I advised!' Emma was shouting now.

Tash shot through from the back office. 'Emma. Leona! Keep your voices down. The door to the high street is open. I don't want the whole of Berecombe hear you arguing like fishwives.'

'Leona is trying to lose me a sale!'

'Emma is the one risking a lost sale!'

Emma turned to her boss. 'Tash, I've got a lot of commission banking on the Morrisons' sale.'

Leona folded her arms and looked smug. 'Oh, that's what this is really all about, isn't it? It's not about caring for your darling clients and getting them the sale you think they deserve. It's all about how much commission you're promised!'

That Leona was bracketing her in the same grasping, venal category as herself had Emma shouting again. 'I. Am. Not. Like. That.' The woman was evil. Pure evil.

'Emma, Leona, please!' Tash roared. 'Sit down, Leona. If you think that couple are genuinely interested and will offer near the asking, then arrange a viewing. But go with them, please. The Morrisons are a sweet couple but they're eccentric and very unworldly. I don't want them taken advantage of. Emma, back office – now.'

Emma sat on a chair in front of Tash's desk. She fiddled with her hair and sucked her teeth mutinously. 'I'm sorry,' she said, eventually, 'but that woman's really got it in for me and I don't know why. She knew I'd lined up Biddy and Arthur for the bungalow and she should have checked with me first. She's deliberately trying to sabotage my sale.'

Tash sat down and placed one hand over another. 'Or trying to get the Morrisons some more viewings?'

'But I *know* that couple who came in. You remember how they tried to do the nasty on Mrs Etham?'

'Yes. You know them. You can also recognize the sort by instinct.' Tash shrugged. 'And that's what Leona has to learn. All the degrees and qualifications in the world won't prepare her for that. She's learning. Remember the mistakes you made when you started?'

'Yeah. I made mistakes, Tash. But I didn't try to lord it over people like little miss swanky-pants out there. I knew I didn't know anything. And was willing to learn. That couple shouldn't be put anywhere near the Morrisons. They'll badger them into submission.'

'Which is why I've insisted Leona does an accompanied viewing. And I'll go along too, if necessary. But we can't deliberately avoid sending viewers to a property they've expressed interest in.'

Emma took her time working out what Tash meant.

'Okay, I know,' Tash admitted. 'Clumsily put, but you understand, don't you Emma? We have an obligation to offer viewings to anyone we feel is a genuine buyer. Leona's couple may well make an offer that's too low. In which case, we advise what the vendor should do. For all we know they may also be cash buyers and be able to proceed even more quickly than Biddy and Arthur can. The Morrisons may prefer to take a cut in price in order to move more quickly. We can't make that decision for them. Only advise.'

Emma blew out a breath. 'I know. She's right, I suppose,' she admitted reluctantly. 'It's just that when she was all over the buyers like a nasty rash and hadn't checked the status of the sale with me first, I saw red. She's got it in for me and I'm—'

'Letting her get to you. Which isn't like you, Em. Look, she won't be here for long. Berecombe's too small for her. She'll move on to Exeter or Bristol. In the meantime, keep an eye on what she's doing, let her make mistakes within reason and do your gloating in private.' As Emma rose, Tash added, 'Oh, and get on the phone to Biddy. Won't do her any harm to know there's another buyer interested. Might make her speed up a bit. We could do with a decision from her.'

'Does anyone succeed in forcing Biddy to do anything?'

'Point taken.' Tash grinned. 'Oh, Leona,' she said as the woman put her nose around the door. 'What can I do for you?'

'There's a Millie in the office. Along with the most divine-looking man who is apparently her husband. Although how she could land something as gorg as that I have no idea.'

'What does she want, Leona?' Tash asked, reining in her impatience.

'They're interested in going to see the Greys' cottage.' Leona put a swift glance Emma's way and sniffed. 'And, after the debacle earlier, I thought I'd check it was okay. Don't want to step on anyone's toes, do I? After all, Emma might have a buyer all lined up already.' It had all the words of an apology but none of the sincerity.

Chapter 53

Tash decided Emma needed to get out of the office and she was the one who accompanied Millie and Jed to the idyllic cottage with the sea views.

As they drew up, she heard them gasp.

'Oh Jed, it's perfect!' Millie sighed.

Emma hovered behind Mr and Mrs Grey as they showed the couple round. She only had to put in a quiet remark every now and again to help things along. If anything, the Greys were being a little too honest and that wasn't always a good thing for a first viewing.

They insisted they stay for tea and cake in the garden again and served Lapsang Souchong in cups which were so delicate they were transparent. Mrs Grey had also made a seed cake.

'It won't compare with your lemon drizzle, my dear,' she said to Millie, 'but it's a good old-fashioned sort of a cake for this time of day. Not too rich and keeps well. And it's so lovely to have visitors to make a cake for.'

Millie bit into a piece appreciatively. 'It's always a treat to eat something I haven't baked myself and this is gorgeous. Do you think I could have the recipe? I think some of my regulars might like to try it.'

Mrs Grey looked delighted. After she'd made sure everyone had what they needed, she sat back and observed her garden. 'We've had such pleasure out of this house,' she said wistfully. Emma could hear tears in her voice. 'It's been the best kind of house in which to bring up a family. It's far enough off the main road not to have to worry about dogs and children running about.'

'Or the chickens,' her husband put in. He took her hand, kissed it and smiled at her.

'Or the chickens. Weren't they good layers? Buff Orpingtons. Nothing showy but good laying chickens. We had ducks for a while but they were the very devil to get back into the duck house at night. Cheeky little things, ducks. But chickens? Nothing like sitting in the garden on a sunny afternoon with your lap full of a warm, fluffy chicken.' Mrs Grey's eyes misted. 'I planted most of what you see, wanted to encourage the birds and the insects.' A fat bee droned by, as if to underline her point.

'The lavender path smells gorgeous,' Emma said.

'It does. Going over a bit now, but full of bees in July. It's a sight to see. And hear!'

'I'd like to learn how to keep bees,' Millie said, putting her empty plate back onto the rusting white metal table and shaking her head in refusal at the offer of more cake.

'Plenty of room for a few hives here,' Mr Grey said. 'Before you go, have a gander to the end of the garden. Ideal spot for beehives. Not too near the house. And beyond the tree line is a stream. We fenced it off when the children were small but when they were older, they spent most of the day down there with Sadie.'

Emma, Millie and Jed looked questioningly at him.

'The springer we had when the children were little.'

'Oh Sadie.' Mrs Grey smiled as she reminisced. 'She was a horror. Never known a dog to get so wet and muddy. And the trouble was, she encouraged the children to come back just as mucky. Still, what's a bit of dirt when they've been happily playing outside all day?'

'You'll be sad to go, Mrs Grey,' Emma said, gently.

The woman sighed enormously. 'It's time, my dear. They've cut the bus services and I don't drive any more so it's impossible to get into town. And I can't keep up with all the dusting the cottage needs.' She turned to Millie, with a chuckle. 'You'll find a house with beams takes some cleaning.'

'And, of course, the land is too much for us now,' her husband added.

'But brilliant for a growing family,' Emma put in, worried the conversation was getting a little negative. 'And you've had the roof re-thatched recently?'

'Two years ago,' Mr Grey said. 'Good chap he was. From over Chideock way. Got all the paperwork so you can have a look. Oh my, it was hot that week. Worked like a navvy, didn't he, Ness?'

'Angus,' his wife chided. 'I don't think you're allowed to say that these days.'

Mr Grey blew out his reddened cheeks. 'Don't know what I am allowed to say any more,' he grumbled. 'Bloomin' PC nonsense.'

'May I ask where you're moving to?' Jed asked and Emma was glad the subject matter changed.

'Got a little place in Colyton to go to. Shops and the doctors just around the corner. Warden controlled.' Angus Grey huffed. 'Not that we need one, of course. Not in our dotage quite yet, are we, Ness?'

'No, Angus, of course we're not.'

Emma hid a smile. The Greys must be in their mid-eighties at least.

Mrs Grey smiled at them. 'Time to make the change. It's time the house had another young family to love it. Lots of little children running about, making the place feel alive again.'

Millie blushed and her hand strayed to her stomach. Emma watched with interest and wondered if she was pregnant. It would explain the need to move; the flat above the café was lovely but hardly ideal to bring up children.

They were all reluctant to move. The cottage had cast a drowsy spell over them. As Millie and Jed drifted to the car, hand in hand, Mrs Grey stopped Emma. 'Angus and I agreed. We'd only sell to a couple who would love the house as much as we have.' Her voice trembled. 'And I think young Millie and Jed are just the people. Try and get them to buy it, my dear, will you? It would make Angus and I so very happy to see the old place go to them.'

Emma smiled. She patted the brown and wrinkled hand on her arm and bent down. 'I'll see what I can do,' she whispered. She watched as Mrs Grey began to collect the tea things and then turned to see Jed put his arm around Millie and kiss her on the temple. The house would be perfect for them. She'd heard Jed was wealthy; he could probably buy three cottages at this price. She let a sigh escape and wondered if she and Ollie would ever get settled. People always said money didn't make you happy but it certainly made life a little easier. She busied herself finding her car keys and when she joined them at the car, a professional smile was back in place.

Chapter 54

For the second evening class, Joel arrived late. He seemed flustered and blamed the traffic on the A30. In Emma's eyes he looked even more gorgeous and a treacherous little wormy thought wished she'd put the flush into his tanned cheeks and it had been her fingers which had disordered his hair.

Fewer students had turned up but Biddy was present, as was Millie, both clutching their Penguin Classics edition of *The Canterbury Tales*.

'Enjoyed it so much, I read all of *The Wife of Bath's Tale*. Corking, it was,' Biddy said, as she settled Elvis down. She opened her copy and Emma saw she had scribbled notes in pencil all over the text. Thrusting the book into Emma's face, she added, 'And look at this bit in *The Knight's Tale*.' She read it out: '"His hair was crisped in ringlets, as if spun of yellow gold." And this bit: "Aquiline nose and eyes with lemon light." And further on it says he has a voice like a trumpet.' Biddy giggled. 'Some might say that about me.' She glared at Emma. 'If they dared!'

'Shall we get started?' Joel opened his notebook. It was one of those expensive moleskin types, Emma noticed and added to his classy look. Looking down, she saw he had on matching black boots under his skinny jeans.

'I'm loving this Chaucer, young Joe,' Biddy boomed. She fluttered her eyelashes at Joel in a positively threatening manner.

'Looks like Joel's got a fan,' Millie whispered into Emma's ear. 'Poor bloke.'

Emma gave Millie a swift grin and opened her own copy, pen poised. She flushed a little. It wasn't only Biddy who had the hots for Joel. There were quite a few women sitting and gazing adoringly at the man, herself included.

'In fact,' Biddy went on. 'It's given me an idea. All those husbands the Wife had. Five! She got through 'em, didn't she?' She winked at Joel who recoiled. He opened his mouth to say something and then closed it again. 'I've been doing a bit of this writing malarkey.' She brought out an A4 lined pad and waved it around. 'Knew all the stories I've got in my head would come in handy sometime. Got lots of experiences. Me and Wifey got skills in common.' She grinned. 'If you know what I mean.'

Joel cleared his throat. 'Are you writing a memoir, Biddy?'

'Memoir?' Biddy drew herself up. 'Not sure the world's ready for that just yet. No, Joe, I'm writing erotica. Going to get it published. Seems to sell from what I can see.'

Emma bit down on another giggle. She could feel Millie's shoulder quivering next to her.

'Well, it can be quite hard to get published,' Joel said, sounding stunned. 'I should know, I've been trying to place something myself.'

Biddy preened. 'Oh, I don't need to worry about that, young

Joe. Got an old mate at one of them big publishers. He owes me a favour.' She sniffed disparagingly. 'Several, if I recall rightly.'

Millie fished out a tissue. Laughing, she snorted into it. 'You would have,' she muttered.

'What girl? What did you say? Speak up. How many times have I told you?'

'I said, good for you.' When she'd got herself under control, she added, 'What does Arthur think?'

For the first time Biddy looked crestfallen. 'Well, he's not completely happy. Said I might bring the council into disrepute seeing as he's a councillor. Promised him I'd write under a what-you-call-it. A sausage-nim.'

'A what?' Joel asked, looking mystified.

'You know, another name. A pen name.'

'Oh, a *pseudonym*.' There was more laughter.

Emma couldn't resist. 'And what name are you going to be writing under?'

Biddy puffed herself up. She took in a deep breath and said, proudly, 'Gertie Gussett.'

Chapter 55

Joel eventually got the class back under control after Biddy's announcement and, apart from her interruptions every few minutes, the evening passed uneventfully. After coffee the class resumed and they began another discussion on *Hamlet*.

'Do you know, this play is full of nothing but sayings,' Biddy was heard to mutter as they opened their playscripts. 'I don't think this Shakespeare bloke had an original thought in his head.'

She kept Joel talking after the class had finished. Millie and Emma helped Amy tidy up the coffee things and then Millie took pity on Joel and prised Biddy away, claiming she needed ask about her apple Charlotte recipe. Amy took a tray of cups through to the main café and Emma found herself alone with Joel.

'Shall we go outside?' he suggested. 'I have the beginnings of a headache.'

Emma smiled at him in sympathy. 'Biddy can do that to you.'

'I think if she'd called me Joe one more time, I might not have been responsible for my actions.'

'That's a Biddy test. To see if you'd rise to the bait.'

'And here's me thinking it would be you who would get me into trouble.' He gave her a long, speculative look. 'Tell you what, I could really do with a cold drink.' He nodded to the Old Harbour. 'Looks a good spot. Care to join me?'

Emma considered what lay in store for her at home. Mum fretting over the ironing, Dad staring glassy-eyed at the television which would be on full volume and, worse, Stevie had cousin Roland round. They'd be holed up in his stinking pit of a room glued to *The Grand Tour* and yelling at one another. A drink in the beer garden of the Old Harbour sounded perfect.

While Joel fetched the drinks, Emma sat at the table and stared over the harbour. It had long since gone dark but it was still warm and the reflection of the lights on the harbour buildings danced in the water. People had begun to retire their yachts for the winter and the area next to the harbour was filling up, the halyards sounding a soft metallic clink in the breeze. As it was midweek and the season was coming to an end, she was alone out here. It was peaceful. It had been a busy day at work and home was always chaotic. She took in a deep, cleansing breath and smelled the sea, with its pungent odour of briny seaweed. Ollie's kind, loyal face loomed into her guilty imagination and she wondered just what she was doing.

'I forgot to ask what you'd like, so you have chilled white wine.' Joel sat next to her, very close. Too close. 'If it's not what you drink, I can take it back. I'm a little out of touch with what young people drink nowadays. All the students in the union bar drink vodka or endless alcopops.' He shuddered. 'Let me know if the wine is good. Not often you get a decent glass in places like this.'

Emma unpicked what he'd said. She was so used to Ollie automatically knowing what she drank she hadn't thought to tell Joel. He thought she was young. She supposed she was, in comparison to him. She hazarded a guess he was around forty. Maybe older.

He reached into the pocket of his linen jacket and brought out a red packet. 'Do you smoke?' When she said no, he added, 'Wise girl,' and lit a long brown cigarette. He concentrated on smoking for a minute, taking in deep lungfuls. 'It's beautiful here, isn't it? I can see why you've never wanted to leave. What incentive would you have?' Flicking ash to the side, he picked up his own glass of wine. 'Not too bad,' he said, sounding surprised. 'And, have you always lived here, my Emma Tizzard?'

She nodded. 'Yes. Dad comes from here. And his parents. And theirs. The closest we Tizzards get to exotic is my Auntie Tessa who's from Birmingham.'

Joel laughed and pointed his cigarette at her. 'And that can be very exotic.'

Emma didn't know what he meant but suspected it wasn't a compliment. She sipped her wine, feeling it burn as it went down.

'Have you researched your very delightful and unusual surname?'

Emma shook her head. The thought had never occurred to her. Boys were common babies in the Tizzard family so the name was scattered around a lot. It had never seemed unusual to her.

'Origins in Tissier.'

Joel leaned closer and Emma smelled the smoke on his

breath. She wondered what it would be like to kiss a smoker. Ollie was a bit of a health freak; he'd never dream of smoking.

'Old French,' Joel continued, looking pleased with himself. 'I had a spare second so I looked it up. Your ancestors were weavers, Emma. Tissier in old French means weaver. Mayhap you came across with the Huguenot protestants?' He reached a hand around the back of her, his fingers resting lightly on the nape of her neck. 'Did you flee your country to escape religious persecution, sweet Emma?' He sighed. 'So romantic. Or are you sturdy Devon stock, my Hardy heroine?'

'I thought Thomas Hardy wrote about Dorset,' Emma said, slightly desperately. She wasn't sure how to take him tonight. The encouraging, enthusiastic tutor had disappeared. This was all getting a bit sleazy and she ought to tell him to get his hands off her. But there was something hypnotic about him. About his honied voice. About drowning in his dark eyes.

He shifted and reached for his wine. 'So he did.' His voice closed. 'Wessex, if we're being pedantic.'

He obviously didn't like being corrected. Emma turned away and drank her own wine. Part of her wished it was cider as she was thirsty.

'Em!' It was Ollie. 'Percy said you were out here.'

Emma stood up, feeling guilt seep out of every pore. 'Ollie. Hi.' She introduced him to Joel. The men greeted one another, Ollie, his normal cheerful self and Joel rather more guarded. 'Better go,' he said and drained his glass. 'Good talking to you, Emma. See you next session.' And he was gone into the night.

Ollie took his place. 'That your tutor? Seems nice. Apart from the smoking.'

Emma nodded.

'What are you drinking?' Ollie peered over in the gloom. 'You on the wine tonight, Em?' he said, sounding surprised. 'Want another?'

She put her arm through his and leaned against him, desperately seeking his comforting presence. She loved him, she really did. So why was she having these thoughts about Joel? She wasn't even sure she liked him. She'd never been more confused.

Ollie, on the other hand, sounded anything but confused. 'Got some news, Em,' he said ebulliently. 'Got a surprise. A nice one.'

Chapter 56

Emma twirled in a circle taking in the luxurious hotel room. 'We can't afford this, Ollie! We ought to be saving.'

He laughed and came to her, taking her hands in his. 'I thought you deserved a treat. You've been working hard and Her Highness or whatever you call her has been giving you grief and I know things aren't always easy at home. Besides, we haven't seen anything of each other, the last couple of weeks.'

'But here, at the Henville? It must cost a fortune.'

'It's only a night's B & B and dinner this evening. You can have it as an early birthday present, if it makes you feel better. And, 'cos it's only down the road, what we saved in petrol, we can spend on cocktails. There's a pool and sauna too, although I couldn't run to any treatments in the spa.'

'Oh, Ollie! Have I told you how much I love you?'

'Actually, no, not lately.'

She flung her arms around him. 'I love you, Oliver Lacey.' They kissed and then kissed some more. Breaking away, Emma eyed him. 'Before we go for a swim, maybe we could do some other exercise?'

Ollie pulled her tight. 'Deffo,' he said and edged her to the sumptuous four-poster bed.

'This has been mega.' At the bar several hours later, Emma lifted her Porn Star Martini and clinked it against Ollie's pint. 'Thank you.' She drank, the alcohol flushing her features. 'And that is delicious.' She set the glass down, eyeing it with pleasure.

'Well, don't give me too much credit for it. Millie said there'd been a last-minute cancellation and she got Jed to agree a deal with his brother.'

'Is that the bloke who owns it? That tall blond guy we saw in the foyer?'

'Alex? Yes. Used to be a banker in the city, or so Millie said. Then he bought this place and has been doing it up.'

Emma looked around, wide-eyed, at their expensive, glossy surroundings. The mixologist, in white shirt and an ornate blue waistcoat, was making another customer something delicious and wickedly alcoholic. He stood behind a deep red mahogany bar which was set against vast mullioned windows. Glass shelves ran across them, set with blue and gold-rimmed glasses which glistened in the subtle light. Nothing as common as optics for the Henville Hotel. Instead, free-standing bottles stood, in regimental rows, on a stone windowsill. The room, itself, was decorated in shades of blue and cream with subtle touches of gold. It was just blingy enough to make it look special. Against the discreet chatter from guests and quiet chinking of glass, a pianist played show tunes in the corner.

'It's lush, Ollie,' Emma breathed and then spotted

something. Squinting to see better, she realized she was right. 'Ollie, that's one of Uncle Ken's paintings on the wall!'

The maitre d' glided up to them and overheard. He raised an eyebrow. 'Mr Henville likes to showcase the works of local artists and considers Mr Tizzard one of the finest,' he said in a strong French accent. 'And you are his niece?'

Emma nodded.

'*Enchanté*. We must take extra special care of you this evening and make sure everything is *parfait*. And now, are you both ready? Your table awaits.'

Emma and Ollie sat in an alcove, slightly hidden away but perfect for people-watching. As he slid a snowy napkin onto her lap, the maitre d' whispered, 'This is the table where we seat, how do you say, our very special guests. Enjoy!'

The food arrived in a sequence of beautifully presented dishes.

'I can't believe they do fish fingers in a joint like this,' Ollie said in delight, as he stared down at his starter.

Emma grinned. 'They don't look like the fish fingers I dish up.'

'And, while I love yours, they don't taste like them either.' Ollie offered her a morsel on the end of his fork.

'They're so good.' She closed her eyes in ecstasy. 'I don't think I've ever eaten food this good. Try some of my langoustine – the garlic butter is amazing.'

'Better have some of that, then.' Ollie gave her a broad wink. 'Might be kissing, later.'

'Certainly hope so. That's if you haven't worn yourself out with the swim and the sauna and all the other exercise we've done today.'

Ollie picked up his wine glass. 'Not a chance.' They clinked glasses and said cheers. Then Emma leaned forward and said, slightly horrified, 'All a bit grown-up, this, isn't it?'

Chapter 57

It began to unravel after the twenty-eight day aged steaks and before the pudding. Ollie, never the most hardened drinker, had had too much wine on top of his pints. It made him garrulous. He began to expound, in onerous detail, about the correct order in which to pack kit for the lifeboat. Emma sat, fidgeting with the stem of her wine glass, and wondered just when he'd got so boring. It was a world away from Joel's sophisticated conversations and she hated herself for letting the thought invade her brain.

'Let's go up, shall we?' she suggested, interrupting him mid-flow.

'You don't want another cocktail?' Ollie looked hurt. 'Or coffee in the bar? Make the most of where we are. Doubt if we'll be able to afford to come back any time soon.'

Emma shook her head. 'I am a bit tired, after all.'

When they got back to their bedroom, someone had turned down the bedcovers and placed two chocolates on the pillow.

'You stay there and eat those,' Ollie said, swaying slightly. 'I've got another surprise for you.' He held up a wavering finger. 'Won't be a tic. Do. Not. Move.'

Emma slipped off her heels and settled back, putting the

unwanted chocolates on the bedside table. She was feeling full and certainly didn't have room for them. In fact, she thought, sliding down on the Egyptian cotton, her eyes closing, all she wanted to do was sleep. She must have drifted off because she woke up with a jolt to find Ollie standing over her.

'Ta-dah,' he cried. 'I'm Ross Poldark and I've come to claim my bride. No, Demelza, do not be coy. I shall be gentle. That is . . .' He swaggered and then swayed a little. 'Until my passion overtakes me and then, alas, I can make no such promise!'

Emma sat up with a jolt. 'Ollie, what do you think you're doing?' She stared at him. He wore white riding breeches, knee-high boots, a loose, frilled shirt which she vaguely recognized as one belonging to his mother and a red waistcoat. In his hand he held what she was pretty sure was Stevie's plastic pirate sword.

'I'm Ross Poldark!' he repeated, hiccoughed, and stumbled over the edge of the rug.

'You've said that.' Emma pushed herself further up against the headboard. 'But why?'

'You love Ross Poldark. You're always going on about him.' He sank onto the bed. 'Thought you'd get a kick out of it. Ross Poldark coming to ravish you.'

'Will you please stop saying Ross Poldark.'

'Sorry.' Ollie was beginning to see he'd miscalculated. 'Thought it might be a bit of fun. We don't have much fun nowadays. Doesn't seem to be going as well as expected.'

Emma began to giggle. She couldn't help herself. It was all so naff. In his amateur dressing-up costume he looked nothing like the Ross Poldark of her dreams. In fact, she realized, she hadn't day-dreamed about Ross ever since meeting Joel. 'I think I'm a bit over *Poldark*,' she blurted out and, too late, saw the humiliation on his face.

'Well that's great, isn't it? I go to all this trouble only to be told Ross Poldark is no longer the hottie. It wasn't all that long ago you dragged me off to Cornwall for a day out. I thought it was because you wanted to be with me but it turned out all you wanted to do was use me to get to your beloved film locations. And now you're telling me that's all finished.'

'Keep your voice down, Ollie, you're shouting.'

He lurched off the bed and squinted down at her. 'You always take me for granted, Emma. You have done for years. As long as we've been going out.'

'That's not true.' Emma swung her legs off the bed. 'I'll get you some water. You've had too much to drink. You're not used to it.'

'I haven't had enough to drink, you mean. You do. You do take me for granted.' He flung an arm in the direction of the door. 'Back down there, in the restaurant. I saw you! You were bored rigid.' He jabbed a thumb into his chest. 'I'm doing something important, Em. I'm saving lives.'

'You're a rookie trainee. You've only been out on practice shouts. I don't think you've saved a life yet, just done a load of training, which I never hear the end of.'

He subsided on to the bed. 'So you *are* bored with me.' He shook his head loosely. 'I knew it.'

'I'm not bored with you, Ollie.' Emma sat next to him and handed over a glass of water. 'It's just that we're leading different lives at the moment. I am proud of you, babe, honest. It's just that we're into different things now.'

'So what gets you going now then, Emma? English fucking Literature?'

It was so unlike Ollie to swear that Emma flinched. 'You're drunk. Go and take all this stuff off and go to bed.'

'Nah. I'm not drunk enough. I've seen how your eyes light up when you mention this bloke . . . Joel? Is that his name? I saw you on the bench with him. You go on about bloody Chaucer and Shakespeare and you call *me* boring?'

'That's the whole point. I don't find Chaucer and Shakespeare boring, but I can't stand listening to you bang on about capsize training any more.' Now Emma was shouting.

'Then maybe we're not meant to be together. We've split up before, maybe it was a mistake to get back together.'

'Maybe it was!'

They stared at one another, horrified by what they'd said but realizing it was too late to retract.

'Let's go to sleep, Ollie,' Emma said, wearily. 'We can talk about this in the morning.'

Ollie shook his head. 'No. It's over. It's finished. For good this time. I've had enough of being taken for a mug.' He hiccoughed and stumbled to the bathroom.

They lay, rigidly apart, in the luxurious king-sized bed. Emma stared glassily at the canopy above. The space in the bed only seemed to echo the huge gulf that had built up between them.

Chapter 58

Emma hadn't seen much point in staying for breakfast; she couldn't face food and Ollie was too hungover to eat. They drove the short distance back to her family home in silence. Ollie dropped her off with a curt nod and she batted off the questions from her mother and Stevie by saying she had to do her reading for the evening class.

Taking a coffee up to the bedroom she'd had since childhood, she stared out at the trees dripping with rain. Sundays were always faintly depressing. Her mother, as it was the only day of the week when the family were guaranteed to be together, always insisted on a full Sunday roast. She started cooking it early in the morning and the house stank of cabbage and roasting meat for hours. As they were all used to eating the main meal in the evening, no one was really hungry at one. Her father was dragged from his greenhouse and Stevie made it plain he'd rather be in bed or on his iPad. They ate in a morose silence, her mother passively furious that she'd gone to the trouble of cooking when no one appreciated it. Her poor mother. They didn't do nearly enough to show their thanks. Emma made herself a promise to pop into The Floral Box and get her some flowers.

She sipped her instant from Stevie's Star Wars mug. For a second, she dreamed of a Sunday morning drinking coffee ground from fresh beans, while talking over the papers with someone who was into politics, current affairs or books. Someone sophisticated and worldly – like Joel. She wondered what he did at the weekends. Exeter was twenty-five miles away. Even if she could afford the petrol, she certainly couldn't afford the price of a frothy coffee in one of the cafés there. She loved Berecombe, but it seemed too far away from anywhere interesting sometimes.

For the first time, a future without Ollie loomed. They'd known one another since year seven, had been going out since sixth form. He'd been part of her life for so long she couldn't imagine it without him. She pictured rocking up at the Old Harbour without him. The empty seat at the table as her mother would no longer be able to ask him over for an evening meal. Being with their group of friends: Amy, Millie and Jed, newly loved-up Tash and Kit. Being there with Ollie but not being *with* him. She imagined him moving on, getting a new girlfriend. Percy's little sister, Leah, had always had the hots for Ollie; she wouldn't hang about before getting her claws into him.

Emma opened the play she needed to read for the next evening class. It was George Bernard Shaw's *Pygmalion*. But she couldn't read. A big fat tear plopped down and smudged the words.

Chapter 59

It was too busy at work to allow herself to be maudlin. September marked the rush to get an offer accepted so there would be a chance to be in by Christmas and Emma spent most of the morning on the phone to the Morrisons. Leona's clients had upset them. The viewers she'd taken over had been less than complimentary about the bungalow and had said so during the viewing – almost certainly as a tactic to put in a low offer. The Morrisons had taken umbrage and had threatened to use a rival estate agent in nearby Lyme Regis and it had taken all Emma's people skills to reassure them and keep them on board. She then had to steel herself to ring Biddy and ask if she wanted to proceed on the purchase. As all Biddy wanted to do was talk about her latest chapter of erotica, Emma ended up exhausted and in dire need of coffee when she'd finished. But the hard work had paid off.

'Biddy and Arthur have made an offer,' she announced, triumphantly to Tash. 'Five grand off the asking price, so I think the Morrisons will accept. And Biddy said it would be a cash sale with nothing to sell depending on it, so it'll go through quickly. Don't know where Biddy gets her money from, but me and the Morrisons are very grateful.' She glared at Leona. 'And it's no thanks to you.'

'On the other hand, maybe you should be grateful to me. My clients probably pushed your Brenda, or whatever her name is, into making the offer.' Leona huffed and turned her back, her rigid shoulders making an eloquent statement.

Tash twisted her lips and made a face at Emma. 'Leona, could you go out to this semi in Otterton Lane? Have a chat with the vendors, see if you can sign them up. Should go in the range of a hundred thou, twenty more if it's in really good nick. Check with me before you give them a definite price, though, please.'

Once Leona had left, Tash made them some fresh coffee and brought it over to Emma's desk. 'Well done you.' She perched on the corner, one stiletto dangling.

Emma took the mug. 'Thanks.'

'You should be proud of yourself. The Morrisons have been messing us about for years and Biddy . . . well, Biddy drove Pete insane when he sold her that house on the hill.'

'How is our esteemed area manager?'

'Trying to find a replacement for Leona so he can shift her off to the Bristol branch. He thinks she'd be better in a city branch. "More suited to the cut and thrust of a buoyant market," I think were his words.'

'Well, she hasn't fitted in here, Tash. And we tried to make her feel welcome but she was a bolshy cow from the get-go.'

'I know. Shame, though. We really need a third member of the team. Maybe a newbie you could train up? I could get you on a management course, if you like. You're definitely ready. Might be a promotion in it.' When Emma didn't reply,

Tash asked, 'You okay?' in an abrupt change of subject. 'I didn't want to ask earlier, with Leona around. You seem upset and it's not just the Morrison sale. You can handle these sort of things in your sleep.'

Emma took in a deep breath. If she said it, it would make it real. She hadn't told anyone yet, hoping Ollie would ring and it would all be a mistake. But it had been two days since their argument and she'd heard nothing. When she blurted out that she thought she and Ollie had split up, Tash held up her hand and insisted an emotional crisis like this deserved lunch at Millie's.

They sat on the terrace in the sunshine and Tash lifted her face to the warmth. 'Better make the most of this. Autumn's coming.'

Millie served them an enormous pot of tea and farmhouse cheddar and caramelized-onion toasted sandwiches. 'Some nice lemon drizzle for pud, freshly made this morning. Lovely with a dollop of clotted.' She put the tray down and added, 'And don't feed the seagulls. They've been a menace this season.'

Emma eyed the food. 'No chance a bird is getting any of this.'

'I thought you were taking a backseat, Mil,' Tash said. 'Letting Petra take over.'

'I like to keep my hand in.' Millie grinned. 'Keeps the staff on their toes. And I've got a meeting with Amy in the bookshop later. Talking Hallowe'en for next month.'

'Sounds good. Keep us posted.'

'Will do.'

'I think she's pregnant,' Emma said, as they watched Millie disappear into the café.

'Do you?' Tash lifted up her sunglasses and peered after Millie. 'That's nice. They'll definitely be wanting the Greys' cottage then.'

'Do you ever stop working?' Emma managed a giggle.

'Soz.' Tash poured the tea, passed her the pink flowery cup and said, 'Come on, then, what are you going to do about Ollie? Tell your Auntie Natasha.'

Chapter 60

'So, you still love him?' Tash asked when Emma had filled her in.

'Yes.' Emma sighed in exasperation. 'Well, I think so. It's hard to know. He's always been around, always been there.'

'Can you imagine life without him?'

'No, but if we've got nothing in common any more and we're boring each other senseless, it can't be enough that I can't imagine life without him.' Emma groaned and put her head in her hands. 'And that sounds as muddled as my thinking.'

'I don't get why you're boring one another. True, you've got different interests now.' Tash waved a toasted sandwich in the air. 'That's a good thing, isn't it? Gives you something to talk about when you get together.'

'It might work with you and Kit but it doesn't seem to with us,' Emma said gloomily, reaching for another sandwich. 'Maybe we don't care enough about each other to be interested.'

'Or maybe you've both just got swept off your feet by these sudden new things in your life and you need to work through it all? Your passion for English Lit will wane in time and Ollie will calm down about his crewing once the novelty wears off. He's just a bit excited about it all at the moment.'

'Maybe. That's if I ever get the chance to talk to him again. I've sent three texts and he's ignoring me.' Emma bit her lip. She couldn't believe Ollie was really serious about them splitting up but it looked like he was, this time. In a bid to change the subject she asked, 'How's the animal sanctuary idea going?'

'Yeah. Good, thanks. We're going over to a place in Somerset to see how they do things.' Tash frowned. 'Lots of paperwork to wade through, though, and it all costs a fortune. The donkeys, alone, cost us an arm and four legs in vet fees. We've just taken on a new puppy. Found in a plastic bag by the side of the road.' Tash's lips thinned. 'How anyone could do that is beyond me. Kit's been bottle feeding her through the nights. You'll have to come and see her. Merlin's so funny, he thinks he's the daddy and he and the puppy curl up together. It's so sweet. Benji would be jealous if it wasn't for the fact he's now become devoted to Kit's mum.'

Emma sat back and grinned. 'Listen to you, talking all things doggy. And you say you don't have anything in common with Kit?'

Tash blushed. She didn't show the softer side of herself to many. 'Okay, okay. I've got involved with that side of Kit's life, but it doesn't mean we have much else in common and we're very different personalities.'

'Maybe that's why it works. You are very different. Me and Ollie are too similar. We're both so easy-going.'

'Em . . .' Tash paused. She picked up the teapot and refilled their cups before going on. 'Do you think there's any truth in what Ollie said, that you take him for granted?'

'No, I don't!'

'You sure, my lovely? Look, I'm no expert when it comes

to relationships. Look at my history. One bloke breaks up with me and goes out with Amy, the other turns out to be a wannabe bigamist.' She shuddered. 'But I know relationships take a bit of work. Kit and I, well, we're still at the starry-eyed phase, but I can see a point when certain things he does will wind me up.' She shrugged. 'And we'll have to find a way round that.'

'Ollie's never irritated me.' Emma drank her tea, thought-fully.

'Hasn't he?'

'No, it's not that. It feels more as if we're drifting apart and that we don't care enough to work things out.' Emma stared into her tea cup as if the answer might lie there. 'He did dress up as Ross Poldark for me though.'

'Oh my God. When?'

'At the hotel. He appeared in this get-up, thinking he looked just like Aidan Turner.'

'And he didn't?'

Emma shook her head. 'Hardly.'

'What did you do?'

'I laughed.'

'Oh Em!' Tash put her cup down on its saucer with a clatter.

'Well, he looked so ridiculous.'

'But he was trying to please you. He'd booked this lovely night away, had taken the time to find a costume and you laughed at him?'

'Wasn't so much of a costume. I think he borrowed the breeches from George Small and he had on his mother's blouse.'

'But he was doing it for *you*. And then you laughed and

he was completely humiliated. Imagine how he felt, Em. Ollie doesn't do stuff like that, he's too straight. No wonder he was angry with you.'

'Yeah. I can see that.'

Tash peered closer. 'There's no one else, is there, Emma? And I don't mean a fictional character.'

'No. There's no one. It's only ever been Emma and Ollie. Ollie and Emma.'

Tash, looking at Emma's blushing face wasn't so sure. She hoped she was wrong.

Chapter 61

Some of the sophisticated gloss of the evening classes had tarnished. Emma hadn't been gripped by *Hamlet* and had got annoyed by his lack of decision. Ollie would have been straight in there, sorted the problem out and then made everyone a cup of tea afterwards. The side of him which she had always written off as boring she now saw as mature and practical. He'd make an excellent RNLI crew member, she realized. Calm in a crisis and focused.

She tuned back in to Joel explaining about *Pygmalion*. 'Of course, it's the play that *My Fair Lady* was based on.'

'Well, we all know that, my boy,' Biddy interrupted.

Emma didn't. She didn't think she knew *My Fair Lady* and said so.

'You must know the film, child. Rex Harrison. "All I want is a room somewhere . . ."' Biddy sang some of the song tunelessly and everyone put their fingers in their ears. '"Oh, wouldn't it be loverly?"' she continued, oblivious of their reaction. 'Used to have a lovely client who liked me to sing to him while we did it. Maybe I'll get me to some classes. They might be grateful for some real singing talent.'

'If we could get back on track,' Joel said and glared at her.

Biddy refused to be silenced and carried on singing in her best cock-er-ney. 'Maybe it would be a good time to take a break?' he yelled over the racket and everyone nodded in relief. They drifted across to the spiral staircase which led down to the café area of the bookshop where Millie had laid on coffee and homemade sausage and chutney rolls. Biddy followed, still humming to herself.

'Emma,' Joel said, 'before you go down, could I have a word?'

Emma looked at Joel in surprise. She was no longer sure how she felt about him. Instead of learned and worldly, tonight he seemed smug and impatient with them all. And slightly sleazy.

'It's how I see you and me, you know.'

Emma frowned. 'What, singing in a cockney accent?'

He came to her and laughed. Running slender long fingers down her cheek, he said, softly, 'And that's exactly my point. I see you as my *Pygmalion* project. Someone to fill with my knowledge. To help explore what our wonderful world has to offer. To mould. You have so much to learn, my little Emma Tizzard. My flame-haired beauty. My very own Eliza Dolittle. Of humble stock but capable of so much more.'

Emma stepped back, insulted. She didn't want to be anything anyone thought she should be. She was her own person and that should be good enough. And how dare he say she wasn't as good as him? She was about to tell him when they were interrupted by Biddy returning.

'Forgot my scarf.' She eyed them beadily. 'Getting chilly of an evening now.' As she picked it up she neared Emma and whispered, 'I don't think it's just knowledge he wants to fill you with, lovie.' She winked. 'Be careful.' Reverting to her normal, overloud voice, she added, 'And, course we know the *Pygmalion* myth really started back with the ancient Greeks when he fell in love with his statue and made her human.' She huffed. 'Typical man, always think they can make us into what they want. Now, young Joel, get me back down these dratted stairs. I'm in need of a coffee and one of those pastries. Not a patch on my brownies, but they'll do.' She offered an arm with a gleam in her eye that would not be defied.

Emma watched as Joel bit back a retort, regained his usual good manners with difficulty, and allowed Biddy to pull him to the top of the spiral staircase. She knew Biddy was more than capable of tackling the stairs unaided but was glad of her intervention. Sinking down onto one of the sofas, she scrubbed at her cheek where Joel's persuasive fingers had caressed. She was desperate to rid herself of the stain of his touch.

She had been insulted and on many levels. She couldn't believe his arrogance, his assumption that he was so much her superior. That had been made patently clear. It had hit the same nerve that Leona had: that a piece of paper proving you'd passed a few exams made you a better person. It didn't make Leona a better estate agent – far from it, in fact. Her self-importance stopped her from listening to what the clients wanted. And paper qualifications certainly didn't make Joel any better than her, Emma thought, or her parents. Short-tempered she might be, but her mother worked hard to look after them all and her father, with only O levels to his name, put in endless hours at the factory to make ends meet. Emma drew herself up, her anger and indignation blossoming furiously. And look at her. Her parents had produced her. She held down a good job, had a town chockful of friends, had a wonderful family and a gorgeous boyfriend. Or had, Emma corrected herself with a sad smile, until recently. Why would she want to be anything other than she was? How dare Joel suggest he *mould* her? In fact, the more Emma thought about him, the sleazier he became. He'd just been on a power trip, influencing those he considered beneath him in order to . . . Emma jumped up, as the horror of what Joel was all about hit her. Rage surged through her veins. 'Sick bastard!' she seethed. 'Using Chaucer to get into my knickers!' Never, in a million years, could she see Ollie acting like that. so dishonourably. Good, kind, straight-as-a-die Ollie, and RNLI volunteer and willing to risk his life for others, Ollie. A gazillion times the better man than Joel. Emma let herself flop back down onto the sofa again. And, for the sake of a few mellifluously uttered literary words, she'd let Ollie slip from her grasp. She thrust her hands through her hair, praying there was some way she could persuade Ollie to come back to her.

Chapter 62

The evening of the carnival was the first cool one of autumn but it was clear and dry.

'At least it's not raining,' Tash said to Emma as they clambered aboard the St Trinian's float attached to the lorry. 'Should be a good turnout. Not sure how warm we'll be in this get up, though.' She tugged her short, pleated skirt down.

'You look great,' Emma said, admiringly.

'We both do. Selfie?'

They posed, ignoring a wolf whistle from George who was getting into the cab.

'Naughty schoolgirls, eh?' he cackled.

Tash gave Emma a worried glance. 'Do you think it's too much?' She looked down at her white shirt, unbuttoned as low as she dared and at the stockings, the tops of which barely nudged the short skirt.

'At least you're used to the stilettoes,' Emma pointed out. 'I can hardly walk in these.' Then she remembered that Tash was still trying to regain her confidence after her relationship with an abusive boyfriend had finished. She was still looking anxious. 'He won't be here, you know, my lovely. He's gone back to Manchester. I asked Marti if she'd seen him around and she said no. And you know how nosy she is. One-woman neighbourhood watch scheme, she is. Besides, you've got your mate Emma to see him off. I'll fight him off with one of these bad boys.' She waggled her giant water pistol. 'Fully loaded and dangerous.'

Tash giggled. 'Yeah. Suppose. And Kit said he'd be around somewhere. I promised to keep the costume on for later.'

'Thatta girl. Switch the lights on, then.'

Tash switched them on and they took a minute to admire the effect. Flashing red, blue and white lights lit up the walls of the school-based float. She grinned at Emma. 'Going to be a good night.'

'You bet!'

'I'll wait until we join the main parade afore I sticks the music on,' yelled George. 'That do? Hold on then. Here we goes.'

The lorry joined the rest of the floats at the top of Berecombe's main street and crawled down behind the main attraction, a futuristic concoction with strobe lights and robots, sponsored by the town's computer firm, Digi-Sol. They were followed by the Carnival Queen's float and, right at the back of the parade, the majorettes. A huge crowd thronged the narrow pavements on either side and the atmosphere was electric.

'Turn the music up, George,' Emma yelled into the back of his cab. 'We're being drowned out by Kraftwerk from Digi-Sol.' George obligingly turned up the music and the Spice Girls yelled out.

Emma and Tash turned to one another, grinned and screamed in unison, 'I wanna, (ha) I wanna, (ha) I wanna, (ha) I wanna (ha) I wanna really, really, really wanna zigazig ah!' And they turned and sprayed the crowd with water.

The procession snaked its raucous way down to the seafront and crawled along the promenade. Emma and Tash alternated spraying the crowds with water and throwing sweets. Emma spotted her parents and her uncle and aunt. Biddy and Arthur waved and clapped and Millie and Jed stood on the corner with Amy. A little further along the front, Emma saw Stevie and Roland, aimed her pistol and scored a direct hit. Their roar of outrage made her night. Tash threw them a whole bag of sweets as compensation.

Once the parade had reached the harbour, there was gridlock as everyone got off and the floats disappeared through the back streets.

'Thanks, George, that was brill,' Emma said, as she dismounted. 'Fab music. Haven't danced like that for ages.'

'I'll see you later at the fair,' he called, as he drove off. 'Gotta try my hand at the coconut shy.' They heard him sing along to Beyoncé as the lorry crawled through the crowds. 'All the single ladies . . .'

'Well, you two make quite a sight.' It was Kit. He took Tash into his arms. 'Hello, gorgeous,' he murmured and kissed her thoroughly.

'Hello, you,' she said and stared up at him lovingly.

'I'll leave you two to it,' Emma said. 'I'm suddenly feeling green and hairy and definitely gooseberry-like. See you at the fair?' She turned and bumped into Ollie, collecting bucket in his hand. She hadn't seen him since their disastrous night at the hotel. It had only been a few days so how had she forgotten the way his hair flopped endearingly into his eyes? His brown face with its sharp features? His newly muscled broad shoulders?

'Hi, Em. Good turnout.'

'Yeah.' Emma was strangled by a sudden shyness. It was awful. Even when they'd spit up before they'd always managed to stay friends. Now it seemed they had absolutely nothing to say to one another.

'Well, best be off. Haven't shaken the bucket along the front yet. Not that I'm allowed to actually shake it, but you know what I mean.'

'Come on, my gorgeous man.' Inevitably it was Leah, Percy's sister. She thrust her hand through Ollie's arm and smirked at Emma. 'Let's get the collecting over and done with and then we can go to the fair.' She gazed wide-eyed up at him. 'You promised me you'd take me on the bumper cars. See ya, Emma.'

As they disappeared into the crowds, Emma stared after them miserably. As she'd predicted, Leah had got her claws into Ollie. She just couldn't believe he'd fallen for it. 'Oh Ollie,' she whispered. 'Have I really lost you?'

Chapter 63

Millie, Jed and Amy gathered her up and insisted she go along to the fair with them. It was the last thing Emma wanted to do but allowed herself to be swept along. She didn't have the energy to decide anything else. A wind had got up and the waves were choppy as they battered the shore. Emma pulled her borrowed blazer tight and shivered.

Millie must have noticed as she put a companionable arm through Emma's and matched her stride. 'Feels like autumn's arrived, doesn't it? I'll have to search out Trevor's doggie coat,' she said, referring to her beloved cockapoo. 'Look, this probably isn't the way to go about it but Jed and I are seriously interested in the Greys' cottage. We're going to put in an offer next week. Do you think they'll accept?'

Emma grinned. It was the one good thing that had happened lately. 'I'm sure they will. As long as it's near the asking price. It was priced pretty keenly for a quick sale.'

'Then I'll tell Jed to make the call first thing on Monday.' She sighed happily. 'I never thought I'd want to move away from the flat above the café but I fell in love with the cottage the minute I saw it.'

'Even with the dusty beams?'

'I'll just have to buy a duster with a long handle.'

'Think they're pretty easy to get hold of.'

'And at least Jed is tall.'

'Ah. Can't say husbands like him are easy to get hold of.'

Millie smiled. 'You're not wrong there. He's one in a million. Although it took me a while to realize how wonderful he really is. Sometimes you just can't see what's right in front of you. You can't see that the perfect person is there, just waiting for you.'

Ollie's face flickered into Emma's mind. He was wonderful too. How could she have not realized? And how could she have not realized how much she truly loved him? He'd been right in front of her all the time. Only she'd been too besotted with fictional heroes like Ross Poldark and fake heroes like Joel Dillon to see his true worth. 'Isn't that the truth?' she murmured, tears prickling.

Millie didn't hear. She hugged Emma's arm. 'I'm so happy, I can't tell you.'

'You don't have to tell me, Millie. It's shining out of you.'

'Ah, thank you, my lovely.' They parted to ease around a big family group. 'There was something else I wanted to say,' she added, as they came together again. 'I don't want the flat to be empty and Petra doesn't want it. I wondered if you and Ollie might like it? I know you're looking for a place of your own. Wouldn't dream of taking any rent but you'd need to cover your bills and, as it isn't very big, they're not too bad. Emma? Are you okay?'

'Oh Millie. You're such a kind, good person.' Emma flicked away the tears.

'I didn't mean to upset you,' Millie floundered as they

stopped walking and faced one another. 'I wasn't sure how to broach the subject. It's just that I'd like someone living there who I know would look after the place. Oh Emma!' She put her hand to her face in dismay. 'I really don't mean it as charity.'

'I know that.' Emma cranked out an attempt at a grateful smile. How could she tell Millie that, a few weeks ago, her suggestion would have been the perfect solution? With just bills to pay, she and Ollie could still save up for a deposit on a house. Maybe one of the starter homes on the new estate? She stared out to a black sea that was looking increasingly churned up. It looked like the first storm of the autumn was setting in. A gust of wind brought with it a foam of salty spray. 'I'll talk it over with Ollie,' she promised, feeling an absolute fraud. She changed the subject. 'And get Jed to call me on Monday and I'll get things put in motion with the Greys.'

'Will do,' Millie promised. 'Come on, let's catch up with the others. I'm in need of candyfloss and one of Barney's toffee apples.'

Chapter 64

The fair had set up in the large cobbled space in front of Berecombe's little theatre. It wasn't a huge affair: a few traditional stalls with a merry-go-round and the dodgems taking pride of place in the middle. These had the town's teenagers thronged around, burgers in one hand, lurid-coloured soft toys in the other. Pharrell Williams blasted out from the dodgems, its bass making the ground vibrate. Emma watched, feeling distanced. She thought she'd never be happy again. Millie spotted Tash and Kit by Barney's candyfloss and toffee apple stall and dragged Jed and Amy over. Emma went to where her parents were standing by the coconut shy. Saying hello to George, who brushed past her bearing three coconuts, she watched Stevie in a grudge match against cousin Roland. Uncle Ken handed over a plastic pint of beer to her father, Tessa chatted to her mother, and their family was complete. Except it wasn't. Ollie should be here. It was just the sort of night they spent together, surrounded by family and friends. Emma remembered the last time the fair had come to town: Ollie had bought her a go at the rifle range and she'd won a furry yellow bear. He'd called it Pringle after her favourite type of crisp and it still sat on her bed. Tears made her vision swim. She missed Ollie so much.

'You okay, bab?' It was Auntie Tessa. She came over and hugged her. 'No Ollie tonight?'

Emma shook her head. She still hadn't told her family the complete truth.

'You've not gone and had another falling out? You two, honestly. Worse than Burton and Taylor.'

'Oh, Auntie Tess,' Emma said, huddling into her aunt's side, 'I don't know who they are.'

'Look them up sometime. It'll be all right, our Emma. Never seen two people more suited to one another. And, it isn't as if you haven't fallen out before, is it, kiddo? You'll get back together again.'

'Well, if it isn't Emma?' It was Joel. He loomed out of the neon flashing lights and stood in front of her, a sardonic smile on his face. He seemed very tall and urban in his pea coat and cap, and slightly overdressed.

Tessa glanced from one to the other with a sharp look. 'I'll leave you to it then, Em. Me and Ken fancy our chances on the Hook a Duck. Give us a shout if you need us.' As one, the Tizzard family drifted off.

Emma stared up at Joel in amazement. He looked completely out of place. After the scales had fallen from her eyes, she'd remained silent during the second half of the evening class and could hardly bear to look him in the eye. Instead, she'd doodled in her notebook and daydreamed horrible fates for him. Shakespearian ones were favoured. They seemed the most gruesome. Drowning in a vat of wine had been considered but rejected as not nasty enough. Now, a red-hot poker shoved up his—

'Emma?' Joel snapped his fingers at her.

God, he was a piece of work. How had she missed it? 'What are you doing here?'

'Patrick suggested it. Said it might be fun, in a slumming it kind of way.'

Emma was pretty sure Patrick had said no such thing. He was far too nice.

'And you have to admit, it's a fantastic experience,' Joel expounded. 'Fairs like this have been going on for centuries.' He looked around, peering down his nose as a teenaged couple staggered past necking cans of cider. 'With one or two exceptions, it could be *Far From the Madding Crowd* or *The Mayor of Casterbridge*. That giddy, childish enjoyment mixed with an edge of danger. I suppose this kind of thing grew out of the traditional country fair. Not one attempt at intellectual pursuit in sight.' He added, without pausing for breath, 'And that was your family?'

Emma interrupted him before he could say it. 'Yes. And not one intellectual thought between them. And why should there be? They're having a night out. Enjoying themselves.' She reined in a lick of temper with difficulty. He was a complete arse.

'Oh, Emma. My Emma. Do I detect crossness? How exhilarating. A temper to match your fiery hair.'

Emma was suddenly angry. More than angry. She was furious. Hands on hip, she squared up to Joel. 'How dare you! How dare you come here making your little intellectual digs and looking down your snidey nose at us all? We may not be able to match you for degrees and qualifications, but not only are we just as good as you, I bet we'll be able to have gallons more fun than you'll ever manage. Why don't you go back to your poncey cafés and bars in Exeter and drink your weight in overpriced coffee and leave the real fun to us!'

'Trouble, Joel?' A tall, slender blonde drifted up to him and put her arm through his possessively.

To Emma's shock she saw it was Leona.

'Oh, it's Erin.' Leona bared her teeth in the briefest of smiles. 'I'd recognize those not so dulcet tones anywhere.' She gave a superior little laugh.

Emma looked from one to the other, the truth dawning. Then she glanced down at Leona's left hand, clutched onto the sleeve of Joel's coat. The third finger bore an enormous solitaire. To her delight, Joel was looking distinctly uncomfortable.

'No trouble, Lee. Emma was just giving me her opinion on the history of country fairs.' He gave Emma a warning look from narrowed eyes. 'This is my fiancée, Leona.'

Emma was beginning to enjoy this. Leona, the woman who had been openly hostile to her for no reason had, apparently, a fiancé who was willing to cheat on her with his students; the very people to whom he had a professional duty of care. She couldn't think of a better karmic revenge. A surge of power overtook her. She could – if she wanted, if she could be bothered – wreak an awful lot of damage here. Giving Joel a wicked look she said, 'Yes, actually we know one another. Quite well, as a matter of fact. Just like you and I do, Joel. Funny how you never mentioned a fiancée.' She let that little nugget drop and then addressed Leona. 'Hello, Leona. I wouldn't have thought this was your scene on a Saturday night. Haven't you got an opera or a fancy restaurant to go to?' She saw the woman dart a narrow look at Joel and then her.

'Well, Erin, I'm sure it's some people's idea of a good time but it's certainly not mine.' The words were bitten out but she was still casting troubled looks at her fiancé. 'And I don't understand, how can you possibly know Joel?'

Emma ignored her question. 'As you well know, it's Emma. And I suppose it's quite brave of you, really.'

Leona's carefully made up lips curled. She looked confused. 'Whatever do you mean?'

'Just that there are an awful lot of people in this town that you've managed to upset. Some quite badly.' Emma shook her head sorrowfully. 'And, you know what we uneducated oiks are like with a drink inside us.' She made her eyes go big. 'We just can't be held responsible for our actions.'

As if on cue, George Small lumbered up to them, at least five pints of Thatcher's Gold along. 'Oi,' he shouted, pointing his can of cider at Leona. 'You're that woman who upset my auntie. Told her her house was falling down and she wouldn't get anything for it.'

Leona drew herself up. 'I have absolutely no idea what you're on about.'

'What's that, young George?' Biddy and Arthur joined them. 'Oh, you're the one, are you? Nearly lost me that bungalow, you did.'

Leona made a small sound.

'George is Mrs Morrison's nephew. And this is Biddy, who is buying the bungalow.' Emma supplied. She shrugged. 'Everyone is related to one another in this town. And, if they're not, they know one another. And look out for their backs. Perhaps it would be wise to get back to the city.' She glared at Joel. 'Both of you.'

'Come along, Lee,' Joel said, edging away and eyeing George's bulky form warily. 'Nothing but the inbred and ignorant here. God,' he added, in disgust, 'it's like the bloody wicker man.'

'I heard that,' Biddy yelled. 'Got the hearing aid turned up. You'd do as well to watch your manners and what you say. I have information that could wreck your career, young Joe.'

'Yes, Joel. Off you go. I could add a few details to the information Biddy has,' Emma added.

They watched as Joel and Leona hurried off. As they went, Emma could hear Leona plaintively asking how he knew her.

'What information?' Arthur asked his wife, curiously.

She touched a finger to her nose. 'We know what he's been up to, don't we, young Emma? Corrupting young bodies when he should be educating minds.' She poked her with an elbow. 'And have you read any more *Wife of Bath*? Deaf, she was. Like me.' Biddy chuckled. 'Swear she's been reincarnated in me. So much in common.'

'I hope you've only had one husband,' Arthur put in, mildly.

'Only the one. And the best.' Biddy kissed him soundly on the cheek. 'Are you ever going to take me on those dodgems?'

'Lead on, fair maid,' Arthur said and winked.

They marched up to the dodgems and pushed past the crowd of teenagers, George staggering after them.

'Was that your tutor and Her Ladyship? Are they a couple?'

Emma swung round to see Ollie behind her. He had a bag of chips in his hand. 'Oh Ollie,' she cried, as she flung her arms around him. 'I love you so much.'

Chapter 65

He took her to a relatively quiet spot along the cliff path above the theatre and they sat on a bench facing out to sea, the waves rolling in. They could still hear the music blaring from the fair but it was muted by distance.

Emma shivered. 'You're not wearing enough clothes,' Ollie chided and gave her his jacket.

'Costume for the carnival parade.'

'I know. I saw you.' He grinned. 'Narrowly avoided getting squirted.'

'It's too tarty, isn't it?'

'I'm not complaining. Chip?'

'Thanks,' Emma said, taking a fat one and blowing on it. 'These are good.'

'Bartlett's. They make the best chips. They a couple, then? This Joel bloke and Her Ladyship?'

'Apparently.' Emma began to giggle. 'And they deserve one another. Would spoil any other couple.'

'You gone off him, then?'

'Oh, Ollie.' Emma snuggled closer to him. 'It was never like that. I just appreciated him opening up my mind.'

Ollie gave a short laugh. 'I don't think that was what he had on his mind to open up, Em.'

'You could be right. Biddy saw through him as well.'

'It's not right, Emma. He shouldn't be taking advantage of students like that.'

'No.' Emma sobered. 'Biddy said the same. He didn't take advantage of me though, don't worry. I just . . . I just got a bit confused. Got my priorities skewed.'

Ollie found her hand and clasped it tightly. 'I did too, Em.'

'I take you for granted, don't I?'

'Sometimes. But I go on about my training too much, don't I?'

'A bit.' She shrugged against him. 'Still love you, though.'

'I love you too. Oh Emma, I don't want to split up. I want us to be together. Do you think we can work something out? I promise not to bang on about the RNLI as much.'

'And I promise to take more of an interest. It is important what you're doing and I am proud of you, you know.'

'I'll try to be interested in Shakespeare, although I can't promise anything.'

Emma laughed. 'Then I'll try not to be boring about it. We've both got things in our lives that are important to us. That's a good thing, isn't it?'

'Do you want to carry on with your studying?'

'I might. I haven't decided yet. It costs a fortune.' She sighed. 'I do love it, though. Tash mentioned there might be a promotion at the office going. You never know, I might do some on-the-job training. Go for management.'

'Way to go, Em. That's fantastic! I can't think of anyone who deserves it more. And, you know I'll support you, whatever you want to do with your life. The world's your lobster, as Biddy says.' Ollie's voice was warm with pride.

'What about babies?' She knew he was keen. 'I'm not sure I can study, hold down a full-time job and have kids.'

'You do want them at some point, don't you?'

Emma thought back to how ecstatic Millie was with Jed and possibly a baby on the way. She thought how happy her mother would be to be a grandmother. 'Yes,' she answered, slowly. 'At some point in the future.' She pictured a baby, with her big hazel eyes and Ollie's shock of black hair. A fuzzy warmth overtook her. He'd make the best sort of dad. 'Oh Ollie, I'd love to have your babies, of course I would.'

Ollie hugged her to him. 'But plenty of time for that, though, eh? We're only kids ourselves. Time for you to get an education first. A degree, if that's what you want.'

'Oliver Lacey, have I told you how much I love you?'

He kissed her, lingeringly. 'I'm getting the idea.' Then he rested his forehead against hers and laughed. 'Can't believe we wasted a whole night in a four-poster, Em. If only you'd been wearing this get-up back then.'

She kissed him back. 'I promise to keep it if you dress up as Ross Poldark again. Only this time, I won't laugh. I'm so sorry about that, Ollie.'

'It's forgotten. Daft idea, anyway.'

'No, it was really sweet of you. And thoughtful.'

They kissed once more, relief that everything was all right between them fuelling their passion.

'You taste of salt and vinegar. Of chips and the cold wind,' Emma giggled and laid her head on his shoulder. 'Delicious.' The picture of Leah, with her hand gripped possessively on

Ollie's arm reared up into her vision. 'And what about Leah?' she demanded, sitting up. 'She didn't waste any time, did she?'

'You jealous?' Ollie asked, obviously pleased.

'You bet I am! Emma said, hotly. 'Don't want my man being pawed by another woman.'

'What can I say?' Ollie said, sounding smug. 'I'm just too much of a temptation.' He sobered. 'Nothing happened, Em. Jeez, I couldn't shake her off though. Wouldn't get the message that there's only one girl for me and that's you.'

'Oh, Ollie . . .' Emma gazed at him, his face impenetrable in the gloom, his black hair lit by the flashing neon lights behind him. 'I do love you.' If she said it often enough, he might believe her. She'd never take him for granted ever again.

'We'll be okay, Emma. We can work through this. It'll be easier when we get our own place. And that will happen, I promise.' He kissed her again, their passion flaming the cold night.

Emma surfaced from the kiss and was about to tell him about Millie's offer of the flat when a high-pitched beep sounded. And then sounded again.

'What is it?' asked Emma, confused. 'It's coming from your jeans pocket.'

'It's my pager,' Ollie said. 'It's a shout.' Thrusting the now cold bag of chips at her, he added, 'I've got to go, I've got five minutes to get to the station. Bugger it, I had something to ask you too. Something really important.' For a second he wavered, then he turned and ran.

'And I've got something to tell you, too,' she shouted after him, watching him sprint down the path. She turned and looked out to sea. The clouds scudded across a clear moon. It looked dark and stormy out to sea. And dangerous.

Chapter 66

Emma thought she might as well return to the fair. Her senses were tingling from Ollie's kisses and she was too wired to sleep. Besides, she wouldn't be able to relax until she knew he was back. This was one of the first real shouts that Ollie had been called to and the knowledge he might be in danger out at sea horrified her. It was all far too real, suddenly. She caught up with Millie and Jed outside Madame Zackerlie's Fortune Telling caravan. A stiff breeze skittered an empty cider can along the cobbles and two drunks shoved past them. To Emma, the fair had lost its appeal. It felt end-of-evening blowsy.

'We thought about going in,' Millie said, nodding to the fortune teller's. 'But then Tessa told us it's really Joyce Biddle from the WI's Knit and Natter Circle.' Sensing Emma's preoccupation, she asked, 'No Ollie? I thought I saw you together a while ago.'

'He's had to go out with the lifeboat,' Emma explained, stuffing the remaining chips into an over-filled bin. She must have been really preoccupied with Ollie, she thought with a smile. She never threw food away and especially not chips. 'There was an emergency. I thought I'd go and wait outside the station for when he gets back.'

'Oh Em, he could be gone for hours.' Millie put a comforting arm around her shoulders. 'And it's getting really cold, that wind is really kicking off. Come back to the flat and you can wait there. You can see the lifeboat station from my lounge window. I'll make us some tea to keep us going.'

'That's ever so kind of you, Millie, but I wouldn't want to take you away from the fair. It's only just getting going.'

'To be honest, I've had enough and I've got to get back to Trevor anyway. I don't like to leave him on his own for too long.' She turned to her husband. 'Jed, do you want to come back too, or are you staying on?'

'I'd quite like to stay for a while longer, do you mind?' A thinner, bespectacled version of Jed waved at them from the dodgems. He had his arm around a spectacularly beautiful woman and she screamed in delighted shock as their car thudded into another. 'There's Alex and girlfriend Eleri,' Jed said. 'Said I'd do battle with him on the dodgem cars. Want to catch up with all the goss from the Henville anyway. Haven't seen them for weeks, they've been so busy at the hotel.' Jed's older brother owned the exclusive Henville Hotel where Ollie had taken Emma. 'I won't be late, though. Promise. Trust me.' He kissed Millie tenderly and strolled off into the crowds.

Millie turned to Emma, with a giggle. 'Don't think Jed has experienced anything quite like the Berecombe fair before. He's enthralled by it all.'

'At least he's not snobby about it,' Emma said, thinking of Joel's insufferably lofty attitude.

They pushed their way through the milling throng and made their way to the steep street leading down to the promenade.

304

'Jed? He's the least snobby person I know.' Millie giggled again. 'Funny, though. It took me a year to realize it. Oof,' she added, as a shock of spray hit them. 'It's getting rough out there. Really high tide too. Wouldn't surprise me if the harbour doesn't flood tonight. Come on, Em, let's get a shifty on and get into the warm. I can show you round the flat when we get there. It won't take long. There's not a lot to it!'

Chapter 67

Trevor the cockapoo gave them a rapturous welcome and followed at their heels while Millie showed Emma around. His cold wet nose bumped against the back of her knees.

'Just the lounge, bathroom, kitchen and bedroom,' Millie explained as they wandered through. 'As you can see, it's completely separate from the café below. There's this tiny box room too.' She opened the door opposite the bathroom. 'It used to be my bedroom when I was little but when my parents . . .' She paused, and Emma could hear the emotion in her voice. 'When I took over the main bedroom,' Millie corrected herself, 'I had shelves put in and it's a bit of a glory hole now.' She closed the door, a thoughtful expression on her face. 'Useful, though.' Turning to Emma, Millie straightened her shoulders and smiled. 'You go on through to the lounge. There's a chair right in front of the window which looks out onto the harbour. You can watch out for the return of the lifeboat from there. I'll bring the tea in. Fancy some carrot cake with it, or is it too late for cake?'

'It's never too late for cake, especially yours,' Emma said and went to sit in the aged and lumpy chair in front of the picture window. She could see the harbour lights from here, through the rain-smeared glass. The lifeboat station had its doors flung open to the night and the interior looked hollow and empty without its bright orange boat inside. The wind hurled itself at the window, making it rattle. Emma shivered and cuddled into the chair.

'That's quite a storm developing,' Millie said, as she brought through a tray of tea and cake. She put it on the coffee table, with a warning look to the dog. 'Make sure he doesn't steal the cake, will you, Em? I'll go and find you something warm to wear. You look frozen.'

Ten minutes later, Emma was curled up, wearing a turquoise blue tracksuit of Millie's and warming her hands around a steaming mug of tea.

Millie collapsed onto the sofa with an exhausted sigh. 'I get so tired at the moment. Wish some of my old energy would make a comeback.' She reached for her tea and hugged Trevor as he jumped up next to her.

'That'll be the baby, I suppose,' Emma said without thinking.

Millie blushed crimson. 'How did you guess?'

'Not difficult.' Emma grinned. 'And Tash always says it's one of the major life-changing events which makes people move house.'

'True. I'd appreciate it if you kept it to yourself for the moment, though. I'm not past the twelve-week stage yet and feeling superstitious.'

'Won't say a word. You'll love the Greys' cottage. What a perfect place to have babies and dogs.'

'Isn't it, though?' Millie settled against the sofa and smiled dreamily. 'I knew as soon as I saw it. Just perfect.' She looked around at the flat's little sitting room. 'I'll miss this place so much. It's been home for as long as I've known.'

'I promise Ollie and I will look after it,' Emma said. 'As long as he gets back,' she added in a whisper. 'If he gets back, I'll promise to never ever take him for granted again.'

Chapter 68

They must have fallen asleep, as Emma woke with a jolt to the sound of the flat's front door slamming shut.

'That wind is really something,' Jed said, as he came into the lounge. He brought the sharp scent of saltwater with him and his face was reddened with cold. 'I was practically blown along the prom. Hello, my love,' he added as Millie stirred sleepily. He crossed the room to kiss her. 'Oh and Emma, I think the lifeboat's about to come in. I saw it heading for the harbour. Think there was a yacht following close behind. Must have been a casualty as there's an ambulance waiting on the harbour road. Emma?'

He received no answer as Emma had shoved on her stilettoes and run out into the night.

She ran the short distance to the harbour, stopping only to take off her shoes and run barefoot the rest of the way. She lurched to a halt where there was a motley collection of people waiting outside the lifeboat station. She recognized the harbourmaster and Paul Cash, the town's only policeman. The rest was a blur of flashing lights and concerned faces.

'What happened?' she asked breathlessly.

'Yacht in trouble in the storm that blew up,' Paul answered.

'Owner broke his arm when the mast went. Family with children too, so everyone's a bit tense.'

The lifeboat was negotiating the narrow harbour entrance now and Emma could see the stricken yacht, its main mast shattered in half, following behind. She hopped from foot to foot, the cold and wet seeping into her bones and watched, impatiently, as the lifeboat was put into its cradle and pulled up the causeway by a tractor. The lifeboat crew looked identical, in their white helmets and yellow waterproofs and Emma couldn't see which was Ollie. A small child in an emergency blanket was handed to a paramedic, with its dazed-looking mother following. They disappeared into the ambulance. A man, his arm in a sling, and an older child, got into a second ambulance which had just made its way down the steep hill to the harbour.

'Where's Ollie?' Emma yelled. No one was listening; they were all too busy dealing with the emergency. She couldn't see him anywhere. Cold, of a far more sinister kind, took hold. What if he had been lost? It happened to lifeboat crew. There was a plaque inside the station detailing those men lost at sea. The list was too long. And every man had been someone's son, brother, father or husband. 'Where's Ollie?' she repeated, desperately. Tears began to fall, blurring the chaos of the night even more.

The helmsman passed her, grinning through his exhaustion. 'He's back there with Will, on the yacht. They stayed on it to motor it into the harbour. And young Ollie spotted the boy in the water. Seconds from drowning, that kid was. You should be very proud of your Oliver. He's done good tonight.'

Emma ran further along the harbour to where she could

see the yacht bobbing high on the spring tide. A crowd had gathered around, watching, as another crew member hauled Ollie up the iron ladder onto the harbour wall. They stood around him, slapping him on the back and teasing; relief that the shout had been successful making them loud and ribald. Emma ducked through and ran to him.

'Oh Ollie.' She grabbed him and put her arms around him, difficult with his bulky kit. 'I love you. I love you. I love you.'

He pushed her away a little and she could see his face was rimed with fatigue. His eyes, however, were alight with the satisfaction of having done a good night's work. 'Hi, Em,' he said, kissing her soundly. 'We've had quite the night. Where were we before we got so rudely interrupted? Oh yes, I had something to ask you.' He went down on one knee and looked up, his grin flashing white in the harbour lights. 'Will you marry me?'

Her answer got lost in the cheers and catcalls of those circled around them. She tugged him back to his feet. 'Oh, Ollie! Yes, of course I will. I'd love to marry you!' He'd just risked his life for others. She might have lost him. Forever. He'd done a very special thing tonight. And, once the adrenaline wore off, she knew he would be casual and diffident about it. She kissed him with all the love she had.

To more ribald cheers, Ollie gathered her into his arms. 'Must be mad to take you on,' he grinned. 'But it's a madness I'll gladly accept.' His kiss made her breathless. Then his face creased in concern. 'Emma, you sure you want to take *me* on? All this, I mean. It won't be much fun, sometimes, being the one who's waiting on the shore.'

'Who knows,' she said blithely. 'I might even volunteer myself. The RNLI take women, don't they?'

Ollie laughed. 'They do, but even they might not be ready for you, my love.' He looked down at her. 'You're shivering like there's no tomorrow. No wonder. You haven't got any shoes on. Come on, let's go and grab a cup of tea.' Loosening his helmet, he took it off and put it on her. Then he swept her off her feet and into his arms. Carrying her towards the warmth of the lifeboat station, they were followed by the cheering crowd.

Emma, pink-cheeked with pleasure and embarrassment, threw her arms around his newly-muscled shoulders and hid her face against his wet neck. 'I love you, Oliver Lacey. Who needs Ross Poldark? You are truly my hero.' And, as she said the words, realized they would be true forever.

PART THREE

Amy's Story

Chapter 69

An early morning sea fret stole around Amy's feet as she struggled to fit the key into the lock of the enormous double doors of the book café. Really ought to squirt some WD-40 in it, she thought, just as it unexpectedly gave way and she fell in. Switching on the outside lights, Amy peered out into the swirling mist which shrouded Berecombe harbour and hid it from view. It was cold this morning and a shiver ran down her spine. Glancing down, she dropped her bags in shock. The pumpkins, which she had spent ages carving and had arranged carefully on the outside step last night, had been destroyed! Getting closer for a better look, she saw that all three pumpkins, which she had whimsically named Mummy, Daddy and Baby Pumpkin had been stamped on. Whoever had done it hadn't even wanted to steal the things; they'd just mindlessly flattened them and made an unholy mess in front of the bookshop.

Amy stared horrified. She had spent most of the weekend taking out the pumpkin innards and carving comical faces into them. It was still only the beginning of October but she had great plans for the shop at Hallowe'en. Getting the pumpkins ready had been hard work, but fun – and it had filled yet another empty weekend. If this is what some Berecombe residents thought of her efforts, she may as well not bother. Tears prickling, she returned to the shop, stowed away her things and went to find a dustpan and brush.

Just as she was putting the pumpkin filled bags into the commercial bins at the side of the building, she heard someone open the shop door. The bell jangled; its sound cutting through the still damp air, and her heart lifted. It was far too early to be a customer, and besides, she hadn't turned the closed sign over yet. It must be Patrick. He often popped in for a chat and an early morning coffee. Hurrying round to the shop front, her heart sank back to it accustomed position when, instead of Patrick's shock of unruly black hair and his dimpled grin, she saw the figure of her mother.

Katrina Chilcombe was holding the shop door sign between her finger and thumb, as if its very touch would infect her. '"Sorry, we've closed the book for today,"' she read. '"Please come back tomorrow for more wise words."' Looking up, she saw her daughter. 'Oh there you are, Amy.' Her lips curled. 'Wouldn't a simple "closed" sign do?' Before Amy could stop her, she turned it over and read, with derision, '"Come in for a lovely read, comfortable sofas, fantastic coffee and yummy cakes." Oh really, Amy? It's hardly professional.'

'But friendly,' Amy wanted to say. 'And sets the tone for how I want The Little Book Café to feel,' but she didn't. As usual, when her mother belittled her, she remained silent. Looking down, she scuffed her shoes in a smear of pumpkin that she'd missed. It was turning into a hell of a Monday morning.

'And where have you been? The place is like the *Mary Celeste*.' Katrina sniffed. 'You really shouldn't leave the place unlocked like that. Anyone could walk in.' She swept past, leaving Amy to follow, stuttering out an explanation about what had greeted her when she'd unlocked.

Katrina turned around, her camel coat swirling around her diminutive figure in the dramatic fashion she'd hoped. 'Well, I told you this was a no-hoper. It's all very well having a business down at this end of town in the summer, but in the winter the harbour is practically deserted. It's not safe at all. Has the heating been switched on?' she added as she pulled her coat collar up to her neck. 'It's very chilly in here.'

'I haven't had a chance to put it on yet.'

Katrina looked around at the stuffed bookshelves, with their tempting selection, at the table that displayed enticing bestsellers, at the vividly-coloured children's section with its balloons and posters, at the spiral staircase leading up to the cosy reading space, and dismissed it all with a sniff. 'Oh I hate this time of year. So dreary.'

Amy couldn't agree. She loved the dark evenings and the cold crisp days. She loved piling on figure-concealing woolly layers and snuggling by a fire with a good book.

'Of course, your father and I had plans to spend the winters somewhere warm when we got older. I always liked the idea of Cyprus. English enough but with *weather*.' She said the last word with relish. 'And then your father went and ran out on us and—' Katrina's lips compressed and her cashmere covered shoulders began to shake.

Amy went to her mother and hugged her fiercely. She may be infuriating and occasionally a bully, but she had never really recovered from the divorce. When Tony Chilcombe had left them to set up home with the lissom – and very young

– Jasmine, Katrina had been left with a substantially reduced lifestyle and had returned to her hometown and a poky two-bed bungalow.

The decree absolute coincided with Amy beginning university and, once she had graduated, she'd joined her mother, a woman who had never really coped on her own. Amy had commuted to jobs in bookshops in Exeter for a while but the travelling had got too much, so when Millie Henville, owner of the newly-opened Little Book Café had offered her the job of managing the shop, she'd jumped at it.

'Oh Mum. Ssh. You've got to move on.' Amy said the first thing that came to her and patted her mother's back. 'It's been nearly ten years.'

'Move on?' Katrina shoved her daughter away with surprising force. 'What, like your father has, I suppose?' She stamped her delicately shod foot in anger and then sighed as her temper distilled into self-pity. 'Who would want a washed-up fifty-seven-year-old like me? Haven't you heard? It's all about the youth now. Oh, why don't you move back in, Amy? I'm so lonely without you. It used to be so cosy with the two of us and it's silly for you to pay rent.'

Amy had lived with her mother for a while but had felt so suffocated, she'd moved out to an attic studio deemed too tiny even for use as a holiday let. It had two windows, noisy neighbours and views over the rooftops of the old town but she had her independence. It made dealing with her mother a little more bearable. Just.

'Think it works better if we live apart, don't you?'

As usual, when her mother didn't get her own way, she went on the attack. 'I don't know why you want to live all on your own.' She sniffed again. 'After all, it's not as if you're ever going to get a man again. Not looking like a lump of lard. Not after Lee jilted you.'

Amy took in a sharp breath. Katrina often pointed out her inability to lose weight but she was rarely vindictive enough to mention the jilting at the altar by Lee Styles. 'Mum,' she said, more tears erupting. 'How could you be so cruel? Maybe that's why I don't want to live with you!'

As if sensing she'd gone too far, Katrina deflated. 'Oh my darling,' she cried, putting a conciliatory and manicured hand on her daughter's arm. She pouted a little. 'I only want you to be happy.'

'I am happy, Mum.'

'Really?' Katrina's eyes widened. She spread her arms. 'Working here? In a *shop*? It's hardly using your degree properly, and you were always such a clever girl.'

Amy had had enough. Time was getting on and she needed to get the bookshop ready for the day. 'Did you come here simply to insult me, or was there a proper reason?'

'Now now, no need to be snippy. I just popped by to tell you that I'm going away for a few days.'

Amy raised her eyes heavenwards. This was the main reason her mother had no money; she was impossibly extravagant. 'I thought you had no money?'

'Oh don't be so ridiculous, Amy. A weekend in an out of season hotel in Scarborough isn't going to break the bank.'

Amy was just about to launch into an explanation that money in had to equal money out when she heard a familiar, softly accented voice.

'Feck, it's cold this morning. Anyone around?'

Chapter 70

'Hi Patrick.' Amy smiled and blushed, aware her mother was watching them avidly.

'Amy. Hi. Couldn't see you. I'm on the early side but thought I'd treat us to a wee coffee and pastry.' He held up a bag. 'Badgered Millie into selling me two apricot Danishes. They've only just come out of the oven. Thought we could go through the spring catalogues. See what you want to stock after Christmas.'

'There's the literary festival in January too. We'd want to stock books by the writers taking part.'

'Ah, so we should.'

'Well, hello there.' Katrina put out her hand. 'Amy has kept *you* very quiet.'

'Not much chance of keeping me quiet,' Patrick said affably. 'Patrick Carroll.' He shook her hand. 'Pleased to meet you.'

'This is my mother, Patrick,' Amy supplied, as Katrina raised her immaculate brows in a silent demand to be introduced.

'As Amy is making such a mess of introducing us, I'll finish the task. I'm Katrina Chilcombe.' She smiled, showing small white teeth. 'How absolutely delightful to meet you. Are you Amy's boss?'

Amy shifted, irritable that her mother should assume, simply because Patrick was a man and older, that he should be her superior.

'Ah sure. I just help out now and again.' Patrick gave Amy a warm look. 'It's your daughter here who's the one in charge and a fine job she does of it too.'

Katrina simpered. 'Really? How very kind of you to say so. And is that an Irish accent I can hear? So terribly charming.'

Patrick gave a modest nod but didn't say anything.

'Mum, I've got to get on. I haven't done anything this morning yet, apart from clean up.'

Katrina made a great show of examining her watch. 'Goodness, yes. I must away. Can't be late for Suki.' She patted her hair. 'Having my hair done before my little holiday,' she said for Patrick's benefit.

'Now, why would you, when doesn't it already look grand?'

'Oh,' Katrina giggled. 'It's true then, the Irish *are* charming.' She caught Amy's glare. 'Right, off then.' Reaching up to air kiss her daughter, she trilled, 'Bye then both. Lovely to have met you, Patrick.' Then she was gone, leaving a Dior-scented whirl in her wake.

'You're not at all like her,' was Patrick's only comment.

'Apparently I take after my father.' Amy caught Patrick's look. 'Thank God.'

He laughed and held up the paper bag again. 'Now, come on, I can't function without coffee at this unearthly hour. Let's eat breakfast and you can tell me why you're running so late.'

Over their coffee and pastries, eaten at one of the scrubbed pine tables in the café end of the bookshop, Amy filled Patrick in on what she had found when she'd opened up that morning.

His blue eyes widened over the rim of his mug. 'That's a shame. I remember you saying you were going to carve them when I came by on Friday.'

'It doesn't make me feel very secure down at this end of town when the days are so short, to be honest,' Amy said, thinking about what her mother had pointed out about the harbour part of town being deserted off season.

'It'll just be kids, Amy. Bored I expect. And sure, isn't the biggest crime around here the theft of the traffic cones from the one way system? Bet that's kids too. A gang of lads thinking they're the big "I Am."'

'A gang?' Amy's voice trembled. 'In Berecombe?'

Patrick put his hand over hers. 'Sure, they'll just be lads, no older than ten or twelve.' Patrick pulled a face. 'Think we can safely assume they're not blessed with imagination. They'll claim there's nothing else for them to do.'

Amy's fears deflated a little. 'You'd think Paul Cash has got enough on his plate,' she said, referring to the town's only policeman. 'What with Tash's court case looming.'

'Is that still happening?'

Amy nodded. 'Poor woman can't move on until it's all sorted.'

'So this Adrian, this ex of hers is up for rape, is that your man?'

'Yes. He did all sorts of horrible things to Tash too but she got out in time, before it escalated. All sorts of – coercive, is that the right term? – behaviour.'

Patrick scowled. 'Can't get my head round men who treat

women like that. And you'd never know, from looking at her, that there was anything wrong in her life. Always seems so in control.'

Amy gathered their mugs and plates. 'Well, she likes to keep things private, does Tash. I'm always a bit scared of her, to be honest. Sharp tongue.'

'Maybe she's had to be like that to survive with this Adrian fella?'

'Maybe. I hadn't thought of it like that. She put their breakfast things on a tray. I'll wash these up and then perhaps we can have a look through the spring catalogue.'

'Grand.' Patrick leaned back on his chair and looped his hands around the back of his head. 'And Amy, if you like, I can come and work in here for a few hours a day. To keep you company and keep the wee beasties away,' he added, casually.

Amy turned, the tray still in her hands. The thought of having Patrick in the bookshop for most of the day was almost too much to contemplate. His suggestion was the best thing that had happened all morning. Admittedly, there had been little competition. 'Would you?' she breathed, trying to keep the love out of her voice. 'Would you really?'

'Of course. That's if you don't mind me hogging the internet and scribbling at something in some dark corner. Oh,' he added, as he warmed to his theme. 'And I need constant refuelling. A writer runs on coffee and carbohydrates, at least this one does. It's pure selfishness on my part. It means I don't have far to go to get at Millie's lemon drizzle.'

As well as owning the bookshop, Millie and her husband, Jed, also ran the café next door.

'Wouldn't it interfere with the next book?'

He paused, appearing to decide what to say. 'Ah, no real deadline for the next and I'm still at the planning and ideas stage, so I can work anywhere that'll have me. If I get here about three I can hang around when it goes dark and you won't have to lock up on your own.' He looked about him, at the still empty shop. 'Not sure how much trade there'll be and you haven't got many talks or children's events on this month, have you?'

Amy shook her head. 'One or two a week until we're nearer Hallowe'en.' She blushed. 'Plus your book signing, of course. I really would love the company. Have to confess to feeling a bit spooked lately. Oh Patrick, it's so terribly kind of you.'

'No problem, darlin'. I like it in here. I like the company too.' His eyes twinkled. 'Now,' he nodded to the tray still in Amy's hands. 'A coffee refill is required and we'll get down to this catalogue.'

Amy beamed. 'Right away!'

Chapter 71

Patrick was as good as his word. He arrived just as the light was beginning to fade from the sky, the white lights along the seaside promenade flickering on to guide his way. He'd often pick up something sweet from Millie's café on the way and would order Amy to sit down and eat and drink, despite her half-hearted protest that she was supposed to be dieting.

Today was no exception. Amy had been rushed off her feet all day and had had no time to dwell on any dark shadows lurking malevolently in the corners. She'd had the order of Christmas stock in and had taken delivery of thirty boxes of books. Patrick had arrived to help with stacking them out of the way and had then taken his now usual seat at the table nearest the door so he could keep an eye out. She was in the middle of unpacking them when the doorbell jangled and Tash flew in, immaculately dressed as usual. Amy never understood how Tash did a full day's work as an estate agent teetering on sky-high stilettos and dressed in a tight skirt suit.

Amy was always a little wary around her. Lee, her ex-fiancé, had been Tash's boyfriend previously and it always made Amy feel awkward. She didn't really know why; Lee had only gone out with Tash for a short while. Then, having sent Amy a text on the morning of the wedding, baldly stating that he couldn't marry her, Lee had left Berecombe to join the navy. He hadn't even managed the text properly – it had arrived too late to stop her turning up at the church. Then he disappeared from their lives, taking whatever confidence Amy had, with him.

'Oh Amy, just the person,' Tash cried. 'Mum and Dad are due back from Portugal at the weekend and I've completely forgotten it's Mum's birthday. I thought you might have a book?'

Tash looked so unexpectedly panicked that Amy laughed. 'We've got one or two.'

Tash laughed too. 'So I can see.' Her brows knitted as she took in the pile of boxes. 'Had a delivery?'

'It's all the Christmas books I ordered.' Amy chewed her lip. 'To be honest, I'm worried I've gone a bit overboard. The shop's been like death lately.'

'Oh, don't worry about that. Berecombe always goes quiet after the carnival, then we get an onslaught of tourists on the run up to half term. It'll pick up, and most of that lot will be pre-ordered Christmas presents or on sale or return, won't they?'

'Some.'

'And I love your new postcard and greetings card selection. That should do well in the run up to Christmas.'

'Yes, I hope so, although I'm holding off from putting out anything Christmassy until after Hallowe'en. Some are prints by local artists. Something a little different, I think. The birthday cards are particularly nice. You'll be wanting one of those, I expect?'

Tash looked blank.

'For your mother? For her birthday?'

Tash slapped a hand to her dark fringe. 'Oh my, yes. A card. How could I have forgotten? I never forget Mum's birthday.'

'Well, you've had a busy few months,' Amy put in, gently.

'You can say that again,' Tash said, with feeling. 'And the autumn rush hasn't helped. Think the world and his wife are trying to buy a house in Berecombe. Work's mad! Doesn't help that we're back to just Emma and me.'

'No Leona anymore?' Leona had worked with Emma and Tash at Hughes and Widrow for a few weeks. 'Didn't she work out?'

'You could say that. Didn't you know? She's been transferred to the Bristol branch. She drove Emma mad so it's no great loss but there's still the same amount of work to do. I'm hoping head office will give us an apprentice. It'll be good experience for Emma to train someone up.'

'Oh, she'd enjoy that.'

Tash laughed again. 'Possibly too much! Now books.' She glanced at the phone in her hand. 'I haven't got long, I'm in between appointments.'

'What's she into? Your mother, I mean. Does she read much? Fiction or non-fiction?'

Tash grimaced. 'She doesn't read much at all, to be honest. Holiday reading mostly.' Tash screwed up her face with the effort of thinking. 'She likes her golf.'

'I've some interesting books on golfing techniques. How to improve your game, the psychological approach to winning, that sort of thing.'

'Oh I don't know.' Tash blew her fringe in frustration. 'Doesn't sound quite right.'

331

'She likes dogs, doesn't she?'

'Well, she's besotted with Benji.'

Amy tapped her biro on her teeth, thinking. 'I might have just the thing.' She led Tash to a display of coffee table books. 'How is Benji? Weren't you looking after him for your mum?'

'Living the high life with Kit's mother. Think Marianne spoils him more than my mother ever could.' Tash grinned. 'Westies put on weight so quickly. When I was taking him running, I'd got him looking quite sleek but he's back to being fat and lazy again now.'

Amy's lips compressed. As someone who easily put on weight, she sympathized with the little dog. Trying not to eye up Tash's reed-thin figure too covetously, she picked up a large book and said, 'I've just put this one out, actually. It came in with the new stock. More of a book to glance through and leave somewhere to impress visitors. A real coffee table job.'

'Sounds like my mum.' Tash took it off her. 'It weighs a ton! What is it?'

'A compendium of facts and figures about dogs. More fun than informative but the photographs are lovely. And, of course, it's got a lovely little Westie on the front cover.'

'Perfect,' Tash declared, without hesitation. 'I'll take it. I usually get her some of her favourite perfume but she'll be picking some up at Duty Free and this will make a nice change. Thanks Amy. Job done.'

'If you go and choose a card, I'll get it gift wrapped and you can pick it all up at book group. You are coming tonight, aren't you?' She led Tash back to the till.

Tash dashed over to the greeting cards, picked one quickly and slapped it on the counter, along with her credit card.

'Thanks Amy. You're a lifesaver. And yes, of course I'll be at book group. Wouldn't miss it for the world. Kit will be there too,' she added, referring to her boyfriend. She took her credit card back and slipped into her bag. 'After all, since that's where Kit and I met, we owe the group a lot.' She blushed a little. 'And we're picking this month's new book tonight, aren't we?' She pulled a face and added sarcastically, 'That's always fun.'

Amy laughed. 'I know, it always takes us an age. But it might be a little easier this time.' She leaned forward and said, conspiratorially, 'There's a rumour Biddy won't be able to come. Think she's in London having deep discussions about the erotic novel she's just written.'

'Thank the Lord! I love the woman but sometimes life is a whole lot simpler without her.'

'Not to mention quieter.'

'Deffo, as Emma would say.' Tash paused before running out. 'Thanks Amy. I mean it. Great book advice and fantastic service.'

The two women smiled at one another, feeling a spark of true friendship for the first time.

'You're welcome, Tash. See you tonight.'

'You betcha.'

Chapter 72

Patrick stayed on after Amy shut the shop and helped her get ready for the book group. She was perfectly capable of organising the seating on the mezzanine level and putting out the trays of wine and glasses but, with two of them, it took half the time and everything was ready far too early.

'Shall we get ourselves to the Old Harbour and grab something to eat?' he suggested at six thirty.

Amy's tummy rumbled in response. She hadn't eaten anything since a quick coffee and slice of Millie's Bakewell tart at three. Looking at her friend, who had become such an important part of her life since he'd joined the book group she'd started in August, she realized two things: one, she knew next to nothing about him, and two, she was completely and irrevocably in love with him. Blushing a little, she said, 'Great idea.'

They sat in a corner table next to the roaring fire. The pub, which in summer was overrun with tourists, was quieter in the autumn. The only people in there were a few locals downing a swift pint before the journey home. Old Davey Pascoe was holding court at the bar, drinking cider and boasting to anyone who would listen about how well his granddaughter, Eleri, was doing at running the newly-renovated Henville Hotel.

Patrick grinned as he set down their drinks. 'Think he's the proud granddaddy. You been yet? Food is supposed to be good, and they do a mean cocktail, so I've heard.'

Amy took a sip of her white wine. 'The Henville? No I haven't been. Emma and her boyfriend Ollie have. Emma said it was lovely.' Amy wrinkled her nose. 'Lush, I think was the word she used. Bit out of my price range, I'm afraid.'

'Well, maybe we should take a look-see one night? Now, what do you fancy tonight?' Patrick fished out a pair of steel-framed specs from his jacket pocket and peered at the chalk board. 'Too cold for a crab salad. Think it'll be steak for me. Nice and bloody.'

Amy was still processing what he'd said about them going to the Henville. Did he mean on a date? He'd said it so casually though. He must mean as just friends. But was the Henville the sort of place you went to as just friends? Emma had said it was pretty exclusive. Patrick treated her with thoughtfulness and was very kind but his vivid blue eyes twinkled at everyone and he treated one and all to liberal doses of his Irish charm. She'd never detected any special favours coming in her direction. She was as sure as she could be – and this was with a painful lurch of the heart – that he regarded her as a friend.

'Amy?'

She blinked, aware he was still waiting for an answer. 'Fish and chips,' she blurted out, without really considering the menu. Bugger it. The diet would have to be put on hold again. Crab salad was what she should have gone for but Patrick had leaped up and was at the bar, ordering their food before she could tell him she'd changed her mind. She admired the view of his back as he chatted to the barmaid. He wasn't overly tall but was compactly built, with broad shoulders tapering to narrow hips and a neat bum covered snugly in indigo denim. Amy blushed again. She shouldn't be thinking about his bottom. Instead, she focused on the effect he was having on the barmaid. She was looking like a rabbit in the headlights in the face of his charm offensive. He's the same with everyone he meets, she thought, sadly. He bestowed no special treatment her way. She mustered a smile as he returned to the table and picked up his pint.

'I suppose you drink Guinness at home?' Amy could have kicked herself. What a thing to say! Why couldn't she behave naturally with him? I need to take lessons in flirting from Emma, she thought. The entire town loved Tash's work colleague, she got on with everyone.

Patrick didn't take offence. 'Ah sure, tis a wee drop of the black stuff for me every time,' he said, in an exaggerated Irish brogue.

'Sorry. That was naff.' Amy blushed to her roots.

'It was a bit. But don't worry yourself.'

'I don't know much about you really,' Amy said, realizing that apart from knowing his novels, she didn't know very much at all; she didn't even know where in Ireland he was from.

'Not much to tell. Born and raised in a little seaside village near Dublin. Went to university. Came over here to lecture in creative writing and that's about it.'

From the way his eyes clouded, Amy was pretty sure that

was definitely not all there was but she didn't press the point. 'What drew you to Berecombe?'

'I like living by the sea. As I said, I grew up by it.'

'Is your home town like Berecombe?'

He laughed. 'It's a lot flatter and sure, it's fine if you like the golf.'

'Golf?'

'Ah sure, Portmarnock is one big golf course. And a grand beach too. The Velvet Strand it's called. But it's all a lot flatter than Devon.'

Amy resolved to google Portmarnock as soon as she got home. 'Sounds lovely. But I suppose you lived in Dublin?' Amy couldn't imagine this urbane, cultured man not wanting to live in Ireland's capital.

'I did. For a bit. Ah look, here's the food.' He nodded. 'Just in time, darlin',' he said to the barmaid. 'We're starving here.'

She put the food down carefully. 'Here you go then, one steak, rare, and fish and chips.' Her face dimpled, prettily. 'Just give me a shout if you need anything and I'll be right over.'

'I bet you will,' Amy thought, mutinously and speared a chip with unnecessary force.

Chapter 73

Amy proudly surveyed her book group. They had gathered, as usual, on the mezzanine level of the bookshop and were sitting against the huge double-height windows. It was dark outside and rain spattered intermittently against the glass. The sumptuous sunsets of August and September had long gone; autumn was rushing into winter with unnecessary haste. It was cosy up here though. Amy had made sure the leather sofas were sprinkled with generous amounts of soft cushions, and she had – now the weather had turned damp and chilly – put some colourful throws out. Her mother, never one to hold back an opinion, had scoffed and claimed the soft furnishings would be ruined within the month. They hadn't been. As Amy had hoped, customers appreciated the welcoming reading area and had taken care of it. She was holding onto this small triumph in the face of her mother's derision. It was a tiny piece of armour in the defence of what was left of her self-esteem.

The book group, taking advantage of the time before the meeting started properly, were catching up with one another and sipping the excellent wine that Millie provided. Amy watched Tash and Emma giggle over something with Tash's boyfriend, Kit. Marti was holding court in a corner, her friends gazing at her open-mouthed in admiration. Amy smiled. She knew Marti was Tash's arch-enemy and it was patently obvious the woman didn't always read the group's book choice but she never missed a meeting and had always been supportive – in her own way.

The book group was the first thing Amy had started up when she began managing the shop and it was the thing she was most proud of. Her heart leapt as Patrick appeared at the top of the spiral stairs which led up from the main shop floor. He put up a hand in greeting before sliding in next to Kit. Patrick had been the first person to enquire about the group and one of the first to arrive at the inaugural meeting back in August. She'd never forgotten the effect he'd had when he'd shaken her hand and introduced himself. She'd been mesmerized by eyes the colour of the sea on a summer's day, and by his wide smile. Her attraction to him had grown, almost without her noticing, over the past weeks. As well as the simple physical attraction, his innate kindness and wicked sense of humour soon added to his irresistible appeal. When he'd let slip he was a writer, she'd ordered his entire backlist and had only just finished his last novel. His work was dizzyingly good; she could see why he frequently topped the *Sunday Times* bestseller list. It was a canny mix of the readable and the literary and she'd stayed up late into the night to read the latest instalment of the history of an Irish family through the decades. She would probably have been safe, had her attraction to him been just physical and that he displayed such kindness, but she was a goner when a man had intelligence too. Covertly watching him now, as he chatted to Kit, she felt a blush steal over her cheeks. She loved him so much. And was one hundred per cent sure she was in the friend zone.

After telling her only scant details of his life in Ireland – she was sure there was more to it – during their pub meal, Patrick, while devouring his steak, had deftly turned the questioning back on her. Amy had found herself telling him all about her parents' divorce and how it had led to her mother's return to Berecombe.

'I was headed for Berecombe Comp but then Dad got this amazing job in Singapore so we all decamped. Big company house, swimming pool. I went to a private girls' school. Mum was in heaven. Then Dad met Jasmine and it all went pear-shaped. Mum was in a bit of a state after the divorce so I ended coming back here too.'

'I suppose your mother wanted folk around who she knew.'

'Something like that.' Having blurted it all out, Amy felt she'd said enough. She looked longingly at the desserts chalked up on the blackboard. 'Do you think we've got time for a pudding?' Patrick had agreed and, from then on, any conversation had centred on food.

Amy gave herself a little shake back to the here and now. If she didn't get the meeting started, they'd never have time to discuss last month's book and choose a new one for October. 'Shall we get started?' she said, clapping her hands to get their attention. 'What did everyone think of our last book, *Demelza?*'

Chapter 74

The meeting slipped along effortlessly. Maybe it was because the book group – after several gatherings – had settled into a routine, or maybe it was the absence of its most troublesome member, the pensioner with a past, Biddy Roulestone.

'So, you were right about Biddy not being here.' Tash said to Amy, as they gathered around the coffee and snacks Millie was putting out. 'It's not like her to miss out on anything going on in town, though.'

Amy grinned into her coffee. 'Must still be in London.'

'It's been a pain in the proverbial, to be honest. We're trying to finalise things on her purchase of the Morrisons' bungalow and now she's gone AWOL. Not even answering her phone and Arthur won't commit himself to anything without his wife's approval.'

'Well, she never makes life easy for anyone,' Amy replied, enjoying this new relaxed friendship with Tash. 'Wonder if she's really talking to publishers?'

Emma bounced up to them and caught the tail end of their conversation. 'You talking about my esteemed client? She's in meetings with a publisher. One of the big five, allegedly.'

'Oh no.' Amy paled. 'So she's serious about getting her erotica published?'

'Deffo. I can't wait to read it, personally. Reckon it'll be the new *Fifty Shades*. Maybe we can read it at book group?' Emma added, mischievously.

'Over my dead body,' Amy said, with feeling. They all laughed.

'It's amazing, isn't it,' Tash put in. 'How some people can dominate any situation even in their absence? Here we are, without a Biddy in sight and we still end up discussing her. One of life's one-offs.'

'Poor Arthur,' they chorused and laughed again.

'So, Emma,' Amy asked, as Tash went off to refill her coffee cup. 'I hear you're all set to move into Millie's flat over the café once she and Jed have bought their cottage.' Millie and Jed Henville were buying an idyllic thatched cottage in a valley just out of town.

Emma deflated. 'That was the plan.'

'What's happened?'

'Mum is really unhappy working for Suki at Klassy Kutz.'

Amy shuddered. 'I know I sound a grammar snob but I've always hated that name, the spelling especially.'

Emma sighed. 'The spelling of the salon name is the last of Mum's problems. Suki keeps making Mum do longer and longer hours and with my darling little bro always in trouble at school, it's wearing her out.'

'It's where my mother gets her hair cut.' Amy thought back to her mother's early morning visit on the way to the hairdresser's. 'In fact, she popped into the shop on the way to a hair appointment this morning at some unearthly hour. I did wonder why she had one so early.'

'Suki claims it's what her clients want. She's got Mum starting at seven now and she does two late nights on top.'

Amy sipped her wine thoughtfully. 'I suppose people want appointments to fit around their busy lives,' she said, diplomatically, wondering just what her mother had to fill her life so much that she needed a hair appointment at eight in the morning. 'Why does that affect you moving out? I thought you and Ollie were desperate to get a place of your own?'

Emma nodded. 'We are. And I mean desperate. You should see the state Stevie leaves the bathroom in. And the stink!' She rolled her eyes.

'I'm an only child and went to a girls' school so wouldn't know.' Amy hazarded a guess; 'I suppose boys of thirteen smell a bit sweaty?'

'Oh, it's not the body odour,' Emma said robustly. 'It's the *deodorant*. Stevie has the hots for a girl in his French class. Every morning he sprays himself from top to toe and probably in other unmentionable places with this lethal-smelling stuff and doesn't bother to even think about opening a window. I go in and nearly pass out from the noxious fumes. Dad used to have an old gas mask from world war two knocking about. I'm seriously thinking of putting it to use.'

'Oh Emma,' Amy said, trying not to laugh. 'Sounds like grounds to leave to me. So why are you hesitating?'

'As well as Mum having a lot on her plate and threatening to leave the salon, Dad's job isn't looking good. There are rumours of redundancies at the vacuum cleaner factory. If that happens, they'll need my wage to help out. And, if Mum leaves Suki's, I'll be the only wage-earner. Plus I'm really trying to do more of the housework to give Mum a break. Trouble is,' Emma added, gloomily, 'my ironing isn't up to Mum's standards and she just tuts and does it all again.'

Amy wanted to put an arm around Emma. She looked so forlorn. Struggling to find something comforting to say, she settled with the inadequate, 'I'm sorry to hear that. I hope something works out.'

'Me too, Amy. Me too.' Emma brightened a little. 'Sorry for going on. Thanks for listening though, you're a really good listener.'

It had been said before. Amy sometimes wondered if the reason she listened rather than revealed something of herself was because she felt she hadn't anything of interest to say. 'Shall we get another drink? Then I suppose we ought to get down to the next bit of the meeting. We've got to decide on the next book.'

'In that case, I'll need fuel. Did I spot cupcakes?'

'Yes.' Amy laughed. 'Millie has been practising for our Hallowe'en party. She's done some iced with a spider web pattern. They're really sweet. In both senses of the word.'

'Lush,' Emma said. 'Gotta get me some of those bad boys.' She went off to find a sugar fix, her troubles temporarily forgotten.

Chapter 75

'Can I make a suggestion, Amy?' Millie said. 'People are so busy during December, do you think we could miss that meeting out?'

'Actually,' Marti raised a bejewelled hand. 'Could I add to that suggestion and say November's not good for me, either. I'm off to Mauritius for quite some time over November and December.' She waggled her head in mock humility and Amy heard Tash, in the seat next to her, grind her teeth. 'I simply must have some sunshine in November or I wither away.'

Millie looked stricken. 'I'm so sorry Amy, I didn't mean to cause a problem.' She gave a Marti a piercing look. 'I only suggested missing out December.'

'Yes and we can't cancel a whole meeting just because one member can't make it,' Tash put in. 'Or we'd never meet up at all.'

Amy could feel the familiar feeling of panic take over her. She was in danger of losing control of the group. Again. She thought rapidly. She really wanted to keep the group going. It was about her only social life, for one thing. But, if Marti didn't come, neither would her group of friends. They followed the woman devotedly although she'd never fathomed out why.

She'd never heard them utter a word in opposition to Marti and they all nodded vehemently whenever she uttered anything vaguely interesting. But they did constitute a large section of the group. And besides, they'd had two meetings a month since August. She really couldn't see the group being in danger of losing momentum if they had a break.

'I don't see missing out November and December being a problem,' she began slowly, still thinking it through as she spoke. 'Why don't we meet again in mid-January? It'll give us all a breather and we can return refreshed in the new year. The days will be lengthening by then too.' She glanced outside as a gobbet of rain spat at the huge windows. 'It's never much fun having to turf yourself out on these cold dark nights. I hope everyone will feel able to come to the Hallowe'en party at the end of the month, though?'

There was a murmur of agreement then Emma piped up. 'Tell you what, if some of us can't go a few weeks without some booky talk, why don't we meet in the pub? Have a less formal chat over a drink?'

'Well, I'm not sure that's a good idea, Emma,' Marti said, looking put out.

'But if you're not in the country, you can't really object to us meeting up?' Tash said sweetly. 'And if you or any of your friends are around when we do meet up, you're more than welcome to come along.'

'I simply don't want the group to split into...' Marti paused, searching for the right word. 'Factions.'

'It's not,' Tash countered. 'It's just a way of keeping the social aspect of the group going.' She appealed to the others. 'And that's one of the things we really like about the group, don't we?'

Amy saw Kit nudge his girlfriend to stop talking before she dug the hole any deeper. She needed to take control before the group really did disintegrate. The animosity between Tash and Marti bubbled underneath every meeting and had done so since the first one. 'I think that's a good compromise,' she said quickly. 'We next meet properly in January. As you've said, Marti, it's unlikely you can make November and Millie, you're quite right, we all have so much on in December. And, if anyone is free and fancies meeting up on a less formal basis, we can go to the Old Harbour, as Emma has suggested. It's quieter out of season than the Lion on the High Street.' Before anyone could object, or put forward another idea to cloud the issue further, she added, 'Perhaps we could bring along a book we've enjoyed, talk about it a little and swap?'

'Great idea, Amy,' Emma said, eagerly. 'We could put the emphasis on reading just for fun.' She went pink. 'I mean, I've loved the books we've discussed but sometimes isn't it nice to just read for the sheer pleasure?'

'Yes, something frothy,' Tash said.

Marti bridled. She took in a great sniff. 'Well, personally I always read to improve myself.'

Laughter rippled around the room. Marti was suspected of never reading any of the books. It didn't, however, stop her expounding on the merits of the text at length.

'Really?' Tash said, in acid tones. 'You must tell me, sometime, how the books we've read have improved you.'

Amy felt the meeting begin to swerve out of control again.

'Genius,' Patrick said suddenly. He'd remained silent until this point. 'The whole thing's genius. This way, we can keep things ticking over until we start again next year. And now, can *I* make a suggestion?'

Amy's heart sank. She thought she'd just sorted everything out. Surely she could have relied on Patrick for support.

'As we're not reconvening until January, could we not read *A Christmas Carol?* A bit of Dickens, nice and spooky for the month of Hallowe'en and it'll get us in the mood for Christmas, so it will.'

'Oh Dickens!' Marti cried. 'Now that's who I call a writer.' She clapped her hands together. 'One of my absolute favourites. Such a towering genius.'

'Oh, what have you read?' Tash asked, innocently.

'Well,' Marti blustered. 'There's the one about the knitters or something isn't there? And there was one adapted for television that I enjoyed tremendously.'

'Oh yes, the knitters. The women who knit, now where was it,' Tash frowned, pretending to remember the details. 'At the doors of the Old Bailey, wasn't it?' She winked at Emma, and Amy could see they were enjoying the joke at Marti's expense.

'That's the one,' Marti sighed in triumph. 'Such a powerful scene. *From Here to Eternity*, I think it was called.'

Amy could see Tash biting her lip to suppress her giggles at Marti's ignorance and, before she could goad the poor woman any further, she intervened. 'Right, that's settled, we read *A Christmas Carol* this month, meet once more to discuss it, enjoy the Hallowe'en party and meet up when we can in the period before January. Sorted.' She said this all in one sentence. Stopping to take a breath, she cast a look at Patrick. 'Thank you,' she mouthed, hoping the love she had for him didn't radiate out with too much ferocity and kill him on the spot.

As she stood at the shop door saying goodnight to the departing book group members, Amy was aware that Patrick remained at her side. She handed over Tash's gift-wrapped book and said, 'It was very wicked of you to tease Marti like that.'

Tash looked chastened. 'Sorry Amy but I can't resist, especially when she's on one of her, "Isn't literature the most marvellous thing," rants. I wouldn't mind so much if she wasn't such a book snob.' She took the book off her. 'Thanks for this. I'm sure Mum will love it.'

Emma joined them, overhearing the conversation. 'Marti'll have a fit when she hears what the working title of Biddy's erotic novel is.'

'What is it?' asked Patrick, Amy and Tash as one.

'Last thing I heard it was *A Tale of Two Titties*.'

'Go Biddy,' Amy said through the laughter. 'You've got to hand it to the woman.' Emma waved goodnight and followed Tash, who was hand in hand with Kit, on the promenade. Amy looked out into the night after them and blew out an enormous breath. It puffed out into the frigid air.

'That's one big sigh,' Patrick said.

'Even without our resident OAP troublemaker, I still have difficulty keeping the meeting in order.'

'You did a grand job,' he exclaimed. 'Sure, it's a thankless task in there some nights. And it's not like a work meeting; they're there for pleasure. You can't play the three-line whip on them.'

'More's the pity,' Amy replied, with feeling. Then she brightened and added, 'Although I think Biddy would rather like a whipping.'

'I think you could be right there,' Patrick said, in mock serious tones. 'However, I, for one, do not want to pursue that line of thought.' He shuddered. 'Now I can't get the image out of my brain!' He held out his arm in chivalrous fashion. 'Can I walk you home, this dark night?'

Amy glanced into the darkness stealing around the corner of the bookshop and shivered. 'Oh Patrick, that would be lovely.' She locked up, checked three times that the door was secured and then turned and put her hand through his arm. She gazed up at his profile. Is there anything so painful as unrequited love, she wondered, feeling the familiar longing for him shoot through her. Stamping on the accompanying pain, she contented herself with hugging his arm to her.

Chapter 76

The last evening class came around far too quickly. It had been a coup to get funding for the short course of four lessons and Amy had been proud to offer them at the book café. The outreach literary study for beginners had been popular, and charismatic tutor Joel Dillon had been even more so. She'd been bitterly disappointed to learn that Joel had, out of the blue, taken an unexpected sabbatical year and had gone to live in the midlands.

'Oh it's such a shame,' she said to Patrick, as she sank down on one of the bright green easy chairs in the children's section, worry etched onto her face. 'It means he can't lead the final session. The group will feel so let down. It's such short notice too, I can't think who could do it instead. It would have been so nice to finish off the sessions and bring it all to a satisfying conclusion. Joel was so popular as well.' She stared hopelessly at the copy of *The Gruffalo* that she was supposed to be putting on display.

'I think that might have been the problem,' Patrick said wryly. He put a mug of coffee on the floor next to her. It was four thirty in the afternoon and trade, although brisk earlier in the day, had tailed off now the October chill clung dankly to the harbour end of town. 'There you go. In your favourite *Persuasion* mug too.'

'Thanks Patrick. You're a star.' Amy positioned the book in its place next to an arrangement of posters tacked onto a background of fake grass.

Patrick perched on a chair upholstered in sky blue. Sipping his own coffee he said, 'That's looking good. I like the plastic grass stuff.'

'Thanks. I'm trying to get something up for the next story-telling session. *The Gruffalo* always goes down well with the little ones.'

'It does when *you* read it to them.'

Amy felt a blush creep treacherously over her face. She couldn't cope when Patrick was nice to her. A peculiar mixture of pleasure and pain consumed her. And, as he was nice to her all of the time, it was reaching danger point. To hide her confusion she picked up her coffee and shoved her pinkened nose in the mug. Something Patrick had said before his compliment now struck her as odd. Putting the mug back down and trying not to long for a biscuit to go with it, she asked, 'What did you mean about Joel?'

'You mean about him being popular?'

Amy nodded.

Patrick scrubbed a hand over his stubble. He pulled a face. 'Ah now, how to put it. He's been a good friend to me,' he paused, 'and I don't like to criticise, but he likes the ladies, does Joel.'

'Well, that's okay, isn't it?'

He gave her a rueful look. 'Not if they're students and he's got a fiancée.'

354

'Oh.' Amy considered what Patrick implied. '*Oh*,' she repeated, as the truth hit her. She blushed anew. 'But it's not actually illegal is it? It's not as if they're children. All students at uni are over eighteen.' She wrinkled her nose. It was all a bit sordid and she was disappointed in Joel.

'Not illegal, no. Not strictly speaking. Frowned upon though. And frowned upon enough for the university to ask him to take this year off or lose his job.'

'Goodness.'

Patrick laughed.

'What are you laughing at? What have I said?' She glared at him indignantly.

'You haven't said anything, my darlin'. You're such an innocent.'

Amy stuck her bottom lip out in a way her mother always disapproved of. 'I'm not innocent,' she protested, not really knowing what he was getting at.

'Good.' The subject seemed closed as he went on to say, 'Why don't you lead the last session? You've a degree in English Lit, haven't you?'

'Me?' Amy shuddered. 'Oh no, I couldn't. What stand up in front of all those people, in front of *Biddy* and teach a lesson?' She shook her head vehemently, her honey-blonde hair flicking out as she did.

'But you'll face a gaggle of three year olds?'

'That's different!'

'Some would say harder.'

'Are you laughing at me again?'

'No, no, I wouldn't dream of it. Just that reading a story to wriggling pre-schoolers isn't my idea of fun. Sure, I'd rather face the adults.'

'Even Biddy Roulestone?'

'Well, every man has his limit.' Patrick smiled at her, his vivid blue eyes wrinkling up in a way Amy found irresistible. 'So, do I take it you want me to teach the final session?'

'Oh, Patrick,' Amy breathed. 'That would be marvellous!'

They spent the next hour discussing the content of the session and decided to focus on women and great literature. It said a lot about Patrick that he wanted to spotlight the likes of the Brontës, Elizabeth Gaskell and Jane Austen. It said equally as much about Joel that he had ignored all women writers.

'And shall I finish up with some Wendy Cope?' 'Good, witty stuff to finish the course off on a high.'

'Unless Biddy offers to read from *A Tale of Two Titties*.'

He shrugged. 'Unless she decides to do that, love her.'

'Thank you so much Patrick. I seem to have spent all afternoon thanking you. You keep me supplied with coffee, you keep me company in the shop and now you've saved the literary course. I owe you.'

'Ah sure, wouldn't anyone do the same if they could, for a friend?'

Amy bit her lip. The friend word again. Much as he put himself out for her which he did on a regular basis, it was only because he saw her as a friend. She felt something shrivel and die a little inside. Trying not to reveal how hurt she was, she gabbled out, 'And thank you for staying and helping me lock up every night. I'm not usually such a wimp but even before the pumpkin incident, I've felt spooked here lately. I don't know why. I didn't feel like this in the summer.'

Patrick gave her a keen look. 'Has anything else happened?'

Amy shook her head. 'Nothing. Well, nothing concrete. Sometimes I feel like someone is watching me but no, nothing else has happened. It's probably a surfeit of imagination, my mother always said it's one of my faults. Too much time with my nose stuck in a book, she moans.' She stuck her chin out. 'I might even put out some more pumpkins as a gesture of defiance. How dare a few vandals spoil the fun!'

'That's my girl. Speaking of locking up, have you seen the time? Come on my darlin' let's get going home.' He held out a hand and Amy took it.

Not wanting to reveal how heavy she was, she half jumped up at the same time as he pulled. It resulted in them standing nearly nose to nose. Amy was so close she could see the flecks of green in his summer-blue eyes and the dusting of freckles on his pale skin. He had red lights in his dark curls and his mouth was full-lipped and kissable. How she wished she could kiss him. But a kiss would spell the death of their friendship and she valued it too much to risk it. She watched as Patrick's pupils dilated until his eyes darkened to the colour of a December sea-storm and then he released her so suddenly she almost fell back.

'Come on,' he said, almost curtly. 'Let's go.'

Chapter 77

Patrick in his role of tutor, was of course, spellbinding. After the first rush of disappointment, the students soon became enthralled in his session on women writers. His twinkly demeanour and soft Irish accent helped.

'Amy, that was fab,' Emma said, at the break. 'Do you know I hadn't realized until Patrick began this evening that Joel had completely ignored all the great female writers. I mean, come on, how could he have not mentioned Jane Austen? She even set *Persuasion* in Lyme and that's just along the coast. I've often jumped off the Granny's Teeth steps hoping a Captain Wentworth would rescue me.' She sipped her wine. 'It's been really good tonight and a fantastic end to the course. I haven't missed Joel one bit.'

'Good, I'm so relieved,' Amy said, gratified. 'Do I take it you weren't a huge fan of Joel's?'

Emma drank some more wine. She flushed. 'Maybe at the beginning. But I saw through him at the end. Creep,' she muttered.

'Do you think you'll go on to do some more studying?'

'I might. Seeing how things pan out at work. Tash has got

me a place on a management course so I'll see how demanding that is first before I take on anything else.'

'Well, there's always going to be standalone talks and seminars here. I'm hoping to launch the new programme of events during the literary festival in January.'

'Thanks Amy. That might be a good compromise. And we can still have booky talks in the pub, can't we?'

'Yes, I'm looking forward to those.' Amy thought about how she struggled with the pressures of chairing the book group meetings. 'Might be more fun.'

'You betcha.'

'How're things at home?'

Emma blew out a breath. 'Interesting,' she said, her mood dulling. 'Mum's decided to take a leap of faith and leave Suki's. She's setting up on her own as a mobile hairdresser. She's wigging like mad but she just couldn't take any more of Suki's demands. Do you know,' she added hotly, 'she wanted her to work Sundays? It was the final straw.'

'That's a great idea. A mobile hairdresser will go down a storm in Berecombe. There are loads of folk who can't get out and about easily. I'm sure they'd welcome it.'

Emma nodded vigorously. 'That's my thinking too. Mum's done a short foot care course too. She's going to offer toenail cutting and foot massages as well. Nothing medical, just a bit of pampering.' She grimaced. 'Can't think of anything worse but Mum's dead excited about it all. Haven't seen her this animated for years. Think she's finally doing something for herself instead of looking after us lot. She's calling it Tops and Toes.'

Amy smiled. 'Spelled with an 's' I hope?'

'Yeah. I insisted.' Emma grinned and finished her wine in one.

'Wish her all the luck in the world. And I hope your father's situation gets easier too.'

'Thanks Amy, I appreciate it.' Emma waggled her empty glass. 'Going to get a top up.' She passed Patrick on the way and gave him a huge kiss on the cheek. 'Cheers Patrick. It's been ace tonight. You even coped with Biddy. Wasn't looking forward to it one bit but I'm really glad I came.'

Patrick came up to Amy. He grinned and clinked his glass with hers. 'Another happy customer.'

'Thanks to you. You've been magnificent.'

'Ah well, it's easy to be enthusiastic about a subject you love. And women's writing is close to my heart. My mother, God love her, was a great reader and loved the nineteenth century women writers.'

'And she inspired you?'

'She did.'

Amy was curious. Patrick took great care to reveal very little about himself. She didn't even know where he lived in Berecombe and had assumed, as he always offered to walk her home, it was somewhere on the way out from the old town where she had her flat. She'd even googled him. It had made her feel a little dirty and she'd found out nothing more than she already knew. Born and brought up in Portmarnock as he'd said, University College Dublin, nine novels published and had lived in England since 2010. She waited for him to expand his answer but, inevitably, he didn't. 'You've got some of Emma's lipstick on your cheek,' she said, to fill the silence. Fishing out a clean tissue, she dabbed at the pink stain. Some of the tissue caught on his stubble and she picked it off. The feel of his skin under her nails was tantalising. They were very close and she could smell his heat. It was almost too much.

'Thanks.' His voice came out gruff.

'You're welcome,' she replied lightly. 'That's what friends are for.'

He seemed to be on the brink of saying something but Biddy, freshly ebullient on her triumphant return from London, loomed towards them.

'Now Patrick, my man,' she boomed. 'Come and settle an argument. Young Emma thinks Austen is the better writer but I'm all for Emily Brontë. And Millie, well Millie can't decide between Mrs Gaskell and Virginia Woolf. Now, they'd make peculiar bedfellows!' She grabbed his arm and route-marched him over to where Emma stood at the buffet table, wine glass in one hand, crab canapé in the other. As it was the end of, admittedly a very short term, Millie had pulled out all the stops and laid on a feast.

Amy watched as the women gathered around him, chatting animatedly. Patrick had always been a popular member of the book group and now his star had risen even further. He'd revealed himself to be a consummate teacher as well as a quietly spoken and informed book lover. She looked on jealously. The other women were so much more at ease with him. Laughing and joking and teasing. She couldn't be like that. Whenever he was near, her senses geared up into turbo-charge and she faltered over every word she uttered. She tried not to talk much at all, to avoid the embarrassment. She was certain it made her appear shy and lacking in confidence. She'd never have the relaxed confidence the others had around him. Sighing, she realized their friendship would never be easy. She loved him too much and it was unreturned.

Sipping her wine to camouflage feeling self-consciously alone, she pondered his remark about his background. So he had a mother who read and who had shared her love of books with him? He'd spoken in the past tense. Had she died? Sticking her nose in her wine again, she reconciled herself to not knowing. It wasn't that she was nosy, she just wanted to soak up everything that had made him the man he was. She'd just finished his latest book; Patrick had given her an advance copy as it wasn't due to be published for another week. Staying up late into the night, she'd gobbled it down. This one was set in the boom of the mid-nineties when the Celtic Tiger economy had exploded. At its heart was a crisis of faith and a troubled relationship between mother and the son who had decided to leave the Catholic church. The mother had retreated into the church community, leaving the family splintered and the son estranged. It had been funny and tragic and masterful. Looking up and gazing over to Patrick, she wondered how much had been written from experience. Patrick caught her staring. Once again, Amy felt heat rising in her face and she looked away. She let her eyes light on the spiral staircase leading up to the mezzanine reading area and fixed her mind back on work. She really ought to decide how she was going to decorate the shop for Hallowe'en, she thought and steadfastly ignored the yearning in her heart.

Chapter 78

Amy spent her next weekend determinedly carving another three pumpkins. Late on Sunday afternoon, when she was in the middle of scooping out the flesh of the biggest one, Katrina called round. Amy let her mother in, conscious that the flat was dusty and the bed unmade. Glancing in at the bedroom before elbowing the door shut, Amy wished it had been a passionate man who had tousled the sheets. The truth was far more prosaic; she always had a book that captured her and took precedence over housework.

Katrina, predictably, wrinkled her nose in distaste. Eyeing her daughter from socked toes to scruffily tied back hair, she said, 'It really wouldn't hurt to run a duster over the place, Amy, and put a comb through your hair.'

'It's Sunday, Mum. I don't tend to go out and no one calls round. Usually.' Amy flicked off the worst of the orange gore into the sink and ran her hands under the tap. Drying them, she turned to face her mother who was eyeing the tower of unread books next to the sofa. 'Would you like a cup of tea or coffee? I've got one of Millie's Victoria sponges too.'

'Is it ground coffee?' Katrina asked, without taking her eyes off the books.

'Instant.'

'Ugh. In that case, I'll take tea.'

By the time it was made, Katrina had perched on the edge of the sofa and was looking through the book which had teetered on the top of the pile. It was the latest top-selling thriller and a particularly nasty tale about a serial murderer. Dressed up in high literary language, it didn't disguise the fact it was all about women being killed in horrible ways. Amy didn't think it was her mother's thing. She proved herself right when Katrina placed the book back into its position with a barely disguised grimace.

'How can you bring yourself to read such things, Amy?' she said, taking her mug of tea. 'And haven't you any proper china teacups? Really, how can you live this way? And so unnecessarily too. You could come home and enjoy a much better standard of living.'

'It's for work, Mum and let's not rehash the old argument about me coming home again.' Amy offered her a slice of cake which she refused so Amy ate it instead. 'To what do I owe this pleasure anyway?' she asked, as she mopped up the cream and crumbs with a finger.

Katrina raised her brows. 'Goodness, Amy, you won't get a man if you continue eating in that manner. What size are you now?'

Amy put the plate down hurriedly. 'I don't know,' she fudged.

'You must be an eighteen at least.'

'Sixteen.' It wasn't a complete lie, she could still get into her size sixteen jeans if she enlarged the waist band with a safety pin and elastic band.

'Oh Lordy,' Katrina cried, clapping her petite hands to her

face. 'It's worse than I thought! I'll drop some diet sheets round at the shop tomorrow. Steak and grapefruit. Not exactly cutting edge but does the trick.' In one swift movement, she rose. She strode the short distance to the kitchenette, found the remaining cake and shoved it in the bin. 'There,' she declared. 'No more temptation!'

'Mum, that was—' Amy was about to say it was her supper but stopped herself in time. If her mother cottoned on that she regularly ate most of a Victoria sponge as a meal, she'd never hear the last of it.

'Well, if it's in the bin, you can't eat it, can you?' Katrina sat down, with the sense of a mission accomplished. 'And,' she added, spitefully, 'you haven't a hope of getting a man as delicious as that Patrick Carroll looking like you do. Darling, he's way out of your league. I mean, if the likes of Lee Styles stood you up at the altar, what hope is there of attracting a bestselling writer?'

Amy was tired. She'd spent all weekend carving the pumpkins, reading a deeply unpleasant book she hated but which she needed to review for the shop, and researching ideas for Hallowe'en decorations. She'd been looking forward to a long bath, the book of her choice and then bed with the latest episode of *Poldark*. She knew, for whatever reason, her mother was spoiling for a fight and Amy refused to give her the pleasure. Looking down, she saw to her horror, that she'd splattered jam from the cake on the front of her grey sweatshirt. Reaching up to tuck a lock of hair back behind her ear, she realized she hadn't washed it for four days. No wonder Lee hadn't wanted to marry her. His rejection, even after eighteen months, still stung. He'd been her only boyfriend.

She'd known he wasn't her dream man but she believed he'd loved her. Not as much as the navy, it appeared. The text, ending their relationship, had only been discovered when she'd retrieved her phone from Katrina's handbag. By that point they'd arrived at the church to be met by Lee's stricken cousin who was best man. It seemed Lee couldn't go through with it and had disappeared into the Royal Navy. Amy had always suspected that Katrina, in some obscure way, had blamed her. She'd certainly never forgiven her, and the mess of arrangements that had to be cancelled had been an expensive nightmare. Amy's confidence, never great, had withered and hadn't recovered.

So, perhaps her mum had a point? Lee Styles was one thing but Patrick was older, sophisticated, worldly. Why would he regard her in any way other than as his slobby, bookish, dull friend? It was always the same. Her mother always cut her where it hurt the most. Trying not to let Katrina see the sudden tears, she said, abruptly, 'What are you here for? I thought you'd gone away this weekend.'

'I did. I had a marvellous time. Oh Scarborough, I love the place! The Yorkshire coast is so bracing at this time of year. The hotel was good, the entertainment last night was just about above average and my room had a sea view.'

'So what's the problem?' Amy could tell her mother was bluffing.

Katrina sniffed a little. 'Oh, baby girl, everyone was in a *couple*. Heaven knows I hadn't expected to find the man of my dreams, quite frankly darling, I don't think he exists, but I'd hoped there might be someone there on their own to chat to. Oh, don't get me wrong, they were all quite friendly in their way but one feels such a spare wheel being the third at a table for two,' she added, mournfully.

'I'm sorry, Mum. I'd assumed you'd gone with a group of friends.'

'No, just little old me, all on my own.'

Amy picked up her mug and sipped her tea thoughtfully. Her mother was often on her own. Since returning to Berecombe she hadn't made any friends; she knew lots of people but none closely. 'You need to work on your social circle,' she suggested, feeling a complete fraud, as she never bothered herself.

'Well, of course, but how? A single man is sought after at any age but a single woman over forty? Invisible and unwanted.'

'I'm sure that's not true,' Amy said, thinking it was more likely to be her mother's abrasive personality that was the problem. 'There's the Knit and Natter group, or the WI? Or volunteering?'

Katrina drew herself up, horror emanating in spiky waves. 'The WI? And, oh Amy really, *knitting?*'

'I don't know what to suggest then,' Amy said a bit feebly, hoping beyond hope her mother wouldn't ask to join the book group. 'University of the Third Age? They do lectures and courses and things.'

Katrina shuddered. She held up a finger. 'Speak no more! I was done with books the day I left school.' She flicked a glance at the pile of them next to her.

Amy felt relief flood through her. No danger of her crowding in on the book group then. A vision of Katrina crowing in delight at her daughter's failure to chair the meetings flashed into her head. 'I'll have a think.'

'Please do try to come up with something more constructive than charity shop volunteering.' Katrina subsided. 'I suppose I'll have to go home now. I've rather been putting it off. It's so lonely.' She batted her lashes at Amy who didn't miss the cunning. 'I'll be all on my own tonight.' She sighed. 'As ever.'

'Then perhaps you *should* join the WI, make some friends. Or learn to knit.'

'Don't be waspish.' Katrina gave her a knowing look. 'That's what happens if you gorge on sugar. You get far too peevish.'

Amy bit her lip. She wracked her brain. 'Then, as it's too late for hosting a foreign exchange student, what about a lodger or running the bungalow as an Airbnb? The spare bedroom has an en suite.'

'A lodger?' Katrina pulled a scandalised face. 'All brown slacks and greasy hair and wet underwear all over the radiators? No thank you.' She tapped a crimson nail on her teeth. 'But an Airbnb you say? So much classier than any old bed and breakfast.' She sat up excitedly. 'You know, that might work! Inviting folk from all over the globe to one's home. Oh yes,' she added, thoughtfully. 'I like the idea of that. I'd need to refurb though. In fact, I'll pop off and start looking through my interior design mags now.'

Amy was about to say that wasn't quite how Airbnbs worked and the bungalow certainly didn't need redecorating but, instead, slumped back and watched as her mother whirled around the tiny flat collecting her coat and bag and listened, exhausted, as Katrina tripped down the stairs on her kitten heels.

Eventually, she roused herself to get back to pumpkin

carving. Tipping the bin lid open, her mouth watered as she spied the discarded sponge. Amy hated wasting food. Little point in beginning the diet tonight, she thought. Peering in, she wondered how much of the cake she could salvage and not be considered very sad indeed.

Chapter 79

The weather, in its quixotic English way, had brightened up over the weekend and a cautious sunshine greeted Amy as she flipped the bookshop's sign to open. She stepped out for a moment to enjoy the view. The sunrise glossed the harbour buildings in pink and the sea was tranquil and quiet. She watched as a gull wheeled overhead, its underbelly plump and glistening. She could hear Petra getting organized in the Millie Vanilla kitchen next door and Radio Two drifted across the still air, along with the aroma of coffee. Amy's stomach growled. She'd given in and eaten part of the cake last night and then had been so disgusted with herself, had put it back in the bin, dropping teabags all over its remains to stop further temptation. She took in a huge lungful of briny sea air. Today was the first day of the new diet. And this time she planned to succeed. Unfortunately, she hadn't had time to stock up on fruit and vegetables and healthy low calorie food. She'd used the last of her milk making Katrina tea yesterday, so had none for cereal and was starting the day running on empty. She took in another breath in the lame hope fresh air would fill her up. At least it had zero calories.

Turning on her heel, she went back into the shop. Today

was going to be busy. On top of the usual morning chores of going through the email enquiries and sorting the post, a large new order was due. Plus, she had to finish preparations for Patrick's book signing that evening. He had refused a London book launch and had asked Amy to host a more low-key signing of his latest book in the shop. In the little back office a display of promotional posters was ready, Amy had ordered a range of freebies well in advance and Millie was providing the food and champagne. Patrick planned to do a short reading, a Q&A session and then the signing. His agent would be attending too. There probably wasn't much more she could do until later but Amy was twitchy. What if she had forgotten something? It didn't help that Patrick had been away for three days, not that she was counting. She'd missed his reassuring presence and it would have been handy to ask him last minute questions. Hurrying to the office and her checklist on the computer, she was waylaid by the phone ringing.

Expecting it to be the delivery driver asking for directions – they always got lost – she answered with half an eye on the computer screen. 'Good morning, The Little Book Café, Amy speaking. How can I help you?'

'Ah now, if you could help that would be grand. I'm looking for Patrick Carroll,' said a woman's strong Irish accented voice.

Amy went on guard immediately. Anyone who needed direct contact with Patrick, his agent and publisher for instance, already had his number. She assumed any family, not that he ever mentioned any, also had it. She found herself going into received pronunciation. 'I'm so sorry, you've come through to a bookshop, not a private number.'

'Oh, my darlin', does Patrick not come into you?'

'Unfortunately not,' Amy thought, ruefully. There had been no coming in any direction and of any sort in their friendship so far. The woman's voice was young-ish – it was hard to tell how young over the phone though. Wife, girlfriend, daughter? Patrick had never admitted to a wife. What if he was married? What if he had been in Ireland with his wife and family these last few days? Amy's throat constricted. Of course a man like Patrick might be married and there would be no reason to tell his dowdy, bookshop-managing friend.

'Hello there, are you still on the line?'

Amy cleared her throat. 'Can I ask who is calling?' she said, stiffly. 'I might be able to get a message to him.'

The woman chuckled. 'Tell the lazy arse when he gets there, he's only gone and left his scarf here. Tell him the next time he's at Dymphna's to collect it. I've tried his home number but there's no answer. He's the very devil to get hold of, so he is.'

'I'll ... I'll be certain to tell him,' Amy said, faintly. He'd stayed with a woman called Dymphna? A young woman with an attractive voice and no doubt attractive, flashing Irish good looks to match. Her imagination ran wild.

'Thank you, my darlin'. Tell him to have a good book launch, won't you?'

'Yes. Yes, I will. Thank you for calling.' Amy put the phone down carefully. She was still frozen in position when her mother hustled the lost delivery driver in and brandished a sheaf of diet papers at her.

Chapter 80

Patrick rushed in apologetically late, five minutes after the signing was due to start and accompanied by Whiz his agent. A nickname, Amy assumed and could see how she came by it. Whiz was a curious creature; a tiny, manic bundle of energy, with spiky red hair and who monopolised Patrick so much Amy couldn't get near. Instead, having made sure every detail was in place, she stood to one side, leant against the Biography and Sporting and Outdoor Pursuits sections, crossed her arms and watched.

It was thrilling to hear the words Patrick had written read out by him. He had attracted a large crowd. The space Amy had cleared near the front of the bookshop was full to capacity and beyond, there were about twenty people standing at the back. Amy glanced across and saw Millie counting heads unobtrusively. She then disappeared through the glass passageway to the café proper, no doubt to check on whether she had enough glasses. There were a scattering of familiar faces. The book group members were there, of course, plus Jed, Millie's husband, and Ollie, Emma's darkly handsome boyfriend. Biddy sat in the front row next to her husband and town councillor, Arthur. To Amy's surprise, her mother had come along and had secured a seat in pole position on the other side of him. Before the reading had begun, Amy had seen her chatting away to a bemused-looking Arthur. Maybe she was here in an attempt at making friends? More likely, it was the draw of free champagne.

The reading was over far too soon and the Q&A began. Whiz chaired it expertly. She might be small but she was fierce. After twenty minutes of routine questions, a large middle-aged man who Amy recognized as Dennis, another town councillor, put up his hand. 'Patrick, elements of your book resonate as being strongly realistic,' he began, a little pompously. 'More so in this one than in any of the others in the series. May I ask if this book is autobiographical?'

Amy held her breath. She tried not to stare too closely at Patrick but found her eyes drawn irrevocably to him. She saw Whiz's one brow rise in query, as if to say, 'You don't have to answer that one,' and then Patrick began his answer.

He started by thanking Dennis for the question and showing his appreciation to him for having bought the book. Amy found herself holding her breath. Poor Patrick, he was such a private man, he must be hating this. She hated herself for wanting so desperately to know his answer.

'Well, Dennis, sure like most people I've had my fair share of conflict and pain, love and success. So I suppose what I do is take a trivial example from my own life and extrapolate how I feel onto a bigger canvas, the larger picture, if you like. I'm Irish and religion played an enormous part in my upbringing, just like Colin's in the book. I took tiny examples from my experiences, examined them and exploded them.'

Dennis wasn't about to give up. 'Are you saying you didn't have a troubled relationship with your own mother?'

Whiz put a warning hand on Patrick's shoulder but he batted it off. To laughter, he said, 'Oh come on, Dennis, name me one Irish boy who didn't have a fallout with his mammy!'

Dennis obviously wanted to pursue the matter but Whiz clapped her hands, announced the end of question time, that the new book was on sale at the cash desk and, after champagne and canapés, Patrick would be available to sign them and answer any other questions. Just not the ones he didn't want to answer, Amy thought, as she watched Whiz stick like glue to Patrick's side and usher him to the back office for a breather. She didn't have time to ponder it any further as she had to push through the crowd and get to the till.

After the initial rush, when she sold over a hundred copies of Patrick's book, it quietened down. It was mid-October and it looked as if people were buying several copies to give as Christmas presents. Then they drifted off to catch a tray of canapés or snaffle another glass of fizz. The noise of talking and laughing was terrific. She began to breathe, feeling a little giddy with success. She might just have pulled off her very first book event. Taking advantage of the lull, she edged around the crowd and opened the double doors. The unseasonably warm weather had continued all day and, with so many people milling around, it was getting tropical in the shop, despite the high ceiling of the original chapel. Amy was beginning to feel light-headed. One or two people cast grateful looks her way and disappeared outside to enjoy the balmy air or to have a smoke. Others followed.

For a second, Amy hovered on the step, looking out to the

seating area where people congregated around the benches. The wide expanse, which linked with the Millie Vanilla Café, overlooked the sea and was dotted with picnic benches and tables. With its drift of white lights, pretty bunting and late-flowering bedding plants, it was tailor-made for an event like this. It gave folk a chance to have a breather and soak up the ambience that the whispering sea provided. She gestured to two of the waiters and asked them to take their laden trays outside. Glancing back into the shop, she was surprised to see it was still crowded. Everyone was having too good a time to want to leave. Amy felt a tiny prickle of pride which withered when she saw her mother heading towards her.

'Hi Mum. Had a good evening?'

'I have, actually, darling. Surprisingly good. Had a long chat with Arthur. He's given me so much advice about running an Airbnb. And I met his wife, Biddy, is it?' Katrina rolled her eyes. 'Quite the character. Oh and a simply wonderful woman called Marti. She belongs to that book group you run. We're having coffee tomorrow. I can't wait to hear all about her next holiday. Did you know she's off to Mauritius?' Katrina gave a little head shake which was meant to appear modest and failed spectacularly. 'She's just my sort of person.'

Amy tried to keep a straight face. It was a match made in heaven. 'I agree. I'm so glad you've come, Mum.'

Katrina looked about her, to see if there was anyone else she could pounce on. 'It's been the most marvellous fun. Do you think you can get me a copy of Patrick's book? I've been telling everyone about how we're *such* good friends.'

'Yes, you can buy one as soon as I get a chance to get back on the till.'

Katrina stepped closer and Amy was nearly annihilated by a waft of Dior. She put a hand up to her mouth. 'No,' she hissed. 'I meant, are there any freebies?'

'None, I'm afraid.'

'Well, can't you have a word with whoever organized this shindig? Surely there must a few free copies knocking about?'

'Mum, I organized this shindig, as you call it and no, there are no free books. Would you like me to buy you one as an early Christmas present?'

'You did all this?' Katrina looked her daughter up and down. 'Oh.' She sniffed. 'Well done, I suppose, although I'd have served a better champagne, of course.'

From her mother, this amounted to the highest praise and Amy took it. She didn't see Tash until she spoke.

'Got to dash, Amy.' She reached over, teetering a little on her stilettos, to kiss her on the cheek. 'I promised Kit I'd be back by nine to take over with the puppy sitting.' She made a face. 'Our latest waif and stray is proving a handful. It's been a fantastic night.' She gave Katrina a meaningful look. 'Everything's gone like clockwork and you did it all by yourself. Amazing evening and it bodes well for the Hallowe'en party. Can't wait!' Waggling her copy of the book, she grinned. '*You're* amazing. See you soon.' Winking but only for Amy to see, she disappeared.

Katrina peered after her, she was too vain to wear the glasses she needed. 'Friend of yours? Mmm, Louboutins. Nice.'

'That's Natasha. She manages the estate agents and works with her boyfriend, Kit, at their animal sanctuary. And yes,' Amy added, realizing it was true. 'She is a friend.'

Katrina plucked at Amy's smart but dull cardigan. 'Grey,

Amy? So not your colour. You need to take a leaf out of your friend Natasha's book. Look how glamorous she is.'

Amy began her defence in saying that her job that night was to be unobtrusive and blend into the background, not to stand out in any glamorous way but her mother had spied another victim and wandered off. She glimpsed Whiz and Patrick return and knew her cue. 'Ladies and gentlemen,' she called, and then repeated it as the volume of chat hadn't decreased. 'Ladies and gentlemen, if you could form a queue by the long table. Patrick is ready to sign your books.' Satisfied, those in the shop had begun to obey, she went outside to round up those still enjoying the night air. She was beginning to feel weary. Just this one last push and then the clearing up and it was over. It had been a long day.

Chapter 81

There had been a long queue. Berecombe readers were enthusiastic and many wanted a one to one chat with Patrick. It wasn't often they could enjoy the company of a bestselling writer. Besides, there wasn't much else on in October.

Once Whiz had chivvied the queue into submission, she held up her tiny hand and bellowed, 'If we could just pause for a moment before launching into the signing.'

From her position at the till, Amy looked up. This wasn't on the itinerary. Patrick should go straight into the signing. A pang of unease stabbed. She'd wanted this evening to go well. It was important to Patrick but also for the bookshop.

'If Amy could make her way over here,' Whiz continued. 'We have a little something to show our gratitude.'

One or two people cheered. Biddy yelled, 'Hear, hear!' and a ripple of applause sounded.

Amy froze. She hated being the centre of attention. A sharp finger poked her in her back and propelled her forward. 'Go on then darling, what are you waiting for?' It was her mother.

Amy's knees shook as she made her way to where Patrick and Whiz were standing. Patrick was smiling broadly. When she reached them, he put his arm around her and Whiz disappeared into the back office again.

'Ladies and gents,' Patrick began. 'Amy has organized this whole event. On top of running The Little Book Café, she's made sure the invites went out, that the event was publicized, that the menu was perfect, and so much more.' He pulled her to him and kissed her on the cheek. 'How did you know I love black pudding? Those little toast things with the black pudding and chorizo on were the business.' Everyone laughed. 'You probably haven't even noticed her this evening but she's worked non-stop making sure the drink flowed, that everyone who wanted a book could buy one – and more besides.' He waggled his brows which made everyone laugh again. 'Thank you to you all, from a poor starving writer and, on behalf of this proudly independent bookshop, for being so generous tonight. And, when you've all staggered off to your beds, this darlin' will be here clearing up.' He stood away from Amy a little and she missed his strong arm around her waist. 'I know you hate the limelight Amy but can you forgive us? We had to say thank you for all you've done.'

To cheers, Whiz produced the most enormous bouquet of lilies and roses Amy had ever seen, along with a large flat box of chocolates in telltale Fortnum & Mason turquoise. Patrick reached down and, from under the table, produced a heavy, beautifully wrapped parcel. 'Set of signed first editions of my books,' he whispered and kissed her cheek again. 'Can't thank you enough for tonight.'

'Don't make me do a speech,' Amy whispered back, stricken. A chorus of, 'For she's a jolly good fellow' began, which Amy strongly suspected Biddy was behind. Then everyone burst into applause. With difficulty she gathered up her presents and slunk back to the till, mouthing her thank yous as she went.

Patrick yelled, over the noise, 'Amy says thank you to you all for coming and helping make it such a good night and she's now getting back to the till to extract more pennies from those of you who still haven't bought the book. Quite honestly, why the feck are you here, if you haven't bought the book?' The champagne-fuelled crowd roared. 'For those of you who *have* contributed to my Guinness fund, we can start the signing.' He raised his glass of champagne to more cheers.

Amy found the tall stool behind the counter and collapsed onto it. Her face burned. She balanced the bouquet on the sales desk and hid the books and the chocolates underneath. She was bursting with pride that Patrick and Whiz had appreciated all her efforts, as had, seemingly, the good readers of Berecombe, but she was mortified. It had been Millie and Petra who were responsible for the delicious food. All she'd done was agree the menu and estimate and order the right amount of champagne. And the rest of it hadn't been all that onerous; she'd loved doing it. Aware three customers were at the till waiting to pay, Amy got back to work. As each one paid, they complimented her – on the event, on running such a great asset to the town, on how helpful she always was. Amy nodded and smiled. She'd had no idea how much Berecombe loved having a bookshop. Fighting brain-fog, she watched how Whiz took over, seamlessly organising the signing. She skipped from standing just behind Patrick, making sure the book that needed signing was open at the correct page, to getting readers to put their name on a Post-it so Patrick could copy it without having to go through the 'how do you spell that?' routine. It should have speeded everything up but it was well after twelve before it finished. As the last few customers began to teeter out of the bookshop doors, Amy put a shaking hand to her head and slipped, bonelessly from the stool.

Chapter 82

A my came to blearily, looking around, disorientated.
'Is she alright?' a voice from a long way away sounded.

'She looks pale. Gave me the right wiggins when she went down next to me,' said another.

'Here's some iced water,' said a third. 'Patrick, try getting her to sip it. Slowly though.' As her hearing focused, Amy thought it was probably Millie.

She tried to sit up, struggling against the arms which held her.

'Oh my darlin' take it easy. You've given us one hell of a fright, so you have.'

Patrick's voice and Patrick's arms which held her. Blinking, she became aware of her surroundings. She reached for the water, her hands over the top of the ones which were holding the glass.

'Nice and slow there.' Definitely Patrick.

She was desperate to sit up but it was safe cocooned in his arms. Besides, her head throbbed and she felt too shaky to move.

'Have you hurt your head?' Whiz asked, with surprising sympathy.

Amy considered the question. Although she had the mother of all headaches, she didn't think she had actually bumped her head. She shook it experimentally.

'I was standing next to her when she fainted. She landed on one of the beanbags from the kid's reading area,' Emma said. 'So I don't think she'll have hurt herself. But she went so quickly I couldn't catch her. One minute she was sitting on the stool behind the till and the next, she tipped sideways, looking green.'

Amy began to feel heat seep into her face. Reluctant as she was to leave Patrick's comforting embrace, she began to sit up. 'Think I'm feeling a bit better.' Patrick and Emma helped her up and sat her in one of the hard chairs leased for the signing.

'Amy, have you had anything to eat today?' Millie asked.

Amy thought and then blushed. 'No,' she squeaked.

'Have you had much to drink?'

Amy shook her head and sipped more water, now held in a steadier hand. 'Nothing alcoholic.' She screwed up her eyes in an attempt to remember. 'I had a coffee first thing but that's been about it. I've been too busy,' she added, apologetically.

'Well, no wonder you fainted,' Millie said matter of factly. 'Do you think you can manage something now?'

'I don't know.' Amy's stomach revolted at the thought of the rich canapés.

'Not party food. I'll make you a sandwich. Ham salad do you? Or tuna mayo?'

'Ham would be lovely, thank you, Millie.' Amy looked up gratefully but she'd gone.

'And once you've eaten and drunk that water, all of it, I'll take you home,' Patrick said, sternly.

'But I can't, I have to clear up,' Amy protested.

'Leave it to us,' Emma said. 'Between me, Ollie and Jed, we'll have it done in no time.'

'I'll pitch in too. Only fair, after all you've done,' Whiz added.

Amy bit back the tears which threatened. 'You're all so good,' she croaked. 'Thank you!'

'What are friends for?' Emma said simply. 'Patrick, get the woman out of the way so we can get started.'

Patrick walked her through the glass corridor to the café proper and sat her at one of the pink painted tables. She could hear Millie bustling about in the kitchen. Her cockapoo padded up to them. As if sensing she was ill, he put his nose on her knee and looked up at her forlornly.

'Hello Trevor,' Amy cooed and stroked his head.

'You're already sounding better,' Patrick said, sounding relieved. 'I was just signing the last book and there was this almighty crash. And there you were, looking like death, lying on the beanbag.'

Amy put her face in her hands. 'I'm so embarrassed.'

'Now why, for the love of God, would you be embarrassed?' When she didn't answer, Patrick took her hands gently off her face. 'You've slaved all day.' He left her hands in his. 'Worked so hard you didn't have time to get nourishment into your body. And your body decided it had had enough. Nothing to be embarrassed about. Sure, it's us who should be embarrassed, letting you shoulder the responsibility. And there's me skedaddling off to the auld country, leaving you to it.'

'But you had to go to Ireland.'

'I did,' he replied, not expanding.

'Oh, there was a message for you,' Amy suddenly remembered, sliding her hands from under his. 'Someone rang this morning. A woman, Dymphna? She said you'd left your scarf at her place.'

'Ah. So I did. I'll pick it up next time.'

Amy, by now feeling a lot stronger but still very empty, was about to ask who Dymphna was, when Millie arrived with the sandwich.

'I've made you a hot chocolate too. Thought the sugar would give you a boost. And there's a slice of cinnamon apple cake.' She gave Patrick a glance. 'I'm sure if you can't eat it all, Patrick will help you out.'

'I will. I'm starving.'

'I'll leave you to it then and go and help the others. And, Amy, don't worry about locking up. I'll do it and leave the key in the café kitchen. You can pick it up from there tomorrow. Petra's always in with the lark.'

Amy felt tears threaten again. To stifle them she picked up the sandwich and bit into it. Although hollowed out with hunger, she didn't think she could face food. However, two bites in and she was eating ravenously. Pausing to drink some more water, she said without thinking, 'I shouldn't be eating like this really. I started a diet this morning.'

Patrick, halfway through the apple cake, looked up. He frowned. 'Is that what this is all about? Are you starving yourself to get thin? For the love of God, why?'

Amy pushed the plate containing the remaining sandwich away. She looked out of the new bi-fold windows Millie had had fitted. They were tightly shut against the night. As the lights were on in the café, she could see only their reflection amid the blackness outside. She imagined looking in from the outside. Two people in an otherwise deserted café, like an Edward Hopper painting come to life. It made sitting close to Patrick feel painfully intimate and yet she was no nearer knowing him. She could sense him staring at her, waiting for her answer.

'You think you're fat,' he said, bluntly.

She looked down at the table and sneaked a tiny piece of ham to a drooling Trevor. 'Well, I am.'

'So that's why you didn't eat today?'

'No! I genuinely didn't have time and forgot. But I do need to diet.'

'Darlin' girl, have you looked at yourself?'

'What do you mean?'

'Do you look at yourself in the mirror?'

'Not if I can help it,' Amy said, in a small voice, suppressing a shudder.

Patrick shook his head. 'How does someone so clever, so talented, so capable, like you have no confidence?'

Amy met his look. It wasn't the time to tell him about Lee. She was still too ashamed about it all. And she didn't want to go into her father leaving, although she suspected that had kicked off the beginning of her insecurities. She went for a try at weak humour instead. 'Have you met my mother?'

'I have.' He smiled wryly. 'But, whatever mess our parents make of our heads, we can outgrow them.' He took her hands again. 'Amy darlin' trust me, you're beautiful and good. Kind and thoughtful. You've eyes a man could drown in and hair he could die lying beside. You don't need to diet.'

Amy loved how his Irish accent escaped sometimes. She

loved his voice. But then she loved him. Everything about him. His intellect, his kindness, his natural ease. Everything. She took a deep breath and went for an answer. 'But I want to make myself happy.'

Patrick leaned back. 'Starving yourself won't do that. Find out what it is that is really making you unhappy, sort that and the rest will follow.' He pushed her plate back to her. 'Now, eat up and nourish your bones and I might even leave you a morsel of this grand piece of cake.'

It was hopeless, Amy thought, gazing at him. Moments like this in Patrick's company made her the happiest she'd ever been. Then she thought about the mysterious Dymphna and wondered how she fitted into Patrick's life. And what about herself? How did *she* fit into his life? He'd admired her eyes and hair and said kind things, but she was still just a friend. And she wanted so much more. Strangled by shyness and a lack of confidence, she couldn't ask any of those questions. It was no good. Patrick had the capability to make her ecstatically happy but sink into the depths of despair at the same time. And she couldn't see a solution. Picking up the remaining sandwich, she ate it without thinking.

Chapter 83

Emma bounced into the bookshop the following lunchtime, closely followed by Tash going at a more sedate pace. 'Amy! Me and Tash are going for coffee and cake to celebrate some great news. Wanna come?'

Amy was still feeling sluggish after the book signing. She hesitated. 'I've got a lot to do. I'm not sure I can spare the time.'

Patrick, in early for once, intervened. 'Sure, Amy there's no one about at the moment, I'll keep an eye on the shop for an hour.' He winked. 'If I get trampled in the rush, I'll come and get you. Go on,' he added, as he gave her a little push. 'Go and have lunch with your friends. You deserve a break.'

She looked at him gratefully. After they'd finished eating last night, he'd given her a lift home. She hadn't even known he *had* a car. It underlined how little she knew about him. By this point she was so exhausted she'd nearly missed the exquisite nearness of him driving her in the dark. Once parked up outside her flat, he'd come round to the passenger side and opened her door. He led her to the front door of the flats, one arm around her and waited until she unlocked.

'Got to give Whiz a lift to her hotel,' he had whispered, his breath misting in the cool night air. The pressure of his arm around her waist had increased for a fraction of a second and she'd thought he might have kissed the top of her head but it was all so swift she couldn't be certain. She'd climbed the stairs to her flat with heavy legs but with a heart bursting with love for him.

'Go on with you,' he urged now, snapping her back to the present.

She followed Emma and Tash into Millie Vanilla's and they bagged the best table in the window, just as a couple were leaving.

'Wonder if they'll go into the bookshop?' Amy bit her lip as she watched anxiously.

'Relax babe,' Emma said. 'If they do Patrick will cope. He could charm the birds from the trees that one, as Biddy likes to say.'

Millie arrived and took their order. She was wearing a turquoise apron with a pretty pattern of pink flamingos and she looked radiant. 'So, curried parsnip soup all round and I'll let you know what cakes we've got later, if you've got room for pudding.'

'*If* we've got room for pudding?' protested Emma, stoutly. 'As if we wouldn't have!'

Millie chuckled. 'Sorry Emma, my lovely. Forgot who I was talking to. Food will be with you in a jiffy.'

Once she'd returned to the kitchen, Emma leaned forward and whispered, 'When do you think she's going to tell people she's pregnant?'

'Millie's pregnant?!' Amy said more loudly than she meant.

'Sssh!' Emma put her finger to her lips. 'She told me a couple of weeks ago but swore me to secrecy.'

'Then perhaps you shouldn't have mentioned it in the first place,' Tash reproved. 'Oh hello Trevor,' she cooed, as Millie's cockapoo padded over for some fuss.

'See?' Emma rolled her eyes. 'All stern with me but if there's a dog about, she goes to mush.'

Amy laughed. It was hard to read Tash sometimes. She came across as completely self-reliant, even a little hard but Amy was learning she could be kind too.

'Great do last night, Amy,' Tash said. 'What a great turn out and brilliantly well-organized. It was fab.'

'Thank you. And thank you for saying so in front of my mother. I often suspect she thinks I'm incapable of doing anything.'

There was an interruption while Millie served their coffee. Amy caught Emma studying Millie's tummy and couldn't help but giggle.

'Ah mothers,' Tash said, sipping her espresso. 'Mine thinks I'm not responsible enough to look after her precious Westie.'

'And mine rejects every ironed shirt I do,' Emma added, mournfully. 'Just not up to her impeccable standards.'

'But they love us really,' Tash said. 'Let's raise our coffees to our sainted mothers!'

Amy obliged but was certain nothing she did would be good enough for her mother. Sometimes she wondered if Katrina even loved her. 'So, you're celebrating,' she said, when they'd put their cups down. 'What's the occasion?'

Tash looked triumphant. 'We have finally, *finally* after many false starts and hiccoughs along the way, completed on Biddy's purchase of the Morrisons' bungalow. Hallelujah to all the gods of estate agents.'

'Oh that's great. Biddy will be pleased. When are they moving in?'

'Not for a while,' Emma put in. 'She and Arthur want to do some work on it first. Then they want us to sell their two houses.'

'Of course. They've not long been married, have they? I suppose Arthur has his own place.'

Emma nodded. 'Biddy promised me if I got them the bungalow, then she wanted us to sell their houses.'

'She wants *you* to sell the houses,' Tash added. She grinned. 'Way to go, Em. You've done a fantastic job.'

Emma preened a little. Natch. 'Oh and the sale of the Greys' completely gorg cottage to Millie and Jed is well on its way too. Should complete by the end of this month. But the best news, the absolute best news, is that Dad's job is safe.'

'Oh Emma, that's brilliant!' Amy exclaimed. 'You've been so worried about it.'

'Whole family has.'

'What's happened?'

'Factory's got a new and long term contract to make old-fashioned carpet sweepers.'

Amy did a double-take. 'To make what?'

'You know, the push and go sort. No power except your own elbow.'

'No disrespect to your Dad but who on earth would want to buy a carpet sweeper?' Amy asked, mystified.

Emma roared. 'Oh Amy, your face! Had the exact same thought, though. Apparently they're the latest must-have retro accessory for hipsters. Along with milk in real glass bottles and record players playing actual vinyl.'

Amy shrugged. 'Well, if it means your Dad has a secure job, I'm all for it. Here's to the humble carpet sweeper.' She looked so perplexed, Emma and Tash laughed.

''Course, it also means me and Ollie can move into Millie's flat above the caff,' Emma said then added, dreamily, 'Can't friggin' wait!'

'I'm really pleased for you Emma,' Amy said and sniffed appreciatively as their soup arrived.

Silence reigned while they paid due homage to Millie's delicious homemade curried parsnip but, once their bowls were empty, Emma slung her spoon down and grinned. 'I love this place. I cannot wait to live upstairs.'

'It's a dream come true for you,' Tash teased. 'Food at your beck and call all day long. You'll never have to cook. You can live on chocolate fudge cake and lemon drizzle.'

'Suits me.' Emma said, practically salivating.

'It wouldn't suit me,' Amy sighed. 'I only have to look at a piece of cake and I put on a stone,' she added, gloomily.

'Gotta admit, I must have a fast metabolism,' Emma said.

'You must have, to process all the crap you eat,' Tash said acidly. She turned to Amy and pulled a face. 'Cheese and onion crisp sandwich for breakfast this morning. I mean, cheese and onion at nine in the morning!'

'And it was yummy-delish,' Emma said.

'I'm like you, Amy,' Tash put in. 'I have to watch what I eat like a hawk or I put on weight. I was really overweight a few years ago, lost it and have lived in fear of putting it all back on ever since.'

This was a revelation to Amy; Tash always looked slender in the tight little suits she wore and Amy said as much.

Tash laughed. 'Nope. There's only one place the stodge ends and that's right on my hips. Emma doesn't know how lucky she is. For the rest of us it's a real struggle.'

'So, how do you keep the weight off?' Amy asked.

'She indulges in marathon bouts of sex with the love-god that is Kit,' Emma sniggered.

'I do apologise for my colleague, Amy. Sometimes I wonder if she's graduated from nursery.'

Amy laughed ruefully. 'Well, even if it's true,' she said, blushing a little as an image of her and Patrick indulging in their very own marathon sex session burst into her brain. 'Not much chance of that sort of exercise for me. Very single at the moment.'

'Or,' Emma piped up. 'A more positive way of saying it would be fun, free, single and ready to mingle.'

'What did I say?' Tash muttered, rolling her eyes. 'Never left the nursery.'

'Ooh, I know what would do it,' Emma squealed, making the couple in walking boots, who had just come in, stare. 'The Slime Run!'

'Oh no,' Amy said, firmly. 'I couldn't manage the Fun Run in August so I'm not even going to consider the Slime Run.'

'Actually, I had trouble with the Fun Run too,' Tash said. 'Wasn't nearly fit enough for it.'

Amy looked at her, amazed. 'I thought you looked incredibly fit.'

'Nope. Really struggled and didn't even complete it.'

'Yeah, but the Slime Run is different,' Emma insisted. 'Goes from the Regent Theatre at one end of the prom to the tip of the harbour. It's a mile tops and all on the flat.'

'Where does the slime come into it?' Amy asked. 'I assume it's something to do with Hallowe'en?'

'Yup. The Sea Cadets run it as a fundraiser. They get dressed up in Hallowe'en costumes and jump out at you at various points along the way and throw gunge all over you. You get sponsored for taking part.'

Tash shuddered fastidiously. 'Sounds tremendous,' she said, in a tart voice and, lifting her pink rose-patterned cup, finished her coffee.

'No, it's great fun, honest.'

'Do you think I'd need to train for it though?' Amy asked.

'Well it never hurts. A bit of training would make running a mile a lot easier. I'll call for you tomorrow night, how does that sound? And, as I always say—'

'What?' Amy asked as Tash grinned; she'd heard it all before.

'The more you run, the more of the goodly cake product you can eat.'

Millie, as if knowing her cue, came to clear their table. 'Now, can I tempt you, ladies? Lemon drizzle, Bakewell Tart, apple cake – or a taster slice each, of all three? It's something new I'm trying as people can never seem to make up their mind what to have. Comes with clotted cream, of course.'

The women looked at one another. As one, they chorused, 'Taster slices!' and then burst out laughing.

Chapter 84

Amy had enjoyed her lunch with Emma and Tash. She'd never been sure what they thought of her at book group. Although she'd been at Berecombe Primary with Tash for a few years, her father had got his dream job in Singapore just before she'd been due to go to the Comp. She and Katrina had gone with him and Amy had been enrolled in an international school. It had meant that, although she'd always felt local, she'd also felt displaced on her return to Berecombe after university, and slightly apart. The tension between her and Tash had evaporated, and Emma was always easy to get on with, but Amy was aware that three was never an ideal number for a friendship group. However, it hadn't seemed to bother anyone yesterday and she'd returned to the shop in high spirits to find Patrick had sold more books in her absence than she'd managed all morning. She'd gone home, feeling as close to happy as she dared; she'd almost forgotten how.

All this vanished the instant she saw the red words daubed all over one of the front windows of the bookshop as she arrived to open up the following morning.

She stood shocked, her head going muzzy with disbelief.

BOOKS ARE CRAP!!! it said. A childish message, it had

been sprayed on with liberal carelessness, the red paint dripping down onto the lovely deep windowsills of the converted seaman's chapel.

Amy was stunned. She clutched her bag to her and, for a second, stood frozen with indecision. Nothing had happened since the vandalised pumpkins. That was, if you didn't count the feeling she often had, but had dismissed, of being watched. She thought she heard a giggle and whirled round. The low sunlight, shining brilliantly from the eastern end of the promenade, blinded her for a second. There might have been a scuffling of feet on the sandy concrete but then all was silent. A gull cackled overhead making her jump. Perhaps that was what she'd heard?

Mustering all the swear words she knew, she muttered them under her breath and concentrated on opening the front door. Carefully locking it behind her again, she headed for the phone. Smashed pumpkins were one thing but this was outright vandalism. Feeling sick, she punched in the number for Berecombe's sole police presence. As she waited for Paul to pick up, she felt her knees tremble and she collapsed onto the stool behind the counter. Had someone got it in for her? But why? And who?

She was trying to scrub the paint off when Patrick arrived. 'Jesus, Joseph and Mary, what the feck is this all about?'

Amy turned and faced him. She was feeling a little calmer now. Still angry but, after her conversation with Paul, more reassured that it had been nothing personal. She'd had to leave a message and he'd got back to her only ten minutes ago. 'I had some visitors overnight and they left me a little message.' She smiled thinly. 'At least it was spelled correctly, even if they do think books are crap.'

'Ah feck Amy, that's awful.'

'Kids apparently, according to Paul. They had a spree all over town last night. We got off lucky. They had a real go at the town hall. They're going round calling themselves The EX Gang.'

'The what?'

'After the first bit of the postcode, I assume.'

Patrick gave a short laugh. 'Not very imaginative then.'

'Or all that bright. If I get hold of them, I'd like to tell them exactly why books *aren't* crap and how they might benefit from reading a few.' She put the cloth down and shoved a frustrated hand through her hair. She gave Patrick a trembling look. 'I'm feeling a bit better about all of this now. This morning I was convinced someone had a vendetta against me. Paul reassured me the gang hit quite a few places, including the boarded-up old Blue Elephant Café, and the theatre. The poor theatre. It's hard enough for them to scrape along at the best of times, without all the expense of cleaning graffiti off.' She shrugged. 'None of the targets have anything in common except they're all in Berecombe.'

'Just kids then, I guess.'

'It's a shame they can't see how hard it is to scrub off.' Amy's voice quivered.

'Oh, darlin' girl.' Patrick enveloped her in a bear hug. He had on a thick Guernsey sweater and Amy clung to him. He smelled of cold air, coffee and reassurance. The roughness of the wool scored her cheek but she didn't care. She just needed to hold onto someone.

'I wouldn't mind quite so much,' she said, reluctantly disentangling herself from his embrace after a few moments, 'but

I still haven't put up the decorations for the storytelling session this afternoon. I haven't got time to scrub this lot off and do that too. Ooh, it's infuriating.' Amy just about stopped herself from stamping her foot.

Patrick kept his hands on her shoulders and looked at her, concerned. 'Have they paid Millie's a visit too?'

Amy shook her head. 'The Old Harbour and the Lifeboat Station escaped too. Millie said she thought she heard something about nine, and Jed came out, but couldn't see anything. It must have scared them off before they had chance to wreak any more havoc.'

'Well, that's one thing. Give me a sec and I'll come and help you scrub.' He moved away and began to push up the sleeves of his sweater. Strong forearms were revealed, covered in black hair. Amy tried not to stare.

She turned back to the graffiti. It was amateurish in the extreme but had a certain bloody appeal as it was painted in red. 'Hang on, Patrick,' she began, as an idea came to her. 'I think we might be able to rescue this without having to scrub it all off today. I don't think I've got time for that anyway.' She turned back to him and grinned weakly. 'Let's not give into the little buggers, let's make it part of the Hallowe'en decorations.'

'How?' Patrick looked intrigued. He shoved his hands into his jeans pocket to beat the chill.

'Last night I made some paper ghosts with a few choice book covers on. I was going to display them inside the shop.' She glanced up at the clear blue sky. 'But it looks as if it'll stay dry today. If we change the wording and hang the ghosts, it might do for today.' She stared back at the message, thinking.

'What about, oh I don't know, Books Are Scary? It's on the lame side but it would mean the least we have to change. Do you think you can find me some red paint? We'll do a bit of vandalism ourselves!'

Patrick gave a broad grin. He tugged his forelock. 'I'm right on it.'

Chapter 85

The storytelling session went down a storm. Even though Amy hadn't decorated fully, as it was still a couple of weeks to go before Hallowe'en proper, there were compliments about how great the shop was looking already. Amy was relieved. The graffiti could have been a disaster. It was not the image with which she wanted to welcome customers, especially children. She'd aimed this storytelling session at a slightly older audience and had told a creepy ghost story. With the lights down low and a hollowed pumpkin glowing on the table next to her, the atmosphere had been deliciously scary. Amy forgot to be herself. Instead, dressed in a black cloak decorated with sparkly skulls and her fingers stained red from this morning's aborted scrubbing, she inhabited Jocasta Howler, storytelling witch and wise woman extraordinaire. Before she began, she'd scanned the audience for possible culprits for this morning's vandalism but these children were all under ten. Surely too young to be out late at night causing mayhem?

Once the last orange-iced pumpkin decorated fairy cake had been gobbled up and the till had rung for the last time, she collapsed onto a beanbag.

Patrick handed her a mug of tea. 'That was wild,' he said in admiration. 'You're a natural, so you are. Maybe you should think about joining the BADS?'

'Berecombe Amateur Dramatic Society?' Amy let a tired giggle escape. 'Thanks for the compliment but I think there's a waiting list.' She gulped her tea gratefully. 'What a day!'

Patrick joined her on the beanbag. They were alone, and with the low October afternoon light striking through the double-height windows on the west side of the shop, it felt very intimate now the buzz of the storytelling session crowd had disappeared.

'You can say that again.' He shook his head. 'I've no idea how you can pull that character out of the bag when you're as shy as a mouse most of the time.'

Amy frowned as she viewed her stained fingers with disgust. It wasn't the first time someone had made that observation. She disagreed. She didn't think she was shy, just reserved. After what had happened to her, with her father leaving and then Lee jilting her, she didn't find it easy to trust people, to open up to them. She wasn't someone who wore her heart on her sleeve but then neither was Patrick. After a pause, she answered. 'I suppose that's why. I pretended to be someone else. I couldn't have done what I just did by being me. It's easier to hide behind someone else.' She laughed again. 'Actually, I quite like Jocasta. Think I'll channel her some more.'

'I think you should.' He gave a dry chuckle. 'Those kids' faces when you appeared out of the dry ice. Some of them really thought you'd appeared out of the caldron.'

'Ooh, that cauldron! Caused me a riot of problems. Found

it at Bridport antiques market. Only just got it back on the bus. It weighed a ton.'

'Well, the kids loved it, especially when the inflatable ghost popped out. And it was just the right story. Not too scary but enough to give them a thrill, with a few giggles along the way. Who wrote it? Sure, it worked grand with you telling it and getting the children to join in, rather than just reading it out.'

'I wrote it.' Amy blushed a little at having to admit to it.

Patrick sat up, admiration etched on his face. 'Is there any end to your talents? *You* wrote it? Are you after getting it published?'

Amy pulled a face. 'I doubt if it's good enough and don't they always say it's nigh on impossible to get children's stuff published?'

'Ah, darlin' girl, you should give it a go.'

'Well, maybe.' Amy was embarrassed. So few people complimented her she couldn't handle it. To deflect attention away from herself, she asked, 'Have you got children, Patrick?' The question came out before she realized she'd asked it. She was amazed at herself. Maybe Jocasta was butting in again? She was desperate to know more about him. After all, he might be married. Might be married to a sexy sounding woman called Dymphna, who had his scarf and might have had his babies. For a second she saw a shadow flit across his good-looking face. Pain. Deep sorrow. She regretted her rash question.

His vivid blue eyes clouded as he answered. 'No. No children.'

There was an agonizingly awkward silence. To fill it, Amy found herself saying, 'Have you never wanted them, is that it?'

Patrick smiled ruefully. 'Now, as a good Catholic boy, I don't think I have an opt out clause.' He stared down into his tea and added, so quietly Amy almost missed it, 'Not that I'm a good Catholic boy.' Visibly, he pulled himself out of whatever dark place his thoughts had led him into. He took a great gulp of tea and nodded. 'It's been grand this afternoon, Amy. Grand. Genius idea to keep the graffiti.'

And that was it. She was shut out again. There was silence for a few minutes then she asked, with a keen look, 'It's very good of you to keep helping out but I've never understood what's in it for you?'

Patrick's lips twisted. He scrubbed a hand over his dark curls. 'Well, there is the fact that I like spending time with you and with the books. That the house I've rented is too echoey when I'm on my own.' He paused and then gave her a direct look. She was almost blinded by its intensity. 'But the real reason is I'm blocked.' He shrugged hopelessly. 'I've written nine novels in fifteen years and now I can't find a thing to say. Can't put a finger to the keyboard. I don't know if I've got another book in me.'

He looked so haggard that Amy wanted to reach over and enfold him in a hug so tight he wouldn't be able to breathe. Just as he'd offered her comfort when she'd needed it that morning. She didn't know what to say; this was way out of her comfort zone. She only had the haziest idea about how writers worked, she thought it just happened. 'But you're always on your laptop when you're in here,' she said and it sounded feeble even to her.

'Oh, I'm the master of procrastination.' He laughed slightly.

'And I'd rather do it here than at home staring at the walls and quietly going out of my mind.'

'I don't know what to say.' Amy had never felt more inadequate.

'Darlin' I don't know if there is anything to say.' He drained his mug and stood up. Looking down at her, his usual charming smile pinned back in place, he said, 'Maybe I should write that children's story with you? Maybe that would do it. Break the block.' Collecting her mug, he strode off in the direction of the office.

Amy had no time to respond. She sat there, a little wormy thread of excitement building. What if they could collaborate on the story? The thought of working with Patrick would make her dreams come true. Well, most of them. Glancing to the office as she could hear him splashing water into the tiny sink to wash up the mugs, her mood sobered as insecurity enfolded like a wet blanket. Perhaps he didn't mean it though? It was probably just a throwaway comment. After all, why would a bestselling, if temporarily blocked, writer want to work with her? Conflicting thoughts flitted crazily through her head as she lolled on the beanbag, staring out, unseeing. She was only roused by Emma, in full running kit, bouncing in from outside.

'Time to start your training, Amy. Go get your gear on.'

Chapter 86

Amy cursed Emma with any energy she had. Which wasn't much. 'Oh yes,' she moaned, as she struggled to flip back the duvet the morning after their run. 'Stretch before and after and you won't feel a thing afterwards. Emma Tizzard, you are a big fat liar.'

She fell back, exhausted with the effort of getting up. Catching sight of the clock radio and its insistent orange numbers nagging her that she was already half an hour late, she swore again. Forcing her aching and leaden limbs into action, she staggered into the shower.

Once at the shop and outside of her first mug of coffee, she felt slightly more human. The feeling didn't last as her mother tottered in on her kitten heels half an hour after the shop opened.

'Oh Amy, what have you been doing to yourself?' Katrina turned her daughter to the light. 'Darling, you look ghastly.' She peered closer. 'You know, a bit of lippy works wonders on winter skin.'

Amy shook her off. 'What do you mean, it's not even winter yet?' Her mother's inference sinking in, she added, 'And I'm not ill. I feel fine. Mostly. I'm just a bit stiff after my first training session with Emma.'

'Your first what?' Katrina gave a peal of laughter.

'Emma is training me for the Slime Run.'

Katrina composed her face to stop herself from laughing again and failed. 'Slime Run? It sounds positively vile. And you,' she looked Amy up and down, her meaning clear. Raising a perfectly tailored eyebrow, she said, '*Running?*'

'It's for charity,' Amy huffed. If she had doubts about anything, Katrina had a way of underlining them and making them double.

'Oh Amy, I agree you need to lose some of the blubber but why not go on a diet or join a gym? Something ladylike rather than huffing and puffing in public. And what are you wearing? That grey cardigan again? And those trousers don't do you any favours.'

Amy relieved her aching legs by perching on a stool. 'Blubber?' she exclaimed. 'Thanks a bunch, Mum. You know, sometimes I'm not surprised that Dad left you. Were you this horrible to him? I'm trying to get fitter and healthier and do my bit for a Berecombe charity and all you can do is insult me!'

Katrina recoiled. Tears welled in her enormous pale blue eyes, so like her daughter's. 'Amy,' she began, 'whatever, I said, I don't deserve that.'

'Maybe you don't Mum but I'm getting mightily fed up of being belittled by you.' Amy had started now. She found she couldn't stop. 'Perhaps, one day, you might start a conversation with me by saying something positive like how I've made this place a success. Not easy when high street shops are closing at a rate of knots and independent bookshops are an endangered species. And perhaps lay off the fashion advice. Trousers and a cardigan is practical when I've got boxes to unpack. They're reasonably smart and perfectly clean.'

Katrina, for once, was rendered speechless. She stood with her mouth open, making a little shocked 'o', two indignant spots of colour staining her Esteé Lauder coated cheeks.

Amy began to apologise but stopped herself. She'd said the truth, maybe not kindly but she'd had enough of Katrina making snide and cruel comments. Some praise and pride in her achievements surely wasn't too much to ask for from her own mother, was it?

'But Amy,' Katrina spluttered. 'I'm always telling people how well you're doing. In fact, I was telling Marti just the other day what a success you've made of the shop.'

Amy was past listening; her stiff and aching thighs were making her crabby. 'I've not got time for this, Mum. I need to get on. Was there anything in particular you wanted?'

Katrina shrank into herself. 'Well, if you're too busy to talk to your own mother, I'll just grab your great-aunt a birthday card and be off.' She teetered over to the greeting cards, picked one seemingly at random, paid cash and disappeared.

As soon as she went, Amy felt awful. She slumped onto the stool behind the counter and thrust her head into her hands. Was it ever going to be possible to have a normal relationship with her mother? She loved her dearly but the woman drove her demented. She was still in this position when the bell on the shop door jingled. She looked up and saw Patrick staring at her in concern.

'Not more vandalism?'

'Only my mother.' Amy straightened and gave a huge sigh.

'Ah, mothers. They know exactly where to aim the barbs, so they do.'

'You can say that again.'

He held up a cardboard box. 'Can I not tempt you with a slice of Millie's Devil's Food cake?'

Amy's mouth watered. She gazed at the box longingly.

'I know, I know, you're on a diet. Have you had any breakfast?' Patrick demanded.

'No.' Amy felt her resolve weakening. 'And I did go running with Emma last night.'

'So you did. You'll be after wanting a coffee too, then.'

'Patrick, you shouldn't sabotage my diet!'

He gave her a keen look, his blue eyes twinkling. 'You know my feelings on the matter. If you've not had breakfast, count this as brunch and have something healthy for dinner.'

It was too much. Amy gave in. Sliding from the stool, she said, 'I can't resist.'

'Now, is it me you can't resist, or the cake?'

'Don't flatter yourself. You're standing there holding a box containing some of Millie's most glorious chocolate cake. There's no contest.'

'Ah sure, I'm an eejit,' he said, in a comically strong Irish brogue. He shrugged. 'You'll be needing all your energy for decorating the shop. Are we going all out Hallowe'en?'

'Oh yes,' Amy said, warmly. 'But first, cake and coffee!'

Chapter 87

As she ate, Patrick cut out bats from black sugar paper. 'So, why does your mammy get to you and, more importantly, why do you let her?'

Amy scooped up the last of the chocolate ganache from her plate with her finger. Licking it, she said, 'Did you know the collective noun for bats is colony, or even better, cloud. Isn't that wonderful?'

'I'll bear that in mind. Now answer the question.'

'Oh well, you know. You said it yourself mothers are the people who know us the best and can hurt us the most.'

'And what does she choose to hurt you about?' He paused in the act of cutting out three small bats in triplicate and sipped his coffee.

'Oh, a myriad of things. Largely driven by the fact I am a huge disappointment to her as a daughter.' Amy sucked her chocolatey finger thoughtfully. 'She used to be fun, when I was little. When she could dress me in pink frills and curl my hair. Before I discovered jeans. I suppose it didn't help that Dad rejected her in favour of the comely Jasmine and stayed in Singapore. The settlement didn't leave Mum very well off so she's trying to maintain vintage champagne appearances on a one bottle a week prosecco income.'

'Great way of putting it,' Patrick smiled. 'Must have been rough on her. I assume the comely Jasmine is younger?'

'And blonde. And, to be fair a PhD. I quite like my step-mother, actually, although I haven't seen her and Dad for over a year.' Amy stared into her coffee.

'Must be rough on you too,' Patrick said, gently.

'Yeah well. If I want an exotic holiday or a stopover on the way to Oz, I've got one all sorted. Every cloud and all that.' Amy's tone was blithe but the hurt slithered through. She sipped some coffee before continuing. 'Mum's also never forgiven me for choosing to live independently. But honestly Patrick, it might seem cruel to leave her on her own but if we lived with one another, I would've strangled her by now.'

'And sure, matricide is never pretty,' he said, dryly. 'There's more than once I considered it myself. In the end I was saved the bother.'

Amy eyed him curiously. She was about to ask him why when the shop door jangled. Getting up to see to the customer, she paused. Maybe if she told him the worst thing about herself he might open up in return? Before she went, she said, 'And then there was the Great Jilting Drama. I was the talk of Berecombe for, ooh, weeks.'

She could sense Patrick staring after her as she greeted the customer and led him to the non-fiction section. After selling him an atlas, she returned to the table, feeling Patrick's eyes still on her. It was a bit of a drastic gamble but if Patrick was to spend any more time in Berecombe, he'd hear about it soon enough. And, at least if she told him herself, she could tell him the truth and he wouldn't believe one of the rumours which had flown about town.

'Talk about dramatic timing,' he said, sitting back and staring at her in disbelief. 'Think you should join the BADs after all. You can't drop a bomb like that and walk off. You were jilted? Or did the jilting?'

'Oh Lee jilted me. Went along with all the plans right up to the morning itself. In fact he palled up with Mum, who had gone completely overboard, as you can imagine. Dad and Jasmine flew over, a couple of uni girlfriends were to be bridesmaids, we booked the church and the reception for two hundred at a hotel near Honiton. I'd even found a dress that didn't make me look too much like an oversized lampshade.' She picked up her mug and drained it. The coffee was cold by now but she needed it. Throughout, her voice had been level but there was no mistaking the humiliation and pain simmering underneath the matter of fact tone.

'So, what happened, darlin' girl?'

Amy's bottom lip quivered. She clattered their mugs and plates together to hide the hurt. 'He wasn't there when I turned up at the church. They'd tried to get a message to me but turns out there's no pockets for a mobile in white shot silk. I'd got as far as the church porch before the vicar and Lee's best man blocked me. Mum gave me back my phone out of her bag and he'd sent me a text. A fucking text to say he couldn't go through with it.' She turned a pale face to Patrick, her huge blue eyes shimmering with tears. 'Mum had to go to the altar and announce it was all off. I don't think she's ever forgiven me the humiliation.'

'And now,' she said as she stood abruptly. 'If we don't get started on these Hallowe'en decorations, it'll be Christmas before we know it.' She'd stalked off to find the stepladder without waiting for his response.

Chapter 88

Patrick stood, with one foot precariously balanced on the top rung of the ladder, pinning up great swathes of fake cobwebs. 'That do?' He peered down at Amy holding the bottom of the ladder safe.

'Brilliant! I love how they're all sparkly. Then folk won't think I just haven't bothered with the dusting. It's perfect, Patrick. You can come down now.' She tried not to be too aware of his rear as it descended and ducked to one side once she was sure he was safely down.

They took a moment to admire the day's work. In the children's book area, the decorations were jokey. Ghost wind-sock puppets made out of paper drifted in the air, a spider trail led to a pin the spider on the web game, with ghost lollipops as prizes. Underneath the display of Hallowe'en-themed books, a pair of legs, clad in striped red and black tights borrowed from Millie, and Amy's Victorian style lace-up boots stuck out from a pile of autumn leaves, complete with a broken broomstick. A profusion of black, orange and white balloons bobbed above. In the rest of the bookshop though, things had taken a more sinister turn. In a dusky corner, a dressmaker's dummy loomed, half unseen wrapped around with a white chiffon shroud. Patrick's paper bats flew along the edge of the mezzanine and a full-sized skeleton lay grinning malevolently in a bed of glittery cotton-wool in the cauldron, surrounded by red-stained candles. The sparkling cobwebs hung from every corner.

Amy pulled a face. 'Too much?'

Patrick shrugged. 'If you're going to do something...'

'I've got some headless figures made from chicken wire to put at the entrance. I've painted them with glow-in-the-dark paint to protect our new pumpkin family against any vandals.' Amy spoke with relish. 'They're really scary.'

Patrick leaned against the ladder and laughed. 'There's no end to your macabre imagination, is there? It's terrifying.' He sobered and gave her an intense look. 'Darlin,' you've not let me say how sad I am for you. About what happened with you and Lee. Sure, it's a terrible thing to have gone through.'

Amy now regretted telling him anything. The gamble hadn't paid off. He hadn't told her one thing about himself she didn't already know, apart from the tantalizing hint that he'd not got on with his own mother. Now, he'd regard her as everyone else did; a failure. A jilted at the altar failure. The last thing she wanted from anyone was pity. And she certainly didn't want it from him. 'Oh, it's ancient history,' she bit out. 'Lee went off and joined the navy. Can you imagine? Let's hope he offered it more commitment.' Forcing a smile, she added, 'And, if you think the Hallowe'en decs are good, just you wait until you see what I've got planned for Christmas!'

Patrick accepted her deliberate change of subject. 'Can't

wait but does it involve more ladders?' He wiped imaginary sweat from his forehead. 'Is now the time to tell you I'm feared of the great heights?'

Amy clapped a hand to her mouth in horror. 'You're not! Why didn't you tell me? Oh Patrick I'm so sorry to make you go up there.'

'You're too easy to wind up.' Laughing, he caught her by the waist and whirled her round. 'Can't say it was my favourite thing to do but it's all done now.'

Amy let him dance her around and around in an impromptu waltz until, dizzy and breathless, she found herself backed up against the Local Folklore and Myth shelves. Breathing hard, they laughed at one another and then the moment stilled. The air shifted. Laughter eased into something else. Something far more potent. Patrick inched closer and pinned her against the bookshelf. She felt the spines of the books pressing into her own. He had a hand either side of her shoulders, his mouth inches from hers. Her breasts rose and fell against his blue sweater. Inside she was molten.

'Ah darlin,' you'd be an easy one to love,' he whispered.

He lowered his chin to the side of her cheek and she felt his stubble rasp against her skin, his breath hot on her ear. Kiss me, she urged him silently. Kiss me and then I can show you all the love I have for you. She held her breath, explosions of desire shooting through her. Screwing her eyes shut, she concentrated on his lovely roughness. Everything was roughness – his scrubby beard, his sweater, all except for his voice. That was as sweet and smooth as honey. Kiss me, she willed but all he did was brush his lips against her cheek. Chaste. Friendly. And only a hint of what might be.

'Fuck. I can't do this,' he muttered. 'You've been hurt enough.'

She felt him leave. A great gulf of emptiness filled the space he'd left. Disappointment tasted like ashes. What couldn't he do? And why? And yes, she'd been hurt but she was ready to love again. But only with Patrick. Only with him. And the man remained a complete mystery.

From somewhere far off came the jangling of the shop bell. A customer. Amy opened her eyes with difficulty, unwilling to descend from the ecstasy she had so nearly tasted. She blinked, looking around. Patrick was nowhere to be seen and a woman was browsing the General Fiction section. Several others joined her. Must be Yummy Mummies afternoon in Millie Vanilla's. They often popped in to restock their reading after a meeting. Amy straightened her much-despised cardigan and tried to ignore the unsatisfied throbbing still claiming her. Taking a deep and calming breath, she went over to see if she could sell some books.

Chapter 89

Patrick didn't turn up at the shop the next day. Or the next. Or even the next. Bereft, Amy sat, flicking through book catalogues and nibbling at peanut caramel cheesecake; a new recipe that Millie was trying out. She consoled herself that the regular nightly runs with Emma would counterbalance the calories. Even a visit from the enthusiastic and very jolly HarperCollins sales rep didn't cheer her up.

It seemed ridiculous but she had no way of contacting Patrick. There had been never been a need to exchange mobile numbers and she still didn't know where he lived in Berecombe. He'd disappeared off the planet. She'd spent her spare time scouring his novels for clues to his life but, after all the exercise she was now doing, found herself nodding off over the books and heading for bed early. Idly cruising the net this morning, she'd had an idea. Googling Whiz, or rather Tabitha Wisley to give her her proper name, she discovered that she worked for Tatton and Brownlow Literary Agency. There was a London contact number. She was punching it in before she could overthink it. The cheerful girl who answered promised to pass a message on but said that Whiz was out of the office for most of the week. Amy replaced the receiver without much hope that she'd get a call back. Glancing at the deserted shop she decided on an early lunch break and set off to walk the short distance to her mother's bungalow. The way she'd left their relationship bothered her. Maybe, if her friendship with Patrick was floundering, she could hope for better from her mother.

As she neared the end of the cul de sac, Amy's heart sank as she spotted the builder's transit parked outside the house. It meant her mother was spending money. Again. Steeling herself, she rapped on the fox head shaped knocker and was greeted by a sniffy, 'Oh, it's you,' as Katrina opened the door.

She followed her mother into the kitchen and sat down at the table while the kettle was put on and tea things made ready. Amy looked around while she waited. The house had never reflected her mother but it had been all she could afford. Property in Berecombe was an astronomic price and bungalows were always in demand. After the divorce, Katrina had never seemed to have the money to do up the bungalow in the way she wanted. The kitchen units were dark oak and dated and the tiles the best tangerine the 1970s could offer. With a pang, Amy recollected the kitchen in the family house in Singapore. Enormous, with shiny white cupboards and a team of servants to keep them that way. The house had come with her father's job. Ultra-modern, with shady raised patio gardens and an infinity pool, it had been a luxurious backdrop to a lifestyle that Katrina had enjoyed to the full. She loved the ex-pat life, the country club dinners and business cocktail parties. She'd been in her element. And while Amy wilted in the humidity, Katrina had bloomed like a delicate frangipani flower. It must have hit her hard to come back to Berecombe and face those who still lived here and knew her before her glittering marriage.

Katrina put the teapot down and arranged the matching teacups. Wedgewood Wild Strawberry. She wouldn't dream of drinking from a mug. For a second Amy had a flare of pride in her mother's stubbornness to cling onto what standards she could maintain.

'I see you're having the work done.'

'Only doing out the en suite and the spare bedroom. If I'm to do Airbnb I want to offer a certain standard.' Katrina picked up her tea cup, little finger crooked.

'You going ahead with that, then?' Amy drank her tea. It was good. Her mother always made excellent tea. Maybe it was because she did it properly. Warmed the teapot, used loose tea.

'Of course.' Katrina arched a brow. 'The income will be welcome and I shall enjoy the company.'

Amy let the barb pass.

'So what brings you here?' Her mother asked as she sipped daintily. 'You very rarely darken my doors these days.'

Amy replaced her cup with care, determined not to rise to the bait. 'I thought we should have a chat.' She took a deep breath and launched in. 'And I'll start with an apology. I shouldn't have spoken to you like that, the last time you came into the shop.'

'No, you shouldn't,' Katrina replied, obviously not wanting to concede too quickly.

'I'm sorry Mum. It's just that sometimes,' Amy paused and let the banging noise from the builder fill the awkward silence.

'Sometimes I get a little,' she shrugged, 'well, a lot to be honest, frustrated that you never seem to give me a compliment. Tell me how well I'm doing. Or even, that I look nice. Every time you open your mouth, all I get is criticism. You never seem proud of me.' Amy stopped, aware of sounding needy.

'Well, maybe I wouldn't have to comment on your appearance if you took better care of yourself. Have you looked in a mirror today?'

Amy sighed. It was no good. Her mother would never change. 'This is pointless,' she said and got up to go. 'I don't know why I even thought to bother explaining how I feel.'

'Where are you going? You haven't finished your tea.'

Amy looked down at her mother. 'Do you realize what you say has such an impact on me?'

'Does it?' Katrina shifted uncomfortably, she looked taken aback. 'I'm only trying to help,' she said plaintively. She put an hand on Amy's arm. 'Why don't you sit back down and tell me.'

'I just have but you came back with another bitchy comment!'

Katrina made a little "o" with her mouth. 'I think you'd better sit down and explain that comment. I've been many things, young lady, but I've never, ever been a bitch!'

Amy slumped back down. What was it with mothers? You immediately regressed to being twelve and surly. 'It's how I feel. I'm fed up with the catalogue of criticism from you.'

'So you said. Do you ever wonder why I say them?' Katrina added, more gently and reached over to take her daughter's hand.

'Often.' Amy scowled.

'Oh Amy, my darling. I want the best for you. The very best

428

that life can offer.' She paused. 'I'm sorry if I come across as critical,' she added, stiffly. 'I don't mean to be. I've been telling everyone how well you're doing with the shop,'

Hope flared. 'Were you?' It was the first time Amy had ever heard her mother come even close to an apology. She settled back onto the hard kitchen chair and waited to see what Katrina would say next.

'Of course. I am very proud of you, my darling. I really am.'

'I wish you'd show it more often.'

'Then maybe I should.' Katrina took in a deep breath. 'I'll try.' Another pause. 'I know I'm perhaps not the mother you wanted or needed.'

'What?' Amy was shocked.

'I've always thought I didn't live up to your expectations. You take after your father. Much cleverer than me. And he left me for someone intellectual. He despised my lack of brain power. I rather think you do too.' Katrina bit her lip, tears not far away. 'You and your father. Always sharing jokes I didn't get, having conversations I didn't understand.'

It was true, Amy thought with a pang. She *had* looked down on her mother. It was hard to believe they shared the same genes. Katrina was all shoes and handbags, the latest lipstick. Books decorated a room; they weren't for reading. Amy had got on far better with her father. They had more in common and he always encouraged her with her studies, backed her all the way in her journey to university. 'I never knew,' Amy stuttered. 'I never knew you felt that way.'

'And when he left us, you were landed with me.' Katrina picked up her cup and, seeing it empty, refilled it, her hand shaking slightly.

Amy was choked. She'd had no idea her mother felt like this. 'You're my mum. You were on your own, I didn't get landed with you. I *wanted* to come back to England with you.' Amy thought of how Jasmine had slipped into her father's life. Had replaced her in the cosy club they'd once shared. It had hurt more than she thought possible. Had left her confidence shattered. It must have done the same to her mother but, instead of bringing them closer, it had riven a gulf between them. 'I should have had more compassion, more understanding,' she said.

'Amy, you were the child,' Katrina said, wearily. 'It was up to me to look after you, not the other way around. But you always seemed so self-contained, so driven. You went off to university without a care.'

'And all the time I was missing Dad so badly, I cried myself to sleep for the first term and a half.'

Katrina gave a wry smile. 'But not me.'

'I missed you too. Like crazy! I felt really guilty, to be honest, about going away and leaving you.'

'I wouldn't have stopped you,' Katrina said, looking amazed. 'I always want the best for you. For you to be the best you can be.' She paused, thinking through what she was saying. 'I suppose that's why I'm hard on you not bothering about your appearance. It's your window to the world, I was always told.'

There was a silence while both women mulled over what had been said.

'You know what,' Amy ventured. 'I've always harboured a suspicion I wasn't the daughter *you* wanted. Not nearly girly enough.'

Karina reached for Amy's hand, her eyes bright with unshed tears. 'You're the only one I've got.'

'And you're the only mum I've got, so ditto. Better make the most of it then.'

They managed a teary laugh.

'I suppose the business with Lee didn't help.' Amy sniffed a little. 'It was all such a mess afterwards. I've always felt guilty that you sorted it all out.'

'Darling, you were hardly in a state to do it.' Katrina shrugged. 'I did what I had to.'

'I'm not sure if I've ever said how grateful I am that you did. I was, you know. I couldn't have got through that time without you. Oh Mum, I know I'm a disappointment to you. I know you'd rather have a high-flying career daughter who married a millionaire and popped out immaculate babies every two years.'

'Amy! How could you be a disappointment? You've never been that,' Katrina added, robustly. She gave a wry laugh. 'In Lee's case, I think he might have fathered the babies but I doubt if he would have managed to make a million. Or stayed around long enough to look after the children. Feckless youth but you seemed taken with him. Although I was never convinced he would have made you happy.' She caught her daughter's astonished look and added, 'The expense of cancelling an entire wedding aside, I rather think you had a lucky escape there.'

'But I thought ... I thought ...'

'Do spit it out, Amy.'

'I thought he was what you wanted for me? A husband, a family. Security. A home.'

'I do want those things for you, Amy.' Katrina paused and poured them both yet more tea. 'Do you want to know what I think?'

'About Lee?'

Katrina nodded. 'About Lee. I think that young man had got it into his head you came from a more monied background than you do. And once he'd realized the pot was rather more empty than full, he scarpered.' She sniffed eloquently, then drank some tea. 'Good riddance, I say. Not the one for you.'

'I wish you'd said at the time!'

'Would you have taken any notice?'

'Probably not.' Amy conceded the point. She'd been so lonely on her return to Berecombe that she'd sucked up Lee's attentions. Better him than be alone. Perhaps she would have been better to nurture a relationship with her mother.

'It's true though,' Katrina replaced her cup with care. 'I do want you to marry well, enjoy a secure life in some sort of comfort.'

Amy chuckled. 'It's the twenty-first century, Mum. I can make my own comfortable, secure life.'

'Living in an attic bedsit and working in a shop?'

'I'm happy in the flat. I love managing the bookshop. And I don't need a man to provide any security.'

Katrina pursed her lips. 'And what happens when you want babies? How are you going to carry a pushchair up all those stairs and what happens with your job? Can you afford child-care? And have you any idea how hard it is to raise a child on your own?'

Amy frowned at her mother. She shook her head in bewilderment. 'I'm not sure I want children. I haven't even thought about it.' Liar, she said to herself, as a picture of a toddler with Patrick's blue eyes and curly black hair flashed into her imagination.

'You girls nowadays,' Katrina said. 'You think you can have it all. You want it all.' She leaned forward. 'And it's not always possible!'

'Did you ever want a career?' Amy had never thought of asking before. Her mother had always seemed perfectly content as the corporate wife. 'Oh Mum, did you regret having me?' Amy clapped a hand to her mouth in horror. 'Is that why you're so horrible to me?'

Katrina sat back, appalled. 'So you really think I'm *horrible* to you?'

Amy nodded miserably.

'Oh my darling, how did we ever get into this pickle?'

'Not being honest with one another, I suppose.'

Katrina got up decisively. 'I can't have my daughter feeling that I'm horrible to her.' She came round to Amy's side of the table and drew her into a Dior-scented hug. 'We need to agree a deal.'

'What's that Mum?' Amy asked, her voice muffled in her mother's bear hug.

'I promise to only make constructive critical comments from now on and follow the rule of three to one.'

'Three to one?'

'One critical to every three positive comments.' She kissed the top of Amy's head and released her to fish out a tissue and delicately blow her nose. 'And now, unless you're awash with the stuff, I think we need more tea. Or perhaps gin? Is the sun over the yardarm yet?'

'Nice try, Mum but it's much too early for gin.' Amy glanced at her watch. She shot up, horrified. 'Look at the time! I've got to get back to the shop.'

A knock came at the kitchen door and a dusty-haired youth in white overalls poked his head round. 'I'll be stopping for lunch now Mrs C.' He grinned attractively. 'Should get that shower in by close of play today.'

'Oh thank you so much, Darren. You *have* worked hard. I'll make sure the kettle's on for your return,' Katrina simpered. 'I'm afraid my daughter,' at this she gave Amy a warm look, 'my *lovely* daughter, has rather monopolised my time this morning.'

Amy watched the exchange and giggled. Her mother was flirting outrageously and Darren looked to be barely into his twenties.

'And chocolate digestives for later,' Katrina added. 'I haven't forgotten they're your favourites.'

'Cheers Mrs C. Crackin.' Laters.'

'Laters Darren,' Katrina waved coquettishly.

'Mum,' Amy said, half appalled, half in admiration. 'You are awful.'

'Well, I've always maintained a little harmless flirtation is good for the complexion. Gives one a glow.'

Laughing, Amy reached for her coat and then paused in the act of putting it on, as a thought occurred. 'What have I got to do to meet my end of the deal?'

Katrina gave her an impish look. 'Do you think you could replace the grey cardigan?'

Chapter 90

Amy was so preoccupied with the conversation she'd had with her mother that, on the training run that evening, she hardly noticed jogging the entire mile along the prom. She thought back to Patrick's advice about sorting out what made her unhappy. Her father hadn't loved her enough to stay around, neither had Lee but there wasn't a great deal she could do about them. Her prickly relationship with her mother had long been a focus for unhappiness and insecurity. She hoped their lunchtime confessional was the beginning of a new start between them and she vowed to do everything possible to make it so. She might even ditch the grey cardie.

'Way to go, Amy,' Emma high-fived her. 'Think you're ready for the Slime Run.'

Amy looked about, amazed that she was at the harbour already. She stood, with her hands on her hips, grinning. 'And I'm hardly out of breath!'

'Well, whatever you had on your mind worked, kiddo. Or maybe it's 'cos you're getting the running bug?' Emma looked her up and down. 'And you've lost weight, did you know? And I hate to say I told you so, but I told you so. Do the run and you can eat the cake.'

Amy felt over her hips. There was definitely bone some-where there that hadn't been evident previously. 'Do you know, I think I have.'

'Fancy running back?'

'Go on then!'

Once they were back in the cobbled square outside the Regent Theatre, Emma said, 'Have to hand it to you, Amy. Didn't think you'd stick it. What were you thinking about just then? Doing psych mind games to get you motivated?'

Amy bent over, breathing hard, gasped out, 'No. Just thinking about something my mother said.'

'Which was?'

'That I'd let myself get dowdy.'

'Dowdy? What a word.' Emma laughed. 'You?'

Amy straightened. 'Yes. Me.' She wiped the sweat from her brow.

'Amy, you're gorg. I'd love hair the colour of yours.' Emma picked up the tail end of hers, now a faded orange and grimaced. 'Pure mouse unless dyed. The red was a big mistake. I'd kill for honey blonde like yours. And those enormous baby blues.'

Amy laughed. 'Think she was more referring to my clothes choice.'

'Ah.' Emma wriggled her nose, embarrassed. 'Well, now you come to mention it, the grey cardie is a bit—'

'Dowdy?'

'Possibly.' Emma grinned. 'Come on, I've got the car parked just up here. Come back for a coffee.'

'Thing is,' Amy said as she fell into step beside Emma. 'I'm so fat. Safer to hide behind layers, I suppose.'

'You've got a bit to lose,' Emma replied, honestly. 'But you're a great shape. Really curvy, in and out in all the right places. Look at me,' she squeezed her hands around her middle. 'Straight up and down. No waist.' She eyed Amy's breasts. 'And Tash and me have always envied your bazookas.'

'My what?' Amy said and then realized what Emma meant. She blushed. 'Oh.' She folded her hands over them.

Emma reached her car and unlocked it. 'And stop doing that. If I had knockers like yours, they'd be out loud and proud.'

Amy slid into the passenger seat, giggling. 'Oh Emma, you do make me laugh.'

'Look, seeing as you're coming back, why don't we see if Mum can do something with your hair? Some layers would bring out the blonde highlights. And she's dying to do a practise mani-pedi on a willing victim.'

'Why would I want a pedicure at this time of year?' Amy asked, wrinkling up her nose. 'My feet are always covered in socks.'

'Oh Amy,' Emma sighed, as she crunched the gears and reversed out of the parking spot. 'How much we have to teach you. You might wear socks or tights or whatever but what happens when a hot man peels them off?' She waggled her brows and made her eyes go huge. 'What happens then?'

Emma let them in to the Tizzard family house, calling to her mum that she was back. Amy followed her along the hall as a teenage boy clattered down the stairs clutching an orange and white rodent.

'Stevie, you had that guinea pig in your bedroom again?'

'Piss off Em, you doosh. She's been keeping me company while I did my homework.'

Emma's brows rose in incredulity. '*You* do homework? Yeah right. And don't swear.'

'Piss off isn't swearing. I've got better words than that.' He took a breath and opened his mouth.

'Steven Tizzard, what have I told you about swearing in this house?' Linda Tizzard emerged from the kitchen. 'Go and put that guinea pig back in the hutch and get ready for bed.'

'Bed? Ah Mum,' Stevie grumbled. 'It's not even nine.'

'And time you were in your bed. It's hard enough getting you up in time for school as it is. An early night would do you the world of good.' Linda glared at her son and then saw Amy standing behind Emma. 'Oh hello.'

Emma grinned at Amy. 'Welcome to the madhouse. This is Amy Chilcombe, Mum. She runs the bookshop next to Millie's.'

'Hello Amy. I've just put the kettle on. Fancy a cuppa?' Linda took Stevie by the shoulders and turned him to their guest. 'Say hello Stevie. Nicely. Amy runs a shop which sells those things with covers and pages in between. You might do well to have a look at one, one of these days.'

'Hi Stevie,' Amy said, embarrassed on his behalf. 'I love guinea pigs.' She tickled the rodent's nose gently. 'He's lovely. I could never have a pet when I was a child. Dad was always moving around with his job. What's his name?'

Stevie eyed her shiftily. He bit his lip as a blush suffused his face. 'Todger,' he muttered. 'I mean Tina. It's a she. Gotta put her away.' With that, he turned abruptly and shot out of the hall.

'My adorable little brother,' Emma said, rolling her eyes. 'I do apologise. The guineas are the only living things he cares about. And even they have to put up with a fair amount of neglect.'

Amy remembered being an awkward teenager and shy. Staying silent, she just smiled.

'Come into the kitchen both,' Linda added. 'I've just been unpacking some new nail colours. Got some beautiful pinks.'

'Mum,' Emma asked. 'Do you think you could do Amy a favour?' She glanced at her friend. 'We need to tart her up a bit!'

Chapter 91

The evening of the Slime Run was damp and foggy. Ideal weather for a Hallowe'en event. Sea mist seeped into the crevices of the old harbour buildings and haloed around the white lights along the promenade. It blanketed the sounds from the sea and shrouded the stars in a dense greyness.

Amy changed at the shop after closing it for the day. The last few days had been frantic. She hadn't given her vandals a thought and hadn't felt spooked at all. She hadn't had the time. Tash had been right, folk were grabbing a last-minute break before winter really took hold. Amy didn't blame them. Berecombe had a charm all of its own in the autumn. The shops were beginning to stock Christmas gift ideas and gearing up for a busy period before going quiet in January. The days were often bright and sunny, with a fresh, metallic light that tempted you out on long walks along the beach or cliff top, giving you a fierce appetite. And, when it was chilly like this evening, the pubs lit their fires and log burners inviting you into cosy corners to warm frozen toes.

Millie was doing a roaring trade with her special hot chocolate. Amy had treated herself to a huge mug of it at lunchtime. With its marshmallows and chocolate sprinkles, it was a meal in itself. She'd had a ham salad on granary too and, normally, would have been wracked with guilt about the calories. As she pulled on a pair of old leggings – no point in wearing anything decent for the Slime Run Emma had said - she realized with glee that they slid on easily. Her legs, always long and shapely, were now beginning to be toned and firm. She'd definitely got the running bug. She and Emma had even discussed training up for a half marathon. There was one organized for the following spring in aid of Berecombe's Arts Centre that Emma's uncle ran.

She went into the little back kitchen and, rubbing the smears off the tiny mirror in there, stared at her reflection. Linda had gone to town on her the other night. Despite Amy's protestations that it was far too late to begin cutting hair, Linda had waved her objections aside with a gleam in her eyes. Amy's hair was now cut into a long choppy bob which, as Emma had predicted, let the natural highlights glow and the waves bounce. Her nails had been painted Sunset Pink and her feet had been soaked in an oatmeal bath. Amy had never let herself be pampered and suspected it might become her second addiction, along with running. For the very first time she could see what her mother had been so enthusiastic about. She vowed to treat them both to a spa day at the Henville Hotel as soon as she'd saved up.

'It's just a shame,' she said to the gorgeous creature staring back at her from the mirror. 'That it's all going to be slimed.' Bobbing her tongue out, she laughed. 'At least it's all for a good cause. And at least Linda showed me how to blow-dry it properly.' Her phone beeped. Retrieving it from her bag, she saw she had a missed call and a voicemail message. Switching off the kitchen light, she stood in the main shop listening. It was Whiz, Patrick's agent.

'Amy, sorry to only just get back to you. I've been on a book tour with Lucy Everett, one of my other authors and it's all been frantic. Patrick gave me a list of people he was happy for me to tell of his whereabouts and one of them is you. He's in Portmarnock. Writing, I hope. He wanted absolute peace and quiet but also needed to do some family stuff. Was very particular to tell you he'd be back in Berecombe soon but he had something important he had to sort out first.' She laughed. 'Bit enigmatic but you know what these writers are like. Love a bit of drama. Anyway, must dash. If this doesn't answer your question, please ring me. Don't mind at all. Toodle-loo.'

Amy stared unseeing at the phone. So Patrick had gone back to Ireland. Family stuff? Was that code for seeing Dymphna with the seductive Irish voice? Was she his wife or girlfriend? Hope flared. Soon to be ex? Was that what he was 'sorting out.' Telling Dymphna he was now wonderfully, gloriously, in love with a dowdy English girl called Amy? She blew out a frustrated breath. Some hope. Replacing her phone, she unlocked the shop doors and went out into the night, wondering at her sanity for loving a man who was so mysterious.

As she walked along the prom to the start line at the theatre, she realized very quickly, that she was underdressed. As she joined others heading in the same direction, she grinned at the fancy dress. Was it to mark Hallowe'en, or a measure to protect against the slime? Either way it added to the fun atmosphere on the seafront. An enormous man dressed in a clown's outfit nodded to her, his friendly greeting belying the sinister grimace he'd painted on in a ragged slash of scarlet. His companion skipped along beside him, dressed from top to toe in black rags, her face painted black to match and topped with a stove-pipe hat. One or two others had gone for the practical approach and wore black bin bags, slit to fit over their head and shoulders. Amy looked down at herself and grimaced. In her baggy t-shirt and leggings, if she got slimed, she'd be soaked.

She followed the noise as 'Monster Mash' pounded out across the theatre's square from a tannoy system and pushed her way through the crowds to join Emma at the starting line. To her relief, she was dressed similarly.

Emma gestured to her t-shirt. 'I thought about nicking Ollie's RNLI kit,' she said, 'but he wouldn't let me. Spoilsport. And anyway, doesn't seem quite in the spirit of the thing. You looking forward to it?'

Amy nodded and grinned. 'Glad I've got a fleece back at the shop though. It's not warm tonight, is it? And that sea fog is something else.'

'I know. It's clear up at Mum and Dad's. Often the way. Thick sea fog down here but clean as a whistle inland.' Emma blew out a long breath and watched it as it puffed white into the chilled night. 'Makes it all the more Hallowe'eny though.'

'So, what can I expect?'

'Well, you just run as fast as you can along the prom, avoiding the slimers. Simples.'

Amy looked along the seafront, currently deserted and swathed in a swirling mist. 'There can't be many places for them to hide, can there?'

'You'd be surprised,' Emma said, cryptically. 'Oh, here goes, Arthur's about to start us off.'

Sure enough, Biddy Roulestone's husband, town councillor, Arthur was standing at one end of the rope which marked the start. To Amy's shock, instead of the gun she expected, the start of the race was announced by a wind up siren. It echoed mournfully around the theatre's cobbled courtyard, bouncing and calling to itself in ghostly fashion. She was so taken aback, she forgot to run. The other runners jostled past her and she found herself at the back of the pack of about forty. Instinct told her she'd be easy pickings for the slimers.

The front runners had only just reached the beginnings of the promenade when two sinister hooded figures, dressed in black, appeared from a doorway that Amy had never noticed before and caught three runners, covering them in neon green gunge. Amy saw Emma dodge and miss it by inches only to have glittery foil confetti thrown all over her. Amy put a spurt on and caught up with the main body of runners. She danced around a lone slimer who bounced from behind the corner of Bartlett's fish and chip shop and heard a yell from her left as the clown got the full bucket load.

Her luck ran out just as she was approaching the end of the prom and nearing Millie's café. She thought she'd got away with it and was getting complacent. Surely there was nowhere to hide here?

Mistake.

Three slimers leaped up from behind the low wall which surrounded the café's terrace. Most unfairly, the clown grabbed her around the waist and ran along with her, holding her in front of him as a shield. Amy took a bucketful right in the face. Dumped unceremoniously, she ground to a halt, unable to see and received the foil confetti treatment too.

Emma couldn't stop laughing when Amy reached the finishing line at the harbour. 'You should get a look at your-self,' she giggled. 'No one would say you were dowdy tonight. Your hair's gone bright green and you've got glittery bits stuck all over you.'

'Glad you think it's funny.' Amy pointed a wavering finger. 'If I see that clown he's a dead man.'

'Percy's well known for his dodgy tactics,' Emma said, still laughing. 'Pulls some stunt every year.'

'Why didn't you warn me?' Amy pulled some confetti out of her hair and went cross-eyed looking at it.

'What, and spoil all your fun? Come on, the St John's Ambulance have donated emergency blankets and the Old Harbour has got burgers with our names on.' She grabbed a silver sheet from a passing man in uniform and wrapped it around Amy's shoulders. 'There. Just about finishes the look. The pub's doing a hog roast, I've heard rumour of mulled wine and Millie's doling out hot choc.'

Amy tucked the blanket around her and grinned. Despite Percy the clown playing nasty she'd had a whale of a time. 'I couldn't believe those slimers,' she complained to Emma. 'They came out of nowhere. Are they marine corps trained or something?'

'Deffo!' Emma giggled again. 'I got away from the slime but I'll be picking this confetti out of places no sane man should see for a month.' She took Amy's arm and they began to walk to the warmth and lights of the pub. There was quite a crowd and the music had just cranked up. From the entrance a silhouetted figure loomed. 'Oh hi Patrick,' Emma said. 'Trust you to turn up when all the slime's been used up.'

'Hello my darlin's,' Patrick said, his Irish accent strong. 'I'd like to say you're looking grand, but I cannot lie.' He shook his head, suppressing laughter. 'The pair of you look a right mess.'

Emma grinned. 'Your powers of observation are legendary. I'll go and find Ollie,' she added. 'I'm hoping he'll have the first round in and I can smell those burgers. Come and find us. Laters babe.'

Amy didn't reply. She was drinking in the sight of Patrick. He wore chinos and a tan jacket. A narrow striped scarf was around his neck. Was it the one he'd left with Dymphna? He looked different. His smile was broader, the dimples deeper, the blue eyes dark and eloquent in the night.

'Hello Amy, my darlin' girl.'

'Hello Patrick.'

Perhaps it was the adrenaline of the night. Perhaps she was just relieved to see him. Whatever the cause, she went to him as surely as a boat heading for safe harbour. Arrowing through the distance between them. Taking his hand, she led him to a dark corner in the deserted beer garden. She didn't care if he was married. She needed to discover how his lips felt on hers. She was desperate to find out how he felt about her. And, if she didn't show him how she felt, she'd regret it for ever. Snatching the collar of his jacket to her, she kissed him with all the love she had.

It was like all the warmth in the world, all the love in the world mixed together and bound with honey. She heard Patrick's breath hitch as he backed her against the wall, pressing his body against hers. She opened to him and they kissed some more. Spiced, exotic, heady honey. She was molten with desire. They gasped for breath but the kissing went on. Patrick's hands found her breasts encased in the wet t-shirt and her nipples hardened under his urgent caresses. He thrust his fingers through her hair and drew her even closer into him.

'Patrick,' Amy said, panting for breath and coming to her senses. She pushed him off. 'I'm covered in muck. Your lovely jacket. Oh my God, it's suede,' she added, horrified. 'And I've got gunge all over you!'

'As if I care about clothes at a time like this,' he growled. 'Bejesus, you've got a kiss on you. Kiss me some more, me darlin' girl.'

So she did.

Eventually it was the cold that stopped them. Despite passion heating the blood, Amy began to shiver violently. She pushed him off again, with a giggle. 'I've got to get changed, I'm wet and frozen. Come to the bookshop, I've got a change of clothes there.'

He gave her one last kiss, his lips reluctant to leave hers. 'And I've got something important to tell you.'

'About why you went to Ireland?'

'Partly.'

They turned, hand in hand, to make their way to the shop only to be stopped by a voice calling Amy's name.

'Amy, is that you? I didn't recognize you. You've lost a hell of a lot of weight. Looking good, girl.'

Amy looked back. She dropped Patrick's hand in shock. 'Lee?' she stuttered. 'Is that you?'

Chapter 92

'**O**h babe, it's so good to see you. Missed you so much!'
'Get your hands off me, Lee.' Amy shoved him away.
She couldn't believe it was him. The cheek of the man, turning
up like this! Her initial shock faded as fury erupted.

'Oh come on babe. That's no welcome.'

Amy smelled beer. Lee was drunk. 'Maybe you should have
thought about what a welcome you'd receive after dumping
me at the altar.' She looked about for Patrick but he'd melted
into the night. It was almost as if their passionate encounter
had been a figment of her imagination. She strode towards
the lights of the pub, not wanting to be alone with Lee. She
wasn't sure she could trust herself not to strangle him.

'Hold up there Amy. Wait for your old man.'

Amy juddered to a halt and gave a short, hard laugh.
Turning on her heel she said, 'My *what*?'

'Your old man.' He took her frozen fingers and rubbed
them. 'You're cold babes. Let Lee warm you up.' He swayed
slightly and a little puff of breath misted into the chilly air.

'Oh Lee, I think you lost all right to that title when you
texted me to say you couldn't marry me. Remember? I was
the one in the big white dress in church. The one with the

flowers in her hand and a set of furious parents. And you couldn't even tell me in person. You sent me a *text* to jilt me!' Snatching her fingers away she tucked her hands under her armpits. 'Have you any idea what you did? The mess that was left to sort out?' She shook her head. It was almost funny. How could she have even entertained the idea of marrying this man?

'Ah look, I know I did a bad but, babe, I didn't have any money, no prospects. I went off to make a future for us both. Do it properly.'

'You what? Oh now I've heard it all. You jilted me without explanation to go off and make your fortune. You are one sad bastard. You're completely deluded!'

'Don't use those big words. I'm back now look,' he wheedled. 'We can start again, can't we, my lovely?' He scrubbed a hand over his buzz cut, a drunken and mystified expression on his thin face.

Amy stared at him, hysterical giggles bubbling through the disbelief that he was here. With a clang that was almost audible, she realized what had happened. Her jaw dropped. 'You've been booted out of the navy haven't you?' she said with clarity. 'And you really thought you could come crawling back to me? Back to Berecombe?' She shook her head slowly, almost feeling sorry for him. He didn't have a clue. 'You sad loser.'

'Don't be cross with me.' Lee's voice took on a pleading, weasely tone. 'It's just a bit of a misunderstanding is all. Me and the navy. Bit of a mistake over leave. I'll sort it.'

'I bet you will. But you won't sort me.' Amy laughed. 'I'm going back into the pub to find my friends. You, Lee Styles, can do whatever the fuck you like.'

'Amy,' Lee frowned. 'That's not ladylike that isn't. You've changed.'

'You bet I have, Lee. I've changed more than could be thought possible.' As Amy said it, she realized how true it was. She never would have had the guts to square up to Lee like this before. A great, soaring swoop of confidence filled her. 'But, even if I hadn't, I still wouldn't have you back. Have a nice life Lee Styles and stay out of mine.' She met Emma at the door to the Old Harbour.

'I was just coming to find you. You okay Amy?' Emma glanced at Lee who had slunk down onto a bench. 'You having some trouble?'

'No trouble at all, Emma. Just laying to rest a piece of my past and, oh boy, didn't it feel good!'

Chapter 93

When Amy opened up the bookshop the following morning, she found a note pushed through the letterbox. It was from Patrick. After her encounter with Lee, she'd gone into the pub with Emma to look for him but he was nowhere to be seen. After getting changed, she'd made herself some tea and waited in the shop but to no avail. Cold and weary, she'd reluctantly locked up and gone home.

Unfolding the letter, she was momentarily distracted by his handwriting: bold with swirling loops and written in indigo ink. Romantic. Old-fashioned.

Darling girl,

I hope you don't think me too cowardly for disappearing. I'm assuming the fella was your Lee and I'm assuming you needed to talk. Alone. Unfinished business? I was trying to be tactful! Awaiting the outcome with no patience whatsoever. But, my Amy, I have to be in LA for the next few days. Big meetings scheduled and rumour of film rights. Also, the book refuses to promote itself, it seems. I promise you I'll be back in Berecombe before long. In truth, I should have flown straight to the

States from Ireland but I had to see your sweet face first. And now we have our own unfinished business. Inside, I'm screaming, yearning to see you, to resolve it, but will have to live on jet-lag and the memory of your lips on mine until then. Darling girl, those explosive kisses! Is it wrong of me to hope or has Lee reclaimed you? Don't ring, it's a conversation that needs to be done face to face and I still have things to explain too. Important things. I need to hold your hand when I tell you. But if you really need to, you can contact me via Whiz. Can you believe I don't have a phone? Can't abide the things. Holding onto the memory of your kisses.

Patrick.

Amy sank onto the stool behind the counter and reread it. It made as little sense as the first time. Bloody Lee, getting in the way! If he hadn't turned up and Patrick hadn't felt a misplaced discretion, their business together would have been very much resolved. She had no doubt. Even though she still knew so little about Patrick, she would have taken him to her bed last night. To not do so would have been the regret of a lifetime. She read the letter a third time. Ridiculously, he'd diverted to see her. For one night. He wanted to see her again. He thought her kisses were explosive! Warmth spread through her as she remembered his lips. He hadn't done too badly either. And he had things to tell her and needed to hold her hand while he did so. Amy's heart sank. That didn't sound good. Maybe he really was married to Dymphna. She blew out a breath and glanced at the clock. She didn't have time to dwell on Patrick Carroll today. She had a class visit from the primary school to host and it was book group that evening. Folding up Patrick's letter, she gave it a little foolish kiss, cursed him for rejecting mobile phones and tucked it safely into her bag.

The school children all had money to spend on a book and swarmed around the shop like enthusiastic and frenzied ants. They were fascinated and horrified by the Hallowe'en-themed decorations in equal measure. It took most of the afternoon to give an explanatory talk on how the bookshop worked, do a short storytelling and another hour to man the tills as each child brought their purchases to the till.

As the last one trotted out, proudly clutching a book, a Hallowe'en lolly and a bookmark that Amy had made, she found a beanbag and sank into it with a mug of tea. Relishing the sudden quiet, she closed her eyes as she gave thanks that she hadn't gone into primary school teaching as she was once tempted. Still, it had been a good afternoon and many of the children had promised they would bring their parents in at half term.

A sound came from the front door. It was still propped open as it had been a sunny, warm afternoon and the press of small bodies had made the shop stuffy. Amy opened her eyes and looked to where the noise had come from. Getting up, she expected to see a teacher and child returning in search of a forgotten glove or bag. She peered out of the door but there was no one in sight. Dusk was settling and a faded sunset imbued the harbour with a flat, orange light. A chill breeze skittered a dried leaf across the terrace. It would be dark soon. Daylight, even on bright days like today, was getting in short supply.

Amy's blood turned to ice as she heard the scuffle of feet and a laugh. Definitely not the giggle of one of the seven year olds who had just left. The old spooked feeling enshrouded her again. Then fury erupted as she saw that one of her glow-in-the-dark wire figures had gone. She'd spent ages making them and still had remnants of blisters on her fingers from twisting the wire into place. She heard another laugh and then a smothered cough. Someone whispered, 'Shut up, you wanker!'

Without making a sound, she stepped out of the shop and pulled the door shut behind her with a bang. Then she stood, hardly daring to breathe in case the ruse hadn't worked.

Voices came from the side of the building, this time less hushed.

'S'okay. We can go. She's shut up shop.'

'Ian, you fuckin' bellend, grab the other end, will ya?'

Three boys emerged from the side alley, struggling to carry the wire sculpture between them as they were crying with laughter. When they clocked Amy standing there, their faces turned to chalk. Dropping the figure, two ran but Amy was too quick for the third. Reaching out, she grabbed his hoodie and held on. When she yanked him round she couldn't believe her eyes.

'Stevie Tizzard!'

Chapter 94

Amy only had time to grab a few glasses and uncork a couple of bottles of wine for the book club. Thankfully, Millie, having seen the police car parked up outside the bookshop, had come in to see if everything was alright and had sorted a few nibbles and crisps.

Amy was still putting glasses on a tray when Emma clattered up the spiral staircase to the reading mezzanine.

'I know I'm early,' she said, her face ashen, 'but I had to come and apologise on behalf of the family. We're all mortified about what the little shite has been up to.' She came to Amy and put a hand on her arm. 'We had no idea.'

Amy straightened. It had been a long day. 'I hope you understand I had no alternative but to call PC Cash in,' she said, embarrassed.

'Of course you didn't! We would have done the same. We're hoping it'll knock some sense into Stevie.' Emma sank down on a sofa. 'Mum's been at her wits end with him since he turned twelve. He dobbed in his mates, then?'

Amy poured two glasses of wine and handed one to Emma. 'Here, I think we both need one of these.' She sat beside her. 'From what he said this afternoon, sounds to me as if Stevie's been tagging along with his mates. Liam and Ian, is it?'

'Those are the ones.' Emma sipped her wine. 'They're not bad kids, really. I just don't get it.'

'Stevie's not a bad kid either,' Amy said, comfortingly. She paused. 'He and I got talking while we waited for Paul to arrive.'

Emma stared at her in amazement. 'Stevie *talked?*'

'Yeah,' Amy laughed. 'Once he started I couldn't get him to shut up. It all poured out. It was a series of dares apparently. It was escalating and all got out of hand the night they daubed graffiti all over the town, so they stopped for a while. Then Liam started up a new set of dares. Stevie was pretty embarrassed when he met me at your house. Put a victim to the crime, I suppose.'

'I wondered why he'd shot off into the garden. Put it down to teenage mardiness.'

'It was probably that too. Don't you remember being so socially screwed up you feel your innards are on show?'

Emma shook her head. 'Not really. I've always been able to chat away to anyone.'

'Well, Stevie's more like I was at that age. Excruciatingly shy. He was terrified, actually, as it was getting out of hand and he couldn't seem to get out. I think, to be honest, he was relieved to get caught. It was a chance to put an end to it. There was talk of stealing cars.'

'No!' Emma was horrified.

'Think it's all been nipped in the bud now though. Paul was saying he's going to set up sessions where the boys have to meet their victims and apologise and then sort out the damage. As long as the parents agree.'

'Oh they'll agree,' Emma said with feeling. 'Mum's been talking to them. Everybody is together on this. It's not the sort of town we want.'

'Then that's all settled then.'

'Mum's grounded Stevie for a million years, taken his Xbox away and she's even been threatening to re-home the guinea pigs.' Emma swallowed some wine.

This time it was Amy's turn to look horrified. 'Oh she can't do that! He loves Todger and Snog. He was telling me how he talks to them. He tells them everything. They're the only things he feels listen to him.'

'I can believe that. They come out with the same guttural grunts and high-pitched squeaks,' Emma added, her natural good humour returning. 'They sound exactly like Stevie.'

Amy was feeling magnanimous in victory. 'Please tell Linda not to get rid of the guineas. I'd feel awful for Stevie if that happened.'

'I'll pass on the message. He should take his responsibilities as a pet owner more seriously. Don't get me wrong, he loves them but he forgets to feed them half the time and doesn't clean them out half enough.'

'That could be a sanction. He looks after them properly or they go.' Amy drank some wine and then put her glass down with a clatter. 'I've just had a thought. Stevie likes animals, doesn't he?'

'Think that's what he's closest to, in terms of evolution.'

'Tash and Kit are always after help at their animal sanctuary, aren't they? Haven't they just taken on a herd of alpacas?'

'Yeah, they were in a right state. Tash was furious. She hates cruelty to animals. She's kinder to animals than she is to most people.'

Amy laughed. 'She's not that bad. Just hides her soft side extremely well.'

'So are you saying we should cast off Stevie and send him to the animal sanctuary as the latest waif and stray? Think even Mum might baulk at that.'

'Not quite. I think Stevie needs something to do. He moaned that Berecombe was boring and they were just livening the place up a bit.'

'Kids always say that though. I can remember saying the same when I was his age. Makes me laugh to think about it now. I mean, we've got the beach and the seafront and the Arts Centre now. Uncle Ken even runs a graffiti painting workshop there for God's sake.'

'Not as much fun as doing your own thing, something that's forbidden, and I suppose you take for granted what you've always known. I had an infinity pool and a tennis club in Singapore and still moaned, on occasion, that there was nothing to do. Dad always said only the boring and unimaginative get bored. Soon put me in my place. Mind you, I always had books.' Amy sipped her wine thoughtfully. 'Maybe mucking out stables would be purposeful work. Give him a direction, some confidence to break away from those who are a bad influence.'

'Sounds more like a reward than a punishment.' Emma finished the last of her wine.

'Perhaps. Well, maybe defer it until Paul's done his stuff, then. And first give Stevie the chance to show you all he can look after animals by keeping his guinea pigs in peak condition.'

Emma swivelled on the sofa and stared at Amy in disbelief. 'I've never heard you talk so much! Since when did you become an expert psychologist?'

Amy gave a wry grin. 'Years of never having the confidence to speak and staying on the sidelines, observing.'

'And that's changed now.' It wasn't a question.

'Yeah, Emma. I think it has.'

'Well, way to go, girlfriend.' Emma high-fived her and Amy, feeling a little self-conscious, reciprocated.

They heard a voice booming up from the bottom of the stairs. 'Anyone around? It's like a bloomin' house of horrors down here, with all this Hallowe'en stuff. Where is everyone, Elvis? Book club is on tonight, isn't it? I'm not coming all that way up those ruddy stairs if not.'

Amy caught Emma's eye and gave her a regretful smile. Their unexpected moment of intimacy was over. 'We're up here,' she yelled. 'Come on up, Biddy.'

Chapter 95

As it was the last formal book group for a while, everyone had made an effort to turn up. Marti and her cronies sat along the three-seater sofa, Kit and Tash sat close together, in a row opposite, with Emma on one side and Millie on the other. Biddy had insisted on a higher chair and Kit found her one from the bookshop proper and manoeuvred it up the spiral stairs for her.

'Thank you, young man,' she said. 'My hips can't cope with levering myself up from those soft sofa things. Take it from me, old age isn't for cissies.'

'Biddy, absolutely no one would take you for a cissy,' he responded with a grin.

Once settled and, with everyone holding a glass, Amy began the meeting. She tried not to notice the yawning absence that was Patrick, the only person not there. She took a breath and launched in. 'Thank you all for coming and supporting the book group and the shop in your own, ahem, very individual, ways. It's been an interesting start to The Little Book Café and I couldn't have made it such a success without all your help.'

'Hear hear,' boomed Biddy. She raised a glass. 'I think we should all say a big thank you right back, girl.'

463

'No, honestly, there's no need for that,' Amy demurred, blushing.

'Here's to Amy,' cheered Emma, her cheeks pink and her eyes sparkling from too much wine.

'I'll second that,' called Tash. 'Or is it thirding?'

Unsuccessfully, Amy tried to stop a chorus of, 'For She's a Jolly Good Fellow', developing. 'Honestly, you lot,' she yelled, holding up her hands. 'But thank you. It's much appreciated.' When the last raucous note had died away, she added, giggling, 'And now, if I may, I'd like to start the meeting.' She waited until everyone had settled. 'As *A Christmas Carol* is so well-known, I'd like us to talk about a theme that leads out of the book, rather than discuss the book itself. I'd like to ask you, what would you would change, with the benefit of hindsight? Just as Scrooge learned from his three ghostly visitors showing him his past, present and future, what have you learned recently?' There were one or two murmurs. Amy held up a hand again. This time in placation. 'You only need to join in if you want to and please don't feel pressured to say something personal. And, if you're really uncomfortable with this, give an insight into Scrooge or one of the other characters.'

There was silence and Amy wondered if she'd gone too far and should have stayed with the concept of a standard book group format. 'I'll go first, shall I?'

'No, I'll go first,' Biddy said.

More murmurs, with one or two comments of, 'That was predictable,' from the Marti camp.

Biddy either didn't hear or, more likely, chose to ignore them. 'Now, don't get your bowels in an uproar, and hear me out. I've had a life packed with incident. Some might say enough incident to fill three lifetimes. I don't regret one thing.

What's more, I wouldn't change anything in the past, even if I could. It's what's made me who I am. And I'm delighted to tell you that *A Tale of Two Titties* will be published next year so I'm not about to change the present or the future either.'

'Thank you Biddy, for getting us started,' Amy said faintly, wincing that the woman had gone off-piste. 'And well done on the book deal. That's fantastic news.'

'Did you decide on a pseudonym?' Emma asked, trying to keep a straight face.

'Humph. Publishers didn't like Gertie Gussett for some reason. Vetoed Fenella Flange too, not that I can understand why. So I've had to go with my third choice.'

Laughter rippled around the group and was just as quickly smothered when Biddy glared at them all.

'And what's that, Biddy?' Amy asked, wondering how the woman could top Gertie Gussett and Fenella Flange.

'I've gone with Darcey Spice.'

'That's great,' Amy said, surprised. 'Actually,' she added, realizing the truth of the matter. 'That's a really good pen name.'

'Especially for a writer of erotica,' added Emma. 'Good stuff Biddy. Hope it sells really well.'

'Had to compromise on the title too,' Biddy huffed. 'It's now called *Adventures in the Skin Game*. You'll stock it here, of course?' She turned her gimlet gaze onto Amy.

'Of course I will,' Amy said, executing a swift U-turn, thinking it would sell well, if only for its curiosity value. 'I'd be delighted to. You'll have to sign some copies and perhaps we can launch it from the shop, too?'

'Thank you, young Amy. Appreciated.'

Before Biddy could steamroll the meeting any further, Amy

asked quickly, 'Has anyone any thoughts on what they might change? About themselves or something else?'

Tash put her hand up and then blushed as she realized she'd done so. 'I want to be less of a bitch. That's what I've learned about myself recently.'

'Oh Tash, you're so not a bitch,' Emma cried loyally.

'Unhappiness makes us lash out,' added Amy. 'I concur with Emma. From what I can gather, you haven't been bitchy just trying to survive.'

Kit put an arm around his girlfriend's shoulders. 'That's exactly what I keep telling her, Amy.' He kissed Tash's cheek with a resounding smack and she blushed some more.

'Actually,' Tash went on. 'Could I say something else? While we're sharing news, I'm over the moon to tell you all that I haven't been called as a witness in Adrian's trial. It's such a relief. They reckon they've got enough evidence to put him away for quite some time. His wife is standing as key witness apparently.'

'Now, that *is* good news,' Biddy said, stoutly. 'Good on you, girl. And good on her. That won't be easy.'

'No it won't, Biddy,' Tash replied, meeting her eyes. 'One brave woman.'

The mood shifted into something sombre and then Marti spoke up. 'Actually, could I get the discussion back on track and confess something? Something I've learned I need to change.'

Faces turned to her expectantly.

She bit her lip before speaking. Looking around anxiously, she said, 'You won't have known but I haven't actually read any of the books on the list for book group. I did watch *The Muppet Christmas Carol* in preparation for tonight, though.'

Everyone roared. 'Oh Marti, bless you,' Tash said,

spluttering. 'We all know you never read a word. If it's any consolation, I often borrow Millie's Spark Notes instead of reading the actual book.'

'She does too,' Millie put in. 'I've had trouble squeezing in the reading as well, Marti.' She gave the woman a kind smile. 'Sorry Amy.'

'Well, what a bunch of complete losers,' Emma exclaimed. She rolled her eyes. 'Am I the only one who always reads the books?' Her voice was squeaky with indignation.

'No child. I read them too,' Biddy protested. 'And I also think, to use your colourful phrase, that you're a bunch of losers.'

Amy could hardly speak for laughing. 'Maybe we'll put *A Tale of Two Titties* on the next reading list? It might warm up January.'

'Ooh! I'll definitely read that,' said one of Marti's friends, hitherto silent at every book group.

'Don't you mean *Adventures in the Skin Game?*' Emma corrected. 'By that prestigious erotic writer, Darcey Spice!'

The hysteria was contagious. Another bottle of wine was opened and shared out.

'Well, seeing as you lot don't even bother to read the books,' Emma said, loftily. 'I'm not confessing to a need to change anything about myself.'

'We all know you're perfect, Em,' interrupted Tash.

'Deffo. I will share some news though. Me and Ollie are engaged and he gave me the ring last night. Got down on one knee and did it properly and everything!'

Amid the chorus of congratulations and cooing over the diamond solitaire, Amy saw Millie slip downstairs. She sat back, willing to relinquish any formality in the meeting. This was far more fun.

Millie returned with a bottle of champagne. 'To toast the happy couple,' she declared. 'Well the half that's with us.' She popped the cork to 'aahs' and 'oohs' and poured out the fizz.

'This has got to be the best book group ever,' slurred Emma. 'Although I'm getting really pissed.' She waved her glass at them all. 'Thanks everyone!'

'Emma,' Millie proclaimed. 'Huge congratulations, my lovely. I hope you'll be very happy with Ollie and enjoy the flat.' She paused and put a protective hand on her stomach. 'I don't want to steal the moment but, seeing as we've completely ignored poor old Dickens all night and we're into sharing news instead, I'd like to say my bit. Jed and I have completed on the utterly delish cottage we're buying.' She grinned. 'Which is just as well, as I'm pregnant!'

Amy sat back and watched the euphoria erupt again. She smiled. Bugger the book group discussion, this was brilliant. Friends getting together, being pleased for one another. Eventually the excitement settled, with just the odd comment and delighted grin – and hiccough from Emma.

'So Amy,' Tash said, when all was quiet again. 'What's your insight into yourself?'

Amy smiled into her champagne. 'Ah, I've had an encounter with my very own, very personal, Ghost of Christmas Past recently. And I'm glad to say it taught me a lot.'

'Which was?' Tash asked, intrigued.

'One, that I'm better at seizing the moment and being brave about getting the things I want than I thought I was.'

'And two?'

Amy gave Tash and Emma a warm look. 'That, with the help of my friends, I'll be successful!'

Chapter 96

After weeks of chilly fog, the day of the Hallowe'en party dawned bright and clear. Forecasters declared a late and unseasonal mini heatwave was on its way for Devon.

Amy wasn't sure how she felt about it. On the one hand, should everyone come who had been invited, the shop would be far too crowded and the good weather would mean guests could overspill onto the terrace. On the other, she'd get far too hot and sticky with all the last-minute rushing about. She didn't even want to think about how hot her fancy dress costume might be. She still hadn't got it. Leaving it too late, the fancy dress costume shop in Sidmouth had run out so she'd got in touch with the Regent Theatre, Berecombe's little theatre by the sea. Having haltingly given her measurements she'd been assured they had something suitable in their costume department and would drop it by later. Worrying she wouldn't get everything done on time as well as serve in the shop, she confessed all to Katrina over one of their now regular coffees.

'Oh darling, why didn't you say? Marti and I will come along and man the shop for you. Marti has tons of retail experience from volunteering in the charity shop and I can read well enough to point customers to the right shelf. You never, know,' she trilled, 'I might even catch the reading bug!'

With half term and the good weather bringing in the crowds, it was just as well she had Marti and Katrina manning the till. Amy was freed up to concentrate on preparation for the party. It was going to be a big affair. Far bigger than the launch party she and Millie had cobbled together back in August. Now she had a comprehensive customer guest list as well as friends and dignitaries from the town. Her first job that morning had been to liaise with Millie and Petra about the catering. That sorted, next she had to make sure the shop was looking at its ghoulish best. The Hallowe'en decorations were, after three weeks on display, looking tired so Amy set about revamping them. It was companionable having her mother and Marti in the shop. Despite her fears that they'd wallow in the shallows of life together, they seemed to have formed a close bond and were bringing out the fun side of each other. Their banter added to the songs she'd compiled with tracks vaguely Hallowe'en-themed. She was cutting out paper bats to replace some of the ones looking decidedly tatty when *Timewarp* came on.

'Ooh, Marti! Remember this one?' Katrina cried, bouncing out from behind the counter and turning it up. 'Come on, wiggle to the left and a jive to the right,' she misquoted and began gyrating her hips.

Amy put down her scissors and laughed as Marti joined in, standing behind Katrina and doing a valiant attempt, her face contorted with concentration.

Biddy chose that exact moment to walk through the door. 'Ooh *Rocky Horror*, my favourite!' she cried. Abandoning her shopping bags and dropping Elvis's lead, she took her place behind Marti. 'Come on, Amy child,' she yelled. 'Join in.'

Elvis danced around, yapping madly and turning in circles in a delirium of excitement. It was just as well there was a lull in customers.

Amy stood up, cramped from bending over paper and scissors. Her mother beckoned to her to stand at the front. As she joined in, she felt Katrina put her hands on her waist, swaying her into the right movements. 'Let's do the Timewarp again!' they yelled.

When it had been replaced by R. Dean Taylor's 'There's a Ghost in my House', they stopped, hands on hips, catching their breath and giggling.

'Now isn't that a grand wee sight!'

Amy looked up. She'd know that Irish voice anywhere. 'Patrick,' she croaked. 'You're back.'

He stood, leaning on the door, arms crossed and grinning hugely. 'I am and too late to join in with the dancing. You looked mighty fine, ladies.'

'Thank you Patrick,' Katrina called.

'You missed book group,' Biddy boomed. 'You missed the best one we've had. And you're going to read my new book, aren't you?'

'Wouldn't miss it for the world, so I wouldn't.' He came and stood with them as they crowded around him.

'I've decided one of your books is going to break my reading virginity, Patrick,' Katrina said coquettishly.

'Is it now? Isn't that great. I'm honoured.'

Amy held back. She'd longed for his return. Yearned for it. Now he was here, she was assailed by a fit of shyness so acute it strangled her. Running a hand through her hair and fishing out fake cobwebs she realized she must look a sight. She'd forgotten to use a brush that morning and her jeans were grubby with dust from scrabbling around on shelves and ladders. At least she'd ditched the dreaded grey cardigan.

Katrina detached herself from the group. Amy could feel her eagle-eyed gaze pinning her to the spot. Had she guessed how she felt about him? 'Patrick,' her mother called. 'My poor daughter has been slaving away since before dawn. I think she's well overdue a lunch break. Do you think you could take the child away and feed her?'

Chapter 97

They collected sandwiches, a couple of cakes and some coffee from Millie Vanilla's and found a spot on the harbour. There was a niche in the wall with a bench, sheltered from the breeze lifting off the sea and in the sun. A few tourists ambled past and the odd dog walker but, apart from the gulls wheeling overhead in a cotton-wool clouded sky, they were alone.

'You've lost weight,' Patrick observed.

'I've been running with Emma. Quite enjoy it.' His presence was still making her mute with shyness. She took a bite of her ham and mustard, squinting in the sun at the coastline on the opposite side of the bay. The October light was peerlessly clear.

'I'd love you whatever you look like. You do know that, don't you, Amy? My darlin' girl.'

Amy put the sandwich down in shock. She swivelled to look at him properly for the first time. 'You – you *love* me?'

'Loved you from the first time I saw you chair the book group. The way you adore books and writers. Your stubbornness in getting some of the members to love reading as much as you do. I love the way you battle your natural reserve to

473

get them in order. Like herding cats, I've always thought.' He picked up her hand. 'I love your goodness and honesty, your endless enthusiasm for that bookshop of yours.'

Amy's jaw dropped open. She didn't recognize this portrait of herself. 'Is that how you see me?' she breathed.

'Ah and sure, that's why I love you the most.' Patrick's eyes twinkled sea-blue. 'You don't know any of this about yourself.' His expression closed. 'But I know you and Lee have history. To my mind, he's a bastard, so he is, for doing what he did. But if he's what you want, then so be it. I'll say my piece and get out of your life.'

'He's not, he's not what I want,' she said, tripping over her words in her haste to tell him. 'Patrick, I don't want him. I never want to see him again. Ever. He's out of my life and I told him so on the night of the Slime Run. He only came back to Berecombe as he's messed up in the navy.'

'So there's hope for me?'

'More than hope!' She flung herself at him, scattering sandwiches to the delight of a gull. It flew down and stole one. Amy and Patrick didn't notice a thing. They were too busy kissing.

Patrick broke away first, breathing hard. 'Never met a girl who could kiss like you.' He ran a hand through her hair, gazing at her, wonderingly. 'Better stop though. Remember I had some things to tell you? Are you ready?'

Amy nodded. 'But first I want to say whatever it is won't make a difference to us, to how I feel.'

He gave her a shuttered look. 'Don't be too sure about that. Eat your lunch while I talk.' Suddenly he appeared nervous. 'Can you eat one-handed? I need to hold the other one and I need to hold on tight.'

The gull returned, looked disappointed there was no more discarded food, cackled madly and soared high into the sky over the sea. Amy watched its flight, its legs tucked tidily against its fat belly. She returned her attention to Patrick. Now she was nervous too. 'Of course,' she said quietly, knowing she wouldn't be able to eat a thing.

'Ah sure, I don't know where to start.'

'At the beginning?'

He gave her a quick look, amused. 'Right then. But I warn you, some bits aren't pretty.' He took a breath and launched in. 'I met Sinead at university. Fell in love, made her my wife by the time we turned twenty-one. My mother loved her, her mother adored me. We married within the church.' He gave a short laugh. 'Both virgins, can you believe? We married for better or worse, for life and, as I said those words before the Father, I believed in them, in God, in the everlasting afterlife. I was a good Catholic boy, y' see. Brought up by a strict Catholic mammy. And I believed Sinead was the love of my life.'

'What happened?' Amy asked in a strangled whisper.

Patrick's lips twisted. 'She died.'

Amy gasped.

'We had seven fine years. She got a job at the university for a while. I started writing. Got lucky. Got the first book published the year after we married. We didn't have much, to be sure, but we were as happy as a body had the right.'

He stared out over the harbour. The tide was out and the boats moored there were keeled over at crazy, drunken angles. Amy was sure he wasn't seeing any of them. She wondered, with a pang of jealousy, what Sinead had looked like.

'When she was diagnosed, we moved back to Portmarnock to help out her Mum with the B&B she runs. Would commute back into Dublin for the chemo. I got close to Sinead's mother. Still am. Still go to see her now and again. The good Lord didn't even grant my darlin' Sinead an easy death.' He looked down, close to tears. Taking in a ragged breath, he said, 'At least we were with her when she went. And, even at the very end and the poor girl was bloated with drugs and ravaged with pain, her spirit shone out. I've never met a finer, braver woman.'

There was silence, filled only by the cheep of a wagtail and the distant laugh of a child. Amy took in a lungful of salty, seaweedy air and waited for him to continue. There was more, she was sure of it.

She was right.

'When she went, so did my faith. How could I believe in a God who would let a woman like Sinead suffer and die as she did? It made no sense and nothing anyone said to me did.' He laughed, hard and short. 'Turned out, *this* was the thing that my mammy couldn't bear. She could watch a beautiful, talented, good woman like Sinead die without reaching her twenty-eighth birthday but she couldn't face a son defecting from the faith. She never talked to me again.' His hand tightened around Amy's. He blew out a breath. 'And I never talked to her again. And then she died and I didn't go to the funeral.'

'Oh.'

'The truth was, I wasn't invited. The evil cow put it in her will that I wasn't to attend. I suppose I could have turned up but I didn't want to put my sisters through it. Didn't want to make a scene. Besides, it would mean going back to the church Sinead and I married in. And, call me a coward if you like but I couldn't face that. Couldn't face any of it.'

He shrugged carelessly but Amy sensed the pain behind it. The latest book had been autobiographic after all. She should have guessed. It radiated truthfulness. 'You've got sisters?' she asked inconsequentially.

'Three. All older.' He managed a weak smile.' Could say that's why I always get on with women best.'

'Do you, are you...?' Amy floundered.

'Do we get on? Ah sure, it's fine now. I don't see them half as much as I'd like now I'm living in England but we're making friends again.' Again, the hold on her hand tightened. 'I'd like you to meet them.'

'I'd like that too,' she said faintly.

'I left the auld country the same year Sinead died. Came over to Exeter first, Joel Dillon got me some creative writing tutoring. When the books took off, I wanted out of the city so I came to Berecombe. Rent a house up on the hill. Belongs to Mike Love and Isadora Bart. Theatre folk. Do you know them? Friends of Millie's, so I understand.'

Amy shook her head.

'Well, the house is perched right up on the cliff. Amazing views and peace and quiet to write. Should be perfect.'

'Should be?'

'Only I can't write. You see there's this woman I can't get out of my mind. She's got hair like honey and eyes like the sky.' He turned fully to her. 'Amy, I didn't think I'd ever love another woman but I love you. Do you think you could love me back, just a little?'

Chapter 98

Amy had lied. She'd told him nothing he could say would alter how she felt. But it had. She felt herself chill despite the October sunshine. She was numb. Besieged by what he'd told her. Full of too much information to process.

'I have to go, Patrick.' She frowned, blinking in the bright light. 'It's a lot to take in, to think about. And there's the shop to look after and the party to organise,' she added in a monotone. She wrestled her hand out of his and one of Millie's blackberry muffins fell onto the floor. The seagulls would have a field day. With a glance at Patrick, not wanting to note his sagging shoulders and defeated expression, she left.

Walking furiously back along the harbour, past Old Davey and his mackerel fishing boat, past the RNLI station and the Old Harbour pub, there was only one place she wanted to be. Ignoring Katrina's anxious questions, she went into the little back office, shut the door and slid down onto the floor. Too stunned to cry, she put her head in her hands. Nothing she had imagined bore any resemblance to what Patrick had just told her. The poor man. So much tragedy in such a short life. A crisis of faith, estranged from his family until recently and never able to reconcile with his mother.

And then there was Sinead.

Amy was older now than Sinead had been when she died. Just. It was almost impossible to get her head around. Amy thought she had problems – her father leaving, Lee, her mother but it was nothing in comparison to what Patrick had gone through. To what Sinead had faced. Sinead. Who Patrick had loved so much. Who he'd named the finest, bravest woman. Amy gulped. How could she ever live up to Sinead's ghost? How could she compete? The perfect woman. One who would stay perfect and never grow old, get lined and wrinkled, put on weight. She'd stay exactly the same, enshrined in Patrick's memory. The love of his life. Every time they argued or he found her lacking, and she was sure both would happen – she knew this from observing her parents' failed marriage – the spectre of the perfect wife would loom over them. Could she love Patrick enough to overcome that? Could he? Frustrated with her selfish preoccupations, she slammed her fists onto the cold hard floor.

And he *still* hadn't told her who Dymphna was!

She waded through the rest of the day on automatic. Batting off her mother's concern, she concentrated on the here and now. And that meant the party. Eventually, she was able to shut the bookshop door and lock it against the world. Making her way wearily to the office, she stared at the dress bag hung on the door. Her fancy dress costume. It had been delivered earlier. Unzipping the protective blue plastic cover, she slid the dress out and pulled it on. She couldn't believe it. Of all the things for someone of her build to wear. Peering into the smeared mirror, she saw her reflection gazing back. The too-tight bodice gave emphasis to her waist and pushed her breasts up to form an impressive cleavage. The silvery fabric made her skin glow and her new hair cut looked slippery and glossy. Too numb to care, she put on the matching satin ballet slippers and sparkly tiara and went out to face the world dressed as a fairy.

Despite her preoccupations, Amy had to admit the party was a roaring success. The gentle weather meant guests could spill out onto the terrace, popping back for more food or drink. She'd sourced a red carpet to make a dramatic entrance and Arthur, Biddy's husband, had found some braziers to run along either side.

'Used them for our beach wedding,' he'd explained, as he lit them. 'Kept the chill at bay.'

Extra heat wasn't needed tonight. It was balmy and warm. The flames shot up into the black sky, the smoke curling up to the dancing stars. The thirty-first of October. Hallowe'en. Witching night. Pagan and elemental. Amy felt her skin prickle as she looked up into the diamond-filled sky. There was something other in the air this evening.

But she didn't have time to dwell on things paranormal. She had a party to host. As usual, Millie had done a wonderful job with the catering. Waiters in black tie shimmied through the crowds distributing champagne, there was a sumptuous buffet including Millie's famous honeyed sausages, tiny nutmeg-spiced custard tarts and bite-sized apple muffins. Amy had made sure orange buckets, overflowing with sweets, had been put out for any Trick or Treaters. Now, with any children long put to bed, the evening became strictly adult. The mixologist from the Henville Hotel had been persuaded by Jed to strut his stuff at the cocktail bar, with a potent cider punch and Bloody Marys in demand.

Guests had taken the fancy dress request to heart. Lots were dressed as ghosts or devils or witches. Others had made far more effort. Amy had to giggle at Biddy dressed as Elizabeth I, with Arthur at her side as Raleigh. Even Elvis joined in, with a tiny Elizabethan ruff around his neck. Emma had come as Demelza, of course, and was accompanied by an uncomfortable-looking Ollie as Poldark. Tash wore a sexy skin-tight black cat outfit, complete with tail and ears and Kit towered over everyone as Harlequin. And Millie was dressed as the Queen of Hearts, her bodice made entirely of a red heart and her full skirts not quite concealing her burgeoning baby bump. Jed, channelling Edward Cullen, never left her side.

Amy watched it as if from far away. She perched on the edge of the children's book table, dislodging her careful arrangement of witch-themed books. She was glad everyone was declaring it a roaring success but couldn't, no matter how hard she tried, join in with the revelling. She'd done the rounds, had made sure everyone had their first glass of champagne in their hand and knew where the buffet was, had accepted the compliments coming her way and then had retreated. She tried to fight the complex emotions welling up and failed. She loved Patrick but didn't know if she'd be enough for him. There was no sign of the man and she couldn't decide if she was disappointed or relieved. Uppermost in the tumult of feelings was a deep conviction that she had failed him. And failed him when he was at his most vulnerable.

Her heart sank as her mother, dressed as Morticia from the Addams family, approached. She looked impossibly glamorous. And slightly drunk.

'Darling, why aren't you joining in? It's the most marvellous party. You have done well. It's a triumph.' She pointed a cigarette, thankfully unlit, in a long, slender holder. 'I think you could have a career in event planning, you know.'

Amy gave her a thin smile. 'I'm quite happy running a bookshop, thanks, Mum.'

Katrina came closer. 'Are you sure? Are you sure, darling? Because you don't look happy to me. Is it Patrick?'

Amy started. 'How did you guess?'

Katrina gave an enormous sigh. 'You'd have to be blind not to see it. You're besotted with each other. So what's wrong?'

'It's complicated, Mum.' Amy shuffled her feet, mutinously.

'When isn't it?' Her mother gave a rueful laugh.

There was a commotion at the door as someone in a green suit and matching hat walked in. A small crowd gathered, laughing.

'Look. He's here, darling. Patrick's just arrived.' Katrina gave Amy a gentle shove. 'Whatever the issue is, talk to him about it. He's one man I can say might be worth the effort. So, go get him,' she said. 'Go get your lovely Irishman.'

Amy stared at her, still unwilling to move.

'Go get him, Amy,' her mother repeated. 'Whatever it is have the courage to sort it out. Don't live your life without love. For my sake, don't be alone.'

Amy's ballet slippers propelled her to Patrick and the crowd that was gathered around him.

'Well,' he was saying. 'If you're going to appropriate a culture, you might as well appropriate your own.' He grinned and then saw Amy. Wordlessly, he took her hand and led her outside.

Chapter 99

They sat on the low wall dividing the terrace from the beach. On one side of them all was colour and drunken laughter and noise. On the other, there was nothing but a black sea sighing gently against the shore and the stars.

Amy gave an enormous and slightly tearful sigh. 'Oh Patrick. I'm sorry.'

'Darlin' girl, what have you to be sorry about?'

'I'm an idiot.'

He took her hands in his. Laughing slightly, he said, 'Of anyone I've ever known, you're the least idiotic.'

'I shouldn't have run off earlier, like I did.'

'Ah sure, you had a lot to think through. 'Tis a sorry tale, that one of mine.'

'You've had to go through so much and all I could think about was how to live up to Sinead.'

Patrick was silent for a moment. 'Amy, I loved Sinead with all my heart. With all my soul. When she died I never thought I'd live through it, let alone love someone else.' He cleared his throat. 'But, you know, no matter how hard the thing is, you get past it. You get through it. Somehow.' His hands on hers tightened. 'I'll grieve for Sinead until the day I die. I can't lie about that. But the past is what it is. I can't and won't change it.' He took her face in his hands and forced her to meet his gaze. 'It's you I love now. Sure, the heart is a wonderful thing. It has an unending capacity to love and keep loving. And I promise you, that's what I'll do with you.'

They kissed. Sweetly. Wonderingly. The sea shifted and sighed with them and a soft breeze whispered at their skin.

When they broke apart, Amy said, 'You've been such a mystery.' She blushed. 'I've got to admit to googling you to find something, anything about you.'

Patrick smiled and put his arm around her, hugging her tight to him. 'Well, I keep my private life private. It helps that Patrick Carroll isn't my real name.' He kissed the top of her head.

'Blimey.'

'Oh I'm a Patrick alright. But I was born Patrick Byrne. Took my grandmother's maiden name when I started writing. I'm a man who likes his privacy.'

'You can say that again,' Amy said, warmly. 'I even read and reread your books to hunt for clues about you. You've never put any of what you told me into your books. Why?'

Patrick winced. 'There's some of it in there.' He shook his head. 'But I was too close, it was too painful to write about. I might be able to now, though. After we've written that children's book. Are you up for it?'

Amy had clean forgotten about the children's book. 'I might be.'

'Oh, and don't I owe you an expensive date at the Henville? You'll be after a cocktail. I hear rumours the ladies like them.'

'I hear they do,' Amy replied, giggling a little. 'Well, I might be up for writing a book with you and a cocktail or two, but only if you answer this one question.'

'Just the one?' He shifted away from her and looked into her eyes with love. Arching a brow with humour, he said, 'Sure. Fire away.'

'Patrick,' Amy paused and took a breath. 'Who is Dymphna?'

'Dymphna? She's Sinead's mother. Did I not mention her this morning?'

Relief surged through Amy. 'Your mother-in-law!'

'Yes. We're still close. In fact, that was the main reason I went back to Portmarnock just. I had to see her to explain I was in love with a beautiful, wonderful English woman.' He grimaced. 'It was hard enough for me to move on, might be nigh on impossible for a grieving mother to see her son-in-law with someone else.' He frowned. 'Why, who did you think she was?'

'It doesn't matter now.' Amy shook her head vigorously and smiled.

'She gave us her blessing, by the way. Lovely woman is Dymphna. Wants to meet you, you know. If you'd like to.'

'Yes, I'd like that. I'd like that very much.' Amy was filled with a sudden, glowing, golden joy. She lifted one of his hands and kissed it and then laughed. 'And Patrick, dressing up as a leprechaun?'

He shrugged and took off his green hat, completely unrepentant. 'It's a form of fairy, did you not know? So we make a good pair.'

'I look awful.'

'Ah, will you hush your mouth, woman. You're stunning. Look at the waist on you and,' he waggled his brows and nodded to her breasts, tightly encased and pushed upwards in the laced bodice, 'you know.'

Amy looked down. 'I suppose it does give me a bit of a cleavage.' She regarded the white and silver tulle dress with more affection.

'A bit she says! And here I am, struggling to keep my hands off you.'

'Then why are you?' Amy said, coquettishly.

'Because there's the wee matter of not knowing how you feel about me.' He sobered. 'Ah Amy, I realize I'm not the catch of the century. I'm older, with baggage. And what's more, I'm a terrible moody eejit sometimes. I'd understand if you want to walk away.'

Amy stopped his mouth with her finger. 'Ah, hush your mouth, man,' she said. 'Wouldn't I be the terrible eejit if I let you go?'

'That's the most awful attempt at an Irish accent I've ever heard. Promise me you will never ever do that again.'

'Only if you kiss me.'

So he did.

A long time later, they sat, hands entwined, watching the night sky and the shimmering stars. Amy let her head rest on Patrick's shoulder and thought she had never been happier.

'Happy Samhain. Happy Hallowe'en,' Patrick said, lazily. 'Did you know it's the night when the spirits pass more easily into the world? That the souls of the dead return to have a candle lit for them.'

'Then we must light a candle for Sinead. What would she say about me?' Amy's voice trembled a little.

'She'd say, be happy Patrick. Be happy with your English

angel.' He put his arm around her, holding her close. He went suddenly rigid, gazing into the sky. 'Did you see that?'

'What?' Amy followed where his finger pointed but could only see the sky, velvet and studded with diamonds.

'A shooting star!'

'Maybe it was Sinead coming back? Giving us her blessing.'

'Ah, that would be it. Stardust and magic are here tonight.' He sighed. 'I love you, my angel, my darlin' girl.'

'And I love you, Patrick,' Amy said, finally having the courage to tell him. She kissed him. 'I love you so very much.'

And the air rippled and shifted around them. 'Be happy,' came a loving whisper, as caressing as the breeze and as soft as the night. 'Be happy.'

Acknowledgements

Grateful thanks go to Tim at Archway Books in Axminster and lovely Bee and Chris at my favourite seaside bookshop, Serendip in Lyme Regis, for helping with information about running an independent bookshop. Lisa Hill – your insights into the life of an estate agent were much appreciated. Huge thanks to Joanna Quinn from the RNLI's College in Poole for taking the time to fill me in with what it takes to be an RNLI volunteer. All mistakes are my own. It's not been the easiest of years to write a book so I must thank everyone at HarperImpulse for their support and patience – and their continuing faith in me. And, as ever, thank you dear readers for buying and reading the books. I hope you love this latest slice of Berecombe cake as much as I enjoyed writing it.